Snowed In

Navessa Allen

Navessa Allen LLC

Also by

The Lunatics: Volume One

Scandal

The Kings of Kearny

Lights Out

Caught Up

Game On

Content Warning

This is an adult contemporary romance with themes of grief and illness. Please see content warnings below:

Death of family members

Mentions of infertility

Mentions of genocide, rape, and assault

Mentions of international adoptions

Mentions of war

Mentions of drug trials and medical testing

TBI/CTE

Therapy and SSRI use

Mentions of potential suicidal ideation

Topics of Grief/Depression/Anxiety

Explicit sex scenes

For Grandma Grace

Chapter 1: Ella

My older sister Jane glared at me, her dark eyes menacing in the glow from the fire. "Let me tell you a story. It starts like this," she said. "'Twas the week before Christmas, and all through the house, not a creature was stirring, except for the megalomaniac four-year-old whose irresponsible aunt fed her twelve candy canes before dropping her off."

I grinned, hoping to lighten the mood. "I don't think that's how it goes."

She shook her head, black hair brushing her shoulders. "It does in this hellish version."

Behind her, Willow, the niece I was an irresponsible aunt to, roared in jolly incoherence. I slanted my eyes toward her and nearly choked. She'd somehow managed to strip naked in the three minutes since we walked through the door, the light brown skin with golden undertones she inherited from Jane now on full display.

What was it with kids her age being allergic to clothing?

Jane caught my expression and turned to follow my gaze. Together, we watched Willow grab the end of the garland that adorned the staircase and take off at a dead sprint. The festive decor pulled loose with surprising violence. Twine snapped. Twigs splintered in half and scattered small, stabby pieces of bark all over the living room carpet.

"Sweet Jesus, no," Jane said.

Willow's long black hair whirled behind her as she raced toward us. The greenery she clutched in her tyrannical little fist left a mess of pine needles and winterberries in her wake that would be a pain in the ass to clean up.

I am never going to live this one down.

As she neared, I caught a familiar tune through the madness and realized that she wasn't incoherent, but scream-singing a badly butchered version of a holiday classic.

"Jangly balls! Jangly balls!"

Oh, God.

Where had she even heard that?

Jane and I reached for her as she ran past, but she managed to evade us, twisting and ducking like a running back at the peak of their game. Sensing freedom, she dropped the garland and fled down the hallway, her singing replaced by a sinister cackle that was unsettling coming from a four-year-old.

I turned back to my sister. "In my defense, I didn't know she could reach the jar I hid the candy canes in."

Jane pointed at me and opened her mouth, but before she could launch into what I'm sure would have been an epic telling off, a distant *thud* came from the back of the house. It sounded like Willow had literally just bounced off a wall.

"I will get you back for this," Jane told me before hurrying off to save her sugar-addled daughter from herself.

"I'm sorry!" I called after her.

She flipped me the bird and disappeared down the hall.

I sighed. What a disaster. I loved spending time with Willow and was usually pretty good with her. Today had been an off day. One I'd pay for. Knowing Jane, it would take me weeks to convince her to let me babysit again.

A pocket door slid open in my periphery. Cropped blond hair peeked out from it, followed, slowly, by the head of my brother-in-law.

"Hey, Dave," I said.

He glanced around the room like he was searching for threats. The lights from the nearby Christmas tree sparkled in the reflection of his black-framed glasses. His gaze landed on me, expression flat. "Go now, Ella. While you still can."

Another *thud* echoed through the house, followed by Jane's raised voice. Dave gave me a meaningful look and slid his office door closed.

I muffled my laughter as I made my escape. Jane wouldn't thank me for it right now.

Outside, the winter wind whipped the freshly fallen snow into a flurry. It spiraled into the spill of fluorescent white shining from the rear floodlights and coalesced into the arctic version of a dust devil. The direction of the breeze shifted, and the mini snow tornado split in two. For a brief moment, it was like I walked past a pair of enchanted winter sprites twining around each other at an Antarctician ball. I could almost hear Jack Frost playing the ice pipes in the distance as he urged them on.

A heartbeat later, the wind died down, and they fell back to the ground, inanimate once more.

I smiled as my boots crunched over the freshly shoveled walkway. Evergreens crowded the driveway, their boughs weighed down by today's snowfall. The steam from my breath hung in front of my face before drifting up and away. I tilted my head back to watch it dissipate.

Above me, stars ripped through the velvety expanse of the night sky like a shotgun blast.

I loved winter. It was my favorite season – a time to gather, to hunker down with friends and family while storms raged outside. Afterward, everything was so clean and bright. It made it easy to ignore, if only for a little while, all the troubles of the world.

The sound of muted whining brought me back to myself. I'd left my truck idling in the driveway. Two dark blobs were pressed against the driver's side window. I moved closer, and the snouts those blobs were attached to came into focus. My rescue Huskies, Fred and Sam, stared at me from the other side of the glass.

I waved my arms at them. "Get your drooly noses off the window."

Sam yipped in response, which taunted a bark out of Fred, which Sam had to answer. By the time I reached the vehicle, they were howling.

I wrenched open the door. "Would you two be quiet? You're going to -"

A deep, keening bay rose to answer them from far too close.

I froze, the hair on the back of my neck standing on end. Sam and Fred shared a panicked look before racing into the safety of the backseat, where they huddled down like a pair of rabbits in a thicket. More howls joined the first, forming an unholy chorus. Low growls punched through the cacophony. A high-pitched yelp rang out like some sort of demonic soprano.

My skin prickled in goosebumps that had nothing to do with the cold. The surrounding woods were carpeted with deep snow, causing sound waves to diffract in a way that made it difficult to judge the distance of the noises. I couldn't tell if the animals making them were a mile away or about to burst through the nearest tree line and rush at me in a seething frenzy of fur and teeth.

The howls broke off, a low, mournful note lingering in the air long after the others fell away.

"It's just coy dogs," I told Fred and Sam.

They didn't look convinced.

I climbed into the truck and shut the door. My thick gloves made it impossible to do much else, so I yanked one off with my teeth, dug my phone out of my heavy jacket, and dialed Dave's number.

"Yo," he said by way of greeting.

"Did you hear that?"

"Your dogs? Or the wolves?"

I sucked in a breath. "They're back?"

"The wolves that the US Fish and Wildlife Service insists we don't have in Maine? Yeah, they're back. A friend of mine said they were sighted ranging down from Canada about a week ago."

"Be careful if you come outside. They sounded close."

"Eh. Sounds are tricky this time of year."

"Still," I said, thinking of Willow.

"Don't worry. I'll tell Jane. We'll be careful."

I put the truck into reverse after we hung up and backed out of their long driveway. The clock on my dash read 6:15. It was a Friday night, and I was a single twenty-three-year-old. If I lived anywhere else in the country, I might be getting ready to go out with friends or swiping right on dating apps. There were fewer options for fun in the northern reaches of Maine, and the thought of eating another dinner alone with my pets sounded a little too depressing right now.

I pulled onto the road and hit the phone button on my steering wheel. "Call Jack Hundel."

A gruff male voice came through the speakers after the third ring. "Y'ello there, Ella."

"Hey, Jack."

One of the dogs let out a low *woof* from behind me.

"You got the boys with you?" Jack's tone changed into the higher register with a slightly hysterical edge that all canine lovers seem to favor when speaking to their four-legged friends. "Who's a good boy? Who's the best boy? Is it you, Fred?" In response, Fred leapt into the front seat and started jump-prancing as he barked. "Or is it you, Sammy?" Sam, not to be upstaged, started howling again. Right behind my ear.

I ducked away from him. "Jack, cut it out. They're not buckled in. If you rile them up any more, they'll wreck the truck."

He cleared his throat. "Sorry. Whatcha up to, kiddo?"

"I just dropped Willow off and was thinking of swinging by before I head home."

"Sure, come on over. I got half a chicken in the oven and just cracked open a beer."

"Homebrew?" I asked, thinking of the delicious dark ale I'd had the last time I dropped by.

"You betcha."

"Any oatmeal stout left?"

"Two. I'll save 'em for ya."

"Thanks, Jack. See you in a few," I said before hanging up.

A four-way stop marked the end of Dave and Jane's street. I paused there and put the truck into park, then ushered Fred into the backseat and buckled both of the dogs in. The roads were a little rough out by Jack's, and I didn't want to risk them getting hurt if I slid into a snowbank. They whined at the constraints at first, but settled down once we got closer to town and they had more to look at out of the windows.

The one set of lights in what passed as the downtown area were red when I reached them. Because of course they were. Three cars sat ahead of me waiting for them to turn green.

I eased to a stop at the end of the line. "Can you believe this traffic?"

Fred and Sam yipped in response.

I reached into the plastic container in my cup holder and dug out a few treats for them as a reward. Yes, I had trained them to bark in response to that exact question. And yes, I still laughed every time. You have to find creative ways to keep yourself entertained in rural areas.

The light turned green. In just a few miles, we were back in the woods, starting the long climb into the foothills. Jack's place was on the opposite side of the valley as my sister's. He lived close to the top of a hill about twelve feet shy of mountain status. The most direct road was so steep that I wouldn't risk taking it now. This soon after a snowfall, you had to begin the ascent going about sixty if you had any hope of keeping enough momentum going to get to the top.

I hadn't been driving fast enough the last time I attempted it, and the tires had lost their grip halfway up the hill. Thank God for the house I had just passed and my years of experience on ice-slicked roads. I'd managed to steer the truck into their driveway during the slide. To anyone watching, I would have looked like a demolition derby queen with nerves of steel, but the truth is I'd been terrified. My hands shook for nearly an hour after, and I'd stayed far away from that road in bad weather ever since.

Taking the long way added another ten minutes to my trip, but I didn't mind; I wasn't in a rush. Plus, the views were nicer along this route, especially after a storm. Two-hundred-year-old stone fences marked the property lines of the houses. Here and there, a merry spill of golden light shone through the forest, offering a brief glimpse of a log cabin or an A-frame in a clearing beyond.

I caught sight of twinkling Christmas lights down a long driveway and had a brief flashback to a snowball fight I'd had there as a kid. The Masons had owned it then. They'd sold the place to the Andrews when I was in middle school and moved to New Hampshire in search of better jobs.

That was a common theme in my area. People moved away to find jobs, or go to school, or to get away from the suffocating monotony of small-town life. Few ever returned, and our population was a dying one as a result.

The truck's engine whined as I navigated switchback after switchback on the climb up. Soon even those brief glimpses of homesteads fell away. Pine trees replaced oaks as I neared the top of the hill, butting right against the road. Their branches crowded out the star-strewn sky and dropped clumps of snow on the roof of the cab.

The road opened up again when I crested the summit. I slowed the truck to a crawl so I could take in the dizzying view. Mountains loomed in the distance, their jagged outlines only visible because of the absence of stars. Resting far below them on the valley floor was the town. Its lights glimmered like the swirling mass of some small galaxy, the pinpricks of white that spread out from it the planets it had pulled into its orbit.

"Would you look at that," I said. I'd lived here most of my life, but sometimes the beauty of my hometown still stole my breath away.

I brought my focus back to the road and shifted into four-wheel low to begin the descent. Jack's was the first driveway on the right. There weren't any streetlights here, so I looked for the red reflector on his mailbox.

The dogs got antsy when I turned off the road. We were at Jack's, and that meant bear hugs and dog treats were about to happen. Fred pulled at his harness. Sam whined as he strained to look out the front window.

"I got it, I got it. Just hold on," I told them. "And don't even think about howling out here."

God only knew what might answer if they did. This side of the valley bordered the wilderness. Like, no one lives beyond this point, you will die if you don't know what you're doing out there, wilderness.

Aroostook County, Maine was the largest east of the Mississippi, with over four million acres of mountains, trees, and waterways. Beyond our town, there was nothing but rugged, mostly impassable terrain dissected by roaring rivers. Instead of humans, it was populated by coyotes, moose, fishers, bears – who were thankfully fast asleep in their dens – wolves, and probably, though the US Fish and Wildlife Service would deny it too, mountain lions.

With the thought of wolves still plaguing me, I drove slowly, searching the tree line on either side of the truck for the tell-tale reflection of eyes. Jack's driveway was unpaved, and thanks to my glacial pace, I gave him plenty of time to hear me coming.

He stepped out onto the front porch as I pulled up. In his mid-sixties, he still stood ramrod straight, with broad shoulders, salt and pepper hair, and a face that was tan even during winter thanks to snow glare. The few wrinkles he had were clustered around his eyes and mouth, a dead giveaway for how much he smiled.

He looked like an instafamous hipster grandpa. One that could out bench-press men half his age. The women of our small town, many much younger than him, considered Jack to be one of the most eligible bachelors in the area. I knew him well enough to say that those women would forever be disappointed. Jack had loved his late wife in a way that would make any other relationship pale in comparison. She'd died the same year as my grandfather; the year Jack would tell you was easily the worst of his life.

When I was younger, I'd called him Uncle Jack, though he was more of a great uncle. Once removed. I think. His father had been married to my grandfather's mother for a few years, so whatever that would make him. Ex-great uncle, maybe?

Their parents' marriage hadn't stuck it out, but even though they were over a decade apart in age, Jack and my grandfather's brotherly relationship had endured the split. Jack had been a constant fixture in my life because of it. After my grandfather's death, I spent a lot of time on this hill with him and his wife, Renee, who had already accepted the finality of her cancer diagnosis and had given up fighting it.

I practically moved in after she passed. Jack and I spent those days felling trees, clearing a swath of forest beyond his home for planting, coaxing tillable soil out of the rocky terrain, and basically working ourselves to the bone to keep from succumbing to grief. Now, three years later, I still came over at least once a week.

Jack yanked open the passenger door as I rolled to a stop. "Where are my boys?"

The dogs barked like mad, nearly deafening me in the enclosed space of the cab. I turned the truck off and freed them from their harnesses, and they shot out of the backseat to race circles around him.

"Nice to see you too, Jack!" I yelled over the racket.

He totally ignored me. "Do you want some...TREATS?"

The dogs fell over each other in their excitement.

I rolled my eyes and went around to the passenger side to join the fray. Jack and I were just pulling apart from a hug when a set of lights flashed through the trees, followed by the sound of tires crunching over gravel.

"That'll be Ben," Jack said. "New neighbor just down the hill. He bought the old Reynolds farmstead and is fixing it up. He's from out west and doesn't know anyone, so I figured I'd invite him over to meet you. You're close in age. Maybe you can introduce him to the other youngins in town."

I glanced toward the vehicle – a lifted Jeep – as it rolled to a stop and the lights cut out. "Sure. They could use some fresh meat. Gossip is running dry with everyone shut up from the storms."

Jack snorted. "Well, go easy on him. Like I said, he's new, and not used to small-town life. I think you'll like him, though. He's artsy-fartsy like yourself."

I grinned. To Jack, artsy-fartsy could mean a couple of things: Ben was either an artist or a craftsman, or identified as a liberal. Which was funny, because while Jack identified as an independent, his political views were pretty "artsy-fartsy" by today's standards.

Jack reached down to ruffle Sam's ears. "Why don't you wait here and introduce yourself? I'll go get these monsters a treat and try to calm them down so they don't maul the poor bastard as soon as they see him."

It was my turn to snort. "Good luck with that."

He disappeared inside the house with the dogs while I readied myself to play the part of Ambassador to the Youngins. I even prepared a brief speech: *"Hi, I'm Ella. Welcome to the middle of absolutely nowhere. Next town is forty minutes thataway. Good news! They have a Walmart there. Oh, and did I mention that I'm one of only fifteen people near your approximate age in this area? Hope you like us, otherwise you're shit out of luck."*

The vehicle door opened, and my nice, witty speech went up in flames, because a very broad shadow stepped out from it. Not down from it, like any normal-sized human would from a jacked-upped four-by-four, out from it. Like the Jeep had to be lifted to reach a height more comfortable for the driver.

He shut the door and ambled into the halo of golden porchlight, and my brain short-circuited for a second. Because I knew who he was: Benjamin Kakoa. Benjamin *freaking* Kakoa. Walking up to me. In my once-removed (possibly?) great uncle's driveway.

To be clear, I didn't know him, know him. I just recognized his face. And his hair. From television. And print ads. And the packaging my running shoes came in. Because he was a famous person. A very famous person.

Two years ago, he'd starred in sports gear commercials and repped luxury watch brands and had even been plastered across magazine pages in shampoo ads. He'd been one of the biggest football stars in the country. And then his older brother, Zach Kakoa, also a football pro, had suffered a seizure while home visiting family in their native Hawaii. He'd been driving at the time. With his wife and son in the car. Tragically, all three had succumbed to their injuries in the resulting crash.

Their deaths had shocked the sporting world, but that was nothing compared to what followed. During Zach's autopsy, the coroner found significant scarring from past traumatic brain injuries, caused by his years of contact on the field. She ruled that these TBIs had been the cause of the seizure.

Ben quit the US Football League the day the findings were released. He was one of many young men who realized the money they were being paid wasn't worth the true cost to themselves. But that wasn't all Ben did. He became a vocal advocate for better safety gear in football, tougher rules that would help protect the players, and higher fines for illegal, dangerous tackles.

Instead of appearing in commercials for luxury brands, he now starred in PSAs paid for by his parents, who were the beneficiaries of Zach's life insurance policy. They had joined the fight alongside Ben, dedicating Zach's money to furthering the scientific study of brain injuries.

The last article I'd read about him said that he was out on the west coast battling the juggernaut that was the USFL. So what the hell was he doing in East Nowhere, Maine?

He strode closer, and my brain short-circuited for an entirely different reason this time, because, and I didn't know how it was possible, he was somehow better looking in real life. I mean, he looked like a football player, sure – well over six feet tall, abnormally wide shoulders, long, heavily muscled arms and legs, an obscenely broad chest – but his face.

Yea gods.

It was his face that landed him those advertising contracts. His father was of Hawaiian and Samoan descent, and his mother was Swedish and Brazilian. He had light brown skin, pale green eyes, impeccable bone structure, arched brows, and a thick head of riotous curls that fell to his shoulders. In all the pictures and videos I'd seen him in, his face had been shaved clean. He wore a short, neatly trimmed beard now.

I needed to snap out of it and greet him, but the sight of him made me worry that if I opened my mouth, all that would come out was a lust-filled, *"Hrrrrrnnnnnn."* It had been way too long since I'd had sex, and I was starting to develop some troubling symptoms of my unintended abstinence.

No way in hell could I introduce him to anyone in town. First off, the last thing this place needed was to be invaded by a horde of paparazzi. Secondly, the women would *murder* each other over him.

Ben extended a hand toward me. "Hi. You're Ella, right? Jack's told me all about you." His voice was also different from the videos: smoother, less stilted, maybe even a little deeper.

I put my hand in his. He had a firm grip, and though he was no doubt trying to be gentle, my knuckle joints still ground together. Thankfully, it was just the right amount of discomfort to jar me out of my lusty thoughts. "I am," I told him. "And you must be the artsy-fartsy Ben that Jack said I would get along with."

He released my hand and glanced toward the house. "Artsy-fartsy, huh?"

"I'm guessing you don't consider yourself an artist?"

"I'm getting pretty good at woodworking, does that count?" he asked. A smile spread over his full lips as he turned back to me.

I forgot my own name for a second, staring up at him.

Brain, I know this is hard right now, but I need you to please ignore how handsome this man is and process the question he asked me.

Belatedly, it complied.

"Hmm...it might," I said. "Tell me, have you ever confessed a deep, undying love for Barack Obama when in Jack's company?"

He frowned a little in response. "I don't think so?"

"A deep, undying love for labor unions?"

His frown deepened. "Huh?"

"Told him you even once voted democrat?"

"We haven't really discussed politics."

I tapped my chin with a gloved finger. "The mystery deepens."

"Uh..." He seemed unsettled, not being in on the joke. I liked that. It put us on more equal footing.

"Well, it's nice to meet you, Ben. I apologize in advance for my dogs. They lose their minds around new people."

With that, I led him up the porch stairs and into the house.

Chapter 2: Ben

The dogs were on me the second I stepped into the house, leaping, sniffing, and whining in such an excited frenzy that it was like there were five of them instead of two. Suddenly I was back on the training field, only instead of blocking tackles, I was fending off a pair of aggressively friendly dogs.

Ella raised her voice over the racket they were making. "Sam, Fred, meet Ben. Ben, I'd advise you not to let them touch you with their tongues. You'd understand why if you saw what else they've licked today."

I might have cracked a smile at that if I wasn't so keyed up.

Where the hell is Jack?

Knowing my gruff neighbor, he was probably in the living room stacking more logs on the fire. I'd made the mistake of telling him I was originally from Hawaii, and now he worried I would freeze to death if the house fell below 80 degrees, regardless of the fact that I also told him I'd lived in the Midwest for a while and was used to the cold.

He'd acted as though this was all brand-new information. Like he had no idea who I was.

I snuck a glance at Ella. She definitely knew who I was. It was obvious from the deer-in-headlights look she gave me in the driveway, though she recovered quick enough. Now I just needed to see what she'd do with this knowledge. If she was good people, like Jack claimed, she'd respect my privacy. But part of me, the part that had grown hard and bitter and disillusioned with humanity, was waiting for her to whip out her cellphone and upload my face and location to Twitter for all the world to see, ruining the peace and quiet I'd managed to find here.

I snuck several more glances at her in between dodging the probing noses of her dogs. She moved to the coat rack, stepped out of her boots, and then shoved down her snow pants, revealing lilac-colored leggings with little white reindeer prancing across them in a horizontal pattern. She was tall, maybe 5'9" or 5'10", with narrow hips and the long, solid legs of a distance runner.

I peeled my gaze away from her and ruffled the fur of the dog trying to dart past my defenses with his plague-tongue. I liked to think that I didn't have a "type", but if I was being honest with myself, that was bullshit. Looking back over my years of dating revealed a definitive pattern of tall, athletic women. Women who could help hold themselves up if we had sex in a shower or against a wall. Women who could wrap their muscular legs around my torso and use their strength to pull me closer, or flex their toned thighs over and over as they rose and fell above me.

I caught movement out of the corner of my eye and looked up to see *this* tall, athletic woman pull off her coat. Beneath it, she wore an olive-green long-sleeved running top. I'd had just enough fashion lessons crammed down my throat over the past decade to recognize how spectacularly the outfit clashed. It looked like she got dressed in the dark.

She glanced down and froze at the sight of herself, eyes wide, lips twitching open in horror. Her head started to turn toward me – likely to check if I'd noticed her fashion faux pas – and I shifted my gaze back to her dogs before she could catch me staring.

I risked another peek a minute later, just in time to watch her pull her shirt down a few inches and rest the hem of it against the fabric of her leggings to double-check that, yes, those colors were truly heinous together. She let it go with a huff, then yanked off her knitted hat. A rat's nest of flame-colored, sweat-damp hair tumbled loose.

She caught a glimpse of herself in the hall mirror, made a choking noise, and raked the mess into a ponytail. "Of all the frigging days," she muttered.

The whole debacle was kind of endearing to witness, but I'd learned that people didn't like to be laughed at when they were embarrassed, so I hid my amusement.

The Huskies had used my momentary distraction to press themselves closer, wiggling their butts so quickly that they almost blurred. One managed to sneak past my guard. A blast of hot, stinking breath hit my nose – the only warning I had before a slimy tongue slipped up the side of my neck.

"Jesus," I said, straightening back to my full height, out of their reach. I loved dogs, but they could be gross sometimes.

"Beer," Ella said, turning toward the fridge. "Only beer can help me now."

In full agreement, I wiped the drool from my skin and followed her into the kitchen. The light was better here, and I caught my first good look at her face as she passed. She had a creamy complexion with olive undertones, strikingly pale blue eyes, and a smattering of freckles across her button nose. She was pretty. Really pretty. Even with matted hair and cheeks a little blotchy from the cold.

She opened the door of the fridge and mostly disappeared behind it as she ducked down to inspect its contents. Mostly being the operative word. Her festive butt was the only part of her still visible. I was suddenly aware of just how long it had been since I'd been around an attractive woman. If Jack walked in now, he'd catch me staring.

"Any oatmeal stout left?" I asked.

She made a pained noise in response, and, without straightening, handed me one over the top of the door.

I frowned and moved to take it.

Jack rejoined us then, stopping beside me to clap a hand on my shoulder. "Don't mind Ella. Her sense of humor takes a little while to get used to. She likes to say things that are only funny if you were part of her conversation from twenty minutes before. Or a week ago." He gave me a long-suffering look and lowered his voice. "I miss a lot of the ones I think I'm meant to get."

"Ah, gotcha," I said. But I didn't really.

Needing something to do to keep my gaze from being drawn back to Ella's reindeer-covered ass, I uncapped my beer and took a healthy swig, savoring the beer's depth and complexity. This was by far the best homebrew I'd ever had.

Jack leaned in and mock-whispered, "She called on the way over and asked about the oatmeal stout. I told her I'd save the last two for her."

Her pained groan suddenly made sense.

"Oh, uh, sorry, Ella. I already took a sip," I told her.

She closed the fridge, the last of the oatmeal stout in hand, and turned toward us, revealing the full glory of her outfit to Jack for the first time.

He spluttered and took an exaggerated step back, hand over his heart. "Holy Hannah! Were you suddenly struck colorblind?"

"I'll have you know that this is the new style, Jack," she said. "Matchy-matchy is out. Clashy-clashy is in."

Jack looked to me, as if for help, and I just shrugged, starting to both understand and appreciate Ella's particular brand of humor. It seemed like the kind that left other people feeling slightly off-kilter but stopped well short of being mean-spirited or turning them into the butt of her jokes.

She turned to me. "It's okay about the beer, Ben. I can share like any other well-adjusted adult."

Jack opened his mouth. I could tell by his expression that something smart-assed was about to come out of it.

So could Ella. "Shut it," she told him.

He chuckled in response and wisely kept his unspoken comment to himself.

One of the dogs moved in then, to press against Ella's leg and look up at her with large, inquisitive eyes.

She leaned down to pet him. "Ready to take a nap?"

The dog sighed heavily, looking past ready.

She turned and led us into the living room.

I liked Jack's place. It was simple, straightforward, a lot like the man himself. The kitchen was small and tidy. A center island with barstools tucked beneath it doubled as the dining area. The living room was dominated by a fireplace made of river rock instead of the traditional brick, with rustic, comfortable armchairs and a couch spread out around it. Down the hallway were a bedroom, a home office, and a bathroom. Upstairs, two more bedrooms sat tucked under the rafters. I doubted the man even owned a television.

My gaze strayed back to Ella, following the swish of her fiery ponytail as she walked. I'd only known her for a few minutes, but I already felt something for her. Sometimes, you meet people, and you just know that there's potential there, be it for unforgettable sex, or intense, burning dislike and antagonization. While Ella was attractive, my intuition told me I could be friends with her. Good friends. That indefinable thing, that "click" was just...there.

I couldn't remember the last friend I'd made outside of football-related circles. As a kid, I'd hit it off with almost everyone I met. I was a good read of people. I was easy-going, quick to trust, and even quicker to forgive. Now I wasn't good with strangers. It was the lack of trust I'd developed. Or so I told myself. Because that's what I hoped it was.

Deep down, I was afraid it was something else. I didn't doubt that I had some level of brain injury, regardless of that "inconclusive" MRI I had after Zach died. I'd had concussions. I'd run head and shoulder first into dudes my size or bigger for nearly two decades, and had them hit me in return.

Just like my brother.

How extensive the damage to my brain was, I had no idea, because I hadn't subjected myself to the more in-depth tests needed to search for signs of Chronic Traumatic Encephalopathy. Would that degenerative brain disease lead me to suffer a life-ending seizure, like Zach? Or slip-slide my way into irrational, uncontrollable anger, paranoia, and violent outbursts, like some of the retired pros I'd met had? Or would I be one of the lucky asymptomatic few?

There was no way to tell. Yet.

Ella sank into the armchair on the far side of the room. The dog trailing her jumped up into her lap like a large puppy and paced in a circle as he tried to find the right spot to lay down. As a consequence, he nailed her on the side of the face with his tail.

She shot a hand up to deflect it on the next pass. "Come on, Fred."

He made two more circles before wedging his butt between her and the arm of the chair, his paws over her lap. He set his muzzle down on them with a heavy sigh and closed his eyes.

She dug the fingers of her free hand into the thick fur on the back of his neck. "I know, bud. Long day."

Jack folded himself down onto the far side of the couch. The other dog, Sam, scampered up from the fireplace and spread out beside him, leaving me with the remaining oversized armchair.

I hesitated to take it, unsure if I was staying. I'd managed to pull my gloves and coat off after walking through the door, no thanks to the dogs, but my boots, which I'd cleaned the snow from before coming inside, were still firmly tied to my feet in case I had to make a hasty getaway. Not that I expected I'd need to – Jack seemed like a pretty good judge of character – but I'd learned over the years that it was better to be prepared to run than it was to get caught out on Instagram by someone looking for their fifteen minutes of fame at your expense.

"You had Willow today?" Jack asked Ella.

She nodded. "Jane and Dave spent the morning finishing up her Christmas shopping and then went home to wrap. The plan was to have some low-key craft time with her at my house, but then she got into the candy canes, and I had to take her sledding to burn off the energy."

Jack arched a brow. "It work?"

"God, no."

"Willow is your niece?" I asked, trying to sift through all the names that Jack had mentioned.

"Yup." She pointed to the mantle of the fireplace. "She's the little girl in the far right picture."

I stepped over for a closer look. In the photograph, a small girl with almost as much hair as I had ran through a field of wildflowers. It was shot in late afternoon, with the sun slanting low, rendering the light that surrounded her a soft, hazy gold. It would have been adorable if not for the manic expression on her face that made it seem less like a peaceful frolic and more like she was sprinting toward the person holding the camera like she planned to tackle them.

"She looks like a handful," I said.

Jack and Ella laughed in response.

"You have no idea," Ella said.

Sounds like Micah.

Grief punched through me at the thought of my nephew. I locked the emotion down and buried it deep before it could show on my face. More pictures spread out along the mantle, and I took my time looking at them, needing a distraction right now.

Next to Willow's portrait was one of Jack and his wife Renee, who I recognized from the much larger photo hanging just down the hall. Beside the picture of the couple sat one of them and their grown children. Next to that was one of Jack and a man that looked about a decade older than him, their arms around each other's shoulders.

My gaze finally settled on a large frame absolutely crammed full of people – a much more visually diverse group of people than I ever expected to see after moving to this part of Maine. I leaned in and picked out Willow and Ella from the crowd.

"Are all these people your family members?" I asked, turning toward Ella.

She nodded. "The middle-aged couple on the left are my parents. The man beside them is my oldest brother, Jacob, with his wife and sons. The woman beside them is my oldest sister, Megan, with her wife, Stacey, on her right. The woman beside them is my sister Jane. Her husband, Dave, is the one holding Willow. Then there's me, my younger brother Charlie, and the baby in the family, Anabel."

Jack's landline rang – another thing I didn't think he owned was a cellphone. He pushed himself up from the couch, carefully, so as not to upset Sam, and went to answer it. I overheard him say hello before he disappeared down the hall, leaving Ella and me alone with the dogs again.

"Are you all adopted?" I asked.

She was the only white sibling in the picture, so she could have been biological, but I didn't think so. Her parents, also white, were both short and had dark hair. She looked nothing like them.

"We are," Ella said. "Mom and Dad wanted a big family but struggled with infertility. It's pretty common to look outside the US to adopt. Jacob is from Somalia, Megan is from China, Jane is from India, Charlie is from Afghanistan, Anabel is from South Korea, and I'm from what's now Montenegro."

I frowned, thinking back to my world history classes as I tried to place her age. "You weren't adopted during the Bosnian War, were you?"

She nodded.

"Damn."

"I was a baby, so I don't remember any of it. Thankfully."

"And your birth parents?"

She shook her head. "I don't know. I haven't looked for them."

"Are you going to?"

Why the fuck did I ask her that? I just met the woman, and here I was digging into some deeply personal shit.

She opened her mouth to respond.

I held up a hand to forestall her. "Don't feel like you have to answer that. I hate it when people I don't know pry into my life, so I'm sorry."

She waved me off. "It's okay. I'm used to it. Our family is different than most, especially around here, so I understand being curious. Plus, it's kind of fair play in this case, right? I probably know more about you and your family history than I have a right to -" She fell silent for a second, then glanced down the hallway, brow furrowing. "Does Jack know who you are?"

I followed her gaze. Jack's voice was distant, like he'd retreated into the bedroom. I doubted he could hear us, but I still lowered my voice, just in case. "I don't think so."

She followed suit. "I thought he might not. He doesn't own a TV, after all, and still gets his news from the local paper, the sports section of which is pretty shit. Then again, the rogue shampoo ad might have snuck into it, and he does know who you are and is just trying to make you feel like a normal person."

"That would be pretty decent of him," I said.

"Jack is pretty decent."

Are you? I wanted to press, but didn't.

"Do you…" She chewed on her bottom lip in a way that suddenly made it hard to focus on anything else. "Do you mind my asking what you're doing here?"

I let out a deep breath and stared down at my beer. That was a loaded question. One I'd anticipated before coming out here. One I'd made up a million answers to. But right now, I just couldn't bring myself to lie. Jack trusted her. She seemed nice enough. Maybe I could risk telling her a little bit of the truth.

I lifted my gaze back to her. "I needed to get away from it all."

There. Simple. To the point. It wasn't a lie, but it could be interpreted in a hundred different ways.

She took a sip of her beer before answering. "Good job then. This is probably the most far-flung place to get away to and still remain in the continental US."

That was exactly why I'd picked this place. "Thanks."

"I'm guessing you want to keep a low profile while you're here?"

I nodded.

"I'll keep my mouth shut," she said. I actually believed her. Especially when she followed it up with, "I'd suggest getting comfortable being a hermit for the next few months. At least until the snow clears. If you plan to stay that long. We get a little gossip crazy up here in the winter. It wouldn't even take anyone recognizing you to set off a firestorm. As soon as a local busybody got a look at your profile and put handsome-man and new-in-town together, you'd be inundated. I can run errands for you if need be. Or interference."

"Thank you for the offer," I said. "I get most everything I need delivered, and so far, I've lucked out with not having to sign for anything I wasn't already prepared to." Oh, the horrible disguises I'd donned. "But I'll let you know if I get stuck."

"Is your address listed under a different name?" she asked.

"It is."

"That's smart."

She opened her mouth to continue, but fell silent at the sound of Jack's voice, drawing closer. He said goodbye to the person on the other end of the line when he reached the kitchen and set the phone down on the island before rejoining us.

"You two getting to know each other?" he asked, carefully retaking his seat around the prone form of Sam. The dog didn't so much as stir.

"Yup," Ella said. "We were just about to start braiding each other's hair before you interrupted us."

Jack nodded. "Good. You should go check out her cabin, Ben. Looks like something out of a magazine. She could have your whole house done up in your style within a week if you unleashed her on it."

Ella raised her free hand and indicated her wild hair and eye-melting outfit. "Yes, I'm quite stylish."

I grinned. "Jack may be jumping the gun. Half of the rooms don't even have sheetrock up in them yet."

Her eyes widened. "Oh, wow. I heard Mabel Reynolds was something of a hoarder before she passed away. Did you have to gut the place?"

"Not really." I pushed off from the mantle and made my way to the free chair, mind made up to stay. "There was definitely a lot of stuff, but it was more like a lifetime of accumulation than mania-driven collecting. I'm surprised her kids didn't want any of it. A lot of the furniture is antique."

"Nah," Jack said. "Nancy's house is already filled to the brim, and Dale is getting ready to retire soon and head down to Florida. Last time I talked to him, he was trying to downsize."

"I still feel guilty for keeping some of the pieces," I said.

Jack gave me a funny look. "Well, feel better knowing that you covered the cost of them when you overpaid for the house."

I groaned response. This was an old argument between us. "Jack, it's a four-thousand-square-foot home on a hundred-acre lot. They were asking way too little for it."

A hundred and fifty thousand had seemed like an offensively low price to me, even with the amount of work it needed. I would have felt like a criminal if I'd paid that for it.

"I didn't realize it was so big," Ella said.

I nodded. "Six bedrooms. Three sitting rooms. A library."

Jack snorted. "And only one functioning toilet."

I tipped my beer toward him. "Fair point, but I'm working on that."

"How far have you gotten with the reno?" Ella asked.

"I'm a little behind schedule," I said. "I had to have the foundation fixed before I could move in, so that set fire to my original timetable."

Jack turned to her. "You should have seen the equipment they brought up the hill for that. Semis hauling massive steel beams. Bucket loaders." He paused for dramatic effect. "A crane."

Ella choked on her beer. "They got a crane up here?"

Jack nodded.

"I hope I never have to go through that again," I said, rubbing a hand over my face. "Once that nightmare was over, I had to get the barn squared away. That's where I'm storing most of the renovation supplies, so I needed it to be temperature controlled. The basement is done, the kitchen is getting there, and the study is right behind it. I got all of the fireplaces cleaned and working before the first snowfall. Some of the electric had to be rerun to replace the remaining knob and tube wiring, and the plumber isn't in for a few more days, hence the lack of drywall. Or more than one functioning toilet. While I'm waiting, I've been stripping the hardwood floors, which are in pretty good shape considering they're a few hundred years old."

Ella frowned. "I feel like we have different definitions of what amounts to a gut job."

I chuckled. "Okay, now that I'm saying all of this out loud, I guess it does sound like one."

Her frown deepened. "How long ago did you move in?"

"Three months."

"Damn, that's -" she glanced at Jack, then seemed to reconsider how to finish the sentence, likely because her original thought had something to do with who I was and how long I'd already managed to hide out here. "That's a really respectable amount of work to get done in that time," she said.

"Thanks. My dad owns a contracting company back in Hawaii. I spent every summer until I moved off the island doing this stuff. It's basically second nature at this point."

"Hey, now," Jack said. "Don't sell yourself short. That's still a hell of a lot of work, even for someone who knows what they're doing." He turned to Ella. "Ben's got a great work ethic. Reminds me a lot of you, kiddo."

I followed his gaze. "Jack said you're an artist?" I asked, latching onto the chance to move the subject of conversation away from myself.

"More of a graphic designer at this point," she said. "I'm the owner and sole employee of Ella Jones Paperie, which I sell through several outlets, including my own website."

"I was wondering how an artist could make a living this far out in the boonies." Too late I realized how that might sound insulting. "No offense."

She grinned. "None taken. This is legit the boonies. To answer the question, you have to get creative. And good at bookkeeping and market research and understanding state and federal tax law. When I first started, I was selling one-of-a-kind paintings and barely scraping by. Two years ago, I switched to prints, which did a little better, and then a little over a year ago I adjusted my products and my target audience, and now most of my revenue comes from greeting cards, calendars, and wedding invitations. I use soy ink and recycled, compostable paper that I source locally, so I'm a hit with the eco-friendly crowd."

"You'd like her work," Jack told me. "Quaint, quirky little forest scenes filled with critters. Most of them are sweet, but some are pretty twisted. My favorite card she did is this Christmas one from last year, with an adorable little squirrel dressed in a holiday sweater staring out of a picturesque winter woodland. You'd expect it to say something cute, but instead the words "I swear to God, if you leave me alone for even a second at our family gathering this year, I will poison your fucking eggnog" was spread out around him in flowery script."

I chuckled and turned back to Ella. "That's pretty good. I bet you sold those by the boat-load."

She looked away from me, her cheeks coloring. "I did. Thanks."

I sobered, fixating on that flush, thinking back to a few minutes ago when she'd made an offhand comment about town busybodies. She'd called me handsome, hadn't she?

Chapter 3: Ella

I made Benjamin Kakoa laugh. Several times. Hard.

This bizarre reality kept me up late last night after I got home from Jack's and was entirely to blame for why I was already awake at – I rolled over to look at my alarm clock. Oh, God, it was five o'clock in the morning. I'd gotten four hours of sleep. Today was going to be rough.

Sam, sensing I was awake, snuggled closer to me. I knew it was him, even in the dark, because while Fred was my shadow during the day, Sam was my cuddlebug at night. I slipped an arm out of the covers, tossed it over him, and closed my eyes, willing myself to fall back asleep.

Sheep. Think of a herd of dumb, fluffy sheep jumping over a white picket fence. I counted one, ten, eighty. The sheep started doing weird little side-kicks to keep my thoughts on them instead of drifting back to -

No! Don't think of him. Watch these sheep. You're getting very tired watching these acrobatic sheep, Ella. Very. Tired. Look, that one did a little back flip! Isn't it adorable? Doesn't it just make you sooo sleeepy?

No. Not even a little. Because I made Benjamin *freaking* Kakoa laugh. And frown. And roll his eyes. Toward the end of the evening, I even got him to join me in teasing Jack.

It's weird, meeting a celebrity. You have this whole persona built up in your head of who they are and how they'll act. Take an ex-football star turned advocate. I'd assumed he'd be stoic, tough, with a dash of toxic masculinity added in to spice it up a bit. That had less to do with Ben's public image and more to do with the acceptance of violence that surrounded the sport of football, both on and off the field.

Watching him laugh at my murder-squirrel Christmas card kind of blew my mind. And made me feel like a complete asshole for making all those assumptions about him. I hadn't been that embarrassed in years. The strength of my blush made my face feel like it was on fire. Then he kept laughing, and, well, I was a red-blooded heterosexual woman, and holy shit that man was beautiful when he laughed. Especially since he did it so unselfconsciously. My raging embarrassment had been immediately eclipsed by raging hormones.

My cheeks burned again thinking of him catching me with that look on my face when he finally stopped laughing. You know, *that* one. That, "Oh, yes, I will gladly climb you like a tree. Now please?" look that is utterly unmistakable.

Ugh. Why did I have to be sweat-slicked and dressed like a weirdo the night I met the hottest man I'd ever seen?

I rolled onto my back and pressed the heels of my hands into my forehead. Fred jumped up on the bed, the mattress sagging beneath his added weight. His hot breath hit my face a second later.

I reached blindly toward him in the dark and grabbed the fur of his neck to give it a little shake. "Lilac leggings, Fred. And an olive shirt. With *this* hair."

That'll teach me to never speed-dress again.

Fred let out the low woof-yip that Huskies were famous for.

"No. Wrong response, boy. Forlorn howling is far more appropriate right now."

He woof-yipped again.

"I have failed in your training."

He whined.

"Better."

Sam shifted on my other side, then the mattress rose and I heard his paws padding over the hardwood. Fred pulled free from my hands and followed him out the door. I was awake, which to them meant it was time to go potty.

I gave up on sleep and turned the light on. It took me an excruciatingly long time to get out of bed. My body was like, "No. What are you doing? We were warm in there. Go back to that place," and actively attempted to sabotage my upward momentum, while my brain was all, "BENJAMIN KAKOA JUST HAPPENED. ARISE, GODDAMN YOU!"

Eventually, I managed to stumble downstairs, where the dogs waited by the front door. I cracked it open just enough for them to slip out. The draft that snuck in was damn near arctic, and the second Sam's tail whipped past, I pushed it shut.

I complained about the dogs, but they were pretty well-trained. My yard wasn't fenced in. The fact that I could let them outside and trust them not to take off and also bark when they were ready to come back in spoke volumes.

I staggered to the kitchen and made myself a strong pot of coffee, all the while thinking about Ben. It had taken work to coax him into taunting Jack with me. I wasn't used to that. It usually only took me a few minutes to get people to relax enough around me that they were cackling with laughter and sharing their deepest, darkest secrets.

Mom said it was because there was something inherently trustwor-thy about my face. Dad said it was because of my self-deprecation. My brother Jacob's wife, Sofia, said it was because I had a sociopath's ability to read people, paired with a pathological need to be liked. She was a clinical psychologist, so obviously I ignored her and went with my parents' explanations. Because she was just joking.

I hoped.

Even with the hard work I put in last night, Ben remained steadfast-ly guarded and quiet in between those small bursts of emotion, letting Jack and I do the bulk of the talking. Whenever the conversation drifted back toward him, he managed to expertly steer it away from himself. I wasn't sure if that was because he was worried I'd somehow slip-up and reveal his fame to Jack, or if he didn't want to tell me anything because he thought I might race home to blog about it, or if that was just how all celebrities had to be to protect themselves.

Not that I could blame them. It must suck to spend your days hounded by paparazzi, unable to even go to the grocery store for your-self. Or make a new friend without fearing that they were only using you to further themselves in some way. Then there was the digital aspect of it, allowing both fans and detractors an outlet to comment on every single moment of a celebrity's life, as it happened.

I read somewhere that it takes a hundred positive comments to overcome the emotional damage that a single negative one can wreak on your psyche. I believed it. I had ten thousand followers on In-stagram and got trolled at least once a week. For painting whimsical watercolors of chipmunks and raccoons and moose. Like, seriously? The span of the moose's antlers is somehow morally offensive to you?

And yet I'd found myself looking closer at my paintings afterward, inspecting the distance between those antlers and wondering if they really were off in some way that I just couldn't see because I created them.

That was nothing compared to what Ben had to put up with. He had well over two million followers – I checked before going to bed last night – and posted about controversial issues like taking a knee during the National Anthem, the societal repercussions of idolizing large, violent men while denigrating any male who shows vulnerability, and the class-action lawsuit that he and a slew of other former players had recently filed against the USFL for downplaying the dangers of the sport to those who played it.

Some of the comments on his feed were so enraging that I almost hulk-smashed my tablet. The kind of vile, racist, bigoted vitriol spewed through the filter of anonymity that makes you lose what little faith you have left in humanity.

No wonder he was so guarded.

It made me that much more determined to get him to loosen up around me. If I ever saw him again. For once, it wasn't because of some need of my own. It was because of him. Because it must be terrible to feel like you can never relax. To always be worried that some small detail about your life that you accidentally let slip might appear on a celebrity gossip site the next morning. The man deserved a break from it all.

The sound of barking pulled me from my thoughts. I went to the door and let the boys back in. They waited patiently on the tile floor of the entryway while I toweled off their feet and legs. Afterward I gave them each a treat from the jar of biscuits on the upper shelf of the coat rack, then left them to demolish them as I went to get coffee.

My kitchen was small, like the rest of the cabin, but it didn't feel cramped thanks to the bright white paint and open shelving. I eyed the shelf containing my mismatched collection of mugs and opted for the largest. I think it was supposed to be a soup bowl, but I'd never used it for that. Instead it served as my coffee version of "we're going to need a bigger boat".

I added a dash of cream and then poured it to the brim. My first sip was heavenly.

A snuffling noise came from the living room, followed by a low, playful growl. The dogs. Sometimes it felt like I was raising two toddlers. Every time I heard an unfamiliar sound, I rushed over to make sure they weren't getting into trouble (they were usually getting into trouble). With so little sleep, my rush this morning was more like the shambling of a freshly turned zombie.

I rounded the couch and found the source of the scuffle. The dogs were sprawled out on the rug near the fireplace, playing tug-of-war with each other over one of their favorite toys. That was one of the good things about having two of them; they could entertain themselves in the morning until my brain came online.

I set my coffee down on a side table and stepped over them. Up here, you had to plan your life around the weather. I kept enough firewood in the house to get me through a week without power, just in case a tree came down on a line from the weight of the snow.

I grabbed a few pieces and stacked them over the kindling already laid out in the fireplace. Five minutes later, a merry glow filled the room, the dogs had ended their game – Sam won – and I was sprawled out on the side of the couch that had the chaise lounge, sipping my coffee and searching through the internet.

Okay, cyber-stalking Ben.

He was still active on social media, with three posts on Twitter from last night after I'd left Jack's. They were retweets. One was from a study by Johns Hopkins on TBIs in the USFL, another was from The Concussion Foundation, and another was from *The New York*

Times on something called CTE. I clicked on each link and spent the next forty minutes reading through the articles. Then I spent another God-knows-how-long clicking on still more links, falling fully down the rabbit hole of brain-related medical research.

It was light outside by the time I picked my head back up. I stared out at the sun glancing off the snowbanks, trying not to feel overwhelmed. This was a lot of information to unpack.

I had known about TBIs, but CTE was a new term for me. Chronic Traumatic Encephalopathy. It was a degenerative brain disorder associated with repeated head trauma. Like, from years of playing a contact sport like football. From what I could decipher through all the medical jargon, your brain cells just started dying off.

The most troubling study showed that nearly all of the brains posthumously tested from former USFL players showed signs of CTE. The author cautioned that there was a bias in the tests, as CTE was suspected in many of the cases, but still. Ninety. Nine. Percent.

Another study examined a large number of ex-USFL players still living, using a combination of brain scanning technology and written and verbal exams. The results were...not great. The scans revealed that 40% had abnormal brain structures, 43% had damage to white matter in the brain – which, thanks to Google, I now knew connected nerve cells between the brain's regions – and 30% had damage to the structures that neurons communicated through. The other tests showed 45% had difficulty with memory and learning. And it didn't even get into the behavioral aspect of CTE.

Altogether, it was a devastating disease, one that couldn't be properly diagnosed until an autopsy was performed. Among the symptoms associated with it were mood swings, memory loss, suicidal thoughts, problems with impulse control, and violent outbursts. Then there were headaches and seizures. The onset of symptoms could vary between just a few years after the trauma, to decades later.

If Zach Kakoa had it, did that mean...

Oh, God. Ben.

I immediately dove back into my phone and tried to find out if he was one of the living players who'd been tested. No luck. They didn't publish names. Next, I searched out interviews he'd given since Zach's death. Again, they were a no-go. Then I stumbled across a video interview with his mother.

The journalist questioning her asked if their family had concerns about Ben.

"*Of course we do,*" she answered. "*He's 28 years old. God forgive us, we put the boys in the pee-wee league when they were eight. That's twenty years of brain trauma.*"

"*But at the time you had no knowledge of the increased risk of CTE in players that start before the age of twelve,*" the interviewer said.

"*We didn't even know what CTE or TBIs were back then. You think that helps me sleep at night? You think that helps my dead son? You think that helps my still-living son deal with the fact that in five years, or ten, or twenty, he might start to lose himself to a degenerative brain disease that could have been prevented by more awareness, or stricter rules, or better protective equipment?*"

I stopped the video, set my phone down, walked over to Fred and Sam, and snuggled down between them, drawing them close with my arms.

"I love you both," I told them. "So much."

Sam licked my face, and for once, I didn't pull away.

Last week I cried after accidentally stepping on Fred's paw hard enough to make him cry out. Part of it was because I had felt so bad for hurting him, while the other part was because I realized I could never be sure that he knew it was an accident and that I was so, so sorry for it.

The dogs were like my children, but I knew there was a difference between them and actual children. I could only imagine how Ben's parents felt. How Ben felt, every day, not knowing what the future held for him.

My face burned with embarrassment again. There I was last night, ogling his good looks and trying to get him to lighten up because of my own stupid need to feel liked.

I immediately abandoned my plan to put him at ease around me and instead adopted the much better plan to leave him the hell alone. I also needed to talk to Jack. He all but forced my number on the poor guy before we left last night, in case Ben wanted help with design choices. From everything he'd said last night, Ben knew what he was doing. He probably wouldn't call, but if he did, I was going to let him decide everything. I wasn't going to invite myself over or him here. I was going to drop the full-blown charm offensive I went on last night and try my hardest to treat him like I would anyone else.

He said he came out here to get away. It was easy enough to guess from what. The media, the trolls. Maybe he needed space and time to deal with the death of his brother, sister-in-law, and nephew. Or to come to terms with his own risk of CTE and what it might or might not mean for him.

I hoped he was able to. I tried to think about it from my own perspective, like if I had to deal with all of that. I had no idea how I would react, or how long it would take me to process through everything.

My phone rang from the couch. I let the dogs go and stood to get it. My sister Megan's name flashed across the caller ID.

I swiped right to answer. "Hey, Megan."

"Hi, Ella," Stacey's voice greeted me. I would have worried that something had happened to Megan if not for the fact that she and her wife were forever calling me on each other's phones.

"Hey, Stace. What's up?"

"We're supposed to get a Nor'easter on the twenty-third and want to get the hell out of Boston before it hits. Is it okay if we get there a day early?"

They were staying with me through Christmas, because with Anabel still in high school, Charlie home from college, and Jacob and his crew all crashing at my parents', the house would be packed. Megan was enough of an introvert that crowding in with everyone else was a non-starter. Staying at Jane's was out, too, because they'd never progressed past the antagonistic stage of their sisterhood. My place was the perfect option. Megan and I had always been close, and because I was so good at reading people, I recognized when she needed to be left alone for a few hours.

I put Stacey on speaker and pulled up my phone's calendar. "So, you'll be here Friday?"

"Yup."

I looked down at my unswept floor just in time to watch a tumbleweed of dog hair roll by my feet, then glanced around at the rest of my house. I wouldn't have called it a disaster zone, but...

"Friday's great!" I said with forced cheer. "What time are you going to get here?"

"Meg, when do you want to leave Friday?" Stacey asked my sister.

"I don't know. Noon?" was her muffled response.

"We should be there by six or seven," Stacey said. "Depending on traffic. We'll call you along the way and give you updates."

"Sounds good."

"Okay, talk to you later."

"Love you guys."

"Love you too," she said before hanging up.

Friday. That would still give me time to finish up printing all my open orders, get to the post office, deep clean my house, set up the spare bedroom, wrap my Christmas presents, and drive over to Walmart to stock up on all the tofu and vegetables I could find. Megan and Stacey were vegan, and I wanted them to have plenty of food options while staying with me.

Right, first I needed to make a list.

My stomach rumbled, as if to say, "No, first you need food, woman."

Chapter 4: Ben

"Boom. Done." I raised my hand and dropped the stain-soaked rag I held like it was a mic. It landed on the tarp beneath me with an uninspired *splat*.

My lower back twinged as I straightened from a crouch. I probably should have taken more breaks instead of spending the entire day doubled over like a pretzel, but I wanted the floors done so I could focus on getting the drywall up, and no one had ever described me as a patient person.

I dug my knuckles into the spasming muscle and examined my handiwork. Even to my biased eyes, it looked good. It wasn't every day you came across 16-inch-wide, 150-year-old floorboards in that good of a condition, and it took me an embarrassing amount of time to find the right stain for them. Too light and they might blend into the room, unseen. Too dark, and I'd cover up all the good stuff. In the end, I opted for a medium-depth varnish that coated the wood in a golden glow and sank into the whorls and knots and other minutiae "imperfections", bringing all that gorgeous detail out.

I left the sitting room and crossed the hall to the dining room, where I'd started staining at five a.m. The day had since bled into afternoon, and the southern facing windows in the dining room bathed the floors in natural light. They looked well on their way to dry.

I pulled my cellphone out of my back pocket, ignored the Twitter notifications crowding the welcome screen, and pulled up my camera. I crouched down, back protesting, and took several shots before finding the right angle. I'd never been a fan of filters, but I used the built-in photo editing tool to darken the image to the point that the detail in the grain popped, then attached the finished picture to a group text with my parents and hit send.

I already knew how they'd respond. Dad would be effusively proud. Mom would love it. My eye for detail came from her. Whenever Dad was in a fix about paint choice or finishing touches, he'd ask Mom, and she always had the perfect solution.

My phone dinged with an incoming text.

I LOVE IT. I bet it looks even better in person. When can I come out to see it???

I sighed. Mom. She was getting pushy about visiting. Even though she'd promised me she'd try to respect my wishes and give me some space. I'd never been great at saying no to her, even less so since Zach died, and I was torn between being annoyed and feeling guilty.

My fingers hovered over the keyboard. What the hell did I say back to her?

While I hesitated, my phone began to rapid-fire chime.

Great job, Ben! It looks awesome. Perfect color to bring out all that character. Ignore your mother. Take your time.

Hani, don't tell him to ignore me! Christmas is in three days. He shouldn't spend it alone!

He asked for space, Klara, and we need to respect that.

Isolation isn't good for humans.

Honey, the man has only been gone for a few months. It's not like he's lived in a shack on the Outer Hebrides for five years.

I read a study yesterday that said even a few months of hermit-like existence can be detrimental to mental health, and with the risk of CTE, Ben has to be more careful than most.

Gee, thanks, Mom.

Klara, Ben is still part of this text. Maybe we don't talk about him like he isn't here?

Oh, sorry, Ben! You know how I worry. Read the study.

She sent the link. It was one I'd already seen.

I've read it, I typed back. *And I'm not a complete hermit. In case you've missed it, the three of us talk almost every day, and I still keep up with my friends back home. Please don't worry about me. I'm doing okay. I've even made a few new friends out here.*

The texts stopped. I waited for Mom's third degree, but it didn't come. Good. Hopefully I'd put off the threat of a visit for another few weeks by mentioning new friends, though "friends" was definitely an exaggeration. Jack didn't know who I really was, and I'd just met Ella.

My phone rang. Dad was FaceTiming me, which he never did alone. Looked like I didn't escape anything after all.

I hit accept.

My parents' familiar faces filled the screen.

Mom leaned in, eyes narrowed. "Who are these friends?"

Well, hello to you too, Mom.

"Jack lives up the hill from me," I told her. "He's in his mid-60s and has no idea who I am. It's kind of a nice change."

"He isn't one of those hillbilly rednecks, is he?" she asked.

I thought of Jack, his lack of a TV and a cellphone, the couple hundred pounds of meat in his basement freezers from animals he'd killed and butchered himself. I immediately decided against telling her any of this. "No, Mom. He's totally normal."

Her brows rose. "Is that it? I thought you said friends. As in plural."

Dad's hand covered their camera, and my screen went dark. "Honey, stop pestering him. He's smart. He'll know to reach out if the loneliness starts to get to him."

"One old man who is probably just as isolated as he is doesn't sound like a healthy social life," Mom said.

I needed to put a stop to this before my annoyance sparked into anger. "Uh, Dad? Your hand is covering the camera, not the microphone. I can hear everything you're saying."

He took it away. "Oops. Sorry, Ben."

Beside him, Mom's expression was full of concern. She opened her mouth, likely to berate or beg me; I didn't have the patience to find out which.

"There's a woman too," I said.

Dad's brows climbed up his forehead. "Oh, really? She pretty?"

"Who cares if she's pretty?" Mom said. "Is she one of those weirdo woodlanders? Or an instagroupie?"

I rubbed a hand over my face. "Mom, where are you even getting these phrases? No. She's totally normal." Well, kind of normal. I thought of Ella's wild outfit and special brand of humor.

Mom stared into the camera. "He's smiling. Hani, why is he smiling? Are you lying to your mother, Benjamin?"

Uh-oh. She went full Benjamin on me. "No, ma'am."

Distrust played over her features. "What's her name, then?"

"Ella."

"Ella what?"

"Jones."

"What's she do for a living?"

"She's an artist. No, a graphic designer." Crap. "Well, a bit of both."

Her eyes sparked like she'd caught me in a lie. "Ah-ha!"

"No, Mom, I swear. She owns Ella Jones Paperie. You can look her up online."

She pointed at me. "You stay right there!" Then she exited screen right, leaving Dad and me alone.

"Sooo...how you been?" I asked him.

He leaned close to the phone, his dark eyes large, "Your mother is becoming a handful. I think I may un-retire."

I nearly choked trying to stifle my laughter. Handful was an understatement. If Mom was this overbearing at a distance, I could only imagine what she was like in person. Poor Dad.

Mom crowded back in next to him before I could say anything else. She had a tablet in one hand, the fingers of her other one flying over the screen.

"Oh, honey, look," she said, pushing the tablet in front of my father.

His eyes crinkled as he smiled. "Well, that's kind of charming. What a cute little fox."

"Told you she was real, Mom," I said, careful to keep the gloating out of my tone. "You guys should check out the birthday card with the moose on the cover."

I might have gone a little overboard looking through Ella's online listings after I left Jack's the other night. I just had to see that squirrel and his death threats for myself. And then after I found it and laughed at it all over again, I read through the rest of her tongue-in-cheek, and, okay, sometimes borderline offensive greeting cards.

I knew they'd found the one I asked them to search for when Dad threw his head back and barked out a laugh.

Mom was slower on the draw, still frowning at the screen. "Wait. I don't get it. Is the moose swearing at the beaver?"

"Yes," Dad and I chorused.

"But why does he have candles on his antlers? Oh, no. I get it. Oh, that is so *wrong*." But then, looking for all the world like she didn't want to, she grinned. And then started to chuckle. "This still doesn't prove that you know her," she said when her laughter subsided. "You could have seen something in the local newspaper about her, for all we know."

My frustration with her came roaring back.

I am a grown-ass man. I will not scream at my mother over the phone.

"When have I ever lied to you?" I asked her.

Her expression darkened. "Seriously? You want to play that game with me, Mr. I-don't-know-where-those-beer-cans-came-from?"

"I was sixteen!"

"The point stands."

"Fine. I'll send you a picture of us the next time we hang out." Anything to get her to back off.

"When will that be?"

"Tomorrow," I said.

Why. Did. I. Say. That? Years of pressure on the playing field, and I faced it like the pro I was. A little harassment from my mother, and I caved like a house of cards. I really should have known better. She was like a dog with a bone when she worried about a loved one. She would not let this go. If I didn't send her a picture tomorrow, she'd probably get on an airplane.

She grinned at me through the phone like a Cheshire cat. Like I'd played right into her hand. "Okay. Talk to you tomorrow. Love you!"

"Love you, Ben," Dad said.

"Love you guys too."

I started texting Dad the moment we hung up. *Please, you gotta help me out here. Mom's stressing me out. I came here to unwind. I need this break. REALLY need it.*

God, if only they knew how much.

I know, Ben, Dad answered. *I'll do what I can. Go easy on your mom, though. We're all she has left, and she's terrified of losing either of us. Every day you're away is a day something could happen to you without her being close enough to help.*

Great. Now I felt like an asshole.

I strode into the kitchen and tossed my phone on the unfinished island. I was mad, at both myself and them. Nothing good ever comes from speaking from a place of anger. Better to cool down before responding. But seriously, I came out here for *me.* And now it was somehow more about my mother's mental health than my own. She wasn't the one who had to live with CTE.

I braced my knuckles on the plywood that currently served as my kitchen counter, bowed my head, and counted to ten. That last thought wasn't entirely fair or accurate. Mom had already lost one son to CTE. If I was diagnosed, she'd have to watch me suffer from whatever symptoms manifested, all while knowing that she and Dad were the ones to put us in football at an early age. She had just lost a son and was worried about losing another. I understood her grief. Her fear. Not a day went by that I didn't miss my brother. Not a day went by that I didn't worry about sharing his fate.

But this goddamn temper of mine was getting harder and harder to control.

After several deep breaths, I picked up my phone.

I'll try to be more understanding, I told my father.

It was the best I could manage.

I flicked the phone to silent and went upstairs. My bedroom was on the second floor, a big behemoth of a corner room, complete with adjoining sitting room and an en suite bathroom that now, thanks to my plumber, had a functioning toilet and shower.

The day he showed up was awkward as hell. I donned another disguise, which consisted of an oversized, ill-fitting, padded sweater that masked my muscle and made it look more like lumpy bulk. A pair of dark contacts and huge, owlish glasses helped. Then there was the grand finale, my hair, which I attempted to comb smooth and pull back into a low, hippyish ponytail.

I could admit that I might have gone too deep into my assumed identity, like an undercover cop that loses sight of where the line is. At one point, I even uttered, "Far out, man" in response to something the plumber said.

So, yeah, that happened.

Maybe my isolation was getting to me more than I'd been willing to admit. At least the plumber was the only one to witness my humiliation. Judging by his muttered "weirdo" when he finally left, he hadn't recognized me either. Thank God for small miracles.

I tugged off my shirt as I walked into my room and then chucked it into the hamper. The rest of my clothes followed. I replaced them with workout gear. The muscle in my back was still complaining, but I had some adrenaline left from my irritation that I needed to get rid of, and the best way for me to do that had always been to sweat it out in the gym. Lifting weights centered me, grounded me, burned off my excess cortisol and replaced it with the good vibes of endorphins.

I'd trimmed down since my football days, and it felt good. I no longer needed to pack the bulk on to pad myself against getting hit by what felt like a battering ram. I'd added more cardio and was surprised to find that I actually liked running. I used to hate sprints. And long distance? Man, forget about it. But it was different when you did it for yourself than when you were forced to by a sadistic training coach armed with a bullhorn.

All of my workout equipment was in the basement; one of the reasons it was the first part of the house I finished. I turned on the sound system in the corner and then hopped on the treadmill, walking for five minutes to loosen the lingering tightness in my limbs. Note to self: spending the entire day in a full crouch is a dumb thing to do. After I warmed up, I jogged for another twenty to get my heartrate going. Once I hit the two-mile mark on my treadmill and that runner's high kicked in, my mind sort of fuzzed out. It was a lot like meditation. I definitely understood how people got addicted to distance races.

Maybe once the snow melted I could ask Jack or Ella if there were any secluded trails nearby. *Safe*, secluded trails. I'd like to avoid coming face to face with a bear, or a moose for that matter. I saw one two months ago, walking through my backyard. It looked primeval. Nothing like the whimsical, be-sweatered creature on Ella's cards. This thing had been almost too big to be real.

I spent the next hour in a circuit. It was shoulders and biceps day. I alternated from curls to presses to underhand pull-ups and through about ten other exercises, pausing every six sets to jog in place or do a series of jumping jacks to keep my pulse up.

Sweat slicked my skin by the time I finished. I was exhausted, but I felt better. Calmer. Able to understand where my parents were coming from and admit that Mom might have been right about a couple of things.

The shower I took after my workout felt like a luxury. I spent an obscene amount of time standing beneath the rainfall showerhead, letting the scalding water go to work on my sore muscles. Reliable hot water had been a pipe dream – pun totally intended – before the plumber worked his magic.

Eventually I forced myself from the warmth of the shower into the cooler air beyond. I tugged on a pair of thick sweats and a long-sleeved shirt, then headed downstairs in search of my phone.

Ella's number was taped to my fridge. Good thing I hadn't put up a stink about taking it from Jack. It saved me the trouble of asking him for it and calling her up out of the blue.

I pulled it off the fridge and punched it into my phone.

Ella picked up on the first ring. "Mom, for the love of God, keep Megan and me out of this. We don't care what you caught Charlie looking at on his laptop. He's nineteen. Boys that age are gross. Actually, boys most any age are gross, but that's beside the point. The point is, you should leave it alone. For all you know, it could have been for some biology class he's taking."

What the hell was she talking about? "Um...Ella?"

There was a long pause on the other end of the line. "This is not my mother. I see that now from the caller ID."

I grinned. "No. Definitely not your mother."

"Sorry, who is this?"

"Ben," I said, flat-out refusing to say my full name on the off chance that I was on speaker and she wasn't alone. Paranoid? Sure, just a little. I'd own that.

"Hi, Stan," she said, voice raised.

"No, Ben," I told her, matching her elevated tone. We must have had a bad connection.

"Guys, it's my friend Stan, I gotta take this."

Oh. She wasn't alone.

There was another prolonged silence, and then what sounded like a door being closed.

"Okay, sorry. My sister and her wife are crashing at my place," she said. "Just to be clear, this is the Ben I met at Jack's the other night?"

"Yes."

"No offense, but I need you to tell me what we drank."

"Jack's homebrew. You graciously shared the last of the oatmeal stout with me."

"Right, sorry. Needed to make sure it wasn't a reporter catfishing me or something to get to you."

I opened my mouth to respond, but didn't actually say anything. I was too caught off guard by the lengths a woman I'd just met would go to protect my privacy.

"You still there?" she asked.

I snapped out of it. "Yeah, sorry. That was smart of you. I really appreciate it."

"No problem," she said. "What can I do for you?"

"Actually, this is going to seem really weird, but I have a huge favor to ask you."

Chapter 5: Ella

I hung up the phone and stared at my closed bedroom door. Benjamin Kakoa just called and asked me to come to his house tomorrow to take a selfie with him to send to his parents. How was this my life?

I double-checked my phone, confirming that yes, I did just get an incoming call from an unknown number, and no, I didn't hallucinate the whole thing. I also didn't ask the very obvious "WTF, Ben?" question that had sprung to my lips.

But seriously, what the fuck? It was such a random thing to ask someone you just met. The fact that he'd offered no explanation was also weird. Like, this felt like a test weird. Or maybe he didn't explain himself because we just met and he didn't trust me with any more information than he absolutely had to give me. Which was fair. But what if he was doing that and was also testing me to see if I pried, or posted something cryptic about it on Facebook?

Argh! I was going to sleep like crap again. I just knew it.

A snuffling sound came from beneath my door, followed by the threat of a whine. The dogs. I'd been up here too long. I was being a bad hostess.

I pulled up Ben's number to save it but hesitated over the contact name. Stan had come blurting out of my mouth when he called because it was the most bland, unassuming male name I could think of on the spot. No offense to all the Stans out there. I don't blame you. I blame your parents.

I decided to stick with that name and saved the contact as "Stan". I was paranoid enough that now that I'd called him that once, it would be safer to always call him that. You know, on the off chance that Megan, who had never once in her life showed even the least interest in spying on me, chose this visit to try to hack into my phone.

I rolled my eyes at myself and went to the door. The dogs stood right outside, waiting to greet me like we hadn't seen each other in a week. I reached down to pet them. "Hi, yes. I missed you too. That was a long five minutes, huh?"

Megan and Stacey were stretched out next to each other on the chaise lounge when I reemerged downstairs. Stacey was of Norwegian descent, and her feet extended a whole foot farther than my sister's. Megan's head rested on her wife's shoulder, her long raven locks contrasting with Stacey's blonde pixie cut. They turned when they heard the floorboards creak under me.

I paused just behind the couch. *Come on, Ella. Time to lie like you've been doing it all your life.*

"That was my friend, Stan," I said.

Megan gave me a look like, *No shit, Sherlock.*

I guess I did kind of scream that name a few times after picking up.

"He's going through a rough patch right now," I told them. "If it's okay with you guys, I'm going to swing by his place tomorrow morning to check in on him. I still want to go cross country skiing with you, though."

Ella Jones: artist, entrepreneur, stone-cold liar.

Stacey smiled. "That's fine. We can go after you get back. Maybe the snow will have started by then." She looked at Megan, her smile widening, a sparkle in her eye. "Won't that be nice? Like skiing through a winter wonderland."

I'm not sure what she expected in response, maybe for Megan to confirm that yes, that did sound romantic AF, or something similarly gushy, but my sister, still grumpy from their long drive, made a decidedly unromantic harrumphing sound instead. "As long as we don't get stuck out in the woods because of it and have to eat the first person to freeze to death just to stay alive. Or get run down by wolves. Or trampled by a moose with a brain worm."

I stared at my sister. "Jesus, Megan. Want to throw in death by mountain lion mauling?"

Stacey put her hands over Megan's ears and stage whispered, "She's just tired."

Megan batted her away.

I laughed and rounded the couch to join them. They'd been here just long enough to drop their stuff in the spare room, listen to Mom complain about Charlie, and then collapse on the chaise in exhaustion before Ben – er, I mean Stan, *STAN* – called.

"How was traffic?" I asked.

Megan scrunched her nose. "Terrible."

"It really was," Stacey said. "We took Route One out of the city, which was a parking lot right up to I-95. We thought it would clear up after the merge, like usual."

"Not so much this time?" I asked.

She shook her head. "Not so much. It's a good thing we left earlier than planned, or we'd still be on the road."

Sam jumped up near their feet, sniffed their socks, and then, with all the drama of the breed, nudged their legs apart with his snout and then whined when they didn't move fast enough for his liking.

"That's dog-speak for 'May I please lay down with you?'" I told them.

"My God. You two are so spoiled," Megan said. But she quickly wiggled over, and when Sam flopped down in the space she cleared, she immediately started to pet him, just behind his ears, exactly where he liked it best.

I narrowed my eyes at her. "Right. So, you didn't do the thing you did last year when you got them both more presents than anyone else in the family?"

I was met with silence. Stacey – from what I could see of her profile – stared at the TV in wide-eyed innocence that I didn't believe for a second. I couldn't even see Megan's face. She'd conveniently turned to lean her head on her wife's shoulder again. Like she was hiding.

I put my hands on my hips. "And you definitely didn't let them unwrap one of those presents early. Like when I was on the phone a minute ago?"

Right on cue, Fred padded around the couch with a brand-new toy in his mouth. He stopped in front of me and started chewing on it. It squeaked with every bite, each sound an exclamation point pronouncing the obvious.

"We can't have dogs in our apartment," Megan said, snuggling closer to Stacey.

"And so you spoil mine. I get it. But how about from now on you don't complain about something you're actively contributing to, grouchy pants."

Her response was muffled and filled with attitude. "I'm not the grouchy pants. You're the grouchy pants."

Stacey met my eyes over her head. "She's *really* tired."

***

"Do you mind watching the dogs while I'm out?" I asked Megan the next morning. We were all a little sleepy after an epic night of wine, card games, and catching up.

"Yes, I mind," Megan answered.

"Wait, what? Seriously?"

I looked at Stacey across the kitchen. She shrugged and went back to sipping her second cup of coffee, opting, like always, to stay out of our sisterly drama. Wise woman.

"Yes, seriously," Megan said. "I love them, but they're a pain in the ass when you're gone. Every time they hear a noise outside, they freak out, thinking it's you, race to the nearest window, and then if it's not actually you, they whine like someone threw all of their toys away and then mope around the house until the next noise comes along. It's depressing as hell."

Fred must have heard the word "toy", because he pranced into the kitchen with his new squeaky, munching on it and looking up at me like it was playtime. Sam joined him, yip-growling around their tug-of-war rope.

Megan pressed her fingers to her temples like a headache threatened. "Also, I just need like five fucking seconds of quiet."

I reached down and gently pulled the squeaking ball out of Fred's mouth. That settled that. Megan was a creature of habit, and was used to the peace and solitude of her and Stacey's dog-free apartment. She got testy when her routine was upended, and after the stress of traffic yesterday, the excitement last night, less than six hours of sleep, and barking dogs first thing in the morning, I could understand why she was already dropping f-bombs. I needed to hightail it out of there with the boys, especially since we'd all be together romping through the woods later. The last thing I wanted was for her to be overwhelmed on her first day here. It might ruin the rest of their trip. Once Megan got into serious anti-social mode, it was hard to snap her out of it.

"Okay. I'll take them with me," I told her.

She exhaled heavily. "Thanks."

Yes, thanks, Stacey mouthed from behind my sister.

I nodded at her.

"We'll be back in a few hours then," I said, and headed toward the front door.

I didn't expect it to take nearly that long at Ben's, but I could head to Jack's afterward to give Megan more time if need be.

I bundled up against the cold – it was only 10 degrees outside, puke – and then opened the door and let the dogs out ahead of me. It took a while for the truck engine to heat up in weather like this, and after I buckled the dogs in, I decided to text Ben.

Hey, it's Ella. I have the dogs with me. I can drop them at Jack's before I head over if you like.

A few minutes passed before he responded. *No, that's fine. I figured you'd bring them. I've already dog-proofed the house.*

LOL, that's adorable. They'll find something to get into no matter what you do. Sorry in advance.

I hit send too quickly and immediately wanted to punch myself in the kidney. Adorable? Really, Ella?

Hopefully he didn't read that and think I meant he was literally adorable. Hopefully he knew it was just an expression. That I used with people I knew. When I was being sarcastic and wanted to tease them about their naiveté. Because he and I went way back, so of course he knew that's what I meant and not that I called him adorable in seriousness.

Oh, God. Why hadn't he responded yet?

After what felt like a small eternity, my phone dinged. *Ha! I'll make sure to close off the rooms with fresh paint on the walls. And put away the fancy china.*

He gave me a "Ha!". That meant he knew it was a joke, right? RIGHT?

I held my fingers over the screen and struggled to come up with a response. Neurotic wasn't a word I'd use to describe myself, but after only a few interactions with this man, I was turning into a hot mess. And not in a good way.

I took a deep breath and typed, *Ok, we're leaving now. See you in a few.*

Straight to the point. No way it could be misinterpreted. Good. I'd stick to texts like this in the future. Because otherwise, neurosis.

I spent the drive to his house deciding how to behave in front of him. "Act like yourself" didn't apply here, since the whole pathological need to be liked thing would be detrimental to the leave-him-the-hell-alone approach I had settled on.

The trouble was, I had no idea how to not act like myself and still seem natural. I didn't want him to think I was a weirdo if I came across as stiff and quiet when I'd been anything but during our first meeting. Not because I worried that it would make him dislike me, but because I didn't want my sudden personality transplant to make him think that I was acting suspicious. Like, in a "My name is Ella Jones, and I'm going to post every word you say to me on the interwebs afterward" kind of way.

Maybe I could just be myself, but...less?

"Ugh, what does that even mean?" I asked the dogs.

Sam craned his head around and gave me a look like, *I'm sorry, hooman. I cannot help you.*

Or at least that's how I interpreted it.

I was on my own then.

In the end, I decided to be more cautious than normal. To stick with self-deprecation and avoid teasing. I didn't want him to think that I was flirting with him either. Or trying to ingratiate myself with him in some way. I suddenly felt for anyone with social anxiety.

I took the back way around the hill again, out of an abundance of caution. The dogs perked up when we neared Jack's driveway, recognizing their surroundings. I rolled past his property, and their excited yips turned into whines. The look Fred gave me in the rearview mirror was borderline accusatory. Their complaining immediately cut off when I pulled into Ben's driveway, because, *ooh, new place!*

I drove slowly, taking in the building's façade. It was a huge, square, Federal-style farmhouse with a wraparound porch on the first floor. The last time I'd driven by, before Ben moved in, it had been yellow, but now it was a crisp, bright white with black shutters to add some contrast. The window frames were also black, and the elaborate corbels that had once connected the columns of the porch and the peaks of the roofline had been replaced with clean, straight pieces of darkly stained wood that matched the decking, giving the place a more modern finish. I really liked it.

It was funny how just a few coats of paint and some small upgrades could change the whole feel of a place. Before, it had looked dilapidated, run down. Now it looked lived in. Not merely a house, but a home. A very large home, that rambled back from its original square frame, telling the story of its past through the various additions that had been added to accommodate for a growing family.

The front door opened as I eased the truck to a stop. I looked away from it before Ben could appear and prepared myself for the reality of seeing him again. It was one thing to tell yourself to treat someone like a normal human when they looked like the offspring of a Polynesian god. It was another thing entirely to stick to that when faced with them.

I glanced back and saw him loping down the steps. He wore boots, faded jeans, and a long-sleeved green button-down. The wind picked up, flattening his clothes to his body, giving me a great view of the copious amount of muscle that rolled and bunched as he walked. It was like the male equivalent of the infamous Marilyn Monroe white dress scene from *The Seven Year Itch*. To make matters worse, his hair was loose, falling just past his shoulders in a glorious, wavy mass that was lighter at the tips than the roots. It fanned out around him like he was in a goddamn music video.

A gunmetal gray sky hung low over us. The smell of snow permeated the air. The wind was cold enough to steal your breath away. And yet, somehow, it was like the summer sun had broken through and shined a spotlight down on Ben. That deep bronze skin. That salt-bleached hair. That mega-watt smile.

"Oof." It felt like I'd been punched in the stomach.

Stop it, I told myself. *Think of all that he's been through. Think of why he's probably here. Not to be ogled by you.*

I took a deep breath, turned off the truck, opened my door, and climbed out. "Hi, Ben."

"Hi. Thanks again for this," he said, coming over to the driver's side.

He towered over me, one of the few men I'd ever met that made me feel small in comparison. This close, the green of his shirt brought out the green in his eyes.

Great. Just wonderful.

"You're welcome," I said, looking away. "You might want to stand back for a second while I let the dogs out. This is a new place, so they might be a little...enthusiastic."

He looked over my shoulder and gave the boys a wave through the window, grinning even wider than before. "Hi, mutts."

They squirmed in response, straining at their harnesses while I reached in and fumbled to undo them.

"Well, I see now that you're going to be a terrible influence," I said.

"Sorry, I really like dogs."

He didn't sound even remotely sorry, and when I looked over my shoulder at him, he was making a *come here, boys* gesture that did nothing to help me in my task.

I shook my head and turned my focus back to the harnesses. Dog people. We were all the same when you got right down to it.

Once they were free, Fred and Sam launched themselves straight at him. He dropped down into a crouch and roughhoused with them for a few minutes before they darted away and took off toward the nearest snowbank, racing each other to be the first one to inspect the rock that stuck out from it. That done, they sniffed a circle around Ben's Jeep, taking extra time on each tire, and then bounded back to him again, briefly, before tearing around the truck, out of sight. From the sound of it, they were plowing through the snow in wild abandon. They raced around the Jeep again and beelined for the woodpile. Then they were back at the rock. Fred peed on the rock. Sam sniffed Fred's pee and added his own for good measure. Finally, they padded toward us.

I leaned down, coaxing them over. "Are you guys all done being -"

Fred got a crazy look in his eye and then took off again, Sam hot on his heels.

I straightened. "Better they get it out now than in the house."

Ben chuckled, nodding in agreement.

"They might be a while, if you want to wait inside." I waved a hand at him. "You're not exactly dressed for this weather.

He gave me a sheepish grin and cupped his hands together to blow into them. "I think I will if you don't mind."

"Not at all. I'm going to play fetch with them for a few minutes to get some of their energy out."

"You need a hat or gloves or anything?" he asked.

Gah. Of course he was super considerate. "I'm good, thanks. I have all the necessary clothing items in the truck."

Necessary clothing items? I sounded like some robot pretending to be me.

Ben, thankfully, didn't seem to notice. "Okay, I'll be inside."

He turned and strolled toward the front door. I watched him go; I couldn't help myself. That butt. The breadth of his shoulders. The way those long legs ate up the driveway.

Hrrrrrnnnnnn.

He turned around halfway to the porch. "Coffee?"

I blanked my face, hoping he hadn't seen my climb-you-like-a-tree expression again. "Yes, please."

I didn't exactly need any more caffeine right now, but holding the mug would give me something to do with my hands once I was inside. Whenever I felt awkward or uncomfortable, I grew hyperaware of them. It was like realizing that no matter where you look, you can always see your own nose. I became consumed with how I should or shouldn't hold them. Did I put them in my pockets? Fold them in front of me? Gently touch my own face?

I whistled the dogs over before they decided to chase after Ben. I kept a bucket of spare toys in the back of the truck. In winter, it was filled with frisbees. They did better skipping over the hard crust of snow than tennis balls or squeaky toys. I'd lost more of those to snowbanks than I could count. Every spring melt, I found about twenty littering the yard.

I spent a good ten minutes flinging a bright green disc across Ben's snow-covered front lawn and driveway before the dogs mellowed enough that I trusted them to go in. Ben met us at the door, opening it wide. I took one look at the freshly-stained floors and grabbed both of the dogs by their collars before they could sneak by me.

"Do you have some old rags I can clean them off with?" I asked.

Ben glanced down at their muddy paws. "I do. Be right back."

He reappeared a minute later with some threadbare towels. I dried the dogs off with them, taking my time. Only once I was sure they wouldn't track anything in or drip all over his floors did we go inside.

I stopped on the front mat and unzipped my jacket while Ben closed the door behind us. The entry and hallway must have only needed cosmetic updates. The staircase was gorgeous, the intricately carved wooden banister polished to a bright gloss. It rose up and away, framing the wide stairs. The walls were a neutral, light gray that contrasted beautifully with the flooring, while the baseboards and crown molding were painted a crisp white.

I bent down to untie my boots and used it as an excuse to check out the hardwood floors I'd heard so much about at Jack's. The planks were well over a foot wide, and they gleamed a rich gold.

"This looks awesome, Ben," I said, straightening.

"You like it?" He took my jacket and hung it on the free-standing wooden coat rack just inside the door. "The stain isn't too light? After it dried, I started thinking about adding another layer."

I shook my head. "It's perfect just like this."

A soft chime came from deeper in the house. He turned toward it. "Coffee's done. Come on in."

I followed after him, the dogs hot on my heels. "Be good," I told them. "No licking the walls or trying to eat plastic."

"They eat plastic often?" Ben asked.

"No, but I just wanted to get ahead of it in case they were thinking of picking today to start."

He chuckled, a deep, bass rumble that I could really get used to hearing.

The hallway was lined with doors, all closed, most likely sealing off the rooms with fresh paint or exposed wiring. At the end, the hall opened right up to the kitchen, which dominated the middle of the house.

The flooring changed from hardwood to dark slate tile as I passed over the threshold. It spread out in a large rectangle, framing the kitchen space. In the middle was the base of an oversized island, unfinished, with a plywood top. There was a fridge, a gas range, and all the framework for lower cabinets, though they didn't have doors, and they hadn't been painted yet. Above the farm-style sink, an oversized window looked out on the back yard. To the left was the barn, and to the right, much further away, the edge of the forest.

It was a nice view now. It would be beautiful in the warmer months.

I stopped at the island and inspected the builder samples spread out on top of it. Paint swatches, wood stains, tiles, and kitchen hardware were clustered together in groups: white with dark blue with silver; black with copper with lightly stained wood; subway tile with butcher block.

"How do you take your coffee," Ben asked.

I looked up to see Fred and Sam on either side of his legs, "helping" him. He didn't seem to mind, one hand idly scratching Fred between the ears, so I let them be.

"Just cream, if you have it," I answered. "Are these your potential pallets for the kitchen finishes?"

"They are," he said, his back to me as he poured. "I'm thinking butcher block for the island countertop and cement for the rest. I like that dark blue paint for the lowers, and then for the open shelving, cast iron supports with the same butcher block used for the shelving to tie it all together."

I imagined it for a minute, moving the corresponding samples together to get the full picture. I could see it spread out in front of me when I looked up again. It would lend the space a kind of understated, industrial farmhouse look.

"What about the backsplash?" I asked.

He turned to me, coffee mugs in hand, and set mine down near my right hand. "Uh...this one," he said, picking up a sample from another pile and moving it over to join those I'd gathered together.

It was a swatch of unfinished cuts of rectangular rock, tiled in a herringbone pattern, light gray in color, with a rough surface and darker veins running through it that would go great with cement counters and slate flooring.

"I want to tile the wall around the window above the sink with it," he said, pointing.

"That's going to be awesome, Ben."

His answering grin lit up his face. "You think so?"

Jesus, buddy, watch where you point that smile.

I nodded. "I don't know why Jack thought I was needed. You've clearly got this."

"Thanks."

"You're welcome."

I wrapped my hands around my coffee mug, thankful for the distraction. The first sip was magical. Exactly the right temperature, not acidic at all, just a nice, mellow bean with the perfect amount of cream.

"Hey, thanks for coming over," Ben said. "I know it was a weird phone call. My parents are worried about me all alone out here, and if I don't give my mother proof that I have human interaction of some kind, she'll hop on a plane and fly out."

And that would be a bad thing, because...? I wanted to ask, but didn't. None of my damn business. "No problem," I said instead. "My sister needed some space anyway."

"Family in town for Christmas?"

"The entire family. Megan and her wife Stacey are bunking down at my place. Megan is the sole introvert in our family, so she needs to have quiet time, which is why they stay with me whenever they're in town."

Ben gave me a questioning look.

"I know when to leave her alone," I told him. "They drove up from Boston yesterday, and after the stress of that, the energy level of the dogs, my excitement to see them, and a night of cribbage, she's pretty wiped out. We're going cross country skiing later, so she needs to recharge her battery before that."

"Makes sense," he said. "What's cribbage?"

I stared at him. "What? How do you not know what cribbage is?"

He smiled and shrugged.

"They don't have it in Hawaii?"

He shook his head, his mane of hair floating around him in a way that made me want to reach out and bury my fingers into it to see if it was as soft as it looked. "If it has, I somehow missed it."

I frowned. "But I thought it was big in the Midwest."

"Might be. All anyone wanted to play in Wisconsin was euchre when I was out there."

"Huh, never heard of it."

He threw his hands up, grinning, and mimicked my disbelief from a moment before. "What? How do you not know what euchre is?"

I clammed up for a second. He was treating me like I swore I wouldn't treat him.

What do I do, what do I do, what do I do?

Maybe acting a little more like myself would be okay after all? Maybe?

"Well," I said. "Clearly it pales in comparison to cribbage, or I certainly would have heard of it before."

He waved a hand at me. "Describe this king of all games."

"No way. I won't be able to do its glory justice. It's way easier to explain while playing. I'll just have to bring a board over next time I – crap, I'm sorry, I'm not trying to invite myself over again."

"You didn't invite yourself over the first time," he said.

Of course he was super polite. Of course. It made me feel like an even bigger asshole for immediately breaking my own promise to myself, and to him, not that he knew it.

"You know what I mean," I said, and, feeling the need to explain myself, I just. Kept. Going. "I can be pushy. And I know you said you hate it when people pry, which is pretty close, so please tell me to back off. Seriously, sometimes I don't even realize I'm doing it. I won't be insulted. I probably need more of that in my life, actually. Most of my family let me bowl right over them because they know how I am and that I don't mean to, like, insert myself into their lives like they don't have plans or something. My brother's wife says it's because...uh, you know what, never mind."

Wow. I almost told him I shared a character trait with sociopaths. That would have been a fun conversation to have the second time meeting someone.

He placed a heavy hand on my shoulder. "Ella, it's fine. It's nice having someone else in the house."

He squeezed me and then let go, and I stared down into my coffee afterward, trying to think of something to say to break this uncomfortable silence.

Too much silence, I realized.

Shit! The dogs!

I whipped my head up. They were nowhere in sight.

"Faaak," I said, the word strangled as I pushed away from the island. "Sam! Fred!"

Ben pointed to an open doorway behind me. "They went that way."

I dashed toward it.

"There's nothing in there for them to get into!" he called after me.

"They'll find something! It's their superpower!"

I skidded to a stop just inside the room. A fire danced in the fireplace, safely tucked behind a large metal screen. Sprawled out in front of it, on thick blankets that looked like they had been set there just for them, were the dogs, both chewing on a piece of rawhide.

"I grabbed a couple of treats from Jack when I told him they were coming over, and he suggested the makeshift dog beds," Ben said from just behind me.

I nearly jumped when he started speaking. For a big guy, he sure did move quietly. Or maybe my panicked pulse had masked the sound of his footfalls. "That was...really thoughtful."

He stepped next to me and shrugged one massive shoulder. "Well, you were doing me a favor, coming over here. I wanted you and them to feel welcome."

Why did he have to be so nice?

My hormones.

Help.

I nodded for a second like an idiot before remembering my manners. "Thank you."

"You're welcome. This is kind of a nice scene, with them snuggled down and the fire going. It would make for a cozy selfie to send to my parents."

Some might say romantic, but I'd be damned if I was going to point that out right now.

"Sure," I said. "This is perfect if you want to include them in it. In most of the pictures I take of them, they show up as black and white blurs. The only time they're still is when they're eating or sleeping." Or shitting, but again, not saying *that.*

Behind the dogs was a comfortable looking leather sofa, with end tables on either side. We set our coffee down on the nearest one and then positioned ourselves so that we were visible in the camera frame, with the dogs and the fire in the background. Even with Ben's freakishly long arms, we still ended up smooshed together to get the shot. I was excruciatingly aware of the heat radiating off of his big body, of the swell of his bicep where it pressed against my arm.

"Smile," he said, and then took the picture.

I looked kind of manic in it. My eyes were too wide. All of my teeth were visible. If he wanted to keep his parents from worrying, I was afraid seeing the face I was making next to their son would have the opposite effect. Maybe I'd get lucky, and they'd be so distracted by the beauty of my dogs that they wouldn't notice the creeper in the frame.

He pulled the phone down and sent the image off.

Not five seconds later, the unmistakable ring of a FaceTime call filled the room.

Ben sighed. "Seriously, Mom?" He lifted his eyes to mine. "I'm sorry about this in advance."

I had just enough time to freak out before he picked up.

Chapter 6: Ben

Ella, it turned out, wasn't great at keeping her emotions from showing on her face. Her eyes flashed wide in what looked like panic as I answered the call. But shit, it was too late now. This was going to be bad enough as it was. If I answered only to hang up on my mother, I would never, *ever* hear the end of it.

"Hi, Mom." I said. "What an unexpected surprise that you immediately called me."

"Show me the girl," she said. "That picture could have been taken with some rando eight months ago."

"I need to pose with a newspaper to show you the date like this is some sort of hostage situation?" Hell, it was beginning to feel like one.

I caught movement out of the corner of my eye and turned to see Ella's eyebrows climbing up her forehead like they were almost surprised right off her face. Great, she hadn't been here ten minutes, and my mom was about to scare her off.

Or maybe I was. My temper was starting to show, and being around a large, strange, angry man wasn't something a lot of women were comfortable with, for good reason.

I hit the mute button. "Sorry," I told her. "My mom drives me crazy sometimes."

She immediately seemed to relax. "Oh, I fully understand. Do you want me to go?"

It was sweet of her to offer. I was tempted to say yes, but then Mom might show up on my doorstep in the middle of the night if I didn't give in to her demands.

I cringed. "Actually, do you mind if I show her that you're here?"

Ella smiled in response. It only looked a little strained. "I don't mind."

"I'm sorry about this," I told her. Again. I was beginning to sound like a broken record.

"It's okay." She pulled her hair over one shoulder and composed herself. "Ready."

I unmuted the phone and looked at my mom. "If I do this, you'll stop, right?"

She nodded.

I swiveled the camera toward Ella and then back to me again, trying to get this over with as fast as possible.

Mom glared at me. "All I saw was a flash of orange. Was it the fire, or her hair?"

Ella pulled a few strands up and stared at them. *"Orange?"* she mouthed.

Well, this was a complete nightmare.

"Mom, you're being ridiculous," I said. And then, to Ella, "Your hair isn't orange."

Dad forced himself into the frame on my screen. "Just show us the girl, Ben. Your mother has her bags packed."

If not for Ella, I would have flipped the fuck out. Worrying was understandable, but this level of emotional manipulation crossed a line.

Anger burned through me like a fire, one that threatened to roar out of me if I didn't get ahold of it. I closed my eyes and counted to ten. Slowly. Twice. When I opened them again, Ella's face filled the small box in the corner of the screen, indicating that my parents could now see her. I must have turned my phone away without realizing it, and Ella, nice person that she was, stepped up and decided to diffuse the situation.

She waved at them. "Hi. I'm here. Now. It wasn't a picture of some rando from eight months ago."

My parents got closer to their camera, their faces filling my screen.

Dad grinned ear to ear. "Oh, so she *is* real."

"Last time I checked," Ella said with an answering smile.

"And she's pretty. Isn't she pretty, Hani?" Mom said.

I snapped the phone back to me. "She is literally standing right next to me and can hear everything you're saying. Please don't embarrass her."

"Ahem." Ella reached out and covered my hands with her much smaller ones. With a surprisingly firm grip, she swiveled them so that the camera was once again facing her. Only then did she let me go. "You're not embarrassing me. Ignore him," she told my parents. "Now, what was that you were saying about how stunningly beautiful I am?"

She managed to surprise a laugh out of them.

"And you've got a good sense of humor too," Mom said, smiling brighter than I'd seen in weeks. "No wonder your cards are so funny."

Ella glanced up at me with a ridiculous, self-congratulatory grin on her face, managing to look like she was swaggering while standing completely still. "This is doing wonders for my ego."

My parents, right on cue, laughed again.

Mom was the first to sober. "How's he doing?" she asked Ella, as if I wasn't standing right here.

Are you fucking *kidding me, Mom?* I wanted to shout. She trusted the word about my wellbeing from a stranger she just met via FaceTime more than my own assurances that I was fine? I was so over this bullshit. What would it take for her to back off? I honestly didn't know anymore. Maybe my therapist would. I made a mental note to call him later.

Ella snuck a look at me. I'm not sure what she saw on my face that made her chew on her lip. A second later, she looked down at the phone, back at me, and then held out her hand.

I gladly passed it to her.

She plastered on a huge grin and lifted the phone. "He's doing great!" she said. She was so upbeat about it that even I believed her. "He's a hit with us locals, and my dogs already love him, which is saying something, because they're tough judges of character. And this place is coming right along. The floors came out so nice, and the kitchen is going to look like one of those HGTV dream kitchens when he's done with it. You guys must be so proud!"

"We really are," Dad said.

Mom remained silent, and I knew it was because she wanted to press the issue.

Ella didn't give her a chance to. "What's the weather like there? Is it sunny? Do you still have leaves on the trees? Is it warm?" She lowered her voice and pulled the phone in close, expression forlorn. "Please describe what warmth is like. I've forgotten."

Another round of chuckling rang through the speaker before Dad indulged her. "It's in the mid-seventies, with a nice breeze off the water."

Ella closed her eyes and made a pained face. "My jealousy. It burns. The high here is twenty today. And that's a warm snap for this time of the year. Two weeks ago, it was minus fifteen." She gazed deeply into the camera. "Please think of us kindly when you look upon the sun."

My parents laughed at this. Again.

Across the room, Fred let out a small woof and clambered to his feet. Ella swiveled the phone around to face the dogs and spent the next several minutes introducing them to my parents. She even had Mom say a few commands to see if the dogs would obey them over FaceTime. They did.

Mom told me I should think about getting a puppy now to keep me occupied when there weren't any other humans around or housework to do. I made a non-committal sound in response. It was the best she was going to get from me right now. Then Ella was through the door and into the kitchen, showing my parents the final choices for the finishes before taking them on a tour of what I'd already done to the space.

I leaned a hip against the doorjamb, crossed my arms over my chest, and watched her expertly distract them. I should have let Jack introduce us sooner. Maybe I could have avoided all this drama with my mom.

Ella exhausted renovation talk and moved on to other safe subjects. A ten-minute conversation followed that I barely took part in. Soon she was saying goodbye and telling my mom that, no, she would never dream of letting me spend Christmas alone.

Her expression changed from ebullient cheer to apology the second she hung up. "I'm so sorry," she said, handing my phone back to me. "I have no intention of forcing you to hang out on Christmas if you don't want to. And I'm also really sorry for totally steamrolling that conversation."

"Ella it's -"

"But your mom looked so worried, and I didn't want you to be uncomfortable or upset, because you looked like you were upset. Kind of mad, but also kind of sad, and maybe like you didn't know how to react. Not that I'm an accurate judge of your expressions. We just met, after all. But I mean, like, in a general way you looked like that. So of course I did that thing I always do and completely took over everything and made it about myself, because I can't ever just shut the hell up and let other people talk when I feel awkward." Her shoulders drooped like all the air had gone out of her. "I'll just go now."

"It's okay, Ella," I told her.

She shook her head. "No, it's not. I'm really sorry, Ben. I had no intention of doing that."

"I'm grateful that you did."

Her mouth snapped shut.

"My mom has been having..." *Am I really saying this right now? Guess I must already trust her.* "...trouble, dealing with me being so far away after my brother's death. She's worried that something might happen to me, like it did him, and she won't be here in time."

"Oh," she said, voice small.

"When I left, she said she'd respect my need for space, but hasn't. At all. And it's been coming between us. If you hadn't taken over that call, we probably would have gotten into another argument. It's like she can't hear me tell her I'm okay. For whatever reason, hearing it from you seemed to help her some. So really, thank you."

"You're welcome then?"

I nodded at her.

"And also, I'm sorry. That's a shitty position for her to put you in."

"Thanks. It is."

It was nice to hear someone else vocalize that. It made me feel less irrational for getting upset. Like it was just a normal response to an overbearing parent and not an uncontrolled mood swing brought on by early-onset CTE.

Sam padded over to me and pressed his wet nose into my palm. I looked down at him, grateful for the distraction, and scratched the spot just behind his ears. He closed his eyes and sighed in doggy bliss, leaning his full weight into my leg.

"Aaand, you're now his new best friend," Ella said.

One side of her mouth was pulled up in a lopsided grin as she watched her dog. My gaze rose from her mouth to trace the smattering of freckles across her nose and cheeks. In this light, her eyes were crystalline blue.

Damn, she was beautiful.

It was obvious the first time we met, even though she was frazzled and still a little sweaty from sledding. Now, with the red blotches gone from her skin and her – definitely not orange – hair worn loose in long, cascading waves, it was impossible to ignore just *how* beautiful.

"Want to see the rest of the house?" I asked her.

Her eyes lit up. "Of course."

I took her through the first floor, explaining the work I'd done so far and what I planned for each space once it was finished. Right now, the house was pretty barren of décor, and it took some imagination to envision what I described. I brought my tablet with us, pulling up images of the furniture I planned to buy, the rugs I wanted to spread over some of the floors in the higher traffic areas, and so on.

Being an artist, Ella had no trouble keeping up. She looked back and forth from the tablet to the rooms around us as I talked, nodding along as if she could see the picture I painted for her with my words. Every now and then, she offered input. Maybe place the chairs here, instead of there, in the sitting room, to maximize the view out of the rear windows, or add a large mirror to the windowless wall in the dining room to give the illusion that the space was bigger, while also bringing in more light from the reflection of the southern facing windows on the perpendicular wall. Every suggestion was insightful and logical, and I'd be an idiot not to implement all of them in the final design.

The dogs followed us through the house, attempting to sniff each new thing they came across. Ella called them to heel whenever she thought they were getting too nosy or rowdy, or to keep them from straying when we entered a room with gaps in the drywall. They instantly snapped to her side when she did.

I opened the basement door toward the end of the tour. Fred and Sam peered into the darkness like they were curious but stayed glued to Ella's side.

I flipped the lights on and led them down. "They're pretty well trained."

"Thanks," she said from behind me. "Huskies are smart, but kind of like the cats of the dog world. Pleasing their humans isn't super high on their list like it is with most other breeds, so starting their training when they're young, like I did, is definitely recommended. And I still let them act like actual dogs and have their fun with new people and places. Like when they met you. You looked like you were in puppy heaven at Jack's, so I let them go a little wild. Had you been a frail old lady, that interaction would have been very different."

I was impressed. The last dog my parents had couldn't be trusted off a leash. Sure, she was a docile English lab that wouldn't dream of biting someone, but she still never listened.

"Maybe if I take my mom's advice and get a puppy you can give me some pointers," I said.

"Absolutely."

We reached the bottom of the stairs, and I flicked on the last set of lights.

Ella stopped short. "Woah. It looks like a Planet Fitness threw up in your basement." And then she was off, disappearing between the large pieces of equipment and muttering to herself as she examined the ones more unfamiliar to her. I caught a flash of red hair over the top of the upside-down leg extension machine. "I mean, what does this one even do?"

I didn't answer, because I was pretty sure she was talking more to herself than to me. Or maybe she was talking to the dogs. One of them gave a little *whuff* in response, like he was taking part in the conversation.

She rounded the benchpress, coming back into sight, and paused at the free weights. Her eyebrows rose as she stared at them. "Can you even...?" she asked, stepping up to the heaviest dumbbell. She put both hands around the handlebar like she was thinking about testing it out, then cocked her head sideways, read the weight stamped into the metal, and let it go like it had stung her. "No. Nope. Nuh-uh. Not today, hernia."

It was only when my cheek twitched that I realized I was grinning like a fool. Funny what a little bit of human interaction could do to a guy that had been lacking it.

Damn it, maybe Mom was right.

Ella paced to the massive ropes coiled on the ground by the back of the room. "Heh," she said, thumbing toward them, "What are these for? Tying up your victims?" Her tone was sarcastic, but before I could answer, she turned fully toward me, her expression morphing into what I hoped was faux panic. Her voice was shaky when she spoke again. "They're not, are they?"

If I knew her better, I would have played along, maybe let loose a maniacal *muah ha ha ha ha* for good measure. But after my earlier outburst of temper, I didn't want to risk appearing even slightly menacing right now. Instead, I smiled in what I hoped was a non-threatening way and shook my head no.

"Jump rope, then? Like, if you only have two people. One does the twirling, while the other jumps?" A wide grin split her face. "I bet you and Jack have pulled off some badass double-dutch sessions with these."

The thought of Jack quick-footing it back and forth as these two-inch-wide ropes flew over and under him was enough to surprise a laugh out of me. "They're battling ropes," I told her. "You take the ends, and with your arms, you get them going in a sinuous motion. Like this."

I picked them up, stepped back, and demonstrated their proper use. Ella had to grab the dogs to keep them from lunging. Right, probably should have warned her. The ropes must have looked like tug-of-war heaven to them.

I dropped them after a second to stop the dogs' torment. Ella's eyes were on the ropes instead of me, her cheeks nearly the same shade as her hair. I couldn't tell if she was blushing, or if the effort of holding her dogs back had brought her color up.

She let them go, and they immediately pounced, each of them trying to pick up their own rope. Must have been the strain.

"How'd you get all this stuff down here and installed without anyone recognizing you?" she asked. Before I could answer, she held up her hands. "Sorry, none of my damn business."

I was starting to regret what I'd said at Jack's about my privacy. I didn't want her to feel like she had to walk on eggshells around me. "It's fine, Ella. I said I don't like it when strangers pry into my private life. That wasn't exactly prying, just an innocent question. And we're not really strangers now, are we? I mean, you've met my parents. One of your children already wants me to adopt them."

She shot Sam a look. "Traitor."

He dropped his rope and stared adoringly up at her, tongue lolling out of his mouth.

"The gym gear came in the containers I shipped my stuff in," I said. "I was able to disassemble it and lug it down in pieces before setting it back up. And, like I told you the other night, I can get most everything else I need delivered. It's lucky the local home improvement store offers truck drop-off, or I'd be screwed. Still, I've had to get really good at making precise measurements while I'm working, so I don't under order supplies."

"What do you do when you have to deal with someone face-to-face?"

"I, uh...I wear a disguise."

Mischief crept into her expression. "What kind of disguise are we talking about here? Costumes? Wigs? Just so you know, I'm imagining an entire closet of spy-grade silicone face masks. You know, like the ones from the *Mission Impossible* movies."

"Nothing that fancy."

She stared at me, eyebrows raised in question.

I sighed. "Fine. I looked like an awkward hippie cosplaying as a praying mantis."

She frowned, her gaze roving over my face like she was trying to picture it. I could tell the second she did, because her mouth started to twitch. It was like the flood that broke the dam. Her lips parted, and she let out a small little chuckle that quickly grew in volume and pitch until she was bent over at the waist, hands on her knees, all but scream-laughing at me.

"I'm not sure if I should be offended or embarrassed right now," I said.

"Oh, God. The *mental image*, Ben," she said as she fought to straighten back up. "Because you're all..." She flared her shoulders out as wide as they would go, flexed her arms, and made a face I'm sure I'd never made in my life. "...and that sounds..." She tucked her chin down, opened her eyes as wide as they would go, and crab stepped toward me.

Then she was laughing again, and I lost it too. I really had looked like a damn fool in that getup.

By the time I calmed down, my ribs hurt. I couldn't remember the last time someone got me laughing this hard. Goddamn it, Mom was right about my isolation after all. I was self-aware enough to admit that I'd been lonely as hell and just suppressing it. And I was probably more secluded than I should be out here.

Even with that awkward phone call from my parents, this morning was nice. Needed. Sharing a cup of coffee with someone, playing with their animals, showing off my hard work, it was these little things that made the difference.

I already got this to some extent with Jack when I visited him, but he was more reserved than Ella. Our conversations tended to be more serious, with long, comfortable pauses where we were left alone with our thoughts. It wasn't like that with her. I couldn't just fade out. Every second she'd been here, I'd been fully tuned in, wondering what she was going to do next.

Do you want to be my friend? I almost blurted.

Like this was preschool, and it was that easy still. I wished it were. Over the past decade, all of my friends had come from the sport I played. My agent. My PR rep. My fellow players. My personal trainer. People I was forced together with at first and then slowly developed relationships with throughout the course of our interactions. It was easier that way than making friends outside of football circles. Those people got it. They understood the stress, the highs and lows, the intensity. And they kept their mouths shut about it all because blabbing to the media or online would cost them their jobs or their reputations.

It was a risk, making a friend who wasn't tied to football in some way. But then again, maybe it would be worth the reward. To have someone in my life totally divorced from that world, to have a person I could talk to about literally every other subject on the planet, would be a welcome distraction, and would probably provide a much-needed mental break.

Ella hadn't once, during any of our – admittedly limited – interactions, given me the vibe that she would ever blab on social media about me. The fact that she'd made up a fake name for me in front of her sister, and then double-checked my identity on the phone in case I was a catfish showed just how much she respected my privacy.

Maybe it was time I started trusting my judgment again.

"Hey, so," I said. "I know your family is in town and Christmas and the following days will probably be hectic for you, but did you want to swing by sometime after, when it all dies down, and bring cribbage with you?"

She immediately sobered. "Are you sure you're going to be okay here on Christmas by yourself? My family spends Christmas Eve and Christmas morning together, but then we break apart during the afternoon and go out visiting other people. It's a tradition in the local area. I always pop in to visit Jack. I could easily swing by here afterward."

"I don't want to impose."

She waved me off. "You really wouldn't be. Megan doesn't do the whole visiting thing. The stress of being around our entire clan for an extended period is too much for her. She usually goes back to my place to chill out, and I try to give her plenty of time to do so. But I don't want to impose on you, either. Like I said earlier, I tend to push myself on people, and I don't want to do that to you. I know you said you came out here to get away."

My first instinct was to tell her not to come over. Not because I didn't want her here, but because I didn't want to upend her life. Then again, she was a grown-ass woman, so if she was saying she wouldn't mind stopping over, I should take her at her word. And act like a grown-ass man and be honest in return.

"You're not being too much," I said. "If you're up for it, please come over on Christmas."

She brightened. "Yeah?"

"Yeah," I said, grinning down at her.

Chapter 7: Ella

Christmas at the Jones house was an *event*. One that required planning, coordination, and a lot of teamwork. Megan and Stacey were staying with me. My oldest brother, Jacob, his wife, Sofia, and their two boys, Evan and Michael, were staying with my parents, along with my two youngest siblings. My father's brother and his wife – Uncle Jim and Aunt Pat – were staying with Grandma Jones. They'd crashed with her every Christmas since Grandpa passed away, in an effort to distract her away from his absence during what had been his favorite time of the year.

My other grandparents, Evelyn and Tom Pritchard, had decided to come up from Oklahoma this year, and were staying in their RV in my parents' driveway. The way Mom complained about Grandma, they hadn't been keeping to it as much as she would have liked.

"If she says, 'Bless your heart' one more time!" she had threatened during our phone call this morning.

It was only going to get more hectic as the day progressed, because our entire family descended upon my parents' house every Christmas Eve and spent the night so we could wake up together on Christmas morning and open presents first thing. It was tradition. And we couldn't change a thing about it, even though it meant that this year there would be fourteen adults, two quasi-adults, three rambunc-tious kids, four dogs, and not nearly enough bedrooms to go around. Most of us would spend the night camped out on the living room floor, which meant we'd be awake late into the evening, followed by a butt-crack-o-dawn wakeup by the kids.

I was going to need to sleep for a week straight when the holidays were over to make up for all the lost shuteye.

I should be at my parents' already, immersed in the chaos. Instead, I'd spent the morning locked in my room, panic-wrapping gifts, be-cause between preparing for houseguests, closing down my shop, and the mega-distraction of Ben Kakoa, I didn't get it done in time.

Megan and Stacey left with the dogs well over an hour ago. Mom had asked them to be team players and stop at the store on the way over, because she'd run out of vegetable stock and carrots for their favorite vegan stew, as well as a few other items that she claimed Christmas would be ruined without.

To say that Megan was unimpressed was an understatement. The thought of wading into the carnage of a grocery store on Christmas Eve made her look physically ill. Thank God for Stacey, who told Megan that she'd be the one to run in, and Megan could wait in the car. After all, someone needed to stay with the dogs while the other acted as a sacrificial lamb. Megan looked only slightly less nauseous at that prospect, but beggars couldn't be choosers.

She tried to get me to relent about taking the boys with them, but for once I stayed firm with her. They would slow my wrapping to a snail's pace. Fred had never encountered a piece of paper that didn't need to be sat on, and Sam thought running away from me with ribbon in his mouth was one of the best games ever invented. I swore they were part cat.

My phone chimed beside me on the floor with a text notification. I craned my head sideways to see it because I was in the middle of tying a rather complicated bow, and if I let it go now, I'd have to start all over.

It was a picture, sent by Stacey, of the familiar black and white blurs of Fred and Sam running through the snow. Behind them, my parents' springer spaniel, Dancer, was mid-leap as he chased after them.

Another text came through from her.

Poor wittle floofywoogins wit his stumpy wittle legs.

What the hell?

I looked closer. There, far behind the rest of the dogs, just barely visible over the top of the snow, was a pair of eyes, a forehead covered in caramel-colored fur, and two tall ears. It was my parents' other dog, Corgnelius the corgi. He looked like a little snowplow trailing after the others. Poor floofywoogins indeed. Then again, judging by the gleam in his beady little eyes, he was having the time of his life.

I shook my head and went back to work on the bow. Another text followed shortly after, and I half expected to see more corgi pictures – Stacey was obsessed – but it wasn't from her. It was from Stan.

My heart skipped a beat.

Merry Christmas Eve. Jack is here. Just challenged him to another legendary round of double-dutch.

I grinned so wide my cheek muscles pinched. I tied off the bow, leaned over, and picked my phone up. *Merry Christmas Eve! Go easy on him. He's old.*

I'm telling him you said that.

Go right ahead.

You sure about that? He finished another batch of oatmeal stout and just gave me a six-pack as a Christmas present. You think if I tell him you called him old, he'll give me yours too?

I TAKE IT BACK. PLEASE DON'T.

You're lucky. The holiday spirit has me feeling kind and benevolent this eve. Three winking emojis were tacked onto the end of the text.

Dear God. Was he flirting with me? Or was this the kind of run-of-the-mill banter I would expect from him if I knew him better? Damn the lack of intent that text messages conveyed!

Thank you, good sir, I texted back, playing along.

My heart beat obnoxiously fast as I waited for his response. It had been far too long since I'd had a crush. I was out of practice. I had no chill.

Nothing else came through, not even the little bubble that indicated he was typing. My fingers hovered over the screen. I wanted to keep talking to him, but if this was where he wanted to leave it, this was where it stopped.

I waited another minute, then heaved a sigh and set the phone down. For the most part, I thought I did okay yesterday. Well, aside from when I'd steamrolled that conversation with his parents, which I was still embarrassed about. After that, I did better. I caught myself when I got pushy. I let him make the call about hanging out again tomorrow night. I stuck to self-deprecation and making a fool out of myself, limiting my more advanced teasing to the Mantis Incident. But, come on, who could blame me for that?

And I did my best not to stare at him. Even when he laughed. Even when he demonstrated the proper use of those battle ropes. Sure, I had to force my face away to tear my eyes from the sight of his flannel shirt pulling taut across his chest as his shoulders and biceps bunched and flexed, but I managed to do it, damn it, and that should count for something.

My phone chimed. It was Ben.

Do you have a timeframe for stopping over tomorrow? I can have food ready if it's around dinner.

This crush I was working on was going to reach monstrous proportions if he didn't start to show some serious character flaws. It wasn't fair that on top of being punch-you-in-the-eyes gorgeous, he was also considerate, polite, passionate about what he did – which I saw firsthand during that house tour yesterday, had a good sense of humor, texted in full sentences with proper punctuation and grammar (be still my nerdy heart), made a mean cup of coffee, shared my taste in beer, and liked my dogs.

Weirdly, the fact that he got pissed at his mom yesterday made him even more attractive. It made him seem real, attainable. Just like the rest of us, this super famous, super handsome man still got badgered by his overprotective parents.

I don't have an exact time. Sorry! I texted back. *Do you want to try to plan for around 5?*

No need to apologize. I know how hectic Christmas can be. Around 5 works. Any dietary restrictions I should know about?

Nope. I'll text you tomorrow afternoon with a more accurate ETA.

Sounds good. Talk to you then.

Before I set my phone down, I sent Stacey a quick, *"He is SUCH an adorable little floof."*, then went back to wrapping presents.

Thirty minutes later, the truck was warming up in the driveway as I brushed the snow off of it. The good thing about nor'easters was that they stuck to the coast. We only got a few inches, whereas Megan and Stacey's friends that stayed in Boston said they had over a foot at the last count, and it was still coming down.

My hamstring twinged as I reached up to the roof of the cab with my snow brush. I'd decided to snowshoe alongside Megan and Stacey on their skis yesterday afternoon, thinking it would be easier to interact with the dogs. It had been, but in the process, I'd pushed myself too hard to keep up with the girls and was suffering for it today.

Once the truck was clear, I loaded the presents and then climbed into the cab. It was good to know that Jack was with Ben. I'd never tell him this, but I agreed with his mom. No one should spend the holidays alone. Not unless they really wanted to. The radio, TV, storefronts, and just about every form of modern media wouldn't let anyone forget that it was supposed to be this magical time of year spent with loved ones. The overload was almost cruel to anyone not able to.

For all Ben's talk about needing to come out here to escape, he seemed happy to have some company yesterday. The pride he took in showing off his hard work, the easy way he bantered and teased, it made him come off as such an outgoing, social person. So much like myself. It was a marked improvement over our first meeting, where I'd done all of the legwork. The fact that he invited me over tomorrow only reinforced my belief that he was in need of some positive human interaction.

Again, I put myself in his shoes. How would I balance my desire for a social outlet with trying to work through a monumental pile of emotional baggage? I had absolutely no idea. My life had been a wonderland of bliss and serenity compared to Ben's. My siblings were all alive and healthy. My family was uncommonly tight-knit. And I was just now realizing that I had the privilege of privacy, security, and safety that came with being a "no one."

I wasn't really the religious type, but I paused for a moment and said a prayer to whoever may have been listening that Ben would be able to take his time and find what he was looking for up here. Closure, or maybe acceptance. Whatever it was that he needed. I prayed that he could find a healthy balance. That no one leaked where he was. And later, once he was ready to go back to the real world, that he wouldn't be sidelined by TBI or CTE. That he would be free to lead whatever life he chose to, and that he found peace and happiness and fulfillment in it.

"Amen, or awomen, or aseveralbeings. Whichever it is," I said when I was done, glancing up at the bright blue sky.

I put the truck into drive and headed out. As soon as things died down, I was going to sort through these feelings and find a way to help, because, like I said, prayer wasn't typically my thing. In my experience, actually standing up and doing something beat well-wishes and positive thoughts every day of the week. For starters, I could donate to the brain injury non-profit that Ben and his parents had set up in Zach's name. Another thing I could do was protect Ben's privacy and well-being with the sulfuric wrath of a mother dragon.

I clutched my steering wheel and snarled.

I am Ella, belcher of flame, safeguard of superstars. Woe be to those who pry.

***

My parents' house was thirty minutes away, on the south side of the valley. The terrain was more hospitable where they lived, with gently rolling hills covered in broadleaf forests, dotted here and there with farmland. Their house sat on the eastern slope of one of those hills, with expansive views of the surrounding countryside.

It was a bucolic setting in the summer. Their front porch looked out upon a hundred-year-old apple orchard, a tree farm, and one of the northernmost vineyards in the country. My mother was an avid gardener. Her flower beds were extensive, and the smell of them in full bloom was something I still looked forward to every year. The sound of the breeze rustling through the nearby willow, paired with the buzzing of insects and cacophonous birdsong was the soundtrack of my youth.

In the colder months, that all faded away. Without many coniferous trees to balance them out, the bare branches of the oaks, hornbeams, maples, and apples that surrounded their house were rendered skeletal against the background of dreary gray winter days. I was thankful that last night's storm had cleared and the sun was out now. It gave me an unobstructed view of the nearby mountains, coated in white.

There was movement in front of the house as I drove up. The dogs raced after a frisbee. Stacey stood nearby, filming their antics with her phone. In the middle of the yard, a snowman came to life under the careful guidance of Jane and my nephews. Their progress appeared somewhat hampered by Willow, who lobbed snowballs at them from behind a nearby stone fence.

The dogs rushed over to greet me when I climbed out of the truck, Corgnelius bringing up the rear. The cute aggression I felt whenever I looked at him was as strong as ever, and I had to fight the urge to scoop him up and smoosh him. Stacey was likewise having difficulty controlling herself. She walked behind him, bent over at the waist as she recorded the way his little nub of a tail blurred back and forth in excitement.

"He is just the *cutest*," she said.

Dancer, my parents' springer spaniel, dropped the frisbee at my feet. I picked it up and flung it as far as I could, not wanting them underfoot when I unloaded presents. I could see myself tripping over one of them and breaking something.

They tore off after the neon-green disc. Stacey continued to film, giggling under her breath. She and Megan really needed to get a new apartment. One that allowed dogs.

"Auntie Ella!" Evan, Jacob's youngest at just four, yelled in his little boy voice as he came flying around the truck. He looked a lot like photos of his dad from this age, only with skin a few shades lighter and a little less curl to his short-cropped locks.

I had just enough time to brace myself before he crashed into my legs and wrapped his arms around my waist in a vicelike grip.

I gave into The Squeezes and leaned down to hug him back. Evan was one of those children whose parents shouldn't bring him out in public. He said please and thank you to everything. He had a habit of waving hello and goodbye to everyone. He asked the most innocent, adorable questions. Every now and then he would look at one of us and say, "You know what?" When we said, "What?" back at him, he answered with, "I love you."

I'd warned Jacob and Sofia that couples probably met him and thought, "My God, what an adorable little boy. Isn't he so well behaved? We should have one of our own!" And then they went off in their little bubble of hormonal bliss and made a Willow.

I could hear her on the other side of the truck. Her laughter had gained a familiar, troubling edge. A second later, there was a loud *splat,* followed by an ear-splitting roar of outrage.

Michael, Evan's eight-year-old brother, hightailed it around the front of the truck and ducked down in the shelter of the wheel well, breathing heavy.

"How you doing, bud?" I asked, straightening as Evan released me.

Michael's eyes were wide. "She just threw a snowball filled with dog poop at Auntie Jane."

I had to bite the inside of my cheek to keep from laughing. It wasn't funny. Really, it wasn't.

"She called it a poopsicle," Michael said.

Stacey made a choking sound from nearby.

I couldn't look at her or I'd lose it.

"You are in *so much trouble*, young lady!" Jane yelled.

I heard stomping and chanced a look through the windshield of the truck to see her marching up the front walk. Willow, laughing uproariously, was slung over her shoulder like a sack of potatoes. As I watched, she stretched out her small arms and started pinching her mother's butt. Hard.

Jane yelped and almost dropped her. "Ow, stop that."

They disappeared inside the house, and I finally looked over at Stacey. We doubled over laughing.

Between us and the boys, we got my truckful of presents safely unloaded. I said a brief hello to Grandma Jones, who was in the living room helping Jane calm Willow down. Charlie was laid out on the couch nearby, sleeping through our niece's tantrum in a way that only combat vets and college students could.

My parents' house was large, to accommodate for our sprawling family, the downstairs even more open than my cabin. I could see clear to the kitchen. Dad and Jacob, both doctors, both wearing sweaters over button-down shirts, both with thick-framed glasses perched on their noses, sat in the breakfast nook, deep in conversation. I couldn't hear them, but from the looks on their faces, they were either talking politics or debating a recent article published in one of the medical journals they both subscribed to. I made a mental note to speak with them about brain injuries later.

Sofia, Jacob's wife, was Italian. Every holiday season, she transformed from clinical psychologist into master-chef. She and Grandma Pritchard had taken command of the kitchen. The center island was dusted with flour, and the two women chatted and laughed together as they rolled out dough for pie shells and bread.

I was tempted to join them, but as I started to take my coat off, Jane gave me a look that froze me in my tracks. She clearly hadn't forgotten the candy cane incident, and her death glare made it obvious that she hadn't forgiven me for it either.

I zipped my coat back up and beat a hasty retreat outside, where Stacey, Evan, Michael, and I got down to the serious business of building snowmen. We kept at it until the sun started to slant in the sky and my aunt and uncle arrived, their car laden down with still more presents and baked goods.

Pat and Jim never had children, so they spoiled us as only doting relatives could. Both were now retired, Pat having been a lawyer, and Jim the owner of a small contracting firm. They did well during their careers. Our summers growing up were spent crawling over the ruins of ancient Greece, meandering up the Scottish coast, or, when we got older, hiking parts of the Pacific Trail alongside them. This summer vacation, they were taking Charlie and Anabel to Norway for two weeks. The lucky little brats.

Pat turned to me once we were all inside. "I meant to tell you the last time we talked that I saw one of your calendars in an article in Marie Clare."

I paused for a second in the middle of taking off my jacket. "Do you remember what month they featured it in?"

"September. It was the calendar with the endangered species theme. They made a point to mention that a large portion of the proceeds go to the World Wildlife Fund."

I shrugged out of my coat and hung it up, thinking back. This explained the early uptick in calendar sales. Every so often, I'd have a huge spike in online traffic for one line of products or another, and could spend weeks trying to track down where it came from, all to no avail.

"Thank you for telling me," I said. "I'll have to add it to the 'featured in' section of the website."

"You're welcome, sweetie," Pat said, giving me a quick kiss on the cheek. Her hazel eyes crinkled at the corners when she pulled away.

For someone who never wanted children, she was one of the most maternal, caring women I'd ever met. It confounded many of the other women in my family for years, until it finally clicked that just because someone was good with children, it didn't mean that they had to have some of their own.

Pat hadn't wanted to sacrifice her career, or her love of travel, or her alone time, or her nightly glass of wine, and she never made any apologies for that. It was wonderful growing up with her as an aunt, because where so much of our society pushed women into motherhood and guilted and harassed those who lacked the desire to have children, here was this happy, successful, regret-free childless woman in my life to counter all of that gendered pressure and show me that I had options.

"Auntie Pat, did you see the decoration I made for the tree?" Evan asked her.

She crouched down to his level. "I didn't, honey. Do you want to show me?"

Evan nodded, took her hand in his much smaller one, and led her away.

Ack. The cuteness was so strong with that child.

I looked away just in time to see Charlie roll over on the couch and blink his eyes open. He was growing his hair out, and it was shaggy enough that he had some serious bedhead going on. In the summer, his skin tanned to a deep brown, but now, in the dead of winter, it was several shades lighter. The bags under his eyes were an uncomplimentary puce. I'd never seen him with bags under his eyes, and the sight set off all of my protective older sister instincts. Our gazes met, and I weaved my way over to him.

"Hi," I said.

He squinted up at me, half-blind without his glasses, which were folded on the end table near his head. "Hi," he croaked.

"How were your finals?"

"Literally the worst."

I grinned. "You're the one who chose such a heavy course load."

"Mhm," he murmured, exhaustion dragging his eyelids back down. "No regrets. Just...so...tired."

"You want to go upstairs and sleep in your bed? It'll be quieter."

Willow, now free from time-out, raced past us, squealing in delight. Michael was hot on her heels, firing a nerf gun at her back. Sofia and both grandmas had music going in the kitchen as they worked. Dad and Jacob sat nearby, watching the news and arguing about foreign policy. It was borderline raucous in here.

Charlie shook his head, mussing his hair even more on the couch cushion, and snuggled back down. "No. This is nice."

I looked around us, at our loud, boisterous family. At our usual semi-organized chaos. "Yeah, it really is."

I left him to his nap and went in search of our missing family members. I found Anabel in her room. It had been painted lilac this time last year. Now it was a deep, charcoal gray, with posters of her favorite rock bands plastered on the walls. She was dressed in all black, sprawled out on her bed with her face in her phone. By looking at her, you'd think she was deep into her rebellious teenage phase, that her moods were as dark and broody as her choices in clothing and decor. You'd be dead wrong.

"Psst," I said from the doorway.

She saw me and leapt from her bed. "Oh, thank God you're here." She gave me a quick hug and then shoved her phone in my face. Much like myself at sixteen, she spoke at Mach-speed. "What do you think this text message means? It's from Tucker. That boy I told you about? The senior? On the soccer team? With the eyes? And the hair?" She grabbed my arm. "The *hair*, Ella."

I did my best to remain serious. "Oh, yes. The hair. I remember the picture. Let's see the text." Not that I was the authority on text messages. Clearly, I needed as much help with them as she did. But she still saw me as her cooler older sister, and I'd be damned if I did anything to spoil that prematurely.

She plopped the phone in my palm, and I dutifully looked at the screen. The text read: *We should hang out during break,* with a smiley face emoji after it.

Oh, I so had this.

"I think he likes you," I told her.

"Really?" She made a high-pitched noise that nearly popped my eardrums.

I wanted to grab her by the shoulders and yell something stupid like, "Of course he does! What's not to like?"

She was easily our most attractive family member, and this was a family filled with good-looking people. She was several inches shorter than me, thin, but athletic, with a curtain of dark hair that fell nearly to her waist, the kind of flawless skin I would have killed for at her age, a heart-shaped face with a pert nose, a cupid's bow mouth, and deep brown, hooded eyes. She was also maintaining one of the highest GPAs in her class, was a star athlete, and had a circle of friends that included jocks, punks, stoners, and outcasts, so, she was, like, perfect? Okay, maybe there was some sisterly bias in there, but if this Tucker kid rejected her...

I would find him.

Anabel stopped squeeing. "What happened? Your face just got weird."

"Nothing," I said, wiping all thoughts of murder from my mind. "You seen Mom?"

She rolled her eyes. "She's probably out on her and Dad's balcony smoking pot with Meg, Dave, and Grandpa."

So that explained where they all were. "Thanks. I'm going to say hi and then help Sofia and the grandmas in the kitchen if you want to come down."

"Sure," she said, looking at her phone. "I'll be there in a bit."

"Anabel, he likes you. Trust me. That's a pretty straightforward text from a teenage boy."

She grinned at me.

This boy better deserve her.

I slipped into the hallway before my expression gave away what I'd do to him if he didn't. As Anabel predicted, I found our last four family members on the back porch, bundled up in heavy winter jackets, smoking dope. Grandpa imbibed because of his glaucoma, Dave for inspiration – he was a staff writer for one of Maine's larger newspapers, Megan because it calmed her down, and Mom because it soothed her hippy soul.

"Hi, guys," I said, trying not to breathe too deeply. It smelled like Woodstock out here.

Grandpa held a joint toward me. "Want a hit?" he asked in his drawling Okie accent.

I waved it away. "No thanks. There's a beer or two downstairs with my name on them, and if I smoke, I'll just pass out."

Mom stepped next to me and slipped an arm around my waist. She was short enough that she could rest her head on my shoulder. I kissed the top of it and wrapped my arm around her back. Like Anabel, she wore her hair long and loose. The difference was that hers was a medium brown shot through with gray that cascaded down to her elbows in a riot of coarse curls.

"Long week? Lots of orders keeping you busy?" she asked me.

Megan shot me a sly look from beside the railing and exhaled a plume of smoke. "That and her *boyfriend*, Stan."

My newfound inner dragon reared her scaly head.

I would incinerate her.

"Oh, yeah?" Dave asked.

"Oh, no," I told him. No, no, no. The last thing I needed was a journalist interested in the new guy in town. The best course of action here was to keep completely quiet about this.

"Is he handsome?" Mom asked, her voice dreamy.

"Okay, I think that's enough for Mom," I said, turning her toward the door. "We still have to get through dinner."

"But I want to hear about my soon-to-be-grandson-in-law," Grandpa said.

I stopped to point at him. "Don't you start."

He grinned, unrepentant, and took the joint from Megan. I came from a family of smart-asses.

"Everyone calm your tits, I was just trying to get a rise out of her," Megan said. "Her friend is hard up, and she's being her typical, I-must-rescue-all-things self."

Thank you, I thought, leading Mom inside. Though that seemed slightly insulting there at the end.

"Yeah, but is he handsome?" Mom asked. She lifted her index finger and booped me on the nose. She was definitely cut off.

"Grandma really got to you, huh?" I asked her once we were safely inside.

Mom straightened, her expression sobering. "Bless her heart," she said, deadpan.

Chapter 8: Ben

I was pulling the ham out of the oven when my phone dinged with a text message from Ella.

Updated ETA: 5:15. Jack's grandkids don't want to let me leave.

I set the sizzling pan on the stovetop, shook off an oven mitt, and leaned over and picked up my phone. *Roger that. Dinner is just about ready. I hope you're hungry.*

FAMISHED. Amended updated ETA: three minutes. These little rugrats will just have to cry it out.

I grinned and set the phone down. Thoughts of Ella's visit kept me distracted for most of the afternoon. I had a lot to do in preparation. Sure, I could have thrown in a couple of frozen pizzas and called it a night, but after all her talk of visiting with family and then opening presents with my parents via FaceTime this morning, I was more than a little homesick, so I decided to make a full-blown Christmas dinner with some of my favorite Hawaiian dishes. I got to work plating them while I waited for her to arrive.

As promised, just a few minutes later, car lights splashed across the front windows. I went to the door to greet her. The outside lights were on, shining like a halo around Ella's truck. She swung her door open and all but fell out of it.

Okay then.

She leaned into the back for the dogs. I expected them to zoom around my yard, but they dropped from the cab and stayed by her side. Maybe she didn't want them running around in the dark. I swear I heard howling a few nights ago.

Together, they made their way toward the porch. The dogs dragged their paws. It looked like Ella was limping. Shit. They were exhausted. I should have expected this after all the holiday antics Ella described. Now I felt like a selfish asshole for asking her to come over.

I'd put a couple of towels on the front mat earlier for her to use on the dogs, and I leaned down and scooped them up before opening the door and stepping out onto the porch.

Ella mounted the stairs and flashed a wide grin. "Merry Christmas!" She looked ready to fall asleep standing, but her tone was so bright and cheerful that my regret eased a little. She sounded like she wanted to be here.

"Merry Christmas," I said.

The dogs picked up their pace and loped toward me. I squatted down to greet them and then used their nearness to towel them off for her.

"Thanks for that," she said.

"You're welcome. You looked like you might be limping."

She made an annoyed sound. "Oh, I'm limping. I pulled my hamstring snowshoeing after I left here the other day, spent yesterday building snowmen and drinking too much spiked egg nog, and then today running around and not eating or drinking enough, so really, I brought this on myself."

I finished with the dogs and stood. "There's aspirin and water inside. And food."

Her expression filled with longing. "Food?"

"And beer."

Now she looked like she might be drooling. "Beer?"

I laughed and let them in. Got to appreciate a woman with her priorities in order.

The dogs sniffed their way toward the sitting room, where I had a fire going and their makeshift beds already set up, a rawhide waiting for each of them. It worked out well the last time they stopped by, and if it ain't broke...

Ella took off her winter jacket and boots to reveal a pair of black leggings and an oversized white cable-knit sweater that fell halfway to her knees, completely obscuring her athletic frame. Her hat followed, and she ran her fingers through her hair and dragged her long locks up into a messy bun. Small tendrils slipped free to frame her face. She brushed them back on reflex. I had to fight a sudden urge to reach out and pull them free again.

"Long day?" I asked when I realized I was staring.

She met my gaze and nodded, smiling like she wouldn't change a thing about it.

"Thank you for stopping by," I said.

"Thank you for having me. Megan looked like she wanted to verbally punch us all in the face when she left Mom and Dad's, so I'm more than happy to give her extra alone time. And as much of an extrovert as I am, I'm beginning to understand why she needs it. There were a lot of people at Christmas this year. This'll be a nice, quiet way to end the day."

I frowned. "Oh. I had an evening of death metal planned."

She cocked her head sideways. "I didn't know you were into Nickelback."

I clutched my stomach and gagged.

She looked at me with an innocent expression, but I could see the threat of laughter in the twitch of her lips and the gleam of her eyes.

I shook my head. The woman was incorrigible. "Come on. Food is this way."

I led her toward the kitchen, where I'd spread out a small buffet of caramelized ham, mashed potatoes, stuffing, gravy, sliced pineapple, green bean amandine, sweet onions, cranberry sauce, poi, and for dessert, haupia – all of my favorite comfort foods. Well, minus the laulau, which I couldn't make because it turned out that taro leaves were hard to come by on short notice in Maine this time of year. The grocery delivery service I used didn't even know what they were when I called earlier.

"This is all I've ever wanted," Ella said, elbowing past me to grab herself a plate and spoon a hefty amount of stuffing onto it.

"By all means, help yourself."

Her head whipped up, an apology written across her face.

"I'm just teasing, Ella."

"My bad," she said. "I'm so tired that I can't understand tone anymore."

I joined her in the buffet line. "This is poi," I said, pointing to the bowl filled with purple. "People tend to either love it or hate it. I made two-finger poi because consistency can sometimes be an issue, and added a little sugar to cut back on some of the earthiness."

"Oh, I love poi." She reached out and dropped a healthy dollop onto her plate. "I had it when we visited the islands when I was in high school. Is that haupia?" she asked, pointing with the serving spoon.

I was taken aback for a second. "Uh...yeah."

"Yasss." She pushed her potatoes aside to make enough room for two pieces of dessert.

If she ate all the food on her plate, I'd be hella impressed. It had grown to linebacker-sized proportions.

We sat down at the folding table I'd set up in the dining room and tucked into the feast, chewing in a companionable silence that was punctuated every now and then by her sounds of appreciation and compliments over the food. She absolutely demolished her dinner. There wasn't a scrap left when she was done.

"You're going to have to roll me out of here," she said, leaning back.

I pushed back in my own chair. "I'd have to stand to do that, though."

I ate too much trying to keep up with her. I'd have to tell my ex-teammate, Shaun, that I'd met a woman who could probably out-eat him. Then again, maybe not. He might try to fly out here and challenge her, knowing his competitive streak.

She opened her mouth to say something, but her words were cut short by a loud, echoing burp in a deeper register than I thought she'd be capable of hitting.

She clamped a hand over her mouth, muffling her next words. "Oh my god, I'm so sorry. Where did that even come from?"

I laughed at her. I couldn't help it; the shocked look on her face was priceless.

She pulled her hand away and grinned at me, cheeks coloring.

"Surprise burps are the worst," I said. I hoped she wasn't that embarrassed. I had an ex-girlfriend break up with me once after she farted in front of me.

Ella's gaze slid back to the buffet. "I think it made room for another piece of haupia."

Right. She had a huge family. They probably still had burping competitions. Judging by the sound she just made, she probably won them.

I thought she was kidding about the haupia at first, but then she heaved herself out of her chair, plate in hand, and limped toward the kitchen. I stood and followed her, carrying my plate to the sink. No way did I have more room. I was a little scared of what might happen if I burped right now.

"Then again, maybe not," she said, gazing down at the delicacy, hand on her stomach, expression wistful. Her eyes rose to mine. "Can I take some with me?"

"Absolutely," I told her. "Take the rest. My present to you."

"Thank you. Oh! That reminds me. I brought you a present." She joined me at the sink and set her plate in it. "I left it in the truck. Be right back."

She turned and made her way toward the front door, her limp visibly worsening with every step. I followed after her. Hamstring injuries could have a lengthy recovery process if you let them get away from you. I knew from experience.

"Do you want me to go grab it for you?" I asked.

She dropped the boot she was trying to lift onto her foot and looked at me with a mixture of pain and relief. "Yes. Thank you. It should be the long narrow package in the middle front seat."

She dug her keys out of her jacket pocket and handed them over to me. I slipped on my boots, unlaced, and stepped out into the chill of the night.

The interior of her truck was riddled with the detritus of the day. Bags full of Christmas presents were stacked floor to ceiling on the front passenger side. With so many family members, it must take hours to unwrap together. No wonder they all stayed over. If they had started opening any later than nine a.m., they'd still be at it.

I snagged the gift-wrapped rectangular present from the middle seat and headed back. Narrow floor-to-ceiling windows framed the front door. Ella stood outlined in the right one, the interior light shining from behind her, throwing her figure in shadow. Her messy bun was bathed in a corona of red-gold.

My steps slowed. I let the imagery wash over me. What would it be like to come home to this? To be greeted by a beautiful woman? The sight was almost painful. Because I didn't think I could do it. I couldn't bring myself to ask someone to share my fate. I'd been out here for months trying to figure out where to go from here, how to move forward with my life, and I felt like my feet were stuck in the mud, preventing me from placing one foot in front of the other. Suddenly, it seemed like I hadn't made any progress at all, despite my therapist's assurances.

Ella was a bright light in a sea of darkness. I was beginning to think of her as a friend. I hadn't let myself progress past that yet, but I did so now. What if that friendship eventually changed? What if I allowed my gaze linger on her? To be drawn into the infectious joy of her laughter? To stop teasing her and start flirting with her? What if we slept together? Started a relationship?

Could I really unload all of my baggage on someone like her? Smother her light with all of the dark shit I didn't tell anyone but my therapist? Anything less wouldn't be fair. Wouldn't be a real relationship. But the thought of crushing that infectious joy beneath whatever symptoms of TBI or CTE I may or may not manifest turned my stomach.

She waved at me from the window, giving me a thumbs-up to say that I grabbed the right box. I took a deep breath of frigid night air and started walking at a normal pace again.

This is ridiculous.

I was just starting a friendship with her. I didn't have to keep my eyes from lingering too long. I didn't have to police my thoughts. I was still enjoying all the feelings of being around a new person that I liked. I was still experiencing the nerves, the anticipation of hanging out more and getting to know each other. And with Ella, that also meant a lot of time spent wondering what she was going to do next, and how hard it might make me laugh.

I needed to stop getting ahead of myself. Stop thinking of worst-case scenarios and instead take this one day at a time, just like my therapist had advised.

I stepped back inside, slipped off my boots, and brought the package to my ear, shaking it. It made a small rattling sound, but felt like a solid board of wood.

"It's cribbage," she said.

I frowned at her. "Wha..hey. You're not supposed to ruin the surprise."

"Fine then. It's a salmon."

"A whole salmon?"

"No. Just a couple of fillets." She glanced at the present. "That were pounded into a perfect rectangle and then frozen. Which is why it's cold. And doesn't smell. Open it quick, before it defrosts."

Our gazes caught and held, for one second, ten. We were very serious adults having a very serious discussion about Very Serious Things™. At what felt like the end of a solid minute, my lips twitched. Or course I'd be the first one to break.

She gave me a blinding smile and took the present from me, heading into the living room where we'd left the dogs.

I kicked my boots off and followed her. The dogs didn't so much as crack an eye open when we walked in.

"Wow, impressive level of dog exhaustion," I said.

She frowned at them. "I think I might have let them play too much the last few days. Huskies are a working breed, and they've been known to hurt themselves by pushing too hard."

She handed the present back to me and moved to Fred – I knew it was him because of the little white splotch on the tip of one ear – and then leaned down to systematically inspect him, rubbing his shoulders, haunches, legs, and paws to check for any sore spots. She repeated the process with Sam. Both tolerated it fairly well, and conked right back out when she got to her feet, looking satisfied they were uninjured.

I went to the couch and pulled the hidden latch in the middle seat. The chairback folded forward to reveal a flat wooden surface with two cupholders built in.

"Is this big enough to hold the board?" I asked. "I figured you'd want to keep them in sight and maybe sit in something more comfortable than a folding chair."

"That's perfect. If you want to open it, I can get it set up while you go grab those beers you mentioned earlier." She sent me a pointed look.

"Deal."

The wrapping was some sort of thick kraft paper with little pine trees and snowflakes printed on it in black. I had a feeling she might have made it herself; it was too nice to be store-bought. I slipped a finger beneath the tape and pulled the paper free to reveal a lightly stained piece of wood with a lot of peg holes in it.

I handed it to her. "What's the little skunk mark for?"

Her grin was a wicked thing. "Oh, you'll see, Ben. You'll see."

The laughter that followed me out of the room was slightly concerning.

I grabbed two oatmeal stouts from the fridge and headed back in. She sat sideways on the far side of the couch, facing the drop-down table, her legs folded beneath her. She'd laid the board out horizontally. Two pairs of brightly colored pegs stuck out from the starting line.

She glanced up at me as I approached. "Sharing your oatmeal stout?"

I handed her one. "Yes. Like a well-adjusted adult."

She snorted, then took a sip. "Oh, God. That's so good."

"Like, Jack could make a lot of money off of it good," I said, folding myself down into the other seat.

"Right? He'd never hand over his recipe, though. Dad and Jacob tinker around with homebrew, and they've been trying to get their hands on it for years."

"Jacob is your oldest brother? The one who looks kind of like Sterling K. Brown?"

She nodded. "And when he realized it, he changed his glasses frames to match the ones Brown wears on *This Is Us*, though he vehemently denies it every time I try to bring it up."

"Ah, yes. Sibling antics," I said, thinking back to all the shit Zach and I did to each other as kids. Okay, and as adults. Kind of hard to get over your rivalry when you're both professional athletes in the same sport.

Fuck, I missed him.

"Jacob is hard to tease," Ella said. "He's too serious by half sometimes. Typical oldest child. He and Dad are both doctors. He started as some fancy surgeon in Boston, but as Dad's gotten older and Jacob started a family, he had the urge to move home and take over Dad's family practice when he retires."

"What do your other siblings do?" I asked. Her family was fascinating to me. What were the dynamics like when you had that many brothers and sisters?

"Megan is the deputy director of a non-profit in Boston that works with LGBTQ+ teens and adolescents," she said. "Her wife is a social worker. They met when Stacey brought one of the children she was working with into the center. Theirs is a very symbiotic relationship. Stacey smooths out all of Megan's rougher edges, where Megan is there to lift Stacey up and stick up for her when Stacey is too quiet or reserved to do it herself. And they both understand the highs and lows of each other's jobs."

"They sound like perfect teammates," I said, reminded of how cohesive the last offensive line I played on was.

"Exactly. They're relationship goals in that way," she said. "Jane and Dave are both journalists. They met at UMF."

"UMF?"

"It's a college about halfway down Maine. Dave writes for the political section of the Maine Journal and Jane freelances. She's been published in a few national press outlets this past year, mostly for taking a unique line on current events. Annabel is still in high school, and Charlie is pursuing his bachelors in molecular biology and will probably go for his doctorate before he's done."

"Sounds like a smart kid."

"He is smart, but its more that he just...loves school. In a way that not many people do. He's one of the few of us who has found his birth mother. Or record of her, at least. She was from Herat, a city in northwestern Afghanistan. The adoption agency wasn't able to locate her, likely because the war displaced so many people, but they knew from the paperwork that she was working class and illiterate. It's driven him to learn as much as humanly possible."

"Makes sense," I said. "Does his experience finding her play a part in why you haven't searched for your birth parents?"

She looked at me.

"Tell me to shut up if you don't want to answer that," I said.

She shook her head. "It's fine. Like I said that first night, I get being curious. And yeah, it is, in part. Me, Charlie, and Jacob all come from war-torn countries. The agency Jacob was adopted from doesn't even exist anymore, and the records have all disappeared. The resulting chaos of war makes it damn near impossible to find people. Charlie was lucky just to track down those few details about his mother. He doesn't know anything about his father."

She fell silent for a second, worrying her lower lip in a way that I now recognized was her tell for mulling something heavy over. "Honestly, I'm more worried about what I might find instead of what I might not."

I took a sip of my beer. "What do you mean?"

"The Bosnian War was...ugly. Not that all wars aren't." She turned to look at the fire. "What if I find my parents only to learn that they were killed in the Albanian ethnic cleansing? Or worse, that they were the ones doing said cleansing?"

"Jesus." I took another deep swig of my beer.

She looked back at me. "And while my skin has olive tones in it, I have bright red hair and blue eyes. That's not a common set of genes from the area. There were outside forces supporting the war. Something like twelve to twenty thousand women were raped by the latest estimates. I've always worried I'm the product of one."

I rubbed a hand over my face. "I am so sorry I brought all this up."

"It's okay," she told me. "Talking about it is better than internalizing it, right? Sorry if it makes you uncomfortable. My family is really open, and I tend to overshare."

"It's fine. I can handle heavy topics."

She nodded. "I figured. I think it's really good what you're doing, by the way. How you bring attention to so many issues that we, as a society, really need to start talking about."

"Thank you."

She picked up the cards and shuffled, and I tensed a little, waiting for her to ask about my family. About Zach. It would only be fair after she just told me so much. Instead, she looked perfectly content to hold such a one-sided conversation. Like she wasn't bursting with questions.

"Have you been to Boston to visit your oldest sister much?" I asked.

"Yup. I go a couple of times a year. Whenever I need a reminder of what civilization is like."

"What do you think of the city?"

"A lot of cool history. Good food. Loud people." She started dealing the cards. "The last time I was there, a cabbie almost hit a pedestrian right in front of me and they both screamed 'Fuck your mother' at each other, which probably shouldn't have made me laugh as hard as I did, in retrospect."

My answering chuckle was cut off by the sound of my phone chiming from inside my pocket. "Sorry," I said, fishing it out.

A slew of texts poured in from my lawyer, saying not to worry, that he and my PR rep were already on it.

On what? I texted back.

He sent me a link, and I spent a few minutes reading in frustrated silence. The Commissioner of the USFL was talking shit about our lawsuit against the league on social media.

Merry Fucking Christmas.

Thanks, Pete. Turning my phone off now, I texted.

I flicked it off and dropped it on the coffee table in front of the couch.

"Sorry about that," I told Ella.

"No worries," she said. "Everything okay? I can keep myself distracted if you need some time."

I shook my head. "The Commissioner of the league is being a prick on Twitter."

She set the card deck on the cribbage board and cracked her knuckles, expression dark. "Want me to create an egg account and call him bad names?"

I grinned. "No need. My lawyer is already on it. We're not supposed to talk about the lawsuit, so the Commissioner might get his ass whooped in court over this."

"Good. That man is such a jackass." She picked the cards back up. "Okay, so, the first thing you should know about cribbage is that it's eighty percent luck of the draw, ten percent desperation, and ten percent raw talent."

I wanted to hug her for moving on so easily.

We played a few practice games, with her teaching me as we went. Cribbage was pretty straightforward. The only thing that tripped me up was the point system. Fifteen-two, four, six? What the hell was that?

"So where'd you go to art school?" I asked as I shuffled the cards in between games.

"I did two years at the Rhode Island School of Design, but then I ended up coming home. My grandfather and Jack's wife were both diagnosed with terminal cancer that year."

I shook my head. "Goddamn cancer. Too many of my family members have had it."

"Mine too. Grandpa had lung cancer, and he wasn't even a smoker. Renee had breast cancer. It went into remission several years before, so we all thought she was clear. Then it came back."

"God, that sucks. I'm so sorry."

"Thanks." She tucked a stray piece of hair behind her ear, expression troubled. "What's super fucked up is that she's listed as a survivor."

I stared at her. "*What?*"

"A lot of medical research organizations and big-name charities have changed the definition of surviving it. So now, if you have breast cancer and you live cancer-free for five years after diagnosis, you're marked as a survivor."

"Even if it comes back and you die from it?"

"Yup. Because it makes them look better. Like they're actually making headway, even though they're not."

I rubbed a hand over my face. "Let me guess, it's all so they can profit off of it?"

She tipped her beer toward me. "Bingo. Long story short, I came home when they got sick and never finished school. The rest was mostly self-taught, though I've taken some art classes up here."

I could sense that there was more to the story, but she'd already shared so much with me that I couldn't bring myself to press her on it, despite my curiosity. "You're really talented."

She sent me a small smile. "Thanks."

"Where do you get your inspiration for the more, uh, controversial cards?"

Her smile widened. "The murder squirrel one was inspired by a friend. She said something similar to her sister-in-law a few years ago before Thanksgiving. Their family is divided down the middle, politically, and there are several loudmouths on each side that like to ruin gatherings by spewing their opinions all over everyone else. I think her exact words were, *I will kill you if you don't show up this year*, and I took that and ran with it."

"Well, you nailed it. I don't think a greeting card has ever made me laugh that hard."

Her expression turned serious. "Ben, if you and your parents don't stop inflating my ego like this, I won't be able to get my swollen head through doorways."

"Too bad. You're really good at what you do, and I'm not going to stop telling you that."

She looked back at her cards, cheeks coloring. "Thanks."

Half an hour later, I found out what the skunk mark meant. If you lost a game, like I just did, and your pegs didn't pass that mark, your opponent will jump up from their seat, nearly upending the board in their excitement, and perform an elaborate dance routine in your living room, their arms akimbo as they hop back and forth while singing, "Iiiiiiiiit's skunkarooney time, it's skunarooney time, with Uncle Frankenstein, it's skunkarooney time!"

Behind her, the dogs lifted their muzzles and howled along with her painfully off-key singing, creating a chorus that made me want to cover my ears.

The display was the most ridiculous thing I'd seen a grown woman do in person. She looked like a demented scarecrow. Like some sort of marionette whose manipulator had gotten into a bad batch of moonshine. Topping it off was the triumphant, gleefully deranged expression on her face that I wished I could unsee.

It was amazing.

My sides hurt from laughing by the time I was finally able to ask, "What the fuck is happening right now?"

"Ow," she said. She fell back into her seat and clutched her hamstring. "I honestly don't know. It's this dance my dad used to do whenever he skunked us, and it somehow turned into another Jones family tradition. Even Jacob does it."

"I hope you don't expect me to."

She levelled her gaze at me. "Of course not. You'd have to skunk me first, Ben."

Was that a challenge?

I narrowed my eyes and stared her down.

She looked away first this time, wincing. "Owww. Totally worth it, but ow," she said, stretching out her leg.

"I have a heating pad for that."

"Bless your heart," she said, and then cackled in a way that reminded me of when Jack said he missed half the jokes she made.

Looked like I'd be joining him.

I grabbed the heating pad from upstairs. Not wanting her to get up, I plugged it in for her, set it to medium, and handed it over.

She wrapped it around her thigh. Her eyes fluttered shut and she leaned way back in her seat, exposing the long line of her neck. A soft moan slipped through her lips.

And there went my mind, straight into the fucking gutter.

So much for not having to police my thoughts.

Chapter 9: Ella

I woke to the dogs whining. It was probably time for them to go out, but I was just so tired. And so warm. But not all that comfortable, I realized. There was a crick in my neck. The right side of my face felt like I was lying on a rack of pork ribs. What the hell was this pillow made of, rocks? I punched it to try to smooth it out, and it *moved* in response, flinching away from me like it was alive.

I jerked upright, suddenly wide awake. A heavy blanket fell away to reveal the sight of Ben's large body spread out beneath me. The flannel shirt he wore was rumpled. His feet hung a foot off the edge of his reclining seat. He cracked his eyes open and rubbed his ribs.

Ribs that I just punched.

We must have fallen asleep watching *A Christmas Story.* The last thing I remembered was Ralphie and Randy being bullied by Grover Dill.

I looked up. The TV was off, and the fire had burned down to ashes, but it was still dark outside. Fred and Sam pushed closer to me, sniffing and whining.

One second, boys. Emergency here.

The middle console with the folding table was back in the upright position, my butt having taken its place. Had I fallen asleep like this, or had my unconscious body inchwormed its way over here and draped itself on top of Ben sometime during the night? I was pretty sure I'd remember this level of snuggling, but for the life of me, I couldn't. I must have done it while sleeping.

My subconscious was a lustful, traitorous bitch.

"Good morning," Ben said, voice low and gravelly.

I scooted away from him. "I just punched you. I'm sorry."

"I'm sure I deserved it."

"We fell asleep."

All hail Ella. Queen of the Obvious.

He grinned. "You first."

"Was there...snoring?"

His grin gained a mocking edge. "Oh yeah. You woke the dogs up with it. I think they thought a bear was trying to break into the house. You quieted down once you decided I made a better pillow than the headrest, though."

I leapt from the couch. My hamstring muscle cramped on landing and I almost toppled over sideways.

Ben sat up. "Are you okay?"

"The dogs! They have to go pee-poop."

I snapped my mouth closed, horrified that I'd let slip the stupid sing-song expression I used when I let them out – *You guys have to go pee-poop?* – and shambled my way toward the front door like an overripe zombie with rotleg.

"Ella Jones," Ben said from behind me. "Are you *embarrassed*?"

"No!" I called over my shoulder as I fled.

His laughter followed me outside.

The dogs raced into the darkness. I shut the door behind me and walked from the spill of porchlight into the shadows at the edge of the deck. My palms hit the railing, and I recoiled. It was freezing out, so cold that it felt like the wood had seared my skin. An image of Flick's tongue stuck to that pole flashed through my mind.

I wrapped my arms around myself and stepped side to side in my thick woolen socks to minimize the danger of frostbite. I couldn't go back in for my boots. Not yet. Maybe not ever. I'd seen a lot of car heist movies. Maybe I could hotwire the truck and peel out of there without ever having to see Ben again.

To answer his question: yes, I was embarrassed. I had been transmogrified from a human woman into a being made of humiliation and regret. So much for keeping my distance. So much for letting him decide things. He invited me over and I moved myself right in. Right on top of him, even.

The front door opened. I did my best to disappear into the darkness.

I am night. You cannot see me, mortal.

Ben walked right up to me, deflecting my Jedi mind powers with an ease that made me fear he was a Sith Lord in disguise. He held out a heavy coat. Not one to look a gift horse in the mouth, I took it and pulled it on. It was one of his, and it absolutely swamped me. God, did it smell good. Like vetiver and sandalwood and frankincense.

"Ella, where are your boots?"

Who had night vision this good? What was he, a werewolf? "Uh...I must have left them inside."

He went back in and grabbed them, and I quickly pulled them on.

"I'm sorry, Ella" he said.

I wanted to shout at him to stop saying my name. Hearing it on his lips made me want to rise up and steal it off of them with my own.

His tone was full of regret when he spoke again. "I didn't mean to embarrass you."

He was too nice. I couldn't do this. I was going to succumb beneath the weight of this crush. My gravestone would read: Beware! Kindness really *does* kill.

I took a deep, steadying breath. "You didn't embarrass me. I embarrassed myself. I'm sorry I fell asleep. I didn't plan to. And I'm sorry for, you know, the snoring. And the sleeping on you." I cringed. "And the punching."

My own night vision had adjusted enough that I saw him lean back against the railing. "I didn't mind." He looked down at me, white teeth flashing in the darkness. "Well, maybe I minded the punching a little."

I didn't respond. I was too busy having an epic internal battle. Did I cling to my shame, an emotion that was so rare for me that it almost felt alien? Or did I take this man at his word and believe that he wasn't secretly annoyed that some strange woman had just couch-crashed in his super-secret bat cave?

"You want to stay for breakfast?" he asked. "It's almost seven."

Poof. All other thoughts disappeared. That hadn't been my eyes adjusting; it was the sun rising.

"In the morning?" I asked, voice shrill.

He frowned. "Yeah. Are you okay?"

"I stayed out all night and didn't tell my sister."

"I'm sorry. I don't like making you lie for me."

I shook my head. "I've decided not to lie. Turns out, I'm no good at it. I'm just going to tell her I was at a friend's and fell asleep. If she gets pushy, I'll go the "Where I was last night is none of your goddamn business" route. She always hated when Mom and Dad tried to police her whereabouts, and turnaround is fair play."

"Then I'm sorry I put you in this position," Ben said.

"You didn't. I did. I made the choice to come over here, and to respect your privacy."

"If it ever gets to the point that it bothers you, let me know. We can stop hanging out."

"Does that mean you want to keep hanging out?" I asked, struggling to keep the unadulterated hope out of my tone.

"If you do," he said, grinning. "It's nice having a new friend."

My heart swelled like the grinch after giving all the presents back. That was it. Put a fork in me. I was done. I'd passed the point of no return with this crush.

"I do," I told him.

I heard a scrambling sound and turned. The dogs raced onto the porch. Sam barreled straight toward us and wedged his body between me and Ben's legs, trembling. You know it's cold when Huskies shiver.

We cleaned them off and brought them back inside. They honed in on what remained of their rawhides while I went in search of my phone. I found it in the kitchen. The battery was almost dead. I unlocked the screen and saw a missed text from Megan around midnight that read: *Hope you just fell asleep at a friend's and aren't bleeding out on the side of the road somewhere. Not waiting up for you any longer.*

Guess she hadn't been that worried after all.

Hey, I texted her. *I did fall asleep at a friend's. Just woke up. Sorry for not letting you know I'd be out all night. Be home in a bit.*

She immediately texted back. *Kind of nice to have the extended quiet last night. No offense. Glad you're safe. Love you.*

Love you too.

I set my phone down and looked up to see that Ben's back was to me. His hair was wild from sleep. I had the strongest urge to reach out and tangle my fingers in it.

This was getting ridiculous.

I told myself, again, that he had come out here for peace and quiet, not to be the object of my lust. It helped clear the fog of hormones.

The fog of sleep remained, and I was thrilled to see him pull a bag of coffee from an open cupboard and begin the motions of making a pot.

We stayed up late last night playing cards and talking. And talking. And talking some more. About everything. From benign topics like where it was safe to trail run once the snow melted to deeply serious discussions about race and politics like the one we'd had before starting cribbage.

We spoke like people who'd known each other for years and had moved past the fear of saying something that might lead to an argument or drive the other away. I'd never clicked with someone like this before, or so quickly, and I was starting to worry that this crush might quickly morph into something *more* if I wasn't careful.

A sharp ringing jarred me from my thoughts: the sound of an incoming FaceTime call.

Ben scooped up his phone and answered it. "Hi, Mom."

"Hi, honey," she said, sounding even more tired than I was.

He bent down to put the coffee bag away, and I caught a glimpse of her over his shoulder. She was as beautiful as the pictures. In her mid-fifties, she had dark hair, light golden skin with pink undertones, and pale green eyes that she had passed on to her son. Seeing them in another person's face had taken me aback the first time we spoke.

"What are you doing up?" Ben asked. "It's like three in the morning, your time."

"I've been awake most of the night thinking about that asshole Commissioner, and I just wanted you to know that our lawyers are working together to –" Her eyes cut left. Our gazes met. I waved. The sleep cleared from her eyes as her expression morphed into surprise. "Is that Ella behind you?"

Realization dawned on me. It wasn't even seven in the morning and I was at his house. We both looked like we'd just woken up. Because we had.

Ben turned toward me in slow motion, his eyes wide, as if just now coming to the same conclusion that I had: this situation could be easily misconstrued.

"*Fuck,*" he mouthed.

Yes, that's probably what she thinks, Ben.

"Why is Ella at your house at," she checked her watch, "six fifty-five in the morning?"

"She came over to drop off my Christmas present," he answered, much better under pressure than I would be.

"Hani, come say hi to Ella," his mother called.

Ben groaned. "Of course Dad's up too," he said beneath his breath.

"She still over there?" I heard his father say.

"*Sorry,*" Ben mouthed at me.

"*It's fine,*" I mouthed back.

I hobbled over to him and leaned against the cabinet so we were both in the camera frame. Looking back at us on the screen were his parents. It was easy to pick out the features he had inherited from them. His skin color was a mixture of both, several shades lighter than his father's and darker than his mother's. The shape of his eyes and their hue came from his mom. He got his wide nose and square jaw from his father. Eyebrows from Mom. Hair from Dad.

Hani's eyes crinkled up at the corners when he smiled, just like Ben's did. "He's not holding you there against your will, is he?"

"Ha. Ha. Ha," I didn't laugh, but said. I leaned closer to the phone and dropped my voice. "Send help."

As I hoped, they lost it. God, these two were easy.

Ben assumed an exasperated expression. "Please don't encourage her."

His parents laughed even harder.

I looked up at him. Our eyes met, and we grinned like co-conspirators.

His mother caught it. "I will gladly encourage anyone that can make you smile like that, Benny."

"*Benny?*" I asked him.

"Don't even think about it," he told me.

In the small insert on his phone screen, my grin transformed into an expression of pure evil. It looked vaguely familiar. Right. Willow made this same face when something diabolical popped into her head. Now the troubling question: had I taught it to her, or had she taught it to me? I was a little worried it was the latter.

One day she would rule us all.

"Don't tease him too much, Ella," Ben's mother said.

I raised my hand in an approximation of a salute. "Scouts honor." The look on my face was a dead giveaway for how full of shit I was. I really needed to get better at mastering my expressions.

"We can talk about the lawyers later," Hani said. "You two have fun with each other." Just in case we missed the innuendo, he winked.

Ben quickly hung up and turned back to the coffee maker. "Well, they think we're sleeping together."

I stared blindly at his back, mouth agape, unable to rid myself of the mental image that just popped into my mind.

***

"Megan, can I talk to you?" I asked my sister several hours later.

Stacey just left the living room to take a shower, much to my relief. I'd been waiting – impatiently – to talk to Megan alone since getting back from Ben's, trying to do it in an organic way, so I didn't offend Stacey. I didn't care if Megan turned around and told her wife every word I said, but part of this conversation might be awkward for Stacey to hear, and I didn't want to subject her to that.

Megan muted the TV and turned toward me on the couch. "What's up?"

I shot a look toward the bathroom and then scooted closer to her, lowering my voice. "You remember that roommate you had freshman year of college?"

She nodded. "Beth."

"Were you in love with her?"

She leaned back and crossed her arms over her chest. "Yes."

"But you two were really good friends."

"Also yes."

"How the hell did you manage that?"

"Honestly?"

I nodded. As much as she and I sometimes bickered, she was the only person in my life that I could have entirely frank conversations with, stuff that I wouldn't say to anyone else, and I doubted that she would either, maybe with the exception of Stacey. She was the one I talked to about losing my virginity. The one who threatened to kill the first boy that broke up with me.

"I managed it by fucking other people," she told me.

Well, all right then. "Did that help?"

"You betcha. It helped me see that there were other fish in the sea, queer women who I could have healthy relationships with, instead of an unhealthy one-sided obsession with the straightest woman to ever straight. Eventually I got over my romantic feelings for Beth and moved on, without torching our friendship. We still keep in touch."

"Damn it," I said. "That's not really an option for me. There aren't enough other people to sleep with up here. Well, ones that I would be interested in sleeping with, anyway. Because those that I would be, I already have."

All two of them.

Maybe I could lower my standards. My friend Jen said Nick Haskell had been pestering her about me. So what if he was missing a few teeth?

"What's going on?" Megan asked.

I sighed. "I have a massive crush on a friend that I think will only ever see me in a platonic way."

"The mysterious Stan?"

I nodded. I didn't bother telling her not to tell anyone else, because now that she knew how I really felt, she would never do that.

"Well, shit," she said. "Sorry for teasing you about him in front of everyone like a total asshole."

"It's okay. You didn't know at the time."

"Why do you think he doesn't like you back?"

"Because he hasn't so much as flirted with me or even looked at me with anything other than friendship. Also, he's totally out of my league."

"Out of your league? Really? Since when do you have low self-esteem?"

I shook my head. "No, it's not that. I guess I didn't mean out of my league. I meant that the world he comes from is so different than ours." The last woman he was associated with in the press was third in line for the throne of a European country. I had no idea if the rumors were true or not, but the point stood.

"What do you mean?" Megan asked. "He from the south or something?"

"I can't really get into it," I told her. "Sorry."

"Okay, fine. Tell me some of his flaws."

I sat there for a solid minute in silence.

Megan finally broke. "Seriously, Ella? The dude has nothing wrong with him?"

"No? At least nothing that I've seen so far?"

"Or are you just living that deep in crushville?"

"Legit possibility."

"Okay, so say you break down and tell him how you feel. What do you think would happen?"

"I think he might want to stop hanging out. I don't think he's looking for anything other than friendship."

"And how would that make you feel?"

"Like abject shit. The last thing I want to do is alienate him. He really seems like he needs a friend right now."

"Good," Megan said.

I stared at her. "Please elaborate on how abject shit is good."

"Because that gives you something to focus on."

"Yeah, so I've tried to focus on similar things when I'm around him, but every time I look at his face, I just -" I lowered my hands to either side of my hips and mimed my ovaries exploding.

Megan frowned. "What is that supposed to be?"

"All of the eggs getting released when I'm in his presence. He is the best-looking man I've seen in real life, by, like, a lot."

"Is that the bias of your crush speaking?"

I shook my head. "Nope. If I showed a picture of him to anyone interested in men, they would try to lick the photograph."

Megan stared at me. "Damn."

"Welcome to my hell."

She chewed on her lower lip for a second, the same way I did when I was deep in thought. Funny how alike we were in some ways, even though we weren't related by blood. It lent credence to nurture over nature.

"I think you should hang out with him more," she said.

"In a ploy to win him over with my stunning good looks and irresistible charm?"

She smiled. "There's that self-esteem."

"Megan, seriously."

She threw her hands up. "I am being serious. When I first met Stacey, it was a struggle to keep from mauling her in public."

"Stacey is, admittedly, gorgeous, so I get it."

"And I still think that, but the more we hung out, the less over-whelming being around her was."

"Because you were mauling her in private?"

She grinned lasciviously. "Oh, I mauled her privates."

I fake gagged. "Too far, Megan."

She rolled her eyes at me. "Think of it like music. You know how you do that annoying thing where when you hear a new song you really like, you play it on endless repeat for a week straight?"

"Yes," I said, ignoring the jibe. Our rooms were right next to each other's growing up. I could see now how that habit would be annoy-ing.

"Why do you do that?" she asked.

"Because of what the music does to me. How the sounds sweep me off my feet and fill my head with images. Music to me is transportive. It makes me feel in color, if that makes any sense."

She shook her head. "It doesn't, but that's not the point. What happens if you listen to that song three months later? Do you still feel the same way you did that first week?"

I had to think about it for a minute. "No. Or if I do, it's to a much lesser extent."

"Maybe Stan is like music. The more you hang out with him, the less his physical beauty will overwhelm you. You'll get used to it, like I did with Stacey. And in the interim, he might manifest a character flaw or two to distract you away from his seeming perfection."

"That might actually work."

She grinned. "Good."

"But what if it doesn't?"

Her expression fell. "Uh...call me and we can try to figure something else out?"

"Deal," I told her.

Chapter 10: Ben

It was two days after Christmas. I couldn't get out of bed.

A crushing pressure kept me there, made up of a debilitating mixture of grief, anxiety, survivor's remorse, and depression. It felt like a physical being with a corporeal form. Some huge, hulking monster that sat on my chest, its paws on my shoulders, pressing me down. All of my hours in the gym were worthless to me now. As hard as I struggled, I didn't have the strength to push it off.

I hadn't suffered a depressive bout like this in months. The setback was infuriating, which only compounded my other negative emotions. I'd been doing so much better lately. This step backward really illustrated that to me now. But then Christmas happened.

The day itself was fine. Between my anticipation to hang out with Ella, cooking, and talking to family and friends, I'd been plugged in, connected. Distracted.

Then Ella left the next morning, and the house suddenly seemed too big. Too quiet. Without the diversion of her and the dogs, my thoughts wandered to Zach. To the last holiday we spent together with the whole family in Hawaii. To my nephew, Micah, racing around my parents' living room, holding Buzz Lightyear high over his head as he made "zooooom" noises. He asked me to read him a bedtime story that night. Not his parents. Not his grandparents. *Me.* I'd felt like the most special person in the whole world.

Watching his eyes flutter shut while I read to him made me want to settle down and have a couple of kids of my own. I walked downstairs afterward to find the rest of the family in the dining room, seated around my parents' large rectangular table, howling with laughter. Zach's wife, Molly, a.k.a. Two Can Sam, a.k.a. Lightest of the Lightweights, a.k.a. Gigglefits McGee, sat at the head of it, her blonde curls frazzled, her brown eyes glazed over.

She'd gotten into the champagne while I was upstairs, and the bubbles went straight to her head. Everything was suddenly rendered hilarious by her buzz. I still had video of "The Incident" as she called it afterward. I watched it earlier, rewinding several times to the part where my dad leaned toward her and muttered, "Ham sandwich." Molly slid to the floor snort-laughing, the rest of us joining along because it was just so ridiculous and her laughter was just that infectious. Chewbacca mask lady had nothing on Molly when she really got going.

I watched the video right to the end, when Zach scooped his tipsy wife up off of the ground and carried her out of the room, followed by a chorus of hoots and catcalls.

When the video was over, I curled into the fetal position in the middle of my bed and sobbed until my tears ran out.

Six months after I shot that video, they were dead.

My eyes were scratchy now, my face puffy, throat sore. I'd cried so much that I was dehydrated. Thanks to the litany of other physical symptoms that manifested whenever a bout of depression hit me this hard, I felt like I had the flu. My head throbbed. I didn't trust my stomach enough to put anything other than bread in it. The sheets beneath me were soaked with sweat.

At least I didn't have the shortness of breath and racing pulse that proceeded a full-blown panic attack. Shut up all alone in the house like this, with no one to help me through it, I'd probably end up hyperventilating myself into unconsciousness.

My phone went off, emitting a shrill tone that reminded me it was time to take my medication. I dug through the rumpled covers around me until I found the phone, then hit 'end' on the alarm. It took a monumental effort to roll over, pop the caps off of several prescription bottles stacked on the nightstand, and swallow the pills with the help of a large swig of water.

I flopped down onto my back afterward, throwing an arm over my eyes.

"This is very common, Ben," Brian, my therapist, told me earlier. "Having setbacks as we lower your dosages is completely normal. Your body needs time to adjust. If these overwhelming feelings persist, we might need to talk about raising your SSRI back up a bit, but we can cross that bridge if and when we get there."

SSRI stood for selective serotonin reuptake inhibitor. It acted by freeing up serotonin – commonly called the 'happy chemical' – for use in the brain. They were a much safer antidepressant for someone who might have CTE than tricyclic ones, which came with strong anticholinergic side effects. Anyone with a potential brain injury or a degenerative brain disorder didn't need help inhibiting parasympathetic nerve impulses – which is what anticholinergic agents did. In laymen's terms, they raised the suicide risk for someone like me.

"Have you been ingesting caffeine or alcohol lately?" Brian had gone on to ask.

Yes, to both. He'd advised me to stop. Immediately. Because they could further compound depression and anxiety. I promised him I would. So far, the man had never led me astray. But goddamn it, sometimes I just wanted to sit back and drink a beer after a long day of working on the house.

I growled in frustration and rolled onto my stomach, clinging to my pillow like it was a life raft. The underlying feeling that made this all so unbearable was the guilt. It always went something like this: I want to drink beer – Zach can no longer drink beer; I want to get over my crushing sadness – Molly can no longer feel crushing sadness; I worry that I'm no longer capable of having a healthy romantic relationship – Micah died long before he could develop romantic feelings for another person.

For every selfish thought I had, there was my brother, telling me to stop being an asshole. At least I was alive to feel depressed. My fear of CTE wouldn't be possible if I were dead. I should have been thankful I didn't have any obvious signs of the disease yet.

I dug down deep and tried to muster some joy at that thought.

Nothing.

Which made the guilt even worse.

You'd think their sudden deaths would remind me that I only had one life to live. That I shouldn't waste this life on negativity and regret. If only I had a choice in the matter. My depression and anxiety had stolen it away from me.

The symptoms started not long after the car crash. As soon as Zach's autopsy was released, I broke my contract and quit the league. And then I began actively speaking out against it. No longer constrained by my old team's strict social media policy, I got political on Twitter. I voiced my opinions. About race. About rape culture. About toxic masculinity.

I was immediately ostracized. Hung out to dry by former teammates and coaches who disagreed with me, or didn't want to weigh in on my "drama". The fans turned on me too. People who had followed my career since college filled my social media feeds, telling me how disappointed they were in what I had become. It left me cut off from the community I had belonged to almost my entire life.

That's fine, I told myself. They made their decisions, and they would have to live with them. Their unwillingness to stand up and do the right thing only served to spur me on. Someone had to act. How many other parents were out there, thinking about putting their kids into children's football leagues without knowing the risk? How much safer would professional players be if only the league enforced tougher rules and higher fines?

Mom and Dad were right there with me after clawing their way out of their own grief. Together, we formed the non-profit. We shot Public Service Announcements. We funded research. There were web-sites to set up, doctors to approach, and studies to retweet. When the league's misrepresentation of the TBI risk to its players first came to light, I found myself joined by more and more men who realized their lives were more important than fame or fortune or the love of the game. Our lawsuit soon followed.

For those first two years, I kept myself so busy that it was easy to miss the early warning signs of my depression. The apathy I felt toward other humans, the mood swings, the insomnia, they could all be chalked up to an agitated state brought on by Twitter trolls and ignorant assholes.

A year ago, the symptoms worsened. They became unavoidable. Inexcusable.

Eight months ago, I almost had a mental break.

Seven and a half months ago, I had my first therapy session with Brian.

"Are you experiencing any severe mood swings? Thoughts of suicide?" he asked me earlier.

A little bit. And no. Even when my depression was at its worst, I didn't think about killing myself. Because how could I do that to my parents? How could I do that to Zach? As much as I resented this never-ending guilt, it had probably saved my fucking life.

My phone went off again, pulling me from my dark thoughts. I rolled over to see a text from Ella lighting up my screen.

Okay, so I have a brilliant idea. AND I NEED YOU TO HEAR ME OUT.

I grinned. For the first time all day. It was fleeting, but it served to remind me that I could still feel positive emotions like amusement.

Hit me with it, I texted back.

You know how you were saying the other night that you're going a little stir-crazy shut up in the house?

If she only knew.

Yeah, I responded.

Well, my cabin sits on about 30 acres, and I have a couple miles of trails winding through them. Did you want to embarrass the shit out of yourself by coming over and learning how to cross-country ski? In a controlled, quasi-safe (see previous comment about embarrassment) environment without the threat of being seen by anyone but me and the dogs?

I'm in, I told her. *But I don't have skis. I'll have to order some first.*

Don't bother. I don't want you to waste the money if you end up hating it and never use them again. I can just borrow a pair from someone close-ish to your height. What are you, like 7'5"?

Ha. I'm only 6'4".

Only 6'4", he says. This was followed by a rolling eye emoji. *When did you want to plan on coming by? Tomorrow looks nice, weather-wise.*

Tomorrow. I couldn't commit to that. Or the next day. Or the one after that. My last depressive bout had kept me in bed for nearly a week. The earliest date I was willing to risk making plans for happened to fall on the last day of the year.

Can't escape the house until New Year's Eve, I told her. *I'm sure you already have plans, though.*

Yeah, sorry. I'm going to be super busy that day. You know, prepping with the girls. Selecting the perfect dress. Deciding which club is throwing the best party. And then I need to have a long, hard think about which of the many, MANY eligible bachelors I should smooch at midnight.

Clubs? Was there some secret underground rave culture up here I wasn't aware of? Or was she going out of town? And why was I suddenly fixated on who she was thinking about kissing?

Another text came through. *#sarcasm. What time did you want to come over?*

Oh, she'd been kidding. Relief flooded through me.

Can we set a time closer to the day of? I asked. I couldn't make a decision yet. Just trying to act normal in this conversation was taking every ounce of my willpower, and I was almost drained.

Absolutely! I'll text you the night before.

I went to set the phone down and caught sight of my Twitter app. The bubble in the top right-hand corner of it said I had over a thousand notifications waiting for me.

"I think it's time to take another social media break," Brian had suggested earlier. "At least until this blowup with the Commissioner dies down or you feel like you're in a better place to interact with others online."

Taking his advice, I tapped the Twitter icon and held it. When the little (x) popped up to delete it, I hit it without hesitation. Next was Instagram. TikTok. Snapchat. I removed each and every social media app from my phone. And then I moved on to my news apps. I didn't think I'd ever seen a positive notification from one of them. It was always headlines like *North Korea Threatens to Annihilate South Korea,* or *Twenty Killed in Latest School Shooting.*

Normally, I thought it was important to keep up with the news. To look, eyes wide open, at this world we lived in. But right now, my mental health needed to be my priority.

Finished with my mass deleting, I tossed the phone away, rolled onto my side, and fell asleep.

***

The next day was a little easier. I got out of bed for a few hours. I didn't drink coffee. I poured all of the alcohol in the house down the kitchen sink. I was able to eat a decent-sized lunch. My morning session with Brian went well – we always switched to two-a-days when I had these episodes.

A few weeks ago, when we first discussed dropping my dosages, he was very upfront about the pros and cons of cutting back. At the time of that discussion, I thought the benefits outweighed the costs. I wasn't sure if I still believed that, but hopefully in the coming days I'd feel better, and it would seem...well, not worth it, exactly, but maybe it wouldn't seem so bad when I was on the other side of this.

After lunch I crawled back into bed, exhausted.

"Don't let yourself dwell on the negativity or ruminate on Zach's death. No more videos of him and his family," Brian said during our afternoon session. "Employ distraction techniques. Watch funny animal videos on YouTube."

"My mom thinks I should get a dog," I told him.

"It's not a terrible idea. Pets have been proven to help combat depression."

After we hung up, I took his advice. What were Fred and Sam like as puppies? I googled "Husky puppies" and then fell down the rabbit hole of baby animal videos. When I was done, I turned on the TV, pulled up my Netflix account, and binge-watched one of their latest shows.

***

The day after that was even better. I got out of bed in the morning and ate a huge breakfast, ravenously hungry. I worked out. The endorphins did wonders to help my mindset. Later, during our afternoon session, I told Brian about Ella. I hadn't been keeping her from him exactly; I just didn't want to bring her up until I was sure that she was someone I might see with frequency. Brian heartily approved of our budding friendship, especially when I told him about the conversations we'd had and how much she made me laugh.

"As long as you don't use that humor as a crutch when you're feeling anxious or depressed," he cautioned.

I assured him that I'd be careful to avoid that.

***

New Year's Eve day, I was up before the sun. I felt good this morning. Not great, but that was okay. Good was a big step forward from where I was a few days ago.

Soon, I'd leave for Ella's. We planned for an early start because a squall was building just across the Canadian border, and it might roll east over the mountains later. I wasn't even halfway through my first winter here and I was already wary of snowfall forecasts. The weather patterns were so unpredictable. Storms had a way of settling into our valley and lingering, hemmed in by the mountains, dumping inches more than the weatherpeople said they would.

I knew we'd be outside most of the morning, and that the fresh air and skiing – and Ella's goofiness – would function as natural mood boosters, but I still planned to work out before I left. I'd take all the help I could get at this point.

I ate another huge breakfast. A frame as large as mine needed constant fuel, and after so many days in a row with a limited caloric intake, there was a risk my body would cannibalize my muscles to burn as energy.

Once I finished with breakfast, I went upstairs and stripped my bed. I'd gone through all of my spare sheets over the last few days. I dumped them in the washing machine, turned it on, and then threw open the windows in my bedroom to air it out. It smelled like an animal den in here. Musky. Slightly ripe. I wished I had something to burn – a candle, or incense, or hell, even sage. I made a mental note to order some later, and in the interim I doused the room in cologne and then closed the windows.

Skiing might trash my legs, so I chose an upper-body routine for my workout. I tired faster than I would have a week ago, and instead of pushing myself, I listened to my body and stopped.

I was stepping into the shower, my muscles already sore and over-inflated from lifting, when I remembered Ella's hamstring. Hopefully she was feeling better by now. I tore my right one in high school, and it took months to fully heal. I'd hate for her to push herself too early and do more damage.

An image of her wrapping that heating pad around her thigh flashed through my mind, followed by the sound of bliss she'd made.

My dick decided that now was the perfect time to stir back to life.

"Is your relationship with Ella entirely platonic?" Brian asked me yesterday.

"Yeah," I'd told him. "Why do you ask? Do you think I'm not ready for anything romantic?"

"I think *you* think you're not ready, which is important, and we should talk about that soon. But the main reason I'm asking is that with this new lower dosage regiment, you might start feeling and experiencing things more intensely. Your sex drive will start to return, for example."

That was welcome news. I'd had a pretty respectable sex drive since puberty. Chalk it up to elevated hormone levels brought on by my involvement in competitive sports. When the depression set in, it plummeted, another symptom I'd overlooked. The meds had only further curbed it.

No wonder the sight of Ella's bliss had stirred something in me. I was less concerned about it now than I was at the time. She was beautiful, and she had arched her back and made a face that could have been construed as sexual. My libido, just waking up after a prolonged slumber, saw it and overreacted.

I reached down, thinking back to a particularly memorable sexual partner I'd had a few years ago, and brushed my fingers up the length of my cock. It swelled even further, straining against my abdomen.

I dropped my hand to my side and leaned back against the shower wall, letting the water run over me, reveling in the sensation of being turned on. The sheer novelty of it. The glorious, borderline painful need to ejaculate.

Jesus. This was worth dropping the dosage for. Hopefully I didn't have any more regressions; I didn't want to up the meds again and lose this feeling.

I washed the sweat from my body and then lingered in the shower, my fingers wrapped around my girth as I stroked myself. All too soon, it was over, my release spilling out of me in a rush that, while it felt damn good, still seemed muted compared to my memories.

I climbed into my Jeep an hour later. Ella texted me a detailed list of instructions in case I lost signal on the way to her house, taking me up the hill I lived on instead of down it, out of what she said was an abundance of caution.

I checked her route on my phone before I left, comparing it against what my GPS wanted me to do. It was a full seven minutes longer, but that was because she had me taking back roads, avoiding town completely, most likely to keep someone from somehow recognizing me through these blackout-tinted windows.

I grinned. Jack was right. Ella was good people.

I decided to forgo my phone's map and instead followed her instructions. She went through all that trouble putting them together, after all. Several of the roads I took were new to me. There was no one else on them – not a surprise in an area this sparsely populated – and so I drove below the speed limit, taking in my surroundings and the distant views of the mountains. It was beautiful up here. Stark. Still pristine. How it must have looked everywhere hundreds of years ago.

Ella's place was so out of the way that I thought I was on the wrong street when I got toward the end of the directions. I hadn't seen a single house yet. Did anyone even live out here? I was just beginning to worry there was a typo in her texts when I noticed a mailbox peeking out of a snowbank. I slowed the Jeep. The mailbox had her house number on it.

I turned the wheel and followed the narrow lane that led into the trees. Pines lined the driveway. Their trunks were massive. It looked like I was driving through an old-growth forest. Up ahead, sunlight streamed through the trees. I passed from the woods into a wide clearing with a squat log cabin nestled in the middle of it. Snow clung to its roof. Smoke curled up from the chimney. The scene looked like something from one of Ella's greeting cards, too quaint to be real.

I knew I had the right house when the front door opened and she emerged from it to stride down the porch steps, her dogs right on her heels. She lifted a hand and waved at me when I rolled to a stop, a huge smile spread over her face.

Seeing that smile lifted my mood from good to great.

Chapter 11: Ella

I was nervous when Ben pulled up. I hadn't seen him in five days, and I worried that all the preparation I'd done to gird myself against his good looks wouldn't be enough.

I stayed on the bottom porch step as his Jeep rolled to a stop, watching the dogs barrel through the snow toward him. He got out of the vehicle and leaned down to greet them. I took deep, bracing breaths in and out, praying that Megan was right and prolonged exposure to him would raise my tolerance, like an assassin taking larger and larger doses of poison, so if an enemy slipped her some, it wouldn't kill her.

Ben rose from his crouch, waved hello, and then pulled a backpack out of the Jeep – probably his snow gear, since he was in jeans and a flannel jacket. He turned and ambled up the driveway toward the freshly-shoveled front walk, backpack thrown over a shoulder, one hand on the strap, the other in his jacket pocket. He looked like he could have been walking a runway.

Jacket by Tom Ford. Backpack by Ralph Lauren. Body by Battle Ropes.

Don't think of the battle ropes!

I shifted my focus away from his broad chest. The dogs jumped around his legs, saying hello to their new friend. Sam had a red frisbee in his mouth, and the way he whined around it could easily be interpreted as *throw it, throw it, throw it!* I had no idea where he found that thing. I thought we lost it three storms ago.

Ben slowed, took the toy from Sam's mouth, curled into himself like an Olympian competing for the gold in discus, and unfurled his upper body, his arm a fulcrum, the frisbee shooting out of his hand at a speed that took even the dogs back. They paused, watching it. If Fred could have whistled in appreciation, he would have. Then they were gone, tearing through the yard as they tried to catch up with it. The frisbee just kept going, defying the laws of physics, gliding above the snow like it was a hoverboard. Yup, we were definitely going to lose it this time. I'd probably come across it half a mile deep in the woods during a summer run.

"Good morning," Ben said from way too close.

I'd been so distracted watching the red blur disappear into the trees that I hadn't heard him approach. He stood by the railing. With me on the lowest step, we were almost at eye level.

I smiled in greeting, trying to think of knitting or folding laundry or whatever inane action would keep my mind in a nice, neutral place. He wore a white beanie pushed back on his forehead, the salt-bleached ends of his wavy locks sticking out from beneath it. His jacket was unzipped a little, exposing the long, muscular lines of his neck.

Vacuuming. Mowing the lawn. Hand washing pots and pans. Think of scrubbing grease, Ella!

"Hi!" I said, belatedly. "Come on in."

I led him inside, leaving the dogs to their search. Ben set his backpack down on the bench and took his jacket off. I glanced quickly away from him.

"This is really nice," he said from somewhere overhead. The man was an absolute giant.

"Thank you."

I looked at the cabin's interior, spread out before us, trying to see it from fresh eyes. To the right was the living room. Comfy couches framed the dwindling fire, with thick-knit blankets draped casually over them, inviting you to sit down and bundle up. To the left was the kitchen, the hallway that led to the spare room, and the narrow stairs that climbed up to my bedroom. Ben would probably bump his head on the exposed beams up there.

"Coffee?" I asked. In my head, I chased the image of Ben out of my bedroom with a broom.

"No thanks. Trying to cut back."

"Anything else? Hot chocolate? Tea?"

"Do you have decaf tea?" he asked.

"I do."

I led him into the kitchen.

"No Christmas tree?" he asked. "Or did you already take it down?"

"No tree. I tried to put one up last year. The dogs were convinced a squirrel was hiding in the upper branches and tore it down an hour after I'd added the last string of lights. It took me forever to find all the pieces of broken ornaments."

I thought that visual would get at least a chuckle out of him. Nothing.

Hmm.

I put the tea kettle on the stove and turned to see him plop down on one of the barstools I kept tucked beneath my kitchen island. He wore a dark t-shirt with a band's logo pulled tight across his chest. The soft cotton hugged his biceps. He had a traditional Polynesian tattoo that started from the elbow of his left arm and disappeared beneath his sleeve. I tried to be as clinical as possible in taking all this in and failed spectacularly.

"How was the rest of your visit with your sister?" he asked.

"Pretty uneventful, aside from dinner at Jacob's house the day after Christmas. All of us crammed into his dining room for a send-off celebration."

"Send off?"

"Jacob spends every January in Somalia, volunteering for a non-profit."

"That's where he was adopted from, right?"

I nodded. "Their dry season is just starting, and with the famines they've had lately, they need all the help they can get. He splits his time between pro-bono doctor work and digging wells."

His eyebrows rose. "Oh, wow."

I turned back around and rummaged through a cupboard for some tea. "Yup. Jacob is a wow kind of guy. Dave, Jane's husband, wrote a pretty amazing article about his work last year, and the whole community has come together to donate to the charity he volunteers for."

"It's great that he has so much support."

I grimaced. "Don't be too impressed. At least some of it is guilt money. Jacob was the first of us to go to school here, and he didn't have an easy time of it. He was the only Black kid in his class and one of three in the whole school. The fact that he was adopted and our parents are well-off didn't help."

"But things are better now?" Ben asked.

I nodded. "It helps that he's one of the few local doctors and these people might have to literally put their lives in his hands at some point. And I do think a lot of that initial shittiness was ignorance. It lends credence to those studies about why people in cities are more accepting of those who don't look like themselves, or pray to the same god, or speak the same language. Exposure to different skin colors and cultures is key. Especially from a young age."

"I'm sure technology has helped with that up here," he said.

"It has to some degree," I told him, grabbing two mugs off the shelf. "This part of Maine felt like we were a decade behind the rest of the country when I was growing up. We only had six TV channels until the late nineties. Now these kids have satellite TV and high-speed internet connections and social media. From a young age, they're exposed to people who don't look or sound like they do. It's like everyone is now being raised in one giant virtual city."

"Hopefully all this turmoil we've had lately is just the death rattle of the older, more intolerant generations."

"Amen," I said. I *really* hoped he was right.

The tea kettle whistled. I turned the stove off and moved it to a potholder to cool down. "What kind of tea do you want? I have chamomile, peppermint, rooibos, and honeybush."

"I'm here for some rooibos," he said.

I plopped a bag of it in one mug, dropped a peppermint bag in the other, filled them with water, and reached across the island to set Ben's in front of him.

A *woof* came from outside. I let my tea steep and went to let the dogs in. They didn't have the frisbee with them. It might have been my imagination, but they looked a little forlorn about that, so I rubbed them down extra good and told them that I didn't care that they couldn't find it, they were still the best dogs in the whole world. They seemed to perk up some after that.

Ben's back was to me when I re-emerged from the entryway a few minutes later. My gaze roved over him as I approached. Maybe if I drank in the sight of him when he wasn't looking, I wouldn't keep getting overwhelmed when he was.

Sam trotted past me and planted himself at Ben's side. Ben reached down and scratched him behind the ears. Fred followed me into the kitchen, where I stopped to pick up my tea. I meant to join Ben on a bar stool, but Fred flopped down onto my feet, keeping me where I was. My toes were a little cold, so I leaned against the countertop and tucked them further under Fred's side to warm them up.

I looked up at Ben. Our eyes met. It was easier this time than it had been a few minutes ago. Megan might be right, after all. I was thankful for that. Because I *really* liked him. Aside from the fact that I found him wildly attractive, he was just my kind of person. He was kind, considerate, witty, and intelligent. Everything all of my closest friends had ever been. I didn't want to screw this up by letting my stupid crush get in the way.

"How much did you get done on the house the past few days?" I asked. He'd been a ghost on his social media accounts, so I assumed he'd been working his ass off.

He broke eye contact and looked down at Sam. "Not as much as I wanted to."

"Let me know if you need help. This is a slower time of year for me in the shop, mostly calendar orders, which I printed a ton of in advance."

He glanced back up. "I might do that. Jack said you're pretty good with a hammer."

"I am. He's taught me a lot. Well, him and YouTube. I did most of the work in here myself."

He swiveled on his stool to take in the open layout. "I bet it's nice and toasty in here even when the power goes out."

"It is. I bet it's a bitch to keep your place warm when it does."

He turned back, grinning. "I have a big ass generator."

"Cheater."

"I'm surprised you don't have one."

I shrugged. "No point. I can just toss the contents of the fridge into the snow to keep them cold, and the house is small enough that I have to carefully monitor the fire, or it'll reach 80 in here and the dogs will melt."

Look at me, having a normal conversation with Benjamin Kakoa and not lusting over him. Hooray for progress!

My newfound platonic mindset continued right through the rest of our small talk – which I dominated – until we finished our tea. Afterward, he headed to the bathroom to change into snow gear, subbing jeans for long johns, which I knew, because he was still tightening the belt of his snow pants when he paced back out, and his t-shirt was hitched high enough that I caught sight of the top of them. A narrow band of lower abs was also exposed. I fled from the sight to my bedroom, where I pulled my own snowsuit on.

"How did you know my shoe size?" Ben asked a few minutes later. We were out on the back deck, shoving our feet into cross-country ski boots.

"I checked the first time I was over at your place," I told him. "Because at first I didn't know if I was looking at a pair of sneakers or sleds designed for toddlers."

Ben chuckled in response. It was the first time I'd heard the sound today, and it ended far too quickly. I felt like I was back at our first meeting, like I was going to have to do the majority of the work. I wasn't upset by it; I just couldn't help but wonder what had changed. Why had he retreated back into his shell? Was it me? Did I do something wrong?

I walked over to the cross-country skis and stepped into mine. I had to rent Ben's gear in the end, because it turned out I didn't know anyone as big as him.

He joined me a minute later.

"I saw an elliptical machine in your Basement of Blood, Sweat, and Jump Rope." I paused for laughter and applause. Again, nothing. "Cross country skiing is a lot like being on one. You lift your foot up, move your leg forward, and sort of glide over the snow." I demonstrated for him.

"I don't use that machine that often," he said.

"Well, then, it's a lot like regular skiing."

"Never been."

Uh-oh. "Ice skating?"

He shook his head.

"Roller blading?"

He held up a hand and began counting off fingers. "Skateboarding, surfing, and snowboarding."

"Okay. I'll start with the basics."

I helped him strap into his skis, handed him his poles, and side-stepped away so I could instruct from a safe distance.

"Wait," he said. "I told my parents I'd send them a picture." He pulled off a glove, unzipped his fancy winter coat, pulled out his phone, and handed it over to me.

"Say cheese," I said, before taking the picture.

I gave the phone back, and he sent the picture off.

"Three, two, one," Ben said.

At one, the phone rang with a FaceTime call. His parents were hilarious.

He hit accept.

"Hi, Benny!"

"Hi, Mom."

"Where's Ella?"

He swiveled the phone to me, and I smiled and waved. "Hi, Klara. Hi, Hani."

"How's he doing so far?" his dad asked. "He fall down yet?" He sounded thrilled by the prospect.

I shook my head. "We just started."

"Ben, hand her the phone so we can watch," his mother said.

"This is going to be so embarrassing, isn't it?" Ben asked, doing as she said.

"Horrifically so, if we're lucky," I answered.

His parents cackled at that like a pair of hyenas. Their son shook his head and assumed a long-suffering expression. I raised the phone toward him and hit the icon that flipped the screen so they would see him and not up my nose.

"Okay, so the best way to do this is to start slow," I told him.

Turned out, for all his athletic prowess, Ben wasn't a fast learner when it came to skiing. His parents and I laughed and teased him good-naturedly while he struggled.

"Should have hit that elliptical machine a little harder," I told him.

"Did you put the breaks down on these things?" he shot back.

I decided to let up on him. We said goodbye to his parents and then got down to learning how to ski.

"Are you sure I'm doing this right?" he asked me ten minutes later. "Your feet are more turned out than mine."

The house was still visible through the trees. We'd maybe gone a hundred yards. Instead of gliding forward, he was ski-lunging, pulling himself forward with his poles, knees dipping nearly to the ground. I was starting to worry that he might pull something critical, and then I'd be the girl who let a world-famous athlete get injured on her watch.

"What I'm doing is the advanced version," I told him. "Where you have to push both forward and sideways at the same time while lifting the backs of your skis over each other. You think you're ready for that right now, hotshot?"

He shook his head in an emphatic NO.

"Let's just focus on moving forward any way possible," I said. I pushed off my poles and slid back toward him. When we were even, I lifted them. "These things are your best friends. Don't use them one at a time like you have been. It'll unbalance you. Try sticking them both in the ground on either side and shove off from them."

He planted his poles in the ground and raised his gaze to mine. "Okay"

"Ready?"

"Ready."

"On three. One, two, three."

We shoved off together. Or, I shoved off. I don't know what the hell Ben did that made him lurch sideways toward me.

If this was a movie, Ben and I would fall together in slow-mo, with more than enough time for him to – with superhuman agility – turn in midair so that it was his large body that absorbed the impact instead of mine. We would land together in the snow, artfully splayed, our limbs conveniently intertwined, our faces just inches apart. The perfect set-up for a kiss.

This was not a movie.

The second I realized he was falling, I dropped my poles and tried to steady him. It was futile. He weighed too much, and he was too unbalanced. Like the coward I was, I let him go and tried to save myself instead, sliding away and to the right. Unfortunately, Ben jerked in the same direction and I took his shoulder to the chin.

Owww.

"Fuck. Sorry," he said.

We stumbled together, tripped up by our gear. His legs slid back and forth as he tried to regain his balance on the unfamiliar skis. He grabbed me to steady himself, but it just made everything so much worse. We fought to stay upright, our movements desperate and jerky. Then he pitched sideways and popped free from one of his bindings. The sudden, unexpected freedom sealed our fate.

We lost the battle and down we went.

Ben didn't turn midair. Our limbs were not artfully splayed. I took an elbow to the left boob during the fall and accidentally bashed my knee into his crotch. I hit the ground first and had no chance to roll away before he came crashing down, half on top of me. My breath exploded out of my lungs. I was left gulping like a fish out of water.

Instead of leaning in for a kiss, we rolled away from each other, both groaning in pain.

"Goddamn it," I gasped, clutching my ribs. He might have seriously bruised a couple.

"Ow, *fuck*," Ben said, curling into himself.

Yup, I definitely nailed him in the balls. And not in a good way.

To make matters worse, the dogs gleefully descended upon on us, yipping and barking and whining and licking our faces because we were too slow to cover them.

"You opportunistic little shit," I wheezed up at Fred, pushing him away from me.

"Sam, no, boy," Ben said, rolling back toward me.

Our eyes met. We froze.

"Sooo," I said in a weak, sing-song voice. "How's your morning going?"

Ben lost it. He rolled over onto his back, arms splayed by his sides, and laughed until tears streamed from his eyes. Sam took the opportunity to flail all over him. Ben had to bear hug the dog to get him to stop. Sam settled in Ben's grasp, tongue lolling out of his mouth like this had been his goal all along.

I would have laughed along with him, but I was afraid to. My ribs screamed in pain.

"God, I needed that," he said when he calmed down. He let Sam go and turned to look at me. "You okay?"

"It's a good thing my boobs aren't fake, or you would've just popped one. You?"

He winced. "I think my left testicle has ascended back into my body cavity."

I snorted out a laugh before I could catch it, then clutched at my side. "Ow, *shit*."

He immediately sobered, clambering up onto his knees to shuffle over to me. "What's hurt?"

"My ribs."

He swore. "I landed on you, didn't I?"

"You did. But it's okay, they're just bruised. Want to help me up and then call it a day?"

He nodded. "Oh, yeah. I'm done."

Twenty minutes later, we were sitting on the couch drinking hot chocolate. I had a bag of frozen peas pressed to my ribs – Ben insisted. He sat beside me, manspreading in a way that told me it was less about taking up space and more about giving his crotchal region room to recover.

"What about snowshoeing?" he asked.

"Yeah, we could definitely manage that."

"But not today."

"Definitely not today. What do you want to do instead?" I wiped my face clean of all expression and turned toward him. "We could listen to some music."

I must not have done a good enough job, because he frowned. "Uh...sure."

I raised the stereo remote and hit play. Elton John's voice rang out through the speakers. Ben sent me an unimpressed look. I opened my mouth.

"Don't you dare," he warned.

"B-B-B-Benny and the jets," I sang at him.

He groaned. "You are the absolute worst."

My answering smile felt feral. I had *so much* planned. "This is nothing, my friend. Nothing, I tell you."

"You know, you're kind of scary when your face gets like this."

I cut the music off. "I think I learned it from Willow."

"That's a frightening thought."

"Hopefully she'll be a kind and benevolent overlord."

He leaned closer and dropped his voice. "When she grows up and takes over the world, you mean?"

I nodded and sat back, away from him. His proximity and my hormones weren't a good combination. "Okay, but seriously though. Do you want to stay and watch a movie or something? I won't be offended if you say no."

He shot me a sly look. "We never did finish *A Christmas Story.*"

I closed my eyes and pinched the bridge of my nose. Embarrassment threatened. "I told you never to bring that up."

"No, you didn't."

"Consider this your warning then."

"What about that new spy-thriller that just came out?"

"Yeah, I'd be down for that."

I pulled up my Amazon Prime account through the TV, found the movie, and ordered it. We talked through the whole damn thing, shooting the breeze, doing stupid voice-overs, and calling bullshit on all the inaccuracies like we knew anything about international espionage.

We kept an eye on the weather throughout, and he left in plenty of time to get home safely before the storm hit. After he left, I took a minute to congratulate myself. That had gone way better than our first few interactions.

Well, minus the whole almost putting each other in the hospital thing.

***

"Can you come over?" Ben asked me a week later. "I need those nimble little fingers of yours."

I nearly dropped my phone.

"I'm having a hell of a time trying to tile behind the toilet," he said.

"Tile. Right."

"What did you think I meant, Ella?" I could *hear* the smile in his voice. Thankfully, he wasn't there to see the blush on my face.

"Nothing! I'll be over in a few," I told him, then hung up before he could tease me.

We'd seen each other nearly every day since New Year's Eve, mostly over at his place, working on the house, but he'd been by here again to go snowshoeing. That had worked out much better than skiing. It had been a perfect, sunny day. Ben had a blast exploring the woods. He went home and immediately ordered himself a pair of snowshoes so he didn't have to borrow my spare pair again – which were far too small for his boat-sized feet.

The next night, we'd met at Jack's for dinner and drinks and cards. Ben had abstained from beer. I kept my mouth shut about it, because I had no idea what his history with alcohol was and didn't know if he'd been imbibing too much lately or something. Part of me was a little worried that I might have been too encouraging about drinking when we first met, and I'd since resolved myself not to bring it up again or drink in his presence, on the off chance that he was a recovering alcoholic.

It was getting easier to hang out with him. The conversation flowed free and fast, covering a wide range of topics, most of which we agreed on. The few disagreements we'd gotten into had been more like civil discourse where we logicked each other into corners that neither of us could get out of. He was so rational that it was easy to see where he was coming from. And him me, I think.

It was maddening how similar our debate styles were. God help us if we ever *really* got into it. It'd be a three-day event where nothing is conceded at the end and everyone goes home feeling fully respected but no less frustrated. The utter lack of passion in our arguments made it a little easier to see that we might better suited to being friends after all.

And becoming friends we were. Our banter game was solid. Our reno projects had proven that we worked well together. It was no longer a constant struggle to keep my head out of the gutter when I was around him. It was only when he caught me off guard that I slipped up. Like telling me he needed my nimble fingers. Or, like yesterday, tugging his sweatshirt off before I had time to look away. I'd been treated to another tantalizing glimpse of abs before turning my head.

Every now and then, he said something that sounded slightly flirtatious or leading, but I was pretty sure that I was just misinterpreting his tone. That my subconscious was trying to sabotage all the progress I'd made.

"Fred, Sam," I called. "Want to go to Mr. Ben's?"

The dogs leapt up from near the fireplace and trotted over toward the front door in answer.

Chapter 12: Ben

It was three weeks into the New Year. Ella should be here soon. We didn't have plans to hang out, but she called earlier and said she had a surprise for me.

My phone rang from my back pocket. I pulled it out, expecting to see her name on the caller ID. Instead, I was met with Brian's. Shit. I'd completely forgotten about today's therapy session.

I picked up. "Hey, man. Ella is about to stop by, so I may have to cut this a little short."

"That's fine," Brian said. "We can make up the time another day, if you need."

"Thanks."

"It sounds like you and Ella have become fast friends. I think every time we've spoken lately, you've mentioned plans with her."

"I've been flirting with her," I said.

"Okay," he responded, with almost no inflection, so I couldn't tell if he approved of this development or not.

"I don't really think it is okay, though," I told him.

"Why's that?"

"Because I don't think I'm in a good place for a relationship right now."

"You've made an incredible amount of progress in the past several months. In my professional opinion, there's nothing to recommend you not becoming romantically involved with someone."

"But I still haven't dealt with this CTE thing."

"In what way are you hoping to deal with it, Ben? The advanced tests we've spoken about?"

"Yes. And the reality that my brain is pretty much a ticking time bomb."

"If you want to schedule the tests, you should," Brian said. "I think it would be good for you to know definitively if there are signs, and if so, how advanced they are. And I think we need to find another way for you to talk about your brain. Bomb isn't exactly the best imagery or the healthiest metaphor. It's not like CTE is going to suddenly explode without warning and shred through all of your synapses in a single day. There will be signs. Early symptoms. Most likely you'll have time to adjust to each one as they manifest."

"Most likely," I said. "But not guaranteed."

"No, not guaranteed. Just like it's not guaranteed that you even have CTE. Can I be perfectly frank with you?"

"Always."

"If I were going through what you are, I'd be scared out of my fucking mind. It's okay to be scared, Ben. No one expects you to just – *poof!* – get over it. In fact, it's okay to be scared about this for years. Because it's a scary thing you're facing. We've talked a lot about emotions, about listening to them and giving in to them, and I know that's been an adjustment for you. You're going to have to work overtime to accept your fear here."

He wasn't kidding. I'd read a book a while back that opened my eyes to the small, hard cage of masculinity I'd been raised in. *Men* don't cry. *Men* don't get sappy. *Men* don't approach a person who hurt them and try to work it out civilly. Anger, violence, lust, these things are okay though, because "boys will be boys". Was it any wonder that after years of bottling everything else up, when men were pushed too far, or felt powerless, or felt like they'd been wronged in some way – real or imagined – they got so angry that they snapped? Violently?

I never realized how much shit I'd kept inside until my first few sessions with Brian, when it had all poured out of me the second another man told me it was okay to be upset.

I rubbed a hand over my face. "Brian, how can I move on with the threat of CTE hanging over my head? How can I ask someone else to take that on?"

"Who's to say you have to move on?" he asked. "Like I said, it's perfectly healthy to continue to be scared about this, whether you have CTE or not. It would be less healthy to let that fear dictate every decision in your life. Some, yes, sure. Like maybe you don't start jumping out of planes just for the thrill of feeling alive, or pick up a hobby that might lead to more brain trauma. But making decisions for a potential partner, or before symptoms manifest, maybe not. And who's to say that anything becomes romantic with Ella? She might not feel that way about you."

The man made a good point. "You're right. She's been nothing but friendly toward me."

"I sense another but here," Brian said.

"But every now and then, I catch a blush on her cheeks. Or a look on her face."

"And you assume they're of a romantic nature?"

I thought back to two days ago, when we'd set up the dining room furniture. At one point I'd picked up the end of the table and swiveled it around into place, having to strain beneath its weight. The way she'd looked me over, the intensity in her gaze, followed by a quick turn away, but not quick enough for me to miss the way her cheeks colored...

"I think they might be," I told Brian.

"And how do you feel about her?"

"I...I'm still trying to figure that out. She's beautiful. In a deceptively innocent, wide-eyed kind of way that pairs hilariously with her wicked sense of humor. The other day I turned my TV on after she left and *Benny and the Jets* just started pouring out of it. I laughed for five minutes straight."

"I'm missing the joke."

"My mom called me Benny on the phone and Ella heard it. Ever since, she's been slipping that song into my life. Last week she locked me out of my phone after trying to hack into it with the intention of changing my ringtone to it."

"So, she's beautiful and she makes you laugh. What else?"

I felt like he was herding me toward something, but I agreed that I needed to figure this thing out between me and Ella, so I decided to play along. "In between the laughter, we keep having these really deep, serious discussions."

"About what?"

"Politics, race, sexuality, religion, the military-industrial complex. You name it, we talk about it."

"Your fear of CTE? Your depression and anxiety?"

The urge to squirm became overwhelming. While I welcomed Brian's directness, one of the unintended consequences of it was the discomfort of being forced to look long and hard at my behavior. "Uh...no. Not that."

"Why not?"

"It goes back to not wanting to get involved with someone while CTE is hanging over my head. She's like this bright light of positivity in my life right now, and I don't want to do anything to snuff it out."

"Has Ella brought CTE up with you? Or Zach?"

Hearing my brother's name was like a punch to the gut. Still. Every time. It took me a minute to recover before responding. "No. She's been incredibly respectful of my privacy."

"And you don't think that she's kept quiet because she's worked at least some of what you're going through out for herself? It wouldn't be difficult to find evidence online and make assumptions from there. The only way to make sure that she hasn't made the wrong ones is to tell her yourself."

Well, shit. I hadn't thought about that. But still... "I don't know if I'm ready for that, Brian."

"Has Ella told you a lot about herself?"

I paused, not liking this change of direction. "She has."

"To summarize, you don't want to get involved with her romantically, because you don't think it would be fair to her. You don't want to be upfront with her about CTE and depression, because you want to keep her humor and lightness in your life. So instead, you're keeping her in a limbo where she continuously puts herself out there and you hold everything about yourself back. In short, you're making all her decisions for her. Tell me, does that seem fair, Ben?"

I exhaled heavily. "No. It makes me sound like a selfish asshole. Goddamn, Brian. You ever think you should have been a prosecutor instead of a therapist?"

"You've always wanted me to be honest with you," he said. "To ask you to examine your own behavior. That's all I'm doing right now. Trust me, I get it. It sucks. My husband just did this to me last night, because I haven't been doing my part around the house or with the kids, and he's had to pick up the slack. Look, I'm not telling you to unload everything on Ella when she shows up on your doorstep today, but I think that maybe, just maybe, it's okay to let her in a little. And to let yourself admit that you might be flirting with her because you're interested in her in a romantic way."

"And you're sure I can't blame that interest on the dosage drop?" I asked, grasping at straws.

"I'm sure."

"I need time to think about everything."

"Totally understandable. Don't rush yourself, Ben. Take all the time you need with this. But a little advice?"

"Shoot."

"If you want to flirt with Ella, flirt with Ella. As long as she's receptive, of course."

We hung up a few minutes later, with plans to talk again in a couple of days. Now was one of those times I wished I could pop open a beer and stare into the fire for a little while, letting my mind go blank. Or jump on the treadmill for an hour. I glanced at the clock. No time. It was three. Ella should have been here by now.

Needing to do something, I paced to the front door, slipped my boots and jacket on, shoved my hair under a hat, and headed out to shovel the walkway. Sure, I'd shoveled it earlier this morning, but we had a flurry a few hours ago, and there was a light dusting over it. Didn't want Ella to slip.

My mind ran in circles as I worked. Of course I'd been flirting with Ella because I wanted to flirt with her. It's not like someone had held a gun to my head and forced me to tease her or slip a few innuendoes into our conversations. I felt like an idiot now for trying to blame my behavior on my meds. But even though I was starting to realize my attraction to her might be more than just physical, I struggled to move past that fact. Every time I tried to picture how our relationship might advance, I ran head-first into a brick wall with the letters CTE spray-painted across it in loud, neon colors. Whatever lay on the other side was completely out of sight, and for that matter, out of grasp.

Ella pulled up several minutes later, while I was still outside, stuck in my own head. I planted the shovel in the snowbank and walked over to greet her. She got out of the truck and shut the door carefully behind her. There was no sign of her dogs as she hurried to meet me halfway.

"Okay, so I did a thing," she said, her expression cagey. "This present I got you, it doesn't have to be permanent. It can just be on a loaner basis, which the person I got said present from fully understands, so there is no pressure for you to keep said present."

I started to walk around her, my curiosity getting the better of me. A loaner basis present? "Ella, you're stalling. Is it in the truck?"

She skirted in front of me and held up her hands. "It is. And I'm stalling because I don't want to do that thing where I-"

"Get pushy?" I finished for her. Jesus, Brian was right. The woman had been going out of her way to accommodate me.

She stilled, hands dropping back to her sides, expression falling right along with them. "Yeah, that."

I took her by the shoulders and leaned down to look into her eyes. From this close, they were as blue as the Mediterranean. "Ella, we're friends now, right?"

"I hope so," she answered.

"Then as my friend, I'm asking you to please stop worrying. Sometimes I need a push, or even a swift kick in the ass."

She chewed her lip for a second as she thought this over. I had a sudden desire to lean forward and pull it out of her teeth with my mouth. For once, I didn't suppress the thought. Her lips were gloriously full, a dusky shade of pink that would probably darken with use.

"But you'll still tell me if I'm too much?" she asked.

"Yes," I said, hating that she thought I'd ever think that about her. I needed to find some way to fix our dynamic. Brian was right; this wasn't fair to her. "Now can I please have my damn present?"

As I hoped, she grinned. She practically vibrated with energy beneath my hands, so I let her go. She bounded back toward the truck, her long legs eating up the ground. I followed after her, letting my gaze slide up those legs. The woman had a great ass. I'd noticed it the first night we met and had avoided looking at it since. The fact that I'd had to avoid looking at it spoke volumes.

Instead of opening the door, Ella stood on her toes and peered in through the window, waving me over. I joined her, confused.

"They fell asleep on the way over," she whispered.

"They? *They?* Ella, what did you do?"

At the sound of my voice – which was elevated because of my surprise – the two little balls of white fluff on the backseat stirred. A small head with triangular ears rose from the one closest to the door. A pair of black eyes blinked open, and a little jaw dropped in a wide yawn, exposing a pink tongue and tiny razor teeth.

"Did you get me puppies?" I asked, tugging on her coat sleeve. I sounded like a little kid. Hell, I *felt* like a little kid. Because puppies!

She smiled. "I did."

I nudged her sideways out of the way with my hip and carefully pulled open the rear door. She laughed at me, but I was too far gone to care. The puppy already awake sniffed the air. The one beside it remained conked out. I tugged off a glove and reached forward to pet the one looking at me, and it immediately started whining as it tried to lick my fingers.

"They're Samoyeds," Ella said. "My friend Jen and her husband raise sled dogs, and right now, they have more puppies than they can handle. I offered to take a couple off of their hands for a few days. If you don't want to keep them here, Jack has already offered."

"I don't have stuff for them," I said, gently petting the puppy. "But yeah, I want to keep them."

"I stopped in town and bought all the supplies you should need."

Of course she did. "What are their names?"

"Jen's kids named them, so don't feel like you have to stick with them. The one you're petting is Boots, and the other one is Doodle."

"Boots and Doodle," I said, testing the names out. As silly as they were, I didn't hate the sound of them. "How can you tell who is who?"

"The collars. Boots' is purple and Doodle's is green. They're both boys."

"Hi, Boots," I said, gently lifting him up. He was so small, and so warm, and so ridiculously fluffy.

Ella leaned past me to wake Doodle with a few gentle pets, then scooped him up too. We stood there next to each other in the driveway for a few minutes, cuddling the dogs and grinning like fools.

I shifted Boots to one arm and wrapped the other around Ella's shoulders, pulling her in for a sideways hug. "Thank you so much for this, and for bringing everything they need. You fucking rock."

Her smile was blinding. "You're welcome."

I released her, even though I didn't really want to yet, and together we got the puppies and all their supplies into the house. She'd bought puppy food, dog bowls, toys, a pet brush, and something she called puppy pads, which were supposed to help with housetraining them.

"Jen said they're already pretty good at letting you know when they have to go to the bathroom," Ella said, laying a pad out by the front door while Doodle sniffed a circle around our discarded boots.

I side-eyed her. "You mean go pee-poop?"

She turned away. "I hate you forever."

Still holding Boots, I scooted around her so I could see her face. "You blush so easily," I said, shifting the puppy to one arm like he was a fluffy little football so I could poke at her cheek with my free hand.

"Stop that." She batted me away. "I do *not* blush that easily."

"Okay, fine, but when you do, it's spectacular. Takes up your whole face."

She stuck her tongue out at me and then leaned down to pick up Doodle.

We spent the next hour laughing and talking in ridiculous voices and making even more ridiculous noises and taking far too many pictures as we watched the dogs explore the first floor of the house.

"It's not just me, right?" I asked her later. "They are uncommonly adorable."

She sat down next to me on the floor of the sitting room, and Boots immediately jumped from my lap into hers. "It's definitely not just you. They stay this adorable all through puppyhood, so you better get used to that cute aggression you're feeling right now."

"Do their tails stay curled like this?" I asked, ruffling Doodle's.

"Yup. But aside from that, they kind of look like polar bears when they get older."

"How old are they now?"

"About ten weeks. You can start training them right away if you decide in a few days that you want to keep them."

I was pretty sure I wanted to keep them, but I stayed quiet about that in case my feelings changed for some reason. Instead, I asked more questions about the breed, how much exercise they needed, and how best to train them. Ella answered me with patience and an amount of detail I was grateful for.

"Just like with Huskies, negative reinforcement doesn't work with them, so yelling will do you little good," she said. "I've found with housetraining, it's best to bring them outside a lot, and bring treats with you, so if they go," she shot me a dark look, "pee-poop," I grinned at her, and she rolled her eyes, "you give them a treat and it lets them know that going to the bathroom outside is good. You don't do that if they go on the puppy pad, and they're smart enough to work it out for themselves even at this age that it's better to go out than in."

"Do I let them sleep in my room tonight?"

"It's really up to you, but I would." She leaned down and lifted Boots from her lap. He immediately tried to lick her face. "Up until today, they've been around their mama and littermates, and they're used to cuddling up to them at night. I have no idea how tall your bed is, so you might want to think about tugging a mattress onto the ground to make it easier for them to get down if they have to. And of course, put some pads in the room." She raised her head, lifting Boots with her so that they were both looking at me with puppy eyes. It was hard to tell who was cuter. "Please let us sleep with you" she said, miming the puppy's voice.

I arched a brow at her. "Really, Ella?"

Her eyes flashed wide as she realized how that sounded. "I meant both puppies. Not me and Boots. That would be unfair to Doodle."

I opened my mouth to keep teasing her, but my phone alarm went off, ruining the moment. Time to take my meds. This would probably be a good segue into bringing up my depression and anxiety. The only thing was, I had no idea how to casually do that.

"Hey, can you watch the dogs? I'm off to down some anti-depressants!"

Ugh. Just no.

I had zero practice with this. I hadn't even told my parents. Mom and Dad would get on the next plane out if they knew. I'd have to ask Brian in our next session if he had some pointers.

"I'll be right back," I told Ella.

"More puppies for meee," she said, leaning forward to pull Doodle toward her too.

I went upstairs, took my meds, and then called Dad on FaceTime as I headed back down. He answered after the third ring, already smiling into the camera. Behind him, sunshine drenched the deck of their house, the lush, tropical forest just visible beyond, like a wall of verdant green. Lucky bastard was outside enjoying the weather.

"Hiya, Benny," he said.

"Hi, Dad. Mom with you?"

"She's inside. One sec. Lemme go find her." There was so much movement on his end of the line that I had to look away or risk getting dizzy. "Klara! Ben's on the phone!"

I heard my mom's distant answer, and within seconds, both of their faces filled my screen.

"Hi," Mom said, waving.

"Ella got me a present, and I thought you two would want to see," I told them. I switched the camera direction and took the hallway toward the sitting room. "Ella! My parents want to see what you did!" I called, giving her some advanced warning.

We found her sprawled out on the floor, laughing as the dogs leapt and stumbled and rolled over her, yipping and growling as they tried to adorable her to death.

Mom shrieked. "Oh my God, puppies!" She grabbed Dad by the arm with both hands and started shaking him, so that he disappeared off the screen with every push and re-emerged with every pull. "Hani, look!"

"I see them," Dad said, laughing at her.

This was the Mom I knew and loved. This woman who got outrageously excited about small animals. The one who borderline assaulted my father whenever she was overcome with joy. It was nice to see a glimpse of her again. It had been far too long.

My stomach sank at the realization. Maybe I wasn't the only one dealing with depression. We'd never been great, as a family, about talking about our feelings. Or at least the negative ones. It felt like it was past time we changed that.

A thought that I'd probably regret popped into my head. I switched the camera so my parents could see me again. "Did you want to come out and meet them?"

In response, Mom started crying. Like, face in hands insta-sobbing. Holy shit.

Ella whipped her head up from the floor, all traces of humor gone. *"Is she crying?"* she mouthed.

I nodded and decided to step out of the room. "Mom, are you okay?"

"I'm fine," she said, waving a hand toward the screen. She was obviously not fine.

Dad slid an arm around her shoulders and dropped a kiss on top of her head. "She's just overwhelmed. She's had a rough couple of days."

That sounded familiar. Was this the reason he'd been so defensive of her when she got pushy with me? The fact that I didn't know made me feel like a jackass. First, my selfishness with Ella, and now this.

"Do you want to call me back later to talk about coming out here? It might be another week before I can host you. I still have to finish the spare room."

"We'll do that," Dad said. "Love you."

"You too," I told him.

We hung up. I left my phone in the kitchen and went back to Ella and the puppies. Doodle bounded over to me and started attacking my left foot with his paws, slapping it into submission. I stopped where I was and let him have his fun, absorbing the sight and letting it balance out some of the shit of today. Ella's present couldn't have been better timed.

"Is your mom okay?" she asked.

I lifted my eyes to hers. "I'm not sure."

"I'm sorry," she said. She looked down at the Boots, who was sprawled out between her legs. "I made my mom cry once when I was in high school. Some horrible comment about how she wasn't my real mom. I think it's the worst thing I've ever said to someone. I felt like garbage for weeks afterward."

"Yeah, this feeling is...not good."

She nodded and looked up. Our gazes caught.

"Do you want to meet them when they come out?" I asked.

Her expression brightened. "Of course. I feel like your mom and I would really hit it off. It must be something about the way she inflates my ego to astronomical proportions every time I talk to her."

I grinned. I could tell she was trying to lighten the mood, get me to smile, and I really didn't want to deny her that.

"And your dad is pretty much the cutest."

"I'm sorry, what? Now I need to compete with my old man?"

"Psssh. I said he's the cutest, not -" she cut herself off, hard, her cheeks flaming red.

"Not what, Ella?"

She dropped her gaze to the puppy and reached out to ruffle his fur. I didn't think she would answer at first, and then she said, "Come on, Ben. You *know* what you look like."

Chapter 13: Ella

This mantra had been running through my mind since I climbed into the truck. I was on my way over to Ben's. Less than twenty-four hours had passed since I almost word vomited how gorgeous I thought he was all over his sitting room. Instead of continuing down that ruinous path, I'd taken a hard right around "You *know* what you look like" and turned it into a joke about how Ben was a giant of a man. I couldn't recall my exact words, but I thought they might have been vaguely insulting.

I must have blacked out from panic. Either that or my brain was trying to save me from the embarrassment of remembering whatever bullshit I made up to cover my near-slip.

It had been touch-and-go for a few minutes after. Ben looked like he wanted to press the issue for some reason, maybe to further embarrass me? Get me to blush again? But that would seem cruel of him, and he'd never shown the slightest inclination for cruelty. Or maybe he knew about the monster of a crush I'd been desperately trying to banish to a vault in the back of my mind.

Crap. That was it. He wanted to press the issue to get it out in the open.

His would probably be the kindest, gentlest rejection of all time. "Listen, Ella. You're an incredible woman. I really like you. But not in that way..." Or something equally flattering before leading into a flat-out denial.

"*Whyyy?*" I muttered.

I rolled to a stop at the one light in town – of course it was red again – and leaned my forehead against the steering wheel. I should have just said it. Told him that he looked like something out of a wet dream. Then he could have gently put me down, I could get over this crush, and we could go on being friends without this stupid tension coming between us.

Maybe I could still say something. Work up my courage and slip my attraction to him into conversation somehow. I decided to practice. "Why, yes, this paint color turned out quite nice. Have you thought about putting the couch over here instead? I sometimes think about you naked, but I'm getting better at suppressing."

Super casual. Definitely not at all creepy.

I needed to call Megan. She was smarter than me. Stacey could help too. With their combined IQs, they might be able to save me from myself. It would have to be tonight. They were both at work now. I'd just have to muddle through today as best I could.

The car behind me honked. I jerked my head up. The light had changed to green.

I waved an apology through the back window and put my foot on the gas pedal. In the rearview mirror, an elderly woman emphatically flipped me off. "Well, fuck you too, Mrs. Barnsdale," I said, recognizing my eighth grade English teacher.

I spent the entire climb out of the valley in a suspended state of dread, terrified that I'd somehow ruined everything.

I didn't go straight to Ben's, but to Jack's first. He was watching the dogs for me again. If Ben decided to keep Boots and Doodle, I'd bring Fred and Sam by and introduce them. I just didn't want to do that prematurely if it didn't work out. My dogs formed attachments much quicker than others. I blamed their sled dog origins and strong pack instinct.

"Thanks for watching the boys," I told Jack a few minutes later.

"My pleasure," he said, leaning down to rub Fred's side. "Those two Samoyed puppies sure are cute. I stopped by Ben's last night and got to spend some time with them. If that man doesn't keep them, I call dibs."

"I'll let Jen know they'll have a home either way." Be cool, Ella. Just be cool. "How, uh, how was Ben doing?"

Jack gave me a funny look. "Probably the same as when you left an hour before?"

"Good, okay, yeah. Just checking."

Jack's lips lifted in an ominous grin. "What'd you do, Ella?"

"What? Nothing! I brought him puppies. I wanted to make sure he was okay with them afterward."

"Yuh-huh," he said, not in the market for the particular brand of bullshit I was selling.

"Okay, well, thanks again for watching the dogs. I'll see you later." I gave him a quick hug goodbye and raced to my truck, pursued by the sound of his laughter.

"Knew you two would hit it off!" he yelled before I could get my door shut.

I jammed the truck into reverse, checked to make sure I was clear of the doggos, and then took off out of there.

That interfering, match-making busybody. For months Jack had been nagging me about finding someone. Dropping wisdom-filled guilt bombs about life being too short to spend it alone. I should have realized he'd meant business. I should have known what he was doing the night he introduced me to Ben. He'd been trying to set us up.

I was so going to get him back for this.

Wait a second. Did Ben know that we'd been set up? He might soon, if Jack mentioned my awkwardness to him, or if he took to teasing him the same way he did me. I needed to get ahead of this and set Jack straight before he made the situation even worse with his good intentions.

Ben was on the front steps when I pulled into his driveway. We planned to paint the spare bedroom he wanted his parents to stay in, and he wore the paint-speckled running pants I'd come to love and loathe in equal measure. Because, dayum, the man's ass looked good in them.

He pointed to the left of the porch. I slowed my truck to a stop further back than normal, assuming the puppies were somewhere in the direction he'd indicated. At the sound of my door closing, two splashes of color emerged from a snowbank by the house. Boots and Doodle. If not for those collars, they'd blend right in.

They caught sight of me and bounded over, barking excitedly in their squeaky puppy voices. My embarrassment and worry evaporated. They looked like someone had animated a pair of overstuffed white teddy bears. Their ears flopped forward and backward with every leap. Those curlicue tails whipped left and right over their hindquarters. Boots hit a patch of ice and slipped, his back legs skirting sideways before he could get them under his control.

The cuteness. It was too much. I leaned down and petted them with both hands when they reached me, trying to contain my overwhelming desire to squee in a way that would make Anabel proud.

Ben ambled off the porch, grinning as he approached. "Don't let them fool you. The little monsters kept me up most of the night."

I would have worried he regretted letting them stay, but he was staring down at them with the kind of open affection that told me they'd already won him over. "Did they cry?" I asked. "Fred and Sam cried so bad the first night I had them."

"They did a little. Mostly they just wouldn't settle down. They wanted to sniff everything, make nests in the blankets, play with their toys, chew my beard." He raked his fingers through his facial hair. "I should shave this thing off."

Now was my chance. I took a steadying breath, and with all the bravery I could muster, I said, "On behalf of womenkind, don't you dare."

He paused, hand still at his chin, gaze shifting from the puppies to me. His lips crooked up on one side in a lazy half-grin I'd never seen before. A grin that made me think of primal things.

"I guess I keep the beard," he said.

Well, this was backfiring. Maybe it wasn't clear enough that I thought he was attractive? That I wanted him? That this was his chance to shoot me down?

"Okay then," I said. I reached down and lifted Doodle. I needed to hold this puppy right now, because if I left my hands free, I might do something awkward with them. Like wrap them in Ben's jacket and mush our faces together.

He picked up Boots, and together we went inside to towel them off.

"I figured I could put the puppies in the sitting room while we paint," he said. "You know, to keep them away from the open cans and the fumes. All their stuff is in there."

"Sounds like a plan."

I shrugged off my coat and turned to hang it up. Something grazed the back of my neck. I froze, sure I was imagining it. A piece of hair must have come free from my messy bun to torment me into thinking Ben was touching me.

There was a tug on the neckline of my sweater. Not my hair. I was either about to be assaulted by a giant spider, or he was actually touching me.

"Your tag is sticking out," he said from just behind my shoulder.

Warmth blossomed along the back of my neck and ran an inch down my spine as he used those long fingers of his to tuck the tag back in. I shivered in response. I knew he could feel it, because he was taking his sweet time pulling his hand back out of my shirt.

"Thank you," I said, a little breathless.

"You're welcome," Ben answered, voice pitched low.

I almost shuddered again, because in that octave, there was a little bass growl to it that *did things* to me.

He stepped away, and the warmth disappeared from my skin.

...or maybe he wanted to push the subject yesterday because he wanted you to be the first one to say something. Maybe he likes you as more than a friend too.

I mentally clamped a hand over the mouth of my subconscious and dropped it into the same deep, dark, inescapable oubliette I kept my crush. I gave them both the finger, Mrs. Barnsdale style, and slammed the lid of their prison shut.

You two play nice now.

"Want some coffee or anything before we get to work?" Ben asked.

I turned to face him, not making eye contact. The only reason my cheeks weren't vermillion was because I was still in shock. "I'll take a glass of water," I told him. Suddenly, I was parched.

He turned and paced toward the kitchen. The puppies tripped over each other as they raced after him. They looked like the world's cutest tumbleweeds. The three of them disappeared around the corner, and I took my time pulling off my boots, my mind a jumble of confusion. Ben's reaction to me mentioning his looks was to give me a sex-on-legs smile and then not five minutes later find an excuse to touch me. He could have just as easily told me the tag was sticking out and let me deal with it myself.

Okay then. Let's stay rational about this, Ella. Let's not freak out or jump to conclusions. The man had been hidden away in the woods for a while. Maybe this was a softcore Stockholm Syndrome situation, and in his captivity, he was turning to the one woman his age in search of comfort. Or maybe I had backtracked and was misinterpreting everything he did. Maybe what seemed like a sexy come-hither look was nothing but a platonic grin. Maybe his fingers lingered in my shirt because he didn't want to accidentally tangle them in my hair and pull some strands loose on the way out.

Yes, let's go with that. Much more likely scenario.

I'd meant what I said to my sister; I didn't have low self-esteem. My face was symmetrical, I actually liked my freckles, and in some lights, my eyes looked closer to aqua than blue. I was tall, in good shape, and while I sometimes wished I had a little more in the chest area, for the most part, I was happy in my own skin. I was pretty. Just a fact. Ben was gorgeous. Also, just a fact. We were not on the same level in the looks department. And that was okay. I'd dated men both more and less attractive than I was, and it had never been an issue.

Maybe I had built Ben up so much to create distance between us that now the thought of him being attracted to me didn't compute. Which was good, because if it did, I might take a flying leap at him.

I gave myself a mental shake and walked to the kitchen. The doors of the hallway stood open, revealing all the progress we'd made. The sitting room now had a full set of furniture. Gone was the dark couch we played cribbage on Christmas Day. An off-white rug with a minimalist pattern took up most of the floor. On top of it sat a much more comfortable replacement that Ben had ordered from Ikea. It was cloth instead of leather, and white instead of brown. He worried about white at first, but then I reminded him that the covers were removable and there was this thing called bleach.

We'd arranged the furniture in a horseshoe pattern, with the couch facing the fire. On each side of it were a pair of armchairs. The ones on the left had light gray cushions and wooden armrests. Those on the right were a light brown leather that matched the color of the armrests, tying them all together. In the center of the horseshoe sat an industrial style table with a wrought iron base and distressed wooden top. The light fixture that hung above it was also wrought iron, with antique bulbs that bathed the room in a soft glow.

Artwork hung on the walls. Soft linen curtains framed the windows from floor to ceiling. Throw pillows and blankets artfully draped over a few of the armchairs lent the space a cozy, inviting feel.

I grinned, proud of our work, as I peered into the dining room next. Another rug with a muted color palette protected the flooring. The farmhouse style table that sat above it was an antique Ben found on Etsy, made of an old barn door that had been stripped, lightly stained, and sealed. The seating didn't match, but that was the intent. Instead, they complemented each other. At the head and foot of the table were round-back wood chairs painted black. On one of the longer sides was a bench, and on the other, three straight-back chairs, also black. The chandelier that hung low over the table was in the shape of a wagon wheel, wrought iron, with the same antique bulbs as the one in the sitting room. A roughhewn oak buffet stood on the far wall, with a black and white painting of a longhorn steer above it.

I walked into the kitchen. The space was exactly what I'd imagined the first time I visited. It gave me serious dream home vibes. To the point that I made Ben promise to come help me tear mine apart after we were done so I could copy a couple of his design choices.

A glass of water waited for me on the butcher block of the kitchen island. I picked it up and chugged it. It did nothing to quench my thirst.

"I'll go get the boys settled," Ben said.

Normally, I would offer to help, maybe play with the puppies a little, take some video of their adorable floofiness to send to Jack or Megan and Stacey, but right now, I needed about fifty feet between Ben and me, self-enforced restraining order style.

He re-emerged several minutes later. "Ready?"

"Yup!" I said, a little more manic than the cheerful tone I'd been aiming for.

He headed upstairs. I followed slowly after him, my focus on the steps beneath my feet to keep myself from staring at his ass. The room we were painting was two doors down from his own, which I still hadn't seen and now had no desire too. Didn't need any accurate images of his bed popping into my mind, thank you very much.

He opened the door and motioned me in. It took up the entire front right corner of the house, with large, double aspect windows looking out at the driveway and forest. Crown molding and base-boards framed walls painted a heinous mauve. It was a color straight out of the seventies – the lost decade of home design. Ben had already laid out throw cloths to protect the flooring and brought in his toolbox and the paint supplies.

"Yikes. What are we covering this with?" I asked him, trying to regain some semblance of normalcy.

"A kind of cool off white with a hint of blue," he answered. "I've already cut the power to the room. You want to help get these lights down?"

"On it," I told him, keeping my eyes averted. Right now, he was the sun. If I looked directly at him, I might burn out my retinas.

I grabbed a screwdriver from the toolbox and made my way to a lumpy, brushed gold light fixture hanging four feet up on the wall. There was another one a few feet away for Ben to tackle. Most likely, they were meant to be reading lamps.

"Your brass is grass, sassafras," I said, placing the tooltip to the screw.

Ben chuckled from a few feet away, a gloriously deep, rolling sound more suited to summer storms than this bright winter day. My pulse picked up in response. I ignored it and got to work.

Five minutes later, I was stuck. I needed one more hand than I had to hold this stupid light fixture in place and get the last screw out. I stood there and spent an embarrassing amount of time trying to find some way around asking Ben to help me. The room was full of the heady scent of his cologne. If he brought it over here, I might try to lick him to see if he tasted as good as he smelled.

My subconscious was clearly winning this war.

He got his light off and started applying painter's tape to the edge of the baseboards, while I remained where I was, deciding whether or not I could stomach the idiocy of holding the light fixture in place with my forehead.

I sighed in resignation. I was going to have to ask.

"Little help here?" I said.

"No prob," he responded.

His words were casual, because, until today, that's how our working relationship had been. We'd assisted each other dozens of times during the reno, our shoulders brushing against each other's, our hands bumping together. It had never been awkward or tense. Until now.

"I just need you to hold the fixture in place so I can get the last screw off without dropping it," I told him.

He approached from behind. The air stirred as he stopped, bringing with it a tantalizing hint of vetiver. His hands slid into view, coming to rest just above mine, his arms on either side of my head, so that I was caged in by them. I took my hands away, and the light fixture slid sideways a little. He stepped closer to hold it steady, his chest pressing against my back, his –

PENIS.

HIS PENIS WAS TOUCHING MY LEFT BUTT CHEEK.

I froze. All that separated us was my whisper-thin leggings and the material of his pants and – possibly? – boxers. For a brief second, I could feel his *entire length*.

Oh, Jesus.

He shifted suddenly, leaning left to either get a better grip on the light or change the angle he held it from, and I felt his dick start to slide away from me. I almost whimpered. My hips swiveled seemingly of their own accord, tracking his motion, desperate to follow.

Panicking, I shifted my legs and moved forward, breaking our contact. Had I really just been a hair's breadth away from grinding my ass into his crotch?

Get ahold of yourself, woman! my brain shouted.

Heh. I'd rather get ahold of him, my libido answered.

Eight months. It had been eight months since another person had made me come, and right now, I realized just how much sexual need could build up in that time. I was breathing like I'd run a set of sprints. My pulse was lodged in my throat. I became hyperaware of my breasts, cradled within my bra. Of the lines of my underwear tracing either side of my sex. My clothes felt too tight. The room was uncomfortably warm.

Unable to stop myself, I turned my head slightly to the left, following the sound of Ben's soft exhalations. Our noses nearly brushed, that's how close he was. Mother of God, was he leaning toward me right now?

Our gazes met. From this distance, his eyes looked like galaxies. In the very center of them were the dark stars of his pupils, surrounded by a nimbus of pale, white gold. Toward the edges, flecks of green appeared, emerald, mint, seafoam, and olive tones intermingling to form an outer corona of vibrant color edged in black. I wanted to launch myself into them and get lost in the expanse just beyond.

"Hi," he said, the warmth of his breath rushing over my lips.

His greeting snapped me out of it. "Sorry, I just..."

I just what? Had to look at you? Needed to see your eyes up close? Wondered if you'd kiss me if I turned this way?

"I stripped the screw tip," I finished, lamely, and ducked out from under his arms to retreat toward the toolbox.

I found the spare screwdriver and swapped out my still perfectly fine one – which he would notice was fine later, UGH – and turned back around. He was standing right where I left him, hands braced on the fixture, shoulders bunched, forearms flexed, traps on full display. If he were a painting, it would be titled *Up Against the Wall,* because that's how everyone would want it when they looked at him.

"You coming back over?" he asked, glancing sideways at me.

I forced myself forward.

"I won't bite." He grinned, a mischievous edge slipping in that I feared he might have learned from me.

I pointed the screwdriver at him. "Don't you dare go Austin Powers right now."

"Hard," he said in an offensively bad English accent.

I laughed. The sound was hysterical, but I was just so grateful that he had broken the tension that I could have kissed him. Still, I was careful not to actually touch him when I ducked back under his arms.

"You know what, on second thought," I said, "why don't you undo the last screw and I'll hold the fixture. You can probably see it better from way up there." I couldn't deal with being framed by his arms right now. Or the feel of his body just inches from mine.

"Sure," he said.

I offered the screwdriver up to him. He took it, and I stepped forward, away from his heat, to hold the fixture in place. He lifted his hand to remove the last screw. His fingers trembled slightly. It took him two tries to fit the tool head into place. I'd worked alongside him for weeks, and I had never seen him fumble like this. His hands were so steady that I'd made jokes about how he could have been a surgeon.

The sight of his shaky fingers completely undid me. It gave me hope. Hope that this wasn't all in my head. That he might be as affected by our proximity as I was.

The screw came loose. I pulled the light fixture off the wall and ducked away to leave him with the remaining wires. I set the ugly brass lamp in the middle of the floor, next to the one he'd removed on his own. That done, I straightened, my mind a total blank, my body on autopilot as I picked up the painter's tape. I turned and walked toward the far edge of the room, hoping to work on the opposite side as him.

Space. I needed space right now.

"Ella," he said, a dark note in his voice that I'd never heard before.

I stopped dead. Turned to look at him. He leaned against the wall, his shoulder propping him up, arms crossed over his chest, biceps straining against his t-shirt. The expression on his face made my pulse flutter. I heard a *thud* and realized the tape had slipped from my fingers.

"Yes?" I said, my voice whisper-light.

"I don't know if this is a good idea."

Brave. Be brave, I urged myself. I took a deep breath. "The paint color or the sexual tension I may or may not be hallucinating?"

He smiled and shook his head. "Even now you make me want to laugh. Goddamn, woman."

"So...it *is* in my head?"

He pushed from the wall and came to me. Hands big enough to palm basketballs rose to cradle my face. His gaze dropped to my mouth. "It's not in your head."

Holy shit.

He brushed a thumb across my lips. I wanted to bite his finger, then drag it into my mouth and curl my tongue around its roughness to soothe the sting of my teeth.

Ben must have seen the open need on my face, because he shifted his thumb away, back to the relative safety of my cheekbone.

"Why isn't this a good idea?" I asked.

He closed his eyes, leaned forward, and braced his forehead against mine. "Because I'm going through a lot of shit right now, and I don't know if starting a physical relationship is a healthy decision."

I had never, ever pushed him on why he was here. Instead, I'd expended endless amounts of energy to keep my usual nosy mouth shut. I didn't know if it was the hormones or the fact that I was just so tired of being so careful, but I decided, for once, to ask the question that popped into my head. To speak the name I'd never heard him say.

"Zach?"

He jerked away like I'd hit him. "Yes."

"CTE?"

He shook his head. "I don't know for sure yet."

Tears sprang to my eyes. I'd always cried easily. I'd always been overprotective of my friends and family. I didn't want anything bad to happen to the people I cared about. Ben was my friend. I cared about him deeply already on that level. The thought of him experiencing even a handful of the CTE symptoms I'd read about was enough to break my heart.

"I'm so sorry, Ben."

I expected him to get awkward, like so many men did around a crying woman. Or to tell me that I shouldn't be upset. He did neither. Instead, he slid his thumbs forward and wiped away the moisture gathering at the edges of my eyes.

"I may not have it," he told me.

"Have you had any tests done?"

"An inconclusive MRI. Nothing since. It was a lot, just getting that one done. I've been building up my bravery for round two."

My tears spilled free. This big man, who looked strong enough to hold the entire world on his shoulders, just confessed to being afraid. No way in hell was I getting this crush back into its prison.

"I'm here if you ever want to talk about it," I told him. "Or if you need someone to hold your hand while you're having the tests done."

"Thank you." He sniffed, grinning. "You keep this up, you're going to make me cry too."

"Trying to stop," I told him with a weak laugh. "Once I turn the waterworks on, it just all comes out." Most of this was for him, but some was a release of all the tension I'd felt the past few weeks.

He lifted the edge of his ratty old t-shirt to blot my cheeks. I knew I was truly upset because not even the sight of his abs was enough to jolt me out of it.

"I have bad days sometimes, Ella," he all but whispered. His gaze moved across my face as he followed the track of his t-shirt.

I gripped his forearm. I *needed* him to understand what I was about to say. "I hope you know that I will never, ever repeat anything you tell me."

He nodded. "I know." And then, so quick it almost sounded like one word, "Ihavedepressionandanxiety."

I took a few seconds to process this, thinking back to our interactions and struggling to find even a single instance where he'd exhibited the outward signs I'd come to recognize. I hated that I hadn't realized he was dealing with this. It was time I redefined my parameters for how someone with depression and anxiety should speak and behave. My narrow experience with them had clearly left me ill-prepared.

"Are you getting treated?" I asked. "I know it's not really my business, but I've had friends and family members who didn't, and the outcomes were unhealthy, to say the least."

He nodded. "I'm on medication, and I talk to my therapist at least once a week."

"Is this why you cut back on alcohol and caffeine?"

"Yeah."

"I thought maybe you were an alcoholic."

His expression darkened. "I got close to that point, before getting help."

"Again, I am *always* here if you need anything. My mom has severe seasonal depression, and Megan has had anxiety almost her entire life. I know a little of what the bad days can be like, so tell me if you need space. Or if want someone to be there with you through them."

He let out a shaky breath. "I will. Thank you."

"You're welcome."

We stood close, our toes almost touching. I wanted to reach out and hold him, comfort him, but after hearing that he didn't think anything romantic would be healthy, I worried he'd misinterpret it.

"Can I hug you?" I asked. "In a friendly way, not an if-it-lasts-long-enough-I-will-eventually-try-to-touch-your-butt kind of way."

He laughed and pulled me into a rib-cracking bear hug.

"I'm sorry if you've felt like I've been pressuring you in any way or angling for a more than friendly relationship," I said. "I've actually been trying to do the opposite."

"You want to be my nemesis?" he asked. He leaned back so he could arch a brow at me. "Could be fun."

I shook my head. "Not what I meant and you know it. I meant that I've been trying not to have feelings for you."

He pulled me back in and rested his chin on top of my head. "Yeah, same."

Chapter 14: Ben

Ella was attracted to me. I was attracted to Ella. But I wasn't sure if I was ready to act on it.

This must have been one of the higher circles of hell. One reserved for amateur sinners who didn't do anything bad enough during their lives to warrant everlasting physical torture but were *juuust* shitty enough that they got to spend eternity sexually frustrated.

Ella left my house an hour ago, as the sun began to set. Upstairs, paint dried in the spare bedroom. We came downstairs after covering the walls with a heavy coat of primer and got to work putting together the furniture I bought for the library. The mood had eased some when we pulled apart from our hug, a sort of cease-fire of sexual tension. We let the puppies into the library with us, and the roly-poly chaos they brought with them worked wonders to distract us.

Now she was gone, and I sat alone on the living room couch, the puppies passed out on me, a fire crackling in the fireplace. There was nothing to keep my mind occupied.

I raised my hand and flexed my fingers, remembering the feel of her waist beneath my palm. This was my fault; I initiated the flirtation. I had no one to blame but myself. When she asked me for help with that light fixture, I turned around to see her holding the ugly thing up, her toned arms on display, and couldn't keep my gaze from sliding down over the rest of her. The t-shirt she wore had ridden up, exposing the slight curve of her hips and her tight, rounded ass.

God bless the person who brought leggings back into style.

Just above the band of them, a couple inches of Ella's lower back was exposed, her skin as pale as cream, the slight dimples on either side of her spine visible. I wanted to drop to my knees behind her and trace them with my tongue.

My attraction to Ella shouldn't have come as a surprise. She was my type, after all. Not just physically, but emotionally and even mentally. It was the strength of my attraction, now that I'd stopped suppressing it, that caught me off guard. I spent the entire afternoon wanting to capture her laughter with my mouth, swallow down that beautiful sound and let her warmth fill me. I wanted to tease her, unendingly, just to watch the color bloom on her cheeks. I wanted to thread my fingers into her hair. I wanted to hear the noises she'd make when I made her come.

She didn't freak out when I told her I had depression and anxiety. Nothing about her behavior toward me changed afterward. It made me want her even more. It made me wish that I'd done what I wanted and kissed her tears away when she cried. It made me want to schedule the tests. To find out once and for all what my fate was so I could finally move forward with my life. And maybe, move forward with her.

My phone rang from the side table. Doodle, who'd been splayed across my lap, jerked awake at the sound and nearly tumbled off of me. Boots, sleeping on his back wedged in between my thigh and the arm of the couch, twitched his head up to glare at the phone. I scooped it up and answered, feeling like I should apologize for disturbing them.

"Hey, Dad," I said. Finally. I'd been worried after not hearing back from them.

"Hi, Ben. I have you on speaker with Mom."

"Hi, Mom. You doing any better?"

"Yes," she said, her voice quiet. "Sorry about yesterday."

I wanted to ask her about yesterday, press her about what "bad days" meant to her, but now didn't really feel like the time. Much better to have that conversation face-to-face.

"You don't have to apologize," I told her. "I know how stressed you've been about me being out here."

"When did you want us to visit?" Dad asked.

"Ella and I put the first coat of paint on a spare bedroom for you earlier. I just need another day or two to get that finished and a few more for the furniture to arrive. Did you want to plan for ten days from now?"

"We can do that," Dad said. "Oh, hey, we finally chose a new staff writer for the website."

"Nice. Who'd you decide on?"

"Veronica O'Leary. She's the woman with the ex-army husband who has TBI from his time in Afghanistan."

"She sounds like the perfect fit. Someone who gets it."

"She is," Mom chimed in. "And she does."

Combat soldiers were right up there with football players when it came to brain injury rates. My parents and I planned to expand the non-profit's website and publish our own articles about the emerging studies on TBI and CTE, and Mom and Dad had been spearheading the hiring of staff while I'd been out here. They asked me to weigh in on some big decisions, but mostly they handled it themselves.

We spent the next thirty minutes talking about plans for the website, shooting another PSA, and the lawsuit against the USFL. Our lawyers had filed an injunction against the league's Commissioner for his Twitter rant, and, thankfully, the judge granted it. Mom, an unforgiving edge to her tone, voiced the hope that in his hubris, the Commissioner would ignore the injunction and get fined, and/or imprisoned, and/or charged with contempt of court.

I sympathized with her. The man was a monumental jackass. He sided with the conservative team owners and the corporate sponsors, always, more their crony than a functioning figurehead. It was obvious what dictated his decisions: greed. The league would lose a lot of money if the courts decided in the favor of the players, which meant that he would lose money. Or get fired. Personally, I hoped he got the axe long before we went to trial. God knew he deserved it.

By the time I got off the phone, the puppies were up and bumbling around the living room, batting at toys, playing tug of rope with each other, and generally being tiny puffs of trouble. It had been a while since they'd gone out, so I pushed up from the couch and coaxed them toward the front door.

I bundled up and then cracked it open. Boots took two steps toward it, got hit in the face with an arctic blast of wind that blew his ears back, and then turned around and took off at full speed back into the house, his little body projecting an almost audible stream of, "Nope, nope, nope, nope, nope."

Doodle was a little braver. He got to the threshold, stepped his front two paws down onto the porch, and then immediately tried to reverse, crying pitifully when he couldn't pull himself back up the step. I scooped him up, set him inside, and closed the door against the wind. He walked over to the nearby puppy pad, squatted down, and peed on it.

"Totally get it, little dude," I told him. I wouldn't want to piss out there either.

My phone dinged from inside my pocket. I pulled it out to see a text from Ella.

Puppy pictures. Need them. Already going through withdrawal over here.

I grinned. *What'll you give me in return?*

We're bartering now? Okay, how about more cribbage lessons so you stop being such an epic loser?

We played best out of three the other day. I'd been blessed with the skunkarooney dance again. One of these days, I needed to stealth record her doing it. The blackmail potential was off the charts.

Hmmm. What else you got? I texted back.

She sent me a picture of Fred and Sam, passed out on her living room floor. From the looks of it, Jack had managed to wear them out. Only a couple of days had passed since I'd seen them, but I missed those hyperactive weirdos. The puppies were adorable, but their personalities hadn't fully developed yet. Fred and Sam had their own presences. I couldn't wait to see how they interacted with Boots and Doodle. Ella told me they were even more puppy obsessed than we were, but I found that hard to believe.

Fair trade, I texted back. *Hang on a sec. I have to get them in the same room.*

I scooped Doodle up from where he was chewing on the laces of my discarded boots, then went to find his brother. Boots was in the kitchen, his paws up on the trashcan like he was going to knock it over for the second time today.

"Come here, trouble," I said, hefting him. He let out a whine and craned his head around to look at the trashcan in open longing.

I brought them into the living room, set them on the blanket by the fire, and took their picture. They looked like they were smiling at the camera. I sent it to Ella.

I JUST WANT TO SQUEEZE THEM, she texted back.

You're that aunt who pinches cheeks, aren't you?

Only Evan and Michael's. If I tried to pinch Willow, she'd seek revenge.

I'm going to have to meet that kid one day.

Woah. Where had that come from? I mean, granted, I'd been curious about Willow since Ella told me about the infamous Christmas Eve Poopsicle Incident, but it was in a vague way. Like, it'd be fun to watch a kid that cute act like such a hellion.

As I stared down at my text, I realized that I meant the words in a more concrete way. I *did* want to meet Willow. And Michael and Evan. I wanted to meet Ella's hippy mom and her grounded dad. I wanted to ask Jacob about his work in Africa. Talk to Jane about freelancing.

I wanted to know all of them. I wanted to watch them interact with Ella. I wanted to see her tease her siblings like she teased me. I wanted to experience the chaos of such a large family firsthand.

I knew the answer to Brian's question now. I knew how I really felt about Ella. This was more than just simple attraction. I wanted to be part of her life. I wanted her to be part of mine.

The question was, what the fuck did I do about it?

My phone chimed with Ella's response.

I'm watching the little hooligan tomorrow morning. Jane has a deadline, and Dave has a meeting down in Portland he can't miss. I'll send you plenty of pictures and updates so you can make a more educated decision about whether or not you want to become one of Willow's minions.

I smiled, looking forward to it. *Sounds good. Stay safe. Don't let her coerce you into petty theft or larceny.*

No threat of that. She has bigger schemes. Like world domination.

I shook my head and set my phone down. The fire was starting to burn out, and it looked like the puppies were right there with it. Boots plopped his butt down and yawned. Beside him, Doodle lay on his side, a toy just out of reach. He halfheartedly batted at it with one paw even as his eyes slid shut.

I now understood why some people made Instagram accounts just for their pets.

"Okay, you two. Time for bed."

I scooped them up and carried them to my room, which, like the sitting room, was relatively puppy-proof at this point. One night was all it took to learn just how much stuff they could get into. My king-sized mattress sat on a low platform that the puppies were able to scramble up and down from. I'd never been a fan of tall beds piled with pillows and squishy mattress covers. I slept on my back, so the firmer, the better.

I set the dogs down on the bed and changed into gym gear. They might be tuckered out, but my mind was still running a hundred miles an hour. I felt wound too tight. I needed the rush of endorphins that came from a hard workout followed by the mindless bliss of exhaustion if I had any hope of falling asleep at a reasonable hour.

I paused to pet the puppies before heading downstairs. "Please don't wreck anything."

I didn't turn the music on in the basement, on the off chance that they managed to knock something large over. They were too small to do that – rationally, I knew they were – but they were so helpless that I was paranoid something might happen to them, and I'd never forgive myself. I needed to get one of those baby monitors so I could keep an eye on them when I wasn't in the same room.

Jesus. I was going to be one of *those* dog owners, wasn't I?

I rolled my eyes at myself and then got down to business. It was legs and back day. Everyone has a favorite workout routine, as well as a least favorite. This was the one I dreaded. Sure, it was fine while I was lunging and squatting and leg pressing and supermanning. It might even be semi-tolerable tomorrow if I drank enough water and ate enough potassium. But being two-day leg sore sucked. You couldn't do anything without feeling it. Sitting down made my glutes scream. Standing back up was quad torture. Taking the stairs required a monumental effort.

I grinned mid-lunge. Last week when I was two-day leg sore, Ella kept asking me to get her things. "Can I have that wrench?", "Have you seen that paint sample anywhere?", "Do you mind grabbing me another glass of water?" It was only as I hobbled out of the room in search of an alleged lost bolt that I thought to glance back over my shoulder. I'd caught her grinning in a way that told me she'd been enjoying my torment just a tad too much.

Evil woman.

Usually when I worked out, my mind went blank, but without the distraction of music, thoughts of Ella continued to creep in. I was in the middle of a set of pull-ups when I remembered her trying to get the last herringbone tile into place on the kitchen wall without having to make another cut, and then the five minutes of swearing that followed when she realized she'd have to. I paused to stretch and thought of the text she sent me a few nights back. *"Hey, I think this would look great in the dining room."* A shortlink followed. I clicked on it, assuming it would take me to an image of a painting or a mirror, but it redirected me to the *Benny and the Jets* video, like it was the new Rick Roll.

There was no way I was going to achieve my usual zen down here in my Basement of Blood, Sweat, and Jump Rope. I gave in and let Ella take over my mind, picturing her holding up that light fixture, remembering the way her hips flared like they were made for my hands to hold onto. What would have happened if I'd fallen to my knees behind her? If I'd turned her around, tugged off those leggings, and given her head up against the wall, one thigh hooked over my shoulder, her fingers buried in my hair as she guided me on?

The woman was so unselfconscious most of the time that I prayed she'd be the same in bed. Would she tell me what she liked? What she wanted?

"Fuck," I muttered, dropping the weights I held. My dick tented my gym shorts.

I gave up on the workout and headed upstairs. The dogs were passed out on the bed, my room still – thankfully – in one piece. I paced into the bathroom, flicked on the light, shut the door behind me, and turned on the shower. It took a minute for the water to heat up. I stripped my sweaty clothes off as I waited. A tendril of steam rose from the spray. I pulled the shower door open. My hand was around my dick the second I stepped inside.

Since dropping my dosages, my sex-drive had been slowly ramping up. I'd kept my masturbatory fantasies to memories of past encounters. Only now was I willing to admit what an effort that had been. How thoughts of Ella kept trying to sneak into them. For the first time, I took the fetters off of my mind and allowed her to take over.

We were back in the upstairs room. I stared at her ass instead of putting up painter's tape.

"Little help here," Ella said.

"No prob," I told her, striding over.

I didn't drop to my knees. Instead, I wrapped my hands around her hipbones and slowly pulled her backward, so she could *feel* how much I wanted her.

"Ben," she said, my name coming out as a moan.

She let go of the light and arched backward, wrapping her arms around my neck. Her fingers dug into my hair, nails scraping over my scalp. The light fixture slid sideways and gouged out a line of drywall that I did not give a single fuck about.

Ella's swanlike neck was bared to me. I pressed my lips against her pale skin and kissed my way up it. She turned her head to the side, giving me better access. I tugged her earlobe into my mouth and slid my right hand forward, across her lower abdomen, toward the band of her leggings.

She widened her stance in invitation and pressed her ass into my erection.

I groaned into her ear and slid my hand into her pants. She wasn't wearing underwear, and I met no resistance as I worked my fingers lower, searching. I slipped them through her soft curls and stopped when she moaned, "There. Right there."

The elasticity of her leggings was a boon, because it kept my hand pressed tight to her as I slid my middle finger torturously slow over her clit, back and forth, around in a small circle, then back and forth again. I lifted my other hand and cupped her small breast over her t-shirt. Her nipple peaked beneath my fingers, and I teased it to the same rhythm that I played on her clit.

Her breathing picked up, hips shifting as she moved with me. I pushed my right hand lower, meeting the slickness of her arousal when I neared her entrance.

"God, Ben," she said, pulling her arms from around my neck to brace her hands on the wall.

I slid a finger inside her. She was tight, but so wet. My fingers were long enough that I reached deep, feeling the muscles of her sex clench around me when my palm hit her clit. I worked my hand forward and backward, letting Ella's hips dictate my tempo. The heel of my palm brushed over that sensitive bundle of nerves with every stroke of my finger, and it wasn't long before she began to make small sounds of pleasure with each pass.

Her hips picked up speed, and I matched them, working her faster, driving my finger deeper, pressing my palm harder. She used the wall to shove her hips into me, framing my dick between her cheeks as she ground into my hand.

"So close," she said, the words a plea.

I added a second finger, and a moment later, she fell over the edge, her hips losing rhythm, head thrown back against my shoulder, eyes squeezed shut. Her mouth fell open as she came, calling my name.

"Ella," I groaned, coming right along with her, spilling myself all over the shower floor.

I had to brace a hand against the tile to keep from faceplanting into it, that's how hard my orgasm hit. When it passed, I was left shuddering.

Holy shit.

If it was that good in a fantasy, what would it be like in real life?

I was suddenly dying to find out.

Chapter 15: Ella

I had no idea how Jane and Dave did it. Babysitting was hard enough. Being a full-time parent...no, I was definitely not ready for that. Aunt Pat had the right idea. Better to just borrow other people's children and then send them back when you need a break.

"Come on!" Willow roared, tearing up the walkway toward her front door.

"I'm coming," I said, dragging my feet as I trailed behind her.

By the time I walked through the door, she'd already stripped off her winter clothes and was clinging to her mother's leg with all four limbs.

"How was she?" Jane asked me.

Exhausting, I almost blurted. Willow's boundless energy was impressive, and after not watching her for so long, I'd forgotten how much she tired me out.

"She was good," I said. "We went sledding this morning before the snow hit, then had lunch, then made a snowman, and spent the afternoon playing dress-up."

Jane grinned. "Yeah, she's going through a phase. Mom said she put a tutu on Corgnelius last week."

This I had to see. "Pics or it didn't happen."

Jane pulled up her phone and showed me the evidence. Sir Corgnelius McFloofikins – his official title – filled the camera frame. A pink mass of tulle spread out from his waist in all directions. He looked scandalized.

"Can you send that to me? Megan and Stacey will lose their minds when they see it."

"Sure. They really need to get an apartment that allows pets," Jane said, her fingers flying over her phone.

"Agreed. Did you finish your article?"

She grinned. "Yeah. Want to have a glass of wine to celebrate?"

"Sure!" I said.

I was thrilled that we were back on good terms. Jane could hold a grudge, and as I'd predicted, it took her weeks to forgive me for the candy cane incident. I knew her extended annoyance was driven by the stress of the holidays and deadlines, and I'd tried to be good about giving her some space, even though I missed her and Dave and Willow. Sometimes Jane and Megan were more alike than I think either of them was willing to admit. I was beginning to suspect it was why they still didn't get along.

We set Willow up in the living room, her favorite show on the TV and the dogs to keep her company, and retreated into the kitchen where we could still see her, but wouldn't have to hear every word of the insidiously catchy songs the cartoon characters sang.

"What's the article about?" I asked.

Jane, her back to me, poured us each a glass of red. "How the USFL is about to lose a lot of money to the players that are suing them."

I nearly choked. "What?"

She turned around, glasses in hand. "You actually gave me the idea, so thanks for that."

WHAT?!

"I did?" I squeaked out.

"Yeah, that conversation you had with Dad and Jacob at Christmas about CTE got my wheels spinning."

Oh, shit. Oh, shit, oh, shit, oh, shit. I grabbed a glass from her and took a big gulp, trying to buy myself some time to think. I had to tell Ben. If I didn't, and he saw that my sister had published an article about him, he'd think I'd betrayed his confidence.

"Jesus, slow down. It's not a shot," she said.

I took one more swig for bravery. "Who's publishing it?"

Please let it be some small news outlet.

She grinned. "The New York Times."

Fuck!

"That's awesome, Jane! Congratulations!" I said with forced enthusiasm. "Cheers!" We clinked glasses. I set mine down on the counter. "One sec, I think I left something in the truck."

"What...Ella, your jacket!" she called as I dashed out of the side door.

I whipped my phone from my pocket and immediately dialed Ben. "Pick up, please pick up." I had so much adrenaline going that I couldn't even feel the cold.

He answered after the fifth ring. "Hey there."

"My sister is writing an article about your lawsuit for The New York Times."

The silence on his end of the line was deafening.

"I didn't tell her anything, Ben. I swear it."

"I believe you."

I let out a shaky breath. "She overheard me talking to my Dad and Jacob at Christmas about brain injuries and got inspired, so this is still my fault. I'm sorry. I'd just met you and was curious about CTE and some of the studies I read. I needed someone to make sense of the medical jargon for me.”

“It’s okay, Ella,” he said. “This isn’t your fault. You couldn’t have known your curiosity would lead to this.”

“I know, but I still feel like it is. I haven’t seen the article yet, but I need to warn you that it’s probably very political.”

He sighed. “Yeah, I figured. I read some of Jane’s articles after you told me what she does. She’s really talented.”

“What do you want me to do?”

He was quiet for a full minute. “What’s her address?”

I stopped dead in my tracks. “You’re not...you’re not going to come over here, are you?”

“I’d like to. I’m sure she could use an anonymous inside source to bolster some of her research.”

“Ben, she’s a journalist. So is Dave. I don’t know what they’d do with the knowledge of you being hermitted up here.”

“You don’t trust them to keep it to themselves?”

“I don’t know. I want to say that I do, but the risk is...”

“The risk is mine to take. What’s her address?”

Holy shit. Okay, this was happening. I gave him the address and then got off the phone.

“What the hell was that about?” Jane asked when I walked back in.

I stared at her, unsure of how to proceed.

“Ella, your face. You’re starting to worry me.”

I took a deep breath. “I know one of the players involved in the lawsuit. He wants to talk to you about your article.”

She nearly dropped her wine. “Are you,” she glanced toward the living room and lowered her voice, “are you fucking kidding me?”

I shook my head.

Realization dawned across her face. "Oh my God. Stan. It's Stan, isn't it?"

I nodded. "Stan is really Benjamin Kakoa."

Eyes wide, she chugged her wine.

"It's not a shot," I reminded her.

She set the now empty glass on the counter and raked her hands back through her thick hair. "Who else knows?"

"No one. Well, Jack, but I don't think he realizes who he is. Ben lives down the hill from him. I met him at Jack's place just before Christmas, which is why I was talking to Dad and Jacob about CTE. Jane, you have to promise me you won't tell anyone. Not even the family." My tone turned brutal, my inner dragon rearing her head. "I swear to God, if you do, I'll never forgive you."

She stared back at me, expression grim. "I wouldn't do that."

"I mean it, Jane."

Her expression darkened. "I won't say anything. I actually have some journalistic integrity, you know."

She did. Damn my mama bear instincts for making me question my own sister. "You're right. I know you do. I'm sorry."

"It's fine," she said. "What the hell is he even doing up here anyway?"

I hesitated. "It's not my place to say."

"Is he about to come bitch me out over this?" She glanced toward her daughter. "That dude is scary."

"He is *not* scary," I said. "He's one of the nicest men I've ever met. And I think he actually wants to help you, be an anonymous source or something, but thanks so much for your assumptions."

She closed her eyes and braced her hands on the island countertop. "I'm sorry. That was a crappy thing to say. This is just a lot to take in."

"I get it. Maybe try to give him the benefit of the doubt from now on, though."

"I will." She opened her eyes and looked at me. "I need to call my editor and get an extension."

"Okay."

She picked up her phone and dialed. "Max? Hi, it's Jane. Yeah. I'm glad you like it. I need you to hold off on doing anything with it. I know. I'm sorry. I may have an anonymous source with insider knowledge of the lawsuit. No. Max, *no*. Do you not understand the meaning of anonymous?"

Some of my dread eased hearing her be so firm with her editor. I picked up my own phone and texted Ben.

She won't say anything.

OK. On the way. Just dropped the puppies off at Jack's.

I grinned. *Good luck getting them back from him.*

He didn't respond. I assumed it was because he was driving. I set the phone down and looked up to see Jane doing the same.

She met my gaze. "This is surreal."

"Tell me about it. I almost had a heart attack when you told me what the article is about."

She laughed. The sound was frayed at the edges. "No kidding. You looked like it."

"I'm sorry for freaking you out. And for snapping," I said. I just got back in her good graces. I didn't want to have another fallout right now.

She walked around the island and hugged me, short enough that she could rest her head on my shoulder, just like Mom. "It's okay. I know how protective you can be." We let go, and she grinned up at me. "Remember the first time you met Dave?"

I smiled in return. "Ah, the threats I made."

Her expression flattened. "Payback is a bitch."

"Jane, don't you dare! It's not like that between Ben and me."

"Oh? You didn't just text him while I was on the phone?"

"I did. So what?"

"Sweetie, your face told me everything I need to know." She patted me on the cheek hard enough to sting a little.

I stepped out of her reach. "Please don't embarrass me."

"I think I've made enough promises for one day, don't you?" Her grin became malicious in a familiar way that suddenly clicked. So this was where Willow got it from.

"Jane."

She cackled in response.

I spent the next ten minutes trying to bargain with her. Right up until the dogs leapt off the couch and started barking at the windows. Ben was here.

"Mommy, truck!" Willow helpfully supplied.

I went outside to meet him, letting the dogs streak past me through the door.

"Hi, you two," Ben said.

He spent a long time crouched down at their level, letting them wriggle themselves close as they threw an OMG-I-missed-you-so-much-where-have-you-been party. Once they calmed down some, they moved on to frantically sniffing him.

"They must smell the puppies," he said, standing.

Our gazes met, and for a second, I forgot why he was here. He wore dark jeans and a white V-neck t-shirt beneath his open jacket. His hair was loose and blowing in the breeze. He was gorgeous. So beautiful it hurt to look at him sometimes. I didn't think I'd ever get over the initial shock of awareness I felt each time I saw him.

"Hey," I said.

"Hey," he answered. He stepped close and lifted his fingers to brush a strand of hair from my face. "It's nice to see you."

I smiled. "It's been less than twenty-four hours since I left your place."

"You shouldn't have."

"What?"

"Shouldn't have left," he said, thumb sliding over my lips.

Oh my God.

A loud knock sounded from behind us, and I whipped my head around. Jane stood framed in the window of the door. She grinned when our eyes met and mouthed, "*Payback.*"

I turned to Ben. "I am so sorry in advance for anything my sister is about to say."

He frowned. "About the article?"

I shook my head. "About us. She owes me from when I first met Dave."

He grinned so wide that dimples appeared on either side of his mouth. "Us, huh?"

I turned and paced to the door, cheeks heating. "Yup."

He chuckled and followed me up the stairs.

The dogs raced past us, back inside, nearly knocking Willow over as she ran to meet the newcomer.

"Be nice!" Willow yelled at them. She was one to talk.

I stepped in and made room for Ben in the doorway. His frame filled the entire thing, throwing a shadow over me.

Willow came to a screeching halt, looking up, up, up at him. "You're *big*."

Ben nodded. "I am."

"I climb you now," she said, then charged at him and immediately started to scramble up his leg.

Jane snorted from behind me. "Like aunt, like niece."

I was going to kill her.

Ben coughed to cover his laugh and leaned down to help Willow. She grabbed onto his forearm and hauled herself up with surprising dexterity. She settled on his back, legs around his waist. Ben hooked his hands beneath her knees to keep her in place, which meant that she didn't have to hold on that well. She lifted a finger and prodded at his shoulder, his back, and then his arm, as if testing his muscle tone.

"Can you throw people?" she asked him.

"What?" me and Jane chorused.

Ben just looked confused.

"I need a thrower," Willow said. It was clear from her tone that she didn't mean she wanted him to toss her up in the air, like any normal child would. No. She was talking about needing someone to throw *other* people, on her command.

Ben's confusion morphed into startled surprise as he looked from me to Jane.

Told you, I wanted to say. And he didn't believe me when I told him Willow was already actively recruiting for her evil army.

"You do *not* need a thrower," Jane said.

Willow sighed and rested her cheek on Ben's shoulder. "Fine. He can be my palandin."

"Your what?" I asked.

Jane frowned. "Palanquin, did you mean?"

Willow nodded.

"Where did she even hear that word?" I asked her mother.

"No idea. The kid is way too smart for her own good."

Willow pulled her head up and pointed over Ben's shoulder toward the living room. "Mush!"

Ben did as his future leader bade, dropping her off on the couch, where she settled back into her nest of blankets and hit unpause on the remote, filling the room with the *Little Einsteins* theme song.

"Hi, it's nice to finally meet you," Ben told Jane when he returned, extending a hand toward her.

"Nice to meet you too," she said. Her brows climbed when her hand disappeared beneath his. "Want anything to drink? Coffee, tea, booze?"

"Water is fine," he said, releasing her.

She flexed her fingers a little, as if testing the joints. "Come on into the kitchen. We'll talk in there if that's okay with you, so I can keep an eye on Her Supreme Majesty."

Ben shot a glance over his shoulder at Willow as we followed Jane out of the room. "You weren't joking," he said to me.

"I never joke about diabolical masterminds," I told him.

"Di-a-bo-li-cal," Willow repeated from behind us in a creepy little kid voice that made it sound like she was savoring this new word.

"That's great," Jane said. "Please expand her vocabulary some more."

Ten minutes later, the three of us were seated at the kitchen table. Paper littered its surface. Ben and I each held a copy of Jane's article. She had notepads and pens and medical journals cluttering up her side.

"This is really good," Ben told her as he set the article down.

My sister smiled a little shyly and didn't meet his eyes. "Thanks."

Ha! It wasn't just me he effected. Even happily married women were susceptible. I felt vindicated in my initial difficulty corralling my crush.

"What do you want me to contribute?" he asked.

"Honestly, whatever you're willing to," she answered, picking up a pen.

"Legally, I shouldn't be doing this, so nothing that could give away who I am."

"Understood." She finally managed to meet his eyes, her own full of sympathy. "I'm so sorry about your brother. I can't imagine what that must have been like. If you want, I can remove mention of him from the article."

I loved my sister for this empathy. So much. Beneath the table, I reached out and grabbed Ben's hand. This was going to be difficult for him. He never talked about Zach, or at least he hadn't with me, and now he might have to do so for all the world to read about.

I meant to give him a reassuring squeeze and then let go, but he surprised me by turning his hand beneath mine and threading our fingers together.

"Thank you, but that's not necessary," he told Jane. "Zach's death was one of the driving factors for so many of us quitting the league and filing this lawsuit, so he should be in it."

"I still don't understand why the league didn't settle," Jane said. "Dragging this out in court is only going to make them look worse."

Ben shrugged one massive shoulder. "They're desperate at this point."

"Can you expand upon that?" she asked, in full journo mode now.

He nodded. "I think the league must feel that if they win in court, the fans won't think they're responsible for what happened to Zach and the other players that have died because of TBI or CTE. Or the ones who are already experiencing what amounts to early-onset dementia thanks to their years on the field. And there are other factors driving them besides that."

"Like?" she asked.

"The USFL has lost a lot revenue as people ditch cable and switch to streaming services. No one wants to pay $120 just for the USFL app," he said. "They're losing viewers at higher rates than they've ever experienced. The fans are fed up with the lack of logical punishment. One player is suspended for three games for ranting about how the senator from his home state is racist, while another suffers no consequences after pleading guilty to domestic abuse. And people are either pissed at the players who took a knee during the anthem for 'disrespecting the flag' or for 'bringing politics into sports' or they're pissed at how the league treated those players and the bullshit ruling that came down afterward. So not only are the fans angry with the league, but with each other. A sport that once united so many people is now dividing them."

Jane's pen flew over her notepad. "The ruling you mentioned, are you referring to the fine players will now face if they continue to take a knee?"

Ben nodded. "Yes. There's another lawsuit about to be filed against that, and I think the players involved are backed by some heavy hitters like the ACLU and even a couple of team owners."

"Really? Do you have anyone I could contact about that?"

"Possibly," Ben said. "I'll have to make some calls and find someone willing to talk."

The two of them spent the next hour in deep conversation about the lawsuit and the league's cover-up of early CTE research. Ben's lawyers uncovered evidence of coercion and intimidation to keep some of the studies from being published. A few weeks ago, the private investigators the players hired found a possible paper and money trail that led from the USFL to falsified, argumentative research papers that claimed there was zero connection between getting repeatedly tackled and TBI. As if they thought by spreading alternative facts and misinformation, they might be able to sway public opinion.

It was a move right out of big tobacco's playbook, from back in the days when they were still trying to cast doubt on whether or not smoking led to cancer. It would have been laughable if it wasn't so enraging.

I let go of Ben's hand at that point and stood to pace the kitchen. I couldn't remember the last time I'd been so angry. My she-dragon was so close to the surface that I felt like I could belch fire.

"You okay, Ella?" Ben asked.

"She's fine," Jane answered for me. "Momma bear mode has been activated."

"More like rage-beast mode," I said, so low they couldn't hear me.

Ben arched a brow at Jane.

"Oh, so she hasn't felt the need to defend you yet?" Jane asked. "Be grateful for that. She can get a bit scary."

"I see that." He turned and watched me pace. He didn't look frightened; he looked...appreciative.

I forced my gaze away from him before my anger morphed into something else.

"Tell me more about this last injunction," Jane said. "The one concerning the Commissioner."

I heard footsteps and turned to see Willow walking toward me. She joined me in my pacing, crossing her little arms over her chest as she glared around the room.

"Who are we mad at?" she asked.

I slowed down so she could keep up. "The Commissioner of the USFL."

"Ben!" she shouted. "Go throw him!"

God, I loved her.

"What did I say about throwing people?" Jane yelled back. She glanced at her watch. "Crap. It's bedtime."

"I got it," I told her.

I took Willow's hand and led her down the hall. I needed a break anyway. To go from Ben never talking about this to hearing how much he'd been hurt by it all made me so mad I felt nauseous. Having to deal with all that toxicity on top of the threat of CTE and his grief for Zach seemed cosmically unfair. No wonder he needed to hide out for a little while. No wonder he'd been absent from social media since Christmas.

The dogs decided to help me with Willow, crowding into the bathroom with us while she brushed her teeth. I tucked her into bed afterward, and Sam, tired from running after her all day, cuddled in close to her on top of the covers, like he was trying to pin her there so he didn't have to chase her anymore. She threw a little arm around his neck and asked me to read her a bedtime story.

"Something di-a-bo-li-cal," she said.

I muffled my laughter and instead chose the most sugar-sweet book I could find.

"Ugh, boring," she told me when I was halfway through it.

I ignored her and kept reading. Eventually, it did the trick. Her eyes fluttered shut and her breathing deepened. I read until I was sure she was fast asleep, then turned off the light and told Sam to keep watch, leaving the door cracked behind me.

Fred followed me out into the kitchen, where Jane and Ben were still deep in conversation. He padded over to Ben's side and plopped down next to him, head on Ben's thigh. Ben immediately reached down to pet him.

"Are you guys hungry?" I asked. "It's nearly seven-thirty."

Jane looked up from her notes. "Dave will be home soon. You might want to duck out now, Ben."

"I don't mind staying to finish," he said.

Jane nodded. "Then don't worry. He'll keep his mouth shut about you too."

"I'm going to make Mom's End of the Week Pasta," I told my sister.

She glanced over at me. "Sounds good. There's a loaf of sourdough somewhere over there if you want to make garlic bread too." She turned back to Ben. "Tell me more about that first hearing."

I worked on dinner while they talked. Mom's favorite dish didn't have a set ingredient list, which made it adaptable. It was called End of the Week Pasta because Mom always went grocery shopping on Saturdays. Friday night, whatever was left over in the fridge from the week before went into the sauce she made.

I found half an onion, a green pepper, some kalamata olives, kielbasa, garlic, and zucchini in the fridge. I dumped them on the counter and went in search of diced tomatoes. A can of red kidney beans sat next to them in a cupboard, and I grabbed them both.

I spent the next twenty minutes dicing, chopping, and straining while water boiled in a pot on the stove. Headlights flashed over the windows as the clock crept closer to eight. I shushed Fred before he started barking, worried that he'd wake Willow.

Dave walked in not long after, looking exhausted from his twelve hours of travel to and from Portland. He dropped his messenger bag inside the door, started to tug his coat off, and then turned to see Benjamin Kakoa sitting at the dining room table with his wife.

His eyes nearly fell out of his head. "Am I being punked?" He looked around. "Is there a camera crew here?"

"Dave, meet Ben," I said. Oh, this was too good.

Ben unfurled from his chair to tower over my brother-in-law. "Nice to meet you, Dave."

"What is happening right now?" Dave asked, wrenching his arm from his coat sleeve to shake Ben's hand.

"Ella's been secretly dating a superstar," Jane said, shooting me a grin.

I pointed the knife I held at her. "Stoppit."

"I'm up here taking a bit of a break from the spotlight," Ben said as he and Dave released each other.

"Well, it's nice to meet you, man," Dave told him. "I'm a huge fan. The work you've done the past few years is amazing."

Ben grinned. "Thank you."

"He offered to be an inside source for the NYT article," Jane told her husband.

"What a fucking scoop," he said. He turned to hang up his coat and kick his leather shoes off. "Anonymous, I'm guessing?"

"Yes," Jane answered. "And if you tell anyone who my source is or that Ben is hiding up here, I will divorce you."

"Okay then," Dave said. "Love you too, babe." He leaned down, planted a kiss on her cheek, and then went to change out of the business formal clothing he'd been trapped in all day.

Jane and Ben finished up while he was gone, with Jane asking for Ben's number in case she had any more questions or needed something clarified when she re-wrote the article. He gave it to her and then rose from the table to join me by the stove.

"Hi," he said.

I looked up at him, thankful our backs were to Jane, because I knew that the look on my face would give her way too much ammunition. "Hi."

"You doing okay?" he asked, voice low so it wouldn't carry.

"Okayish," I said. "You?"

He exhaled. "Okayish too. I think."

"That was a lot."

He frowned. "Too much?"

I moved the wooden spoon to my left hand and wrapped my right one around his elbow, careless now of what Jane thought. "No. Not too much. Never too much."

He leaned toward me. "Come over tonight."

I stared at him from inches away. "I thought you didn't...?"

He shook his head. "It doesn't have to be like that. Truthfully? This was almost too much for me. I could use some company after it all."

"I'll come over," I told him.

Chapter 16: Ben

I stepped out of the front door at the sight of Ella's truck turning onto my driveway. The night air nipped at my skin with teeth made of frost. I took a deep breath, feeling like my lungs were about to freeze. Our local news station warned that temperatures were going to plummet over the next few days as a polar vortex roared down from Canada.

They had a name for it up here: killing cold.

Ella pulled into the golden nimbus of porchlight and put the truck in park. She cut the engine and hopped out, and I took the stairs down to meet her.

She turned to me as I approached. "I am wearing the world's ugliest underwear."

What the fuck?

Her breath misted in front of her face when she spoke. "I thought I would throw that out there now, since you said yesterday that you don't think that, uh..." she looked at me, shifted her gaze toward the vicinity of my belt, and then gestured back and forth between us several times, her hand at crotch level, "...that this is a good idea."

I started to smile but bit my lip when I realized she was dead serious.

I will not laugh. I will not laugh.

Ella opened the back door of her truck. "Anyway, I felt like there was some tension at Jane's earlier, maybe, and after everything you just talked about, I'm not sure if you're emotionally vulnerable right now, and I don't want to take advantage of that or anything."

I wasn't emotionally vulnerable, but it was sweet of her to care so much about my mental state that she was trying to sabotage herself with the mention of hideous panties. And yet, somehow, it made me want her even more. How to tell her that her plan was backfiring?

She unbuckled the dogs. They jumped down, gave me sniff in greeting, and then raced out into the night, crashing through the snow.

"Is your underwear supposed to be a deterrent?" I asked, unable to keep the teasing edge from my tone.

She shut the truck door and turned to me. "Yes. Or, they would be, if you saw them." Her eyes squeezed shut for a second. She looked like she might be wincing. "They're, like, Great Aunt Muriel level ugly."

I ambled over and smiled down at her. "I don't have a Great Aunt Muriel."

"Then picture the largest, plainest pair of threadbare women's underwear you possibly can." She held out her hands to demonstrate their size. Impressive. "Now cover them in paint stains – long story, please don't ask."

I wanted to ask. So bad.

"And imagine them on the oldest woman you know."

I couldn't do that. My head was too full of her to think of anyone else. "And you're wearing them because?"

"I found them in the way back of my underwear drawer. They were the last clean pair. It was either them or nothing."

My mind came to a screaming halt. I suddenly hated these underwear with the fiery wrath of a dying star about to turn supernova. If not for them...

"I really don't like doing laundry," she continued, unaware of my internal struggle. "You should know that about me. Like, if we stay friends for long enough, I will eventually try to lure you over to my house with the promise of tasty treats and then withhold them until I can convince you to wash my clothes for me."

"Tasty treats?" I asked, my gaze roaming over her. My mind was stuck in the gutter. All I could think of is what could have been if not for these allegedly hideous undies. "Are we talking food, or something else?"

She looked up at me, eyes wide. "Food?"

"You sure about that?" I asked, taking a step closer.

The dogs barreled back into the floodlight and squeezed between us, doing their damnedest to ruin the mood with their whining and panting.

"We better go in," Ella said, breaking eye contact. "I swear I heard howling at Jane's when I left."

I gave up on my attempted flirting and led them toward the porch. "Really?"

"Yeah. One of Dave's friends is a ranger, and he says the wolves are back."

I stopped at the door and looked down at her. She was close, really close, like she was trying to hide behind me. Her gaze shifted from right to left, searching the darkness beyond the safety of the porch. "Not a fan of wolves?"

She shook her head. "They're right up there with bears when it comes to predators I'd least like to meet in person."

"I saw a grizzly from a car once. Damn thing was nearly as big as the vehicle."

"We don't have them here. Ours are smaller. But they're even better at climbing trees because of their size, and they can run faster than a human could ever hope to." Her expression turned grim. "Plus, razor claws of doom and machete teeth."

"Thanks so much for the nightmare ammunition."

"Just trying to share the misery."

"Right. We need puppies."

She nodded. "Only baby floofs can help us now."

We stepped inside, toweled off the dogs, shed our winter layers, and headed toward the sitting room, where I'd corralled the puppies before she arrived. The sound of their muffled cries echoed from inside. Fred and Sam took off toward the door and started frantically sniffing the crack beneath it. Every few seconds, Fred straightened and looked back at Ella like, *"Mom! Puppies, Mom!"*

"I know, bud." She stepped next to him and took him by the collar. "But we have to be gentle because they're little."

I did the same to Sam, and when they calmed down, Ella opened the door a crack, just enough so that we could all see each other. Fred and Sam lost it, pulling against their collars and whining like I'd never heard before. They worked each other up until they started howling.

Boots, on the other side of the door, plopped his butt down, tipped his head back, and let out a prolonged, answering squeak.

Fred and Sam stopped to stare at him.

"Is he...is he trying to howl?" Ella asked.

"Uh, yeah, I think he is."

Come on, little dude. You can do it.

Sam howled again, and Boots threw back his head and squeaked some more in response. Beside him, Doodle seemed to concentrate, really hard, and then uttered a little whine-growl as if he was testing it out before he lifted his muzzle skyward and let forth a high-pitched, "*A-roo-roo-roo-roo-roo.*" Boots did his best to mimic him, and soon all four dogs were howling together like their own little wolf pack.

Ella and I managed to live through it, proving that no, you cannot be killed by cuteness.

We let the dogs greet each other in stages from there. Ella told me this wasn't Fred and Sam's first time meeting puppies, and while they'd been good with them before, you never knew how the puppies would behave, whether or not they'd be aggressive and cause a reaction in the older dogs you didn't expect.

Everything went pretty well, considering their size difference. The dogs sniffed and danced around the puppies once we let them freely intermingle. At one point, Fred splayed his front paws and dropped down, butt still in the air, then sprang up and away like he wanted Doodle to play chase with him. Doodle ran away in sheer terror instead, cowering behind my left foot.

I scooped him up and gave his ears a ruffle. "You're okay."

"You're really good with them, you know," Ella said. "I'm glad you decided to keep them."

"Me too. And thank you again. I feel like I owe you so much. For the dogs, and for all the help you've put in with the house."

She gave me a look I'd never seen before. "You can pay me back in tasty treats." She waggled her brows, just in case I missed the insinuation.

I nearly dropped Doodle. "Ella!"

"What? You started the flirting! Are we not doing the flirting?"

I grinned and set the puppy down. "I thought you didn't want to take advantage of me."

"Fine, I'll stop."

I closed the distance between us and raised my hands to cup her cheeks. Her hair was loose, and my fingers slid easily into the silken strands, coming to rest at the back of her head. "Don't stop."

She let out a shaky breath and leaned into me. Her hands wrapped around my arms, just above my elbows. She slid her right one up until her fingers brushed the edge of my tattoo. Goosebumps rose in their wake as she traced the bottom of the design.

"How far up does this go?" she asked.

"Stay the night, and I'll show you."

She sucked in a breath. "I thought you didn't think this was a good idea."

"That was before I knew how well you could handle all my shit."

She shook her head within my grasp. "It's not shit."

A well of emotion bubbled up within me. Hope. Longing. Appreciation. Desire. I liked her. I wanted to be with her. She heard a lot tonight, and she didn't run away. Her light hadn't been dimmed by my darkness. She still wanted me.

Brian thought I was ready for this. And I was finally ready to agree with him.

"I want this," I said. "I want you."

She leaned in. Her hands disappeared from my elbows and came to rest on my shoulders. They bunched in the fabric of my t-shirt as she stood on her toes and pressed her lips gently against mine.

I nearly groaned into her mouth.

One of the puppies started yipping like a maniac. We broke apart to see Doodle running circles around Fred, who spun in place, trying to keep the puppy in sight while Doodle attempted to leap up and grab his tail.

"That won't end well for you," Ella said, stepping away to scoop Doodle up.

I stared at her profile, my gaze lingering on her freckles before moving down, tracing the outline of her breasts, the narrowing of her waist, the swell of her hips.

"Stay," I said.

Her focus remained on the puppy, her fingers scratching under his chin. "Okay," she answered softly.

The word ricocheted through me. I wanted to pick her up, fireman style, and sprint up the stairs with her. Instead, we calmly separated the dogs, careful not to touch each other on the off chance that it set off some unstoppable chain reaction. I told her where the puppy food and spare bowls were. She took Fred and Sam across the hallway into the library to get them settled, while I stayed with Boots and Doodle.

We met at the bottom of the stairs a few minutes later. I took her hand and wordlessly led her up them, forcing myself to keep a normal pace. My pulse thrummed, sending adrenaline and lust coursing through me. I turned left at the top of the stairs, opened my bedroom door, and let go of her hand so she could go in first. She paused just inside, inspecting the room. I shut the door and went to her, wishing she was wearing leggings instead of jeans.

"This is nice," she said.

"You're nice," I told her.

She laughed, the sound nervous, and started to turn.

I put my hands on her hips to stop her, thinking back to the fantasy I'd dreamt up last night and wanting to experience it for real. She stilled in my grip. I pulled her backward, wrapped my arms around her waist, and then dropped my lips to her neck. This wasn't a fantasy, though, so of course her hair was in the way. She impatiently pushed it aside, exposing a long line of creamy skin.

I brushed my lips over it.

She jerked away, snorting. "Your beard."

"Are you ticklish, Ella?" I asked, angling my chin toward her and wiggling my jaw as I leaned in.

"Yes!" She tried to squirm out of my grasp.

I let her go and gave up on replaying that fantasy. This was more fun anyway.

She came to a stop near the foot of the bed, her hair disheveled. The neck of her t-shirt was pulled sideways. Her chest rose and fell as she sucked in heavy breaths. Those blue eyes were wild when they met mine, pupils blown out from lust.

Fuck it.

I walked over to her, picked her up under the armpits, and tossed her onto the bed.

She shrieked mid-air, then laughed when she bounced off the mattress. Her hands went to the hem of her shirt, and she tugged it off in one fluid motion. The bra she wore was beige and entirely unremarkable. I was thankful for that, because I didn't want anything to distract me away from the sight of her toned stomach, her defined shoulders, that long, swan-like neck.

I put a knee on the edge of the mattress and crawled toward her on all fours. Her eyes danced as she watched me come. When I got within touching distance, she grabbed my shirt and pulled me closer. I had to brace my hands on either side of her thighs to keep from falling. She met me halfway, covering my mouth with her own. Her lips parted, tongue pressing out, seeking access.

She was taking the lead, and it turned me the fuck on. There was nothing sexier than a woman who knew what she wanted and pursued it with such single-minded intensity.

I opened my mouth and let her in. Our tongues brushed across each other. She moaned into my mouth, hooked an arm around my neck, and dragged me down on top of her. I rested my weight on my forearms to keep from smothering her. Beneath me, her legs spread as wide as her skinny jeans would allow, our hips fitting together as her tongue continued to ply mine with expert precision. My dick strained against the constraints of my boxers and jeans. I shifted my pelvis forward, so she could feel how much I wanted her.

She broke off the kiss, gasping. "Too many clothes."

I sat up and all but ripped my shirt off. The open hunger on her face as she took in the lines of my muscles made every sit-up and bicep curl I'd ever done more than worth it. I barely repressed the desire to flex for her.

Her gaze rose, taking in the tattoo that climbed up my left bicep, whorled over my shoulder, and snaked down to cover both of my pecs in a series of stylized enatas, tikis, ocean waves, spearheads, and shark fins, the spaces between swathed in bands of black.

"It's beautiful," she whispered, her tone reverent.

"You're beautiful."

Her gaze moved from my chest back to my stomach. She traced the outline of an ab with her finger. "You could do my laundry on these things."

I cocked an eyebrow up. "In exchange for tasty treats?"

She grinned, nodding. Her nimble fingers slid down, nails scraping lightly over my skin in a way that made me shudder. They came to rest on my belt. Below it, my dick strained toward her. She started to undo my belt, one-handed, while her free hand rubbed up and down the length of my bulge.

I needed these pants off. Now. Hers too.

I reached out and fumbled at the button on her jeans, my fingers trembling.

Her hands disappeared from my waist. She clamped them onto my wrists, stopping me.

I froze. "Sorry. Too fast?"

Horror spread across her face. "I forgot about the underwear."

Holy shit, she'd been telling the truth. I laughed before I could stop myself. "I thought you were kidding about them."

"I wish." Her tone was grim. "Ben, they are so bad."

"Okay, now I really have to see them."

She closed her eyes in resignation and released me. I got her top button undone with a flick of my fingers and then started to slide her zipper down, curiosity making strange bedfellows with the lust still coursing through me. More of her skin was exposed, and while I could have spent hours staring at it, or dropping kisses on it to find out just how ticklish she was, I was too distracted by the frayed elastic band of her underwear.

I kept unzipping. They were cotton, the fabric a mottled taupe that leaned more toward brown in the darker areas. What the hell?

I moved the zipper lower, and a splotch of orange was revealed. Lower still. A dab of blue-green-gray that reminded me of drowned things. I reached the end of the line and spread the sides of her pants open. A Rorschach-style kaleidoscope of colors stared back at me.

"How the fuck did you even do this?" I asked.

She groaned and covered her eyes. "I used a folded-up rag to wipe up paint one day, and the underwear was stuck inside it from static. I tossed them in the wash with the rest of my paint rags and they came out looking like this. I was going to throw them away, but then I had a vague idea of doing something with them, making some sort of artistic statement full of ennui and existential angst." She pulled her hands away and looked up at me. "You know, because I'm so dark and moody."

"Oh yes. I know," I said, fighting back a smile.

"I threw them into my underwear drawer afterward so I wouldn't forget about them, and then promptly forgot about them. Until today."

I stared at her. "You're going to need more than an ugly pair of panties to make me not want to sleep with you."

Her mouth popped open in response. Then her eyes darkened and her lips lifted in a downright indecent grin before she straight up launched herself at me. I caught her out of the air and spun us, one arm around her back, the other braced on the bed so I could lay her down on the comforter. Our mouths crashed together, almost violently.

I dragged myself away from her and gripped the band of her underwear and pants. I paused, looking up at her.

"Take them off," she said.

Yes, ma'am.

I dragged them down her legs. She squirmed out of them, arching her back at the same time so she could reach behind herself and unhook her bra. It came off a second later, leaving her gloriously naked before me.

"I want to trace your tattoo with my tongue," she said, her gaze running up my left arm.

I looked down at her. "Funny. I was just thinking about doing the same to your vagina."

She barked a laugh, and then spread her legs, exposing herself to me, just as unselfconscious as I hoped she would be.

I dropped to my knees, hooked my elbows beneath her legs, and tugged her to the edge of the bed. Her pubic hair was a few shades darker than the hair on her head, trimmed so that I had an unobstructed view of the delicate folds of her sex, of the moisture that already glistened there.

She slid her legs up and rested her calves on my shoulders, then chuckled darkly.

I paused to meet her eyes.

"My legs fit into the divots in your shoulder muscles exactly like I imagined they would."

I turned my head and kissed the inside of her knee. "You imagined this?"

She let out a shaky breath. "Yes."

I should have taken my time, traced my way up her leg, licked and kissed and bit the inside of her thighs until she begged me for it. But I did none of those things. Instead, I spread her wider and leaned forward to suck her clit into my mouth.

Chapter 17: Ella

"**B**en," I moaned, arching up off of the bed, my amusement forgotten.

I wanted to look down at him, watch him, thread my fingers through his hair. But I couldn't, because – *holy fuck* – he was good at giving head. He knew exactly where a clit was, just how to tease and taunt, lavishing it until I neared the point of overstimulation before dragging his mouth lower so he could slide his tongue into me.

I dug my hands into the covers and spread my knees further, giving him even greater access to me. His mouth returned to my clit, and a finger slicked into my wetness, replacing his tongue.

"You're tight," he said, voice so low I could feel it vibrating into me. "And so wet."

"You're going to talk me to climax," I warned him.

His finger dove deeper, mouth returning to my aching flesh. "You taste so good."

I raised my hips to meet him.

"Do you want to come like this, Ella?"

"Yes," I said, panting. "And again with you inside me."

In answer, he redoubled his efforts to send me over the edge. My heels pressed into his back, giving me leverage. I bunched the sheets in my fingers, nails digging in. He set a rhythm with his mouth that my body quickly caught, and soon my hips shifted back and forth with every pass of his tongue. Heat gathered in my core, spreading outward to light my nerve endings on fire.

"Ben," I gasped. "I'm so close."

He latched his lips onto my clit and sucked. It was like someone poured gasoline on the fire. White light flashed behind my closed eyes. Pleasure roared through me. I lost the rhythm, giving myself over to it as wave after wave dragged me under.

I was still reeling when Ben pulled away to stand. Normally after an orgasm, I was sated, damn near lethargic, but the sight of him pulling off his jeans and boxers shot a thrill of adrenaline through me that had me immediately ready for round two.

"Are you on birth control?" he asked.

"Yes. And it's been eight months since I've been with anyone. I got tested afterwards, so I know I'm still clean."

He wiped his thumb over his glistening lower lip and then sucked it into his mouth, eyes closing as he savored the last taste of me.

Oh my God.

He opened his eyes and pulled his finger free. "I have you beat. It's been over a year for me, and same."

My gaze slid down his body. His dick was proportional to the rest of him, so, it was huge. Good thing I already came, because it had been so long since I'd done this that I wasn't sure if I'd be able to stretch comfortably around him otherwise.

"Condom?" he asked.

I lifted my gaze back up, taking my time before I answered. He was the most beautiful thing I'd ever seen. The muscles, the tattoo, the face, the eyes, the empathy, the humor, the kindness. Everything about the man was gorgeous. When our eyes met, I shook my head. "No condom."

"How do you want it?" he all but growled.

Holyfuckingshit.

"However you want to give it to me," I told him. I was desperate now.

His eyes smoldered. "Missionary then. I want to see your face when I make you come again."

I moved backward on the bed, watching him crawl toward me, relishing in the sight of his shoulders bunching and flexing as he prowled closer. My head hit the pillows, and I collapsed down, shifting my legs apart to make room for him.

I had been wrong. I had been *so* wrong. I thought because we were clinical and respectful when we disagreed that there'd be no passion between us in the bedroom. It was a lie I told myself to keep from thinking of this. My final attempt to put him once and for all into the category of "friend".

I wanted him now with a fierceness that shocked me. It was primal, this feeling. Some completely unevolved need that was downright cavewoman in nature. The look on Ben's face as he lowered himself onto me reflected it, which drove me even further toward the edge.

Our hips met, and he slid the head of his dick down over my folds, torturously slow, before fitting it to my opening. Ice green eyes stared into mine, his brow furrowed in concentration. He shifted his hips forward, barely, just enough to push inside.

I lifted my lips and kissed him. His tongue slid against mine. I dragged my nails down his back and grabbed his ass. He groaned into my mouth and deepened the kiss. Slowly, he shifted his hips forward, pushing just a little bit deeper. I felt a slight pressure, like my body didn't know whether or not it could accommodate him, and I broke our kiss to lay back down and force my muscles to relax.

Ben felt the resistance, so he took his time, working himself in, then sliding out to coat himself in my slickness. When he pushed back in again, it was easier.

He paused, dropping his forehead to mine, eyes closed. "God, you're tight."

"God, you're big," I shot back.

I was staring straight up at him, so I saw his eyes crinkle up as a smile split his beautiful face. I raised my fingers to trace the lines, and he turned his head and kissed the inside of my wrist. His beard tickled, but not as much as it had on my neck.

I shifted my hips forward, taking him a little deeper. His lips parted over my skin. Very gently, he bit me. That part of my body had never, ever been erogenous, but the sight and feel of his teeth latched onto me sent a thrill of lust straight to my core.

I shifted my hips again, craving the feeling of being full to bursting with him. He released me with a gasp and leaned forward to meet my thrust, pushing another glorious inch in. We worked like this for a few minutes more, until he was buried to the hilt inside me and both of us were breathing heavy.

"You feel. So good," he said, eyes wide open as he looked down at me.

"So do you," I told him.

I ran my nails lightly up his back, urging him on. His pupils edged out the ring of green around them as he pulled almost all the way out of me. He slid back in, slowly, driving me crazy. I could tell from his clenched jaw that he was being careful with me, holding back.

"Harder, Ben. I'm not a doll. I won't break," I told him.

He took me at my word, pulling out again and then driving into me, hitting part of my cervix when he was fully seated. I had never had this happen, only read about it. All the articles said it would either hurt, or be the best thing I'd ever felt. I was so turned on that I didn't feel an ounce of pain, only bliss.

My eyes rolled back. "Oh my God, Ben. Right there."

He kept one arm braced by the side of my head. The other dropped to my upper thigh. He squeezed it, holding me in place, and drove into me again. I hitched my hips up, needing more, and his hand moved further down, shoving beneath me so he could grab my ass and pull me closer. He lifted my hips clear off the bed, like I weighed nothing. I relished in the feeling of it, bracing my hands on the headboard to give myself more leverage as I met his next thrust.

He leaned down and dragged my earlobe into his mouth. "Ella," he rumbled, then began to set a deliberate, driving pace.

I'd had sex. A decent amount of sex, I'd say. But Ben was by far the largest man I'd been with, and the feel of him sliding so deep was different than anything else I'd ever experienced. He brushed along my cervix with every stroke. Soon a pressure began to build within me. Instead of pleasure being centered around my clit, like it usually was, it felt like this stimulation was coming from much deeper, somewhere past even he could reach.

He picked up the pace slightly, his lips dropping to my neck, his fingers gripping my ass. My breathing gained a rough edge. The muscles of my thighs started to shake. Beads of sweat formed along the back of my neck.

Holy hell, what was he doing to me?

"Ben," I said, tone full of warning because I was actually a little concerned about what was about to happen.

My muscles clenched around him deliciously.

He shuddered and slowed.

"What are you doing? Please don't stop."

He pushed into me, teeth scraping over the skin of my neck. "I'm really close, Ella."

I shivered beneath him. "So am I."

"Where do you want me to come?"

"Inside me. I want to feel you."

He pulled halfway out and slammed into me. My spine arched off the bed. The moan that slipped through my teeth was close to a whimper.

The pressure was unbearable now.

"Are you okay?" he asked.

"Yes. Do that again."

He thrust into me again. I had to clench my jaw shut to keep from screaming.

"Look at me, Ella."

I stared up at him as he drove into me. His brows drew down in concentration, even as his lips lifted in a lopsided grin. The sight made me wish I'd never closed my eyes.

"Again," I said.

We found our pace together, faster than before. Harder than before. Our breaths turned ragged. Within me, the pressure reached a crescendo.

He thrust into me one final time, and my orgasm hit so hard that I nearly blacked out. My entire body seized up around him, thighs gripping his sides, inner muscles clenching so hard he could barely move. It was like every single cell of my being came at the same time. I now understand why the French called this *la petite mort,* the little death. I wasn't sure if I'd ever felt so alive, or so close to dying.

"Fuck. Ella," Ben said.

His dick stiffened and swelled within me. I'd closed my eyes when I came, and I snapped them open just in time to watch his face as he climaxed. The sight sent an aftershock of pleasure rolling through my core, and I moaned aloud with him and ground my hips into his.

Afterward, we lay sated in his sweat-slicked sheets. He was still inside me. We breathed so hard it sounded like we'd just finished a set of wind sprints.

"Well," he said, matter-of-factly.

"Do not make me laugh right now, Ben. It will get *so messy*."

He grinned in response, and I had to look away.

"Shower?" he asked.

I nodded. "Necessary at this point."

He had to help me from the bed. My legs were jello.

"If I have another orgasm right now, I'll probably have a heart attack," I told him.

We got into the shower together. He made me come again. I somehow managed to live through it.

***

I was glowing. Positively radiating contentment. So deliriously happy that not even the sound of the dryer buzzer blaring out from my bathroom could make a dent in my mood. If not for the fact that it would drive the dogs berserk, I'd be singing.

Two days ago, Ben and I had sex. Mind-blowing sex. Sex that was in turns gentle, rough, sweet, funny, and so intimate that I didn't think I'd ever felt that connected to another human being. Every time I remembered the look on his face as he came, a little shiver of pleasure ran through me.

I switched the laundry, hauled the clean clothes up my stairs, folded them, and then retreated back downstairs into my little art studio tucked in the very back corner of the house. It was a closet of a room, but I kept most of my supplies stowed elsewhere, so only a desk and a chair and whatever medium I was working with on a given day cluttered it up when I used it.

Today I'd laid a throw cloth over the middle of the room, on top of which sat my easel. I'd come in here this morning thinking to start a new line of artwork for next year's calendar series. Yeah, that wasn't happening. On the canvas, Ben came to life in watercolors, his portrait painted in greens and blues and golds. I used warmer hues of each, because I couldn't think of him without picturing the technicolor lights of summer.

I stood in the doorway staring at it for a full minute, a stupid, self-satisfied grin on my face.

My phone chimed from the desk. I nearly tripped in my rush to reach it. The name "Stan" lit up my screen.

What are you doing? he wanted to know.

Painting, I told him.

Painting what?

Did I answer honestly? Was it weird that I was painting him? Screw it. I was too happy to be neurotic right now.

You, I answered.

Really? Can I see?

Sure, but it's not done yet. I can send you a picture.

Don't bother.

Huh?

Out in the living room, the dogs started barking. I peeked out the window and saw his Jeep coming up the driveway. My stomach erupted in butterflies as I raced down the hallway.

"Go get him," I told the dogs, yanking the front door open.

They raced out into the snow.

I shoved my feet into my boots, tugged on a jacket, and followed them.

He climbed out of the Jeep to pet the dogs. I all but sprinted down the front walk. Behind him, Boots and Doodle batted at the rear window with their little paws like, "*Lemme out, lemme out!*"

Ben straightened as I neared him. Just in time.

"Hi," I said, taking a flying leap at him.

He caught me out of the air with an, "*Oof!*"

I wrapped my legs around his waist and clung to him like a spider monkey, peppering the side of his face and neck with kisses.

His chest rumbled with laughter. "Glad there's no awkwardness between us now."

"God, you smell good. You want to come inside and then come inside?"

His answering groan went straight to my core. The hands that held me up slipped to my ass, pulling me close, so that I couldn't miss the way his dick swelled in response.

I heard a muffled *yip* over the sound of my racing pulse and craned my head around to see Boots and Doodle watching us from inside the Jeep with their tongues hanging out.

Awkwaaard.

"The dogs," I said.

He let me go, and I slid down him. His erection pressed between us in a way that made it difficult to think about anything else.

"The dogs," he repeated, his expression dazed as he stared at my mouth.

A thrill of power shot through me. There was something infinitely satisfying in knowing that I drove him to distraction the same way he did me. I'd been absolutely useless since we'd gotten naked together. I burned dinner last night because I was distracted by my memories. The skin on my fingers pruned in the shower this morning because I was so lost to daydreams of *next time*. Every hour or so, I stopped whatever I was doing to giggle.

Ridiculous.

I rose onto my toes and pressed my lips to his, briefly. "The dogs," I said, pulling back. "Doodle looks about ready to diddle on your car seat."

The lust cleared from his expression. Nothing like the threat of puppy piss on leather to snap a man out of it. He jerked away from me and pulled open the back door. It was too high for the puppies to jump safely down from, so we each took one and placed them gently on the ground. They were immediately swarmed by Fred and Sam, who sniffed them over like concerned parents. I could almost hear them consoling the puppies about the discomfort of car rides.

Ben leaned against the Jeep and then reached out and pulled me to him, turning me so that my back pressed against his chest. One long arm wrapped around my waist. The other snaked across my shoulders, and I was enveloped in his warmth. I let out a contented sigh and settled in to watch the dogs tumble after each other through the snow.

"I came over here because I want to talk to you about something," he said. He sounded serious.

"What's up?"

"You know how my parents were going to fly out here next week?"

I nodded.

"Well, we pushed the date up. They're on a flight out right now."

I stiffened in his embrace, nervous about meeting them in person so soon after our relationship had changed. "Okay. And the reason for this was?"

"I scheduled the advanced tests for CTE. I'm going to meet them in Boston tomorrow."

Holy shit.

I turned within his arms. "How are you feeling?"

His expression was drawn. "Honestly? Terrified."

I wrapped my arms around his waist and hugged him, burying my face in his jacket. So many words crowded together in my mind, of comfort, of consolation, but I hesitated to say them, feeling like none were worthy.

"I've been terrified about this for months," he told me.

I hugged him harder.

He dropped a kiss on top of my head. "The fear isn't going away, or getting any better. If anything, I'm worried it's getting worse. I don't want to be crippled by anxiety-induced procrastination. I can't live like I have been, trapped in ignorance. That's not a healthy place for me to be. Not while battling depression. The only way to move forward is to actually know once and for all what my future might look like."

I didn't tell him it was going to be okay. Because it might not be. I didn't validate his fear or worry. He was intelligent, and more in tune with his emotions than most men I knew. Plus, he had a therapist who had probably done a way better job of helping him unpack all these feelings than I ever could. I also didn't offer to go with him, though I wanted to. We'd only been friends for weeks. We'd only been lovers for days. My tagging along would be selfish, filling my own desire to be there for him. And if we were photographed together? The paparazzi might go nuts. I could be identified, and then his cover here would be blown.

Instead, I said the only thing that seemed like it fit. "Whatever you need, I'm here. To watch the puppies or clean the house or just to be there for deliveries. Seriously, anything, Ben."

His arms tightened around me. "Thank you. I already asked Jack to watch the dogs and look after the house. But I'll let him know you're available for backup."

A question jumped to the tip of my tongue. I pulled away and looked up at him. I wanted to read his features, to gauge whether or not I pushed him too far on this, so I could stop before upsetting him any further. God only knew how stressed he must be on top of the fear, and I didn't want to force him to talk about this if it made it worse.

"What tests are you having done?" I asked.

The wind caught a strand of my hair, blowing it in front of my face. He tucked it behind my ear before answering. "Some of them are pretty new. Like, not approved by the FDA new."

"Are they safe?"

He nodded. "As safe as any of the others. For one of them, I'm not the first stage of their human guinea pigs. My results will add to the two dozen military vets and ex-USFL players they've already tested."

"How is it different from the MRIs and cognitive tests?"

"They inject you with a molecular tracer that bonds with the abnormal proteins that lead to CTE and then scan your brain. It's the one that shows the most promise, because they also scanned the brains of people with Alzheimer's and noticed an actual difference between the two."

"Are you having the others done too?"

"Yeah. I'll be gone for a few days at least."

His expression tightened as he lifted his gaze and looked out at the dogs.

My own fear crept in as I stared up at him. He might have CTE. This big, strong, caring man might one day be brought low by a degenerative brain disease. His depression might get worse. He could end up with mood swings. Memory loss.

The thought made me want to break down sobbing. I pulled free and turned away from him before he could see it on my face. He was already afraid. No need to add my terror to his.

"Fred, what are you even doing?" I called, thankful for the distraction of the dogs.

Fred held a frisbee in his mouth, just over Boots' head. Whenever the puppy jumped up to bite it, Fred moved it just out of reach. Like he was teasing him.

"I swear they're like human kids sometimes," I said, marching through the snow toward them. "Give me that, you jerk." I took the frisbee from him and chucked it across the yard.

We stayed outside for several minutes, playing with the dogs, not speaking, distracted by our thoughts, the air between us heavy with unspoken words.

I led him inside when the puppies started to flag. We dried the dogs, stripped off our winter gear, and then watched as the little ones took off into my house, sniffing all the new things. Fred and Sam trailed after them in a way that made it look like they were giving a tour.

And this is where we stand when we're waiting to be fed.

Over here, you can see our dog beds, artfully arranged.

This is where Mom keeps all of our toys.

Yes, you may play with my squeaky.

Doodle chewed on the toy with a mania that was impressive given how tired he'd looked outside. The good thing was that his little mouth wasn't capable of squeezing it all the way, so the squeaks coming from it were both quiet and few and far between.

"Can I see that painting?" Ben asked.

"It's back here," I told him, leading him down the hallway.

He followed after me.

We were just passing the bathroom door when his fingers curled over my shoulder.

I paused and turned to him.

The pressure between us snapped.

We moved toward each other at the same time, our lips crashing together. His hands were in my hair, pulling me close, while my own fumbled at the buttons of his shirt. We turned sideways together, bumping into the doorframe as we squeezed through it.

He let go of my face and lifted me onto the washing machine. My fingers were too slow. I gripped his shirt and tore it open, popping buttons. He wore a white undershirt beneath it. I pressed it up with shaking hands and reveled in the feeling of touching him skin to skin again.

He grabbed the top band of my leggings. I shifted my hips so he could tug them and my underwear down over my butt. The cold metal bit at my fevered skin but did nothing to cool my ardor. I wanted him. Now. Hard. Deep inside me. I needed to be so full of him that all thoughts of CTE were driven from my mind.

Ben tried to tug the garments the rest of the way off, but my underwear tangled in the fabric of my leggings and got caught on my left ankle.

I let out a growl of impatience. "Leave it."

He straightened and sealed his lips over mine. His hand cupped my right breast, fingers plying my nipple through my t-shirt.

I didn't need or want foreplay right now. I'd spent the entire day in a heightened sense of arousal, and now that he was here, touching me, I was soaking wet and desperate for him.

I broke the kiss and popped open the button of his jeans. His hands shook as he shoved his pants and boxers down just enough to free his dick. Then he wrapped his fingers around his length and fit himself to my opening. The spin cycle kicked on as he slid into me, and the centrifugal motion vibrated through both of us. Then his mouth was on me again, his tongue sliding against mine as his dick pushed deeper. The angle of my hips made me so tight that I could feel each delicious inch of him filling me up.

I was a little sore from our first time, but the pain only served to heighten my pleasure.

"More," I said. I wrapped my legs around his lower back and pulled him in.

We'd been careful with each other before, learning what we liked, taking our sweet time. This was nothing like that.

I clung to Ben's shoulders. He grabbed my hips and set a hard rhythm that pushed me so high, so fast that light burst behind my closed eyelids. I wrenched them open and broke the kiss, leaning back to brace my hands on the top of the washing machine, using it as leverage to shove my hips forward to meet his thrusts.

The sight of him pounding into me proved my undoing. My clit became hypersensitive. Pleasure gathered deep inside of my core from where he stroked in and out of me, over and over again.

I arched my back, and his lower abdomen hit my clit with every thrust.

His pupils dilated, mouth dropping open as his eyebrows furrowed. Inside me, his dick stiffened and swelled. "Ella."

I tumbled over the edge first, keeping my eyes open even as I lost myself to the pleasure that burned through every nerve of my body and synapse of my brain.

My inner muscles clenched around him as I came, spurring on his own orgasm. He thrust hard into me, once, twice, and then lost the rhythm, slowing as he leaned forward and braced his forehead against mine.

I wrapped my arms around his shoulders and pulled him closer. It was only when he kissed me and I tasted salt on my tongue that I realized I was crying.

He must have tasted my tears too, because he pulled back to look at me. "Did I hurt you?"

I shook my head.

He nodded, understanding heavy in his eyes.

The washing machine cut off, rendering the sound of his deep breaths and my muted sniffles loud to my ears.

His gaze ran over my features as if he was trying to memorize them. We didn't say anything else. The threat of CTE had swelled to monstrous proportions between us and taken all of our words. How could you possibly voice the enormity of it? What could you say to make it better?

Silently and gently, he leaned in and kissed the tears from my cheeks.

Chapter 18: Ben

In Aroostook County, you're always aware of the remoteness of the area. It's more than the obvious lack of people and buildings.

The wind that blew down from the alpine ridges carried a pervasive scent of snow and some indefinable mixture of stone and pine and inhospitable wilderness. The bitter cold felt dangerous. With no light pollution, the night sky seemed closer, like I could reach up and touch the stars.

They were still out in all their glory this early in the morning, dimmed only a little by the sliver-thin sickle of waxing moon that sat low over the tree line. I stared up at it for a minute after shutting the rear door of the Jeep. It was easy to imagine, standing here in this land of rivers and mountains, how the local tribes might have worshipped it in the same way that my ancestors had. Maybe they even had their own version of Hina in the Moon.

The wind picked up, a blast of subzero air buffeting me. I brought my gaze back down to earth and headed toward the house. Boots and Doodle met me just inside the door. I scooped a puppy up in each hand, then pulled the door shut behind me with the toe of my boot and went to put them in the vehicle.

I started it thirty minutes ago, leaving the engine running while I loaded it. In all that time, the temperature gauge had barely moved off of its lowest reading. It was still cold inside, so I settled the puppies on a little nest of blankets in the back seat and went to lock up the house.

The wind pulled at me as I made the short trip to the front door. It tugged at my hair with insistent fingers until several strands were loose. One hit me right across the eyeball, and I had a sudden urge to cut it all off. But then I remembered the feel of Ella fisting it in her hands while I fingered her in the shower the other night and thought better of it.

The wind hit me in the face again as I turned back to the Jeep, wiping the small grin from my lips. It would be nice to get a little bit further south. The temperature in Boston today was supposed to reach a balmy thirty-nine degrees. Ella was jealous when I told her. It hadn't gotten above freezing here in weeks. I almost asked her to come with me and experience it for herself, but didn't. That would have been selfish. She had a life, a business. Who would watch the dogs on such short notice? She'd have to shut down her digital storefronts. Work like a maniac to get all her open orders out.

And me asking her would have been unhealthy too. Because the driving factor behind it was for her to be my emotional crutch. To lift me up with her positivity and inexhaustible enthusiasm. To act as a go-between for me and my parents if shit got awkward or tough. That wouldn't be fair, to her, my parents, or myself.

I climbed into the jeep, cupped my hands, and blew some warm air into them before I gathered the courage to touch the steering wheel.

"You two seen my gloves?" I turned and saw Doodle chewing on the finger of one. "Gimme that, you little destructicon."

It took me several minutes to pry it away from him, mostly because I was trying to be gentle and didn't want to hurt his little teeth by pulling too hard. I tugged the gloves on afterward and glanced at the rest of the stuff crowding the vehicle. Everything I might need for the trip was packed. My duffle bag full of clothes sat in the way back, with more spare blankets and a two-way radio in case I broke down somewhere without cell reception. I'd thrown my backpack into the passenger seat after loading it up with snacks and water. My phone had an entire day's worth of podcasts downloaded onto it to keep me entertained during the long drive.

I just needed to drop the puppies and a spare set of keys off at Jack's. I'd taken care of everything else. I was ready. Well, as ready as I'd ever be for what I was about to put myself through.

Jack stood on the front porch when I pulled up. Together we got the puppies and all their supplies inside before he offered me a cup of coffee for the road.

"No thanks," I told him. "Trying to cut back on caffeine."

"Your parents excited to see your place after your sight-seeing trip?"

"They are. Thanks again for offering to put the bed together for them while I'm gone." It was supposed to get there tomorrow.

"No problem," he said.

I rubbed the back of my neck, feeling shitty for all the lies of omission I'd told him over the past several months. "Hey, so, I'm not going down there to sight-see."

He looked at me in a way that made me feel like he wanted to nod in a *Well, no shit* kind of way, and I wondered, for the hundredth time, whether or not he'd known who I was all along. Only one way to find out.

"I'm going to have some tests done," I told him.

His expression darkened. "Cancer?"

"No. A possible brain injury."

"Ah."

"I used to play football."

He angled his head sideways. "You don't say."

"Jesus, man, do you know who I am?" Too late I realized the words made me sound arrogant.

Jack broke into a grin and patted me on the shoulder. "Course I do. You think I'm some hillbilly out of touch with the world?"

"Uh…"

His smile widened, a mischievous gleam in his eye that reminded me of Ella. "Everyone always forgets I have a laptop in the office and cable internet."

"Well, damn, Jack. Why didn't you say anything?"

He shrugged. "Figured you came up here to get away from all that. Thought you might just want someone to bullshit with."

"I did. Thank you."

He nodded. "No problem. Good luck with the tests. I can look after the house and hang onto the dogs as long as you need."

I pointed at him. "Hey, now. I know you have puppy envy. I see what you're doing here."

He put his hands up in an innocent gesture I didn't believe for a second.

The Jeep sat idling outside, so I didn't linger, saying a quick goodbye to him and my boys before bracing the chill of the morning once more. I backed out of his driveway, took the big hill down into town, and then started the long journey south out of Maine. Mom and Dad's flight touched down in Logan at three, so that gave me plenty of time to get there. I left an hour earlier than necessary to factor in rest stops and the odd chance I hit traffic on the interstate.

The first hour went by pretty fast, my mind preoccupied with all the things I still needed to do today: the drive ahead, picking up my parents, checking into our hotel rooms, trying to find somewhere to grab dinner, and mostly, the conversation I needed to have with them about my depression and anxiety. I focused hard on that, planning out what to say and trying to predict how they'd react. It was better than fixating on the reason we were meeting in Boston in the first place.

My phone rang around eight, Ella's name flashing over my screen. I paused the podcast I had on and picked it up.

"Good morning," I said.

She answered with a loud yawn. "Hi, sorry. Good morning."

"You just wake up?"

"God, no. I've been awake since four."

Yikes, even earlier than me. "How come?"

She was quiet.

"Ella?"

"Just thinking about you. How are you feeling this morning?"

"Better than yesterday."

After our quickie in her bathroom, we spent the rest of the afternoon on her sofa, wrapped around each other, not talking much, binge-watching TV and playing with the dogs to distract ourselves.

"That's good," she said.

"I think deciding to do this relieved a lot of stress I hadn't even been aware of."

"I get that. Some of the worst anxiety I've ever had was when something big loomed on the horizon. Like when I decided to stop painting one-offs and start selling stationery. Oh, God, sorry. I know it's not nearly the same as what you're going through, but I-"

"I know, Ella," I said, softening my tone as I cut her off. Her voice had started to take on that slightly panicked edge it got when she worried she'd said something offensive or offhand, and I'd learned from experience it was best to stop her before she started in on herself too hard. "You're just trying to relate. It's understandable. I'd do the same thing if our roles were reversed."

She exhaled heavily. "You are so frigging sweet, do you know that?"

I grinned. "You might have mentioned that once or twice."

"I mean it, Ben. You give me the adult, sexual version of cute aggression."

"Is that even a thing?"

"Sexgression? No, that sounds predatory. Cuteousal?"

"Ella, I'm trying to drive here," I said, laughing. "What the fuck is cuteousal?"

"Cute arousal. Duh."

"Too bad you're not here to show me what cuteousal looks like," I teased.

Her tone turned low and sultry. "Oh, I'd show you, all right."

An image of her pretty little mouth wrapped around my dick flashed through my mind. And now I was driving with a semi. I checked my speed and slowed down some. It would be really fucking awkward to get pulled over right now.

"Again, trying to drive here," I said.

"Let the record show that you started it."

"Fair."

We were quiet for a few minutes, the silence between us stretching and becoming slightly uncomfortable.

"Ben?"

"I'm still here," I told her.

"I'm sorry you're going through this."

I let out a heavy breath. "Thank you."

"I should have said it yesterday, but I kind of internalized a lot of it and turned slightly neurotic."

"You're saying it now, and that's all that really matters."

"I hope everything goes okay tonight with your parents. Just remember all the tips Brian gave you for talking about it with them."

"Thanks. I will. I even wrote them down in case I need some cues to keep me on track."

"That's smart. It can be so hard to focus in the heat of the moment." She paused, and I swear I could *hear* her mulling over what she wanted to say next. "So, I was thinking that maybe I don't call or text you for the next few days. I'm sure you'll have a lot to process one way or the other, and I don't want to stress you out by making you feel like you need to get right back to me or dive into things you might not be ready to. Just...know that I'm here, whenever you want to talk or to hang out when you get home."

"How are you this fucking considerate?"

She laughed. "I could say the same thing to you. It's part of why I like you so much. You know, aside from your self-deprecation, cooking skills, and the fact that you look like the living amalgamation of every wet dream I've ever had."

"You're not so bad yourself," I said.

"What? With this orange hair of mine?"

I sighed. "My mother really needs to apologize for that one."

"No way. I'm just kidding. Your mother has more than made up for it with all the times she's told me how incredibly wonderful I am in literally every other way. Tell your parents I said hi?"

"I will. What are you up to today?"

We talked for another half an hour, her telling me about the orders she needed to get to the post office and the graphic designs she planned for her next wildlife calendar series before filling me in on all the latest Jones Family Drama.

Jacob would be home from Somalia in a few weeks. Charlie hated one of his new college professors. Megan and Stacey were thinking of moving apartments so they could get a puppy. Anabel had a new boyfriend. Ella tried to enlist my help with scaring the kid if he hurt her baby sister at any point in the future. I was pretty sure she was joking, but I still told her I wasn't going to be complicit in the harassment of a minor. She called me a spoilsport.

Jane's article would be published soon, and her editor at the NYT sounded like he was salivating over it. I made a mental note to warn my lawyer about it. He'd either be pissed or super behind this. Either way, I didn't regret my decision to be her source.

I'd heard so much about these people over the past several weeks that I felt like I knew them. I wanted to know them. I wanted to immerse myself in one of the loud, boisterous gatherings that Ella had talked about. I thought about calling her back after we hung up and inviting myself over for Jacob's coming home party, but decided against it. I shouldn't make plans, not knowing what my mental state would be like by then. And that day should be about him. They didn't need me coming in and distracting away from everything he'd accomplished. Maybe down the road I could ask Ella to plan a big dinner party with her family so I could meet them in a more relaxed, natural way.

I realized that I was thinking about us in the long term and cut myself off, hard. I couldn't go there right now. I couldn't get those expectations up. First, I needed to have these tests done. Then, I needed to process the results. My own mental and physical health had to be my priority.

I felt selfish for placing myself above everyone else, still, even after all the times that Brian had told me I needed to, that it was okay to be my own number one. Part of the reason I was in this position in the first place was because I'd pretended to be okay for so long. Big tough men didn't get depressed. Big tough men didn't get sad. They didn't have anxiety. Especially not big tough famous men. Because public image was king.

Sometimes I wished I could go back in time and shake my younger self.

I spent the rest of the ride listening to the episodes of *Stuff You Missed in History Class* that my publicist recommended. In between each, I made phone calls. I chatted with my parents during their layover in Chicago, checked on how the puppies were behaving for Jack, and then called Brian. Together, we formulated a game plan for the coming days. I felt better when we hung up. Like I might actually get through this without completely shutting down or reverting back to my darkest days of depression. The fact that he promised to clear his schedule and jump on a plane if I needed him to had a lot to do with it. It reminded me, again, that I wasn't alone in this, that I had support, people like him and my parents and Ella and Jack that would be there for me.

Traffic picked up as I neared the city but didn't slow to a slog until I turned onto Route One just outside of Boston. Who puts a two-lane road with traffic lights leading straight into a city?

Because of the delay, I barely got to the airport in time. Mom called when they deplaned, and I pulled up to the curb just as they stepped out of the terminal. She wore a floral scarf over her hair and huge sunglasses, ala Jackie Kennedy, no doubt worried she might be recognized. It could happen; she was the face of the charity.

If anything, the getup only made her more conspicuous. People waiting nearby turned to look at her, their gazes tracking her movements, wondering who hid behind the disguise. She wheeled her luggage straight to the Jeep and all but dove into the front seat, leaving Dad to put their things in the way back.

"Nice shades, Mom."

She lowered her glasses and looked at me. "Bond, Klara Bond."

I smiled and leaned over to hug her, glad to see this glimpse of humor returning.

"I missed you so much, Benny," she said, squeezing me hard.

"I missed you too, Mom."

She turned and peered into the backseat. "No Ella?" She looked disappointed.

I shook my head. "She didn't want to impose. And I didn't want to put her through this with us."

Mom nodded. "I understand."

The rear door opened and Dad folded his large frame into the backseat. He buckled himself in and then reached forward to clasp my shoulder. "Hi, son."

"Hey, Dad."

"We should go before someone sees you," Mom said. "I can't believe you didn't put a hat on."

Let the mothering begin.

I grinned as I pulled away from the pickup zone. "Thanks for coming out on such short notice."

"Of course," Dad said.

"Did you guys sleep on the planes at all?"

"A little," he answered.

Mom made a disgruntled sound. "He slept the entire flight from Hawaii to LA."

"I'm guessing you didn't?"

"No. The new meds I'm on give me insomnia."

Well, that was a revelation. "What meds?"

"Antidepressants."

I guess we were jumping right into this then. "My SSRI gave me pretty bad insomnia when I first got on it."

I saw her turn and look at me out of the corner of my eye. "You're on antidepressants too?"

"Yup, have been for a while. But can we pause this conversation until we get to the hotel? I need help navigating out of this maze," I said, handing her my phone.

She pulled up the map app and punched in the hotel's address. We were quiet the rest of the ride, other than her instructions of "turn left here" or "there's a merge up ahead, and you need to be in the right lane".

You could tell how old the city was just from all the twists and turns we took to get to our destination. Nothing ran in a straight line here. The roads were so narrow that they couldn't have been widened much since the days when horses and carriages had been their main source of traffic.

"Well, we survived, and that's all that matters," Dad said when I parked.

There had been a few close calls there. Boston drivers were fucking scary.

Mom gave him *A Look*. She wasn't a fan of car-related jokes, for obvious reasons.

"Sorry, you know what I meant," he said.

I pulled on a hat and sunglasses before getting out of the Jeep. Mom and Dad checked us in. I'd booked the rooms under Dad's name to be safe.

I hid in a dark corner of the lobby while they spoke to the desk clerk and tried to make myself look smaller than I was. It didn't work. A bellhop spotted me almost immediately, doing a double-take as he walked toward the door. He turned, midstride, and beelined straight toward me.

"Hey, man," he said, extending a hand. "I'm a huge fan."

I plastered a smile on my face and shook his hand. "Thanks."

"I follow you on Twitter."

I nodded. This could go one of two ways. He either agreed with me, or he didn't. I stood there, stressing out as I waited for the other shoe to drop. Being so removed from recognition for so long had made me rusty at this. I was more nervous than normal – something I really didn't need right now.

I should have stayed in the fucking Jeep.

"Thank you for all the stuff you link," the guy said. "We were gonna put our boys in the local peewee league, but after reading all of those articles about brain injuries, we put them in baseball instead."

Well, shit. "You're welcome."

He nodded and then looked around the lobby. "You park in the garage underneath the hotel?"

"Yeah."

"In the back corner of it, there's an elevator no one uses because it's so damn far away from everything. Takes you right up to all the floors, though. If you're trying to fly under the radar, you might want to stick to that from now on. It's way down that hallway," he said, pointing.

"Thanks. I will."

"No problem, man. Keep up the good work."

"Will do."

Dad came over a minute later, eyeing the retreating form of the bellhop. "What was that about?"

"He told me the articles I linked on Twitter kept him and his partner from putting their boys into peewee."

"That's amazing, Benny," Mom said, joining us. "It makes me so happy whenever someone tells us we've made a difference."

"It's a pretty good feeling," I said.

Together, we walked toward the back elevator. I kept my head down and hunched my shoulders, but I'd learned early on that a guy my size draws eyes no matter if he's famous or not. Still, the few people we passed moved along without comment, and I hoped they didn't recognize me or Mom.

We settled into our neighboring rooms upstairs. Mom and Dad showered after their long day of travel while I unpacked my stuff and looked through the menus of the nearby restaurants. I texted Ella to tell her we'd made it safely, and she sent me a smiling emoji in response. I wanted to call her. I wanted to see her. I was nervous about talking to my parents.

My feelings about tomorrow were even bigger than that, almost unquantifiable. Was it so wrong for me to want to lean on Ella just a little? To let her distract me from all of this?

In the end, I decided against calling or FaceTiming her. Instead, I gathered my courage and went to my parents' room and knocked on their door.

"So, about those meds," I said to Mom after Dad let me in.

"I've been on them since the day after Zach, Molly, and Micah's funerals," she answered.

I nodded, thinking back. Try as I might, I couldn't pinpoint behavior changes or signs that might have told me she was struggling. Not ones that couldn't be chalked up to grief or anger. Then again, I'd kept so busy ignoring my own feelings that I might have been blind to everyone else's.

I sat down on the couch in their suite. "I got on mine seven months ago, after nearly having a mental break."

Dad tucked into the chair across from me. "What happened?"

"Did something trigger it?" Mom asked.

I shook my head, turning to her as she sat on the other side of the couch. "Nothing really triggered it. It was more like rock bottom of the downward spiral I'd been on since the accident."

Mom's expression crumpled. "I'm so sorry we didn't know."

I shook my head. "Don't be. It's not your fault. I hid it pretty well."

Dad leaned forward, resting his elbows on his knees. "Is that why you came out here?"

"Yeah," I said. "I had to get away from home. Everywhere I went reminded me of them. I felt like I couldn't move forward or deal with my grief when I was crippled by it just by passing our old high school, or the courts where we played basketball with our friends, or the movie theatre he used to work at."

"I understand," Mom said, her voice quiet. "But I wish you had told us."

I sighed. "I didn't really know how to talk about my emotions. We haven't been great about that, as a family."

She frowned. "That's not fair."

"Klara, it is," Dad said. "When we're happy, sure, but not when we're mad, or sad. I bottle everything up. You get distant. And the boys learned that from us."

Mom sat back and let out a heavy breath. "How do we fix it?"

Dad shrugged. "Simple. We start being honest with each other."

Chapter 19: Ella

*B**en is getting tested today.*

I couldn't think about anything else. I couldn't do anything but worry. I sat in front of my computer, Photoshop open, with the latest draft of the month of January for my wildlife calendar series filling the screen. I hadn't touched the mouse in half an hour.

Sam, my little empath, stood next to me, his head on my leg. I curled my fingers into the fur on his neck, feeling like my grip on him was the only thing holding me together. If I let go, I'd curl up in a ball and start sobbing.

This was terrible. The worst I'd felt since Renee started to go down-hill. And it brought up all of the associated emotions. I was crippled by them. To the point that I recognized I might need some professional help to pull myself out of it.

"Come on, bud," I told Sam.

I paced out into the living room and curled up on the chaise, and Sam bounded up next to me. Fred, right behind him, jumped onto the footrest and sprawled out next to my legs. I opened my phone and checked, for the millionth time, if Ben had been spotted in Boston yet. It looked like no. Thank God. The last thing he needed on top of everything else was the attention of the media.

Feeling only slightly better, I pulled up my sister-in-law's number and hit the call button. It was Saturday, so she shouldn't be working. Not unless a client needed an emergency session.

She answered on the third ring. "Hey there, stranger."

"Sofia?" I said, my voice raw.

"Ella? What's wrong?"

"Can I come over?"

"Of course. Are you okay?"

"No, but I can't get into it over the phone or I'll lose it."

"I understand. Come on over. We're home."

"Thank you so much."

We hung up. I forced myself to stand. I got all the way to the front door and started pulling on my winter gear on before I looked down at myself. When was the last time I showered? The day before Ben left? Had I been wearing these pajamas since that night? I pulled the fabric of my shirt up and smelled it.

Ew.

Sam pressed against my leg and whimpered. I must have looked as bad as I felt.

"I'm okay," I told him, though why I felt the need to lie to my dog about my mental state was beyond me.

I dropped my snow pants and went to shower. I scrubbed myself under the hot water until my skin turned red. Afterward, I pulled on clothes without really looking at them and braided my hair because I didn't have the bandwidth for anything else. Then I was out the door, tugging on my heavy coat as I went. I blasted the heat in the truck while the dogs went pee-poop. It was still frigid in the cab when I pulled out onto the road, but I didn't have the patience to wait any longer.

I forced myself to drive the speed limit to Sophia and Jacob's place: a decent-sized colonial farmhouse down in the valley closer to town.

Snowmen dotted their yard – a sign that the boys had taken full advantage of their recent snow days.

Sophia met me at the door. She wore leggings and a large sweater that swamped her small frame. Her thick, curly hair fell loose around her in perfect ringlets that I'd always been covetous of. Even with copious amounts of hairspray, I could never achieve them. She looked polished and put together. I felt like shit in comparison, guilt at letting myself fall apart warring for dominance with all the other emotions battling it out in the gladiatorial arena that had become my mind.

She reached out and hugged me. "Hi."

"Hi. Thanks again for this."

We pulled apart, and she handed me a couple of towels to clean the dogs off with. The second they were free, they raced past us in search of my nephews.

"You look like hell," she said.

I wasn't insulted. I needed her bluntness right now. "I feel like hell."

Evan came around the corner of the hallway, Fred hot on his heels. "Auntie Ella?" He beamed when he caught sight of me, then started running.

I scooped him up and hugged him to me, trying to keep my tears at bay.

"Are you sick?" he asked when I set him down. "You don't look good."

"Not sick," I said. "Just sad."

He frowned for a second, staring up at me, and then his expression brightened, as though he'd just had a great idea. He turned and raced upstairs.

"What's he doing?" I asked his mom.

Sofia shrugged.

He came back holding his teddy bear and offered it up to me. "Mr. Bear always makes me feel better when I'm sad."

Oh, Jesus.

I reached out and took it. Moisture gathered in my eyes, threatening to spill over. "Thank you so much, Evan."

Sofia leaned down and kissed him on the forehead. "You are so sweet to share Mr. Bear with Auntie Ella."

He kissed her back, then turned and headed into the house.

"Come on. I have ice cream," she told me.

We walked down the long hallway to the kitchen, pausing by the living room so I could say hi to Michael, who sprawled out on the floor, playing with Sam, while his brother and Fred crowded together in an armchair watching cartoons.

Sofia's phone rang from the kitchen island as she pulled the freezer open. She turned to pick it up and answered in Italian. It must have been her mother. She was the only person I'd heard her speak nothing but Italian to. With her sisters, it was usually a mix of Italian and English. With her dad, straight English.

They chatted for several minutes while Sofia found bowls and spoons for the two of us and then scooped us out healthy dollops of Cherry Garcia.

"How's Ma Trocci?" I asked after she hung up.

"Better now that Bernadetta is back at home to help with the bills."

"She's your youngest sister, right? The math whiz?"

Sophia nodded. "The place she interned with just offered her a job. It's some high-end wealth management firm in Boston, so she should be able to start making some headway in her student debt."

"I thought she had all those scholarships."

"She did," she told me, pausing to take a bite of ice cream. "But Harvard is still outrageously expensive, and they didn't cover all her costs. At least she was smart enough to take up our parents' offer to live with them for a while. Renting a decent place in Boston is almost as expensive as New York, and she couldn't swing that while also paying off her loans, even with the healthy salary she's now making."

We were quiet for a few minutes as we tucked into our ice cream. I stared down into mine like it could solve all my problems. Maybe it could. A food coma sounded good right now.

"What's going on, Ella?" Sophia asked. "I don't think I've seen you this down since Renee passed."

"Can I ask you not to repeat this to the family?"

"I'll give you full client privilege."

"You remember me talking about my friend Stan at Jacob's going away?"

She nodded.

"Well, he has some past head trauma and is having tests done today to see if he might have signs of Chronic Traumatic Encephalopathy."

Her eyes widened. "Oh, damn."

"Yeah."

"Is the threat of chronic illness bringing up all those memories of Renee and your grandpa?"

I nodded.

"He's not just a friend, is he? You two are romantically involved?"

Her intuition was so next level that when we first met, I thought she was psychic. "Very recently."

"Okay, so what are you hoping for here? Do you want me to help you sort through all these feelings?"

"Please," I said, my tone skirting the line of begging.

"The first step is acknowledging them. Tell me what you feel."

"I'm terrified that the tests might come back positive. And I keep going worst-case scenario with it."

She set her ice cream bowl in the sink. "What is the worst-case scenario?"

"That he has scarring, that he has tons of abnormal proteins, and that his brain is already showing signs of deterioration. It kills me to think of this sweet, generous, caring man having uncontrollable outbursts, or becoming violent, or suffering from memory loss, or..." I leaned forward, head in my hands.

"It's okay," Sophia said, coming over to hug me while I cried.

"And I also feel like an asshole. Like, how do I have any right to be so torn up over this when I'm not even the one going through it?"

She pulled away. "You really like him, don't you?"

"Yeah," I told her.

"Ella, look at me."

I craned my head sideways.

She cupped my cheeks and met my eyes, her own full of empathy. "Your feelings are valid. Your feelings matter. If Jacob were going through the same thing as Stan, I would be doing the emotional equivalent of shitting myself. The threat of a chronic, debilitating illness is terrifying. It's okay to be afraid for him. It doesn't mean that you're putting your fear above his in any way."

"But-"

She let me go and shook her head. "No buts here. Feel the emotions. If you try to suppress them, you'll only make things worse for yourself. I'm a professional here; I think I know what I'm talking about."

I grabbed a napkin from the countertop and blotted at my face. "Right. You're right."

"You don't always have to be strong for everyone, you know. You don't always have to be happy, bubbly Ella."

"I know that," I said on reflex.

"Do you? Because whenever I see you sad or angry, you apologize for it."

I paused, mulling over her words. "Do I really do that?"

"Yes. And whenever someone you care about is sad or angry, instead of talking about it with them, you bend over backward to find some way to distract them or make them laugh."

Megan's comment from Christmas Eve sprang to my mind. The one that alluded to me having a savior complex. Was she right? Was Sophia? I looked back at my interactions with Ben. A troubling pattern began to emerge. He told me about the Commissioner of the USFL, and I cracked a joke about an egg account. He was clearly struggling New Year's Eve, and I made a fool out of myself for him. And then there was the day he told me he was getting tested.

"I think it's why you can't be around your mom much this time of year," Sophia said. "You know that no amount of joking or self-deprecation can pull her out of it for more than a few minutes."

"Can we please not talk about Mom right now?" I asked. "I'm already sad. I don't want to be pissed off too."

"I understand."

Unable to stop myself, I said, "Have you seen her lately?"

Sophia nodded.

"How is she?"

"Same as she always is this time of year. She still refuses to listen to your father or me."

I raked my hands through my hair. "How do I...how do I stop doing this? Feeling like I need to save everyone?"

She pulled up her phone. "I can send you a list of emotional exercises I think will help, but you may want to talk to someone other than me about this."

"And my sociopathic ability to read people?"

She shot me a grin. "I was kidding about that."

I stared at her. "Sophia! I've been freaking out over it."

She chuckled. "Sorry. I thought you knew how to take a joke."

I glared at her. My phone dinged with an incoming email. I looked down to see she'd sent me a rather large PDF file. My glare disappeared. "Thank you for this."

"You're welcome. Let me know if you have questions about the exercises or want help with them."

"I will."

"Right now, I think we need to focus on your path forward through this current situation," she said. "You need to feel these emotions. But with balance. If you start to get overwhelmed, like you clearly were when you got here, stop whatever you're doing. Get up and do some jumping jacks, take the dogs outside, or even watch a bunch of videos of people doing dumb things on YouTube. Distraction techniques can be really beneficial in the short term."

"Okay."

"When you're able to, go all the way to the end of that worst-case scenario."

I reached out and grabbed Mr. Bear off the counter, clinging to him like a shield.

Sophia caught sight of my expression and softened her tone. "It doesn't have to be today, or even tomorrow. But Ella? You need to chase that path, and instead of dwelling on how horrible it will be, find solutions. Say he might have memory loss. You could search for some brain exercises that have proven effective for Alzheimer's patients. Things like that."

"I...I think I can manage that."

"I think so too. You're a helper. You have been for as long as I've known you. That desire to take action, to do something to make things better is your best ally right now. Especially after Stan's diagnosis. However it turns out."

"Are there ways I can help him in the short term?" I asked.

She nodded. "There are. One way is to encourage him to feel whatever losses he might have. Loss is like a wound, and grief can be considered the healing element. The bigger his loss, the longer it might take for him to heal, so expect him to be down for a while."

I chewed my bottom lip for a minute. "So, he has depression and anxiety. Could heavy grief be dangerous for him?"

"You mean could it make him suicidal?"

Oh, God. "Yes."

"It might, Ella. There's really no way to tell. Everyone is different. But yes, I'd say the chance is higher. Does he have a therapist?"

"He does. And he told me that during his lower points, he talks to him every day."

She nodded. "That's good. He should stick tight to that. His therapist might adjust the dosage of any medications he may be on too, which might alter his mood in the short term. Does he have anyone with him right now? He probably shouldn't be alone either."

"His parents are with him."

"He might need them to stay for a while," she said. "With brain injuries, as with diseases like cancer, there can be a lot of collateral loss. Like the financial burden of medical bills, the inability to trust yourself in social situations, or not being able to work or drive. These will be future losses for him, things his doctors will eventually tell him he has to consider, which can cause something called anticipatory grief."

"Anticipatory grief? I've never even heard of that."

Her expression softened. "Renee went so quickly after her diagnosis that there wasn't really time for me to bring it up with you. Basically, once Stan's initial grief is over, he'll have all these microcosms of it. The important thing is to keep to the same process of healing. He needs to allow himself to feel each potential loss ahead of time and accept the reality of it. This will really help him when it comes time to actually experience the loss. And he needs to realize that he'll have setbacks. That some days he might feel fine, and then the next he can't get out of bed because he's so sad."

"Is there anything I can do to help him with that?"

"You might experience it right along with him," she said. "Apply the same techniques to your own emotions. Grieve, accept the potential loss, and, for you, find a way to help him do the same. Whether that's as simple as staying with him on his bad days, or encouraging him to feel his emotions. Men often struggle most with that."

"Okay. Thank you so much for this."

She reached for her phone again. "You're welcome. Here, I have some more exercises for you. And some links if you get stuck and can't reach me for whatever reason."

My own phone dinged several times from beside me.

"Do you have anything to help me through the next few days while I wait to hear from him about his results?" I asked her.

She arched a brow. "I got some horse tranquilizers I could douse you with. Put you under for at least 48 hours."

"I can't tell if you're joking or not, but if you're not, yes, please."

She grinned. "You knew I was joking. Okay, so here's what I'd recommend..."

We talked until I ran out of questions. When we were done, she invited me to stay for the rest of the afternoon. We huddled together for a long time in the kitchen and planned out Jacob's welcome home party. When the sun finally broke through the clouds, we shoved ourselves into our snow gear and went out to add another snowman to the village cluttering up their front yard. Afterward, I read a sleepy

Evan his favorite book. He conked out on the couch halfway through the third chapter. Michael and I sat close by him on the living room floor and played a few quiet rounds of Mario Kart on Jacob's old game console. Michael kicked my ass, the little game shark. Later, I helped Sofia make her mother's recipe for *pasta fazool,* and she taught me some Italian while we worked – mostly swear words, which she insisted were the best introduction into any language.

I left her house feeling much better than I when I'd arrived. When I got home, I sunk down onto the couch, let myself be terrified until I couldn't take it anymore, and then pulled up the YouTube channel for a vocal competition and watched all of the auditions.

I went to bed earlier than normal, worn out from the emotional rollercoaster I'd been stuck on the past few days.

I fell asleep thinking about Ben.

And woke up to what seemed like a nightmare.

Chapter 20: Ben

Mom stared down at me while two lab assistants positioned my legs on a PET scan table, concern etched into her features. "How you doing, Benny?"

"About how you'd think," I answered.

She gripped my hand and stayed there with me until they told her she needed to go stand behind the glass like everyone else.

"I'll be right over there with your father," she said, leaning down to hug me.

I couldn't really return the gesture, what with my head being held in place by pieces of foam and my chest strapped down to keep me from moving during the scan.

"Okay," I said.

She left, and I was alone in the room.

What a fucking day. I woke up exhausted, having barely slept. My parents and I had stayed up until almost midnight, saying all of the things that we should have over the past two years. How Mom and I both hid our depression, how it affected us. How we should have been better at sharing our grief and our fears with each other. How we should have talked over our frustrations with each other for hiding things, for pushing too much, or for pulling away.

Was it a perfect conversation in which we resolved all of our issues? Nope. At points, we argued. We yelled. Mom cried. Dad stalked out of the room. I nearly punched a wall. It was awkward and uncomfortable and at times fucking painful. But it needed to happen. We were all better for it now.

Even though we had more shit to unpack and work through – likely with the help of a therapist – I already noticed a difference. I didn't hide my early morning phone call to Brian from them. Mom and Dad hadn't hidden their fear from me throughout the day. They'd butted in to ask the specialists questions until they felt like they had a better understanding of the tests and what to expect from the results.

I checked into the clinic at 9 a.m. and met with what seemed like half their staff of doctors. We reviewed the entire battery of tests I needed. They went over the costs in great detail, including what my medical policy would pay for and what it wouldn't. Thank fuck I'd invested my USFL money well, because even with most of the bill covered by insurance, I was still going to be out of pocket a large sum. After agreeing to undergo all of the recommended tests, I signed more paperwork than I had to buy my house.

And then it began. First up were the cognitive tests. Math. Essays. Comprehension. Recall. They started simple enough and then got progressively harder, until I felt like I was back in college, which I guess was the point since they were trying to gauge my memory and reasoning.

Next came a barrage of physiological exams. They tested my balance, fine motor skills, and even my nerve responses. I ran on a treadmill for a while with about a hundred sensors strapped to my body and a breathing tube taped over my mouth.

"Just relax," they said.

"You ever tried running with a fucking breathing tube?" I tried to yell back. It came out garbled. Probably for the best.

Afterward, they moved on to emotional tests. They pushed and prodded at me to make me sad, and then angry. I still think it was unethical to have me watch Zach and Molly's first dance at their wedding while instruments read my brain waves. What right did these strangers have to my grief? And did the fact that I got sad and also pissed register on their test? Was that an expected emotional response to something like that, or would it count as a mark against me?

That I didn't know the answer and they wouldn't tell me when I asked wasn't helping my current mental state, which was completely trashed thanks to the shitshow that unfolded during our lunch break. I got a phone call from my publicist halfway through my meal. Someone had taken a picture of me walking into the clinic, and it had already been picked up by a local news channel. She was in full-blown damage control now, circulating a story that my parents and I were here to inspect the clinic in relation to the charity. That we were considering donating to it and wanted to see what tests they could conduct here, etc, etc.

It didn't matter. I knew how this circus went. A national news outlet would pick it up soon. Celebrity gossip mongers would have one take, the mainstream media another, and the suits running the sports networks would probably scramble to put together an entire panel of football commentators to pour over why I was here and whether or not they should believe the story they'd been fed.

I hadn't needed Mom to point out the fact that being a recluse up to this point wouldn't help me out at all. But she had, in an *I told you so* kind of way that made my usually cool-as-a-cucumber father snap at her.

We were all pretty close to our breaking point.

It was almost a relief to get away from them this afternoon, aside from the fact that it was only because I'd spent the past several hours in scanners. The MRI came first. They didn't like the results of the inconclusive one I had after Zach died and decided to re-do it with their own specialist. Then there was the two-hour CT scan where they imaged my entire brain.

The one I was getting ready for now was the last test of the day, the new one I'd told Ella about that might render all of the others moot. Before getting strapped in, a nurse had injected me with a radioactive tracer – which I hoped wouldn't give me cancer further down the road. Now I got to lay here for another couple of hours without moving, while my future was unveiled to the watching doctors.

"Here we go, Ben," a woman's voice said over the speakers. "Remember, try not to move."

"Got it, Dr. Souza," I told her.

The table I rested on moved, sliding me into a tunnel so narrow that my shoulders brushed the sides. Good thing I didn't suffer from claustrophobia or the stress of today might have reached heart attack levels. I still experienced a slight moment of panic when the table came to a stop. No one likes to feel trapped. Deep breaths saw me to the other side of it, and I tried my best to relax while the sound of machinery started up around me.

Dr. Souza had been great about explaining this one to my parents. She went into a lot of detail about how the tracer they injected me with worked by bonding to the abnormal tau protein that leads to both CTE and Alzheimer's. The key difference in how the diseases manifested was that in the former, the tangles of tau usually appeared around small blood vessels and rarely formed beta-amyloid plaques, which was what could make this test so critical for suspected cases of

CTE. If I had any of those tangles in my brain, they should light up like Christmas trees in the scans.

Please, God, don't let my brain light up like a Christmas tree.

Time passed slowly in the tube. The seconds felt like full minutes, the minutes like hours, and the hours like small eternities. Soon, I lost track of them. Had I been in this thing for twenty minutes? Forty? Three hours? I couldn't tell anymore.

I tried to focus on the clicks and beeps and whirs of the machine's components to distract myself. It worked for a little while. And then the anger of being outed by someone with a smartphone returned. I told myself to let it go. To stay calm. That there was no way that person could have known what I was doing here. That if they had, they wouldn't have taken the picture.

Brian taught me this technique of rationalizing and empathizing with people and their choices to keep from getting angry. It wasn't really working right now. Because no matter who took the goddamn picture or for what reason, the last thing I needed was media attention while trying to get through this.

I could just imagine the crowd that would gather outside when the story broke, the questions they would hurl at me as I exited the building later. Maybe the clinic had a back door or a garage I could escape through. Who knew what my mental state would be like then? I'd hate to lose my shit, punch someone, and make all of this worse.

I turned my thoughts to Ella to try and calm myself down. I was so used to talking to her every day that it felt weird that we hadn't spoken. Several times I'd had the urge to text her updates just to keep her in the loop. But what would be the point?

Hi, Ella. I had to take a math test. Without a calculator.

She'd just worry. Or try to make me smile by responding with, *That is cruel and unusual punishment! What sort of cockamamie hospital are you at???*

I hoped she was doing okay, that she'd found some way to deal with her own worry and stress. During my phone call with Brian this morning, he'd actually encouraged me to use her as a crutch if the tests came back with bad news. Told me that her humor and her teasing would be good distractions in the face of a CTE diagnosis.

I just...

I still didn't know if I could do that to her.

He'd been the only one to witness my lowest points. I didn't want to drag her down with me. She should be free and happy and unencumbered by an attachment to a man that might one day develop an explosive temper. Or lose his way while driving and terrify her when a search party had to be called out. I'd seen those silver alerts for seniors with Alzheimer's. CTE could have the same effect.

"All done, Ben," Dr. Souza said over the speakers.

Shit. So soon? Once we finished here, they were going to go over all of my results and then sit me down for a consultation. I wasn't fucking ready for that yet. Wasn't there another test they could do? Some way to delay this a little longer?

"You okay, Ben? Your vitals are spiking," Dr. Souza said.

"Get me out of this fucking coffin," I growled.

My breaths were ragged, a familiar weight settling on my chest that I couldn't seem to push off. A panic attack threatened.

"Get him out!" Mom yelled.

The table beneath me whirred to life and began to slide out of the tube. My arms trembled from the effort to keep still. As soon as I had enough room, I started pulling sensors off of my arms. A lab tech hurried in and undid my restraints.

"Thank you," I told him, sitting up.

"No problem. I get it."

Do you? I wanted to shout in his face. How could he possibly get it?

Mom shoved through the door and rushed over to me. She wore open fear on her face. What had she heard the doctors saying?

"Just give me a minute," I told her.

I jumped off the table. I needed out of this room. Out of this place. But I couldn't leave, because the fucking paparazzi were probably parked outside. Instead, I escaped to a back hallway with windows that faced the Charles River. The city of Boston spread out before me, the roofs of the low buildings covered in snow, the skyscrapers glittering like jewels in the sunshine.

Dad followed after me, leaning a shoulder against the wall as I paced. He didn't say anything, just stood there, offering me the steady strength of his presence and turning away anyone else that tried to join us. Including Mom.

"I'll pay for that one later," he said.

I paused to look at him. He was tall, still broad like me, though his middle had softened in his retirement. Three years ago, his hair was as long as mine, but it was thinning some around his face, and he'd decided to cut it. It was hard to look at him now. Because Zach had kept his hair short. His skin had been almost as dark as Dad's. He'd had the same nose, nearly black eyes, rounded cheeks, and slight indentation in his chin. If you compared pictures of them from the same ages, they looked like twins. Seeing Dad now was like seeing the ghost of my brother. Of what he might have looked like if CTE hadn't stolen him from us.

Dad's eyes were pinched, brow creased in worry. What was this like for him and Mom? Waiting to find out if your surviving son might share the same fate as the one you'd already buried seemed like cruel and unusual punishment.

I walked over and hugged him, hard. He squeezed me back. When I pulled away, there were tears in his eyes.

"Whatever happens, Benny, your mom and I are here for you," he said, clasping my shoulders.

"I know Dad, thank you."

"And we -" His eyes snapped to something over my shoulder. "Shit," he said. He never swore. I started to follow his gaze, but he used his grip to keep me facing him. "Don't look. Keep your head turned and walk back down the hall through the doors."

"Is someone outside with a camera?" I asked, a slow, steady rage beginning to build within me. We were on the first floor, and with these huge windows, it would be easy for them to film us. They might have caught that whole exchange. They might have been close enough to see my dad crying.

He knew better than to lie to me. "Yes."

"Still frame or a video recorder?"

"Big TV style camera."

I stiffened in his grip. "I'll fucking kill them."

"No, you won't. That will only make things worse. Come on." He threw an arm over my shoulders and dragged me away, careful to shield me with his body.

We hid out in Dr. Souza's office while the clinic's security dealt with the cameraman. It was a small, tidy space with a desk, a computer, several filing cabinets, and enough chairs to go around. Mom and Dad spoke with my publicist while I sat in the corner with my head leaned back against the wall, trying to keep myself together.

An hour later, Dr. Souza joined us. She was a short, compact Latina woman who spoke with an authority and efficiency that had made me instantly trust her. She was also detached, clinical, and very obviously a scientist more than a doctor. I was glad it was her giving us my results. I couldn't take the looks of pity and empathy I'd seen from some of her peers.

"Your memory results aren't what we'd hope for in a man of your age," she said.

"What does that mean?" Mom asked.

Dr. Souza looked at me as she answered. "My colleague, Dr. Baptiste would like to speak to you further when we're done here, to go into greater detail about each reading and talk about treatment options. The good news is that your comprehension and reasoning are well within the expected range."

"Any other good news?" I asked.

She nodded. "Physiologically, you're fit as a fiddle. We detected no loss of balance or cardiovascular anomalies, and you have good blood flow through your brain when exerting yourself."

Was that it? Was that really the only good news she had for me?

She turned to her desk and picked up a folder. "The way you responded to the emotional stimuli does give us some small cause for concern," she said, turning back to us. "The speed with which you became angry indicates that your flashpoints are much lower than we would like, but the fact that you didn't lash out when angered does show promise. We still recommend behavioral therapy."

"On top of the therapist I'm already seeing?" I asked.

"Yes." She opened the folder and handed my parents and me a stapled stack of paper each.

I glanced down and caught a few of the headings on the first page: Withdraw, Distract, Reorient, and Reassure.

Mom tried to take my hand, but I put it on my knee instead, worried that I might accidentally break her fingers if I squeezed too hard.

"I won't beat around the bush with you," Dr. Souza said. "The MRI and CT scans show signs of past concussions and traumatic brain injury."

It felt like she'd punched me. I dropped the stack of papers and leaned over, elbows on my knees. Dad reached out and put his hand on my shoulder.

"The PET scan highlighted tau clusters," Dr. Souza told us. "They're not as dramatic as a lot of the other cases we've seen, but they're there, and in areas of the brain that would explain your severe bouts of depression and anxiety."

What she was telling me was that at 28 I was already showing symptoms of CTE.

Beside me, Mom began to sob.

I just sat there, looking down at the crack in the tile beneath my feet, not really seeing it. Not really feeling anything. A numbness had settled into me. Because this was worst-case scenario.

My life as I'd known it was fucking over. The happy, goofy, trusting kid I'd been was gone forever, and God knew what kind of man CTE would turn me into.

Chapter 21: Ella

"Oh my God," I whispered, my hand over my mouth as I stared down at my phone.

Across its screen splashed a series of photos of Ben and Hani in a hallway of the rehabilitation center in Boston where he'd had his testing done. In one, they hugged. In the next, Hani was crying. And then the final one showed him leading his son away as though he had to physically support him. They were still shots from a video. I pulled it up, fingers shaking as it played out. By the time it ended, I was crying.

Oh, no. Oh, no. Oh, no.

The story was from six o'clock last night. What time had I fallen asleep to have missed this? I read through the accompanying article in a near panic, my eyes flying over the screen as I tried to keep from fearing the worst. It became apparent quite quickly that the writer didn't really know anything, that they were only jumping to the same conclusions that I was based on how upset Ben and his dad looked.

I clicked on another link, and then another and another, until I found the story that started it all. A smaller Boston news channel first broke the news that Ben was at the clinic. No wonder I had missed it. The piece was pretty neutral, citing Ben's PR rep and her statement that Ben and his parents were visiting the clinic because of their charity.

I read several more stories, searching for answers that no one seemed to have. Eventually I landed on a YouTube video from the biggest sports network in the country. Six large men in suits sat around a half-moon table discussing Ben's absence from the limelight, his appearance at the clinic, and how they didn't believe his PR rep. Not after the photos of him and his dad surfaced. The panel was split between empathy and dislike. Some of them sided with the league against Ben and all the "trouble" he'd made for the sport, while others defended him. The round table erupted into argument toward the end, and, God, it was so ugly.

I set my phone down before I broke it.

Sam whimpered from beside me on the bed and scooted a little closer. I threw my arms around his neck and hugged him. I hated those men. I hated them all. Even the ones on Ben's side. Because they had agreed to go on national television and have this debate about him in the first place. How dare they do this to him? How could they treat a fellow player, *hell*, a fellow human like this when all he'd ever wanted was to make things safer for other people?

My phone rang. I let go of Sam and scrambled to pick it up, praying it was Ben. It was Jane.

"Hi," I said.

"Holy shit, Ella. I called you three times last night. Where have you been?"

"I slept through it. Sorry, I was exhausted."

"Did you see the news?"

"Yeah."

"The story I wrote is being published tomorrow."

My fingers tightened on my phone. "What?"

"I'm sorry. I can't call the editor and ask him to postpone it again. He'll know something's up. He's a reporter, after all. And he wouldn't do it even if I begged. The timing is too perfect for him to delay."

"Do you think it's going to make this worse?" I asked, voice small.

Jane sighed. "Yes. Because with Ben already in the spotlight, it'll probably turn the ongoing media frenzy into a dogpile."

"I don't know whether or not I should warn him."

"Does he have CTE?"

"I don't know. I haven't heard from him yet. Either way, this is horrible timing. I don't want to make him more stressed than he already is. But would knowing this is coming ahead of time be better? Or is he so out of it that there's a chance he might miss it completely?"

"I'm sorry, Ella. I don't know what to tell you. The article wasn't supposed to be published until Thursday, but they want to jump on the bandwagon and put it out there while the story is relevant to current headlines."

I had to take several deep breaths before responding. "Sometimes I fucking hate the kind of people you work with."

"Trust me, so do I. Again, I'm so sorry. Can I do anything else? Do you need anything?"

"I don't think so..." I began, then changed my mind. "Actually, yes. Come help me get these open orders done. I'm closing down the shop for a while." I needed to be ready to drop everything in case Ben called.

"I'll be there in thirty," she told me.

We hung up. I checked my other messages. Nothing from Ben. I tried not to panic.

Jane pulled into my driveway just as the sun broke over the mountains. Together, we printed and put together my open orders, carefully packaged them, and put them into boxes and mailers. She ran them to the post office for me on her way home while I went through the long process of putting all my storefronts on vacation mode.

And then I waited for Ben to call.

One day passed. Nothing.

Day two, the media frenzy over Jane's story hit. It was so bad I had to delete my news apps.

Ben still didn't call.

Three days passed. I applied distraction techniques to keep my mind occupied. I bundled up and took the dogs snowshoeing, careful not to overdo it this time.

I'd read a study a while back about how two hours a day in nature could cure you of everything, and while I thought that was a bit inflated, it definitely helped me a little. Once I was back inside, I got a fire going and focused on staying positive. I read articles about young engineers solving the world's problems. A kid still in high school discovered plastic-eating bacteria that might clean up our oceans. Another found you could kill the invasive kudzu vines eating the entire south using helium.

Four days passed. Not even those feel-good articles or exercise helped my mood. I broke down and called Jack.

"Is he home?" I asked.

"He is, kiddo," Jack answered. "But I only know because his dad came by to tell me when they got back from Boston yesterday. I still have the dogs, so I'm guessing they're a little preoccupied."

"How did Hani seem?"

Jack was quiet for a while before answering. "Not good, kiddo. I'd get ready to hear some bad news."

My panic became a living, breathing thing. I could feel its fingers digging into my chest, searching for my heart. It whispered terrible things to me, giving voice to all of my greatest fears.

Five days passed without word from Ben.

I read and re-read every PDF Sophia sent me. I applied *all* of the techniques she suggested to help me cope with the emotional storm that raged inside of me.

A whole week went by.

On day eight, I got a text.

Ella, this is Hani. Are you able to come to Ben's?

On my way, I texted back.

I was out of the door in a flash.

I'd been ready for this. Had prayed for this. A bag with a week's worth of clothes sat on the passenger seat of my truck. Anabel was going to watch my place and the dogs for me while I was gone. Mom and Dad told her no boys. I told her just don't have sex in my bed.

I texted her as the truck warmed up.

Be right over, she texted back.

What?! Don't you have school?

It's Saturday.

Oh. Sorry.

God, I was out of it.

Just in case it took her some time to get here, I let the dogs out to go to the bathroom. When they were all cleaned up and back inside, I hugged and kissed them both before telling them to be good for Auntie Anabel.

And then I was off, locking the door and sprinting back to my truck. I forced myself to drive slowly. It had snowed again last night, and I was so emotional and exhausted that I didn't trust myself on the slushy mess the roads had turned into. It took me an eternity to get to Ben's. I yanked my keys out of the ignition as soon as I rolled to a stop and then ran up to the front door.

Ben's father opened it, almost as tall as his son. His face was drawn, his clothes rumpled like he'd been wearing them for a few days.

"Hi," I said.

He opened the door wider to let me in. "Thank you for coming over."

His voice was quiet, so I lowered my own. "You're welcome. What do you need?"

"We're running low on food."

I followed him to the kitchen, keeping my million and one questions to myself. Because priorities.

He stopped at the island counter and turned to face me. "Ben and Klara are both sleeping."

I nodded, not trusting my voice to hold out if I spoke. It was the middle of the day. They were both asleep. Not a good sign. Especially when added to the fact that now we were in better light, it looked like Hani hadn't slept at all. His dark eyes were bloodshot. His face had an ashen hue to it. All traces of the laughter that I'd once seen in his eyes was gone.

Together, we wrote out a shopping list.

Deep breaths, I told myself as I climbed back into my truck. *Don't jump to conclusions.*

Maybe they were just emotionally exhausted. Maybe they were recovering from the buildup of stress leading to the tests. Maybe this was how Ben and Klara and Hani manifested relief.

But I didn't really believe any of that. I was just shoving the lies down my throat to keep it together while I bought milk and bread and eggs and all the other essentials.

Like always, I ran into several people I knew at the store. One was a high school friend of mine who was back in town to visit her folks. She held me hostage for several long minutes in aisle seven as she caught me up on all the latest drama of her big city life. I nodded along, impatiently, praying for her to just shut up.

I hightailed it out of there afterward, flat-out ignoring whoever it was that called my name in the parking lot.

Hani helped me unload the groceries when I got back to Ben's, his movements slow and lethargic like he was sleepwalking. I was putting the bread in a cupboard when I saw him pause out of the corner of my eye. He stood in front of the fridge, holding the milk, staring at a photo of Ben and Zach stuck to its door. The fingers of his free hand shook as he placed it over the picture. He bowed his head, shoulders heaving as he started to cry.

I couldn't lie to myself anymore. This was what full-blown grief looked like.

I stepped forward and placed a hand on his shoulder, remaining quite but present, letting him know that at least he wasn't alone.

He straightened back up after a few minutes, wiping at his face. "I'm sorry."

"There is absolutely no need to apologize to me."

"Thank you for coming."

"I can stay as long as you need. My schedule is clear."

He hesitated. "I don't want to impose."

"You wouldn't be. Really. I'd rather be here doing something to help you than freaking out by myself at home."

Hani's face crumpled. "It's bad, Ella."

Oh, God. Deep breaths.

"I thought it might be."

"Did he tell you about the tests?"

I nodded.

"They found tau tangles in his brain. Enough that they think it was complicating his depression and anxiety."

I managed to get myself to one of the kitchen barstools before my knees gave out. I was still nodding. Why couldn't I stop nodding?

"And maybe his memory and emotions," Hani added.

I leaned forward, elbows on the island, and squeezed my eyes shut to keep the tears in.

Ben.

It was Hani's turn to place a hand on my shoulder. "He and Klara...they're not doing too well right now."

I took a shuddering breath and pushed it down. All my grief, my rage, my fear. I bundled them together and dropped them into the same deep, dark hole I used to hide my crush monster in. Later, I could let them out, but right now, Hani needed me. Ben and Klara needed me.

My emotions safely stowed away, I sat up, scrubbed at my eyes, and looked over at Hani. "Has Ben been talking to Brian?"

"Every day. I make sure of it." He paused for a few heartbeats, voice softening. "I took his phone from him when the Times published their story."

"My sister feels terrible about that," I said. "They pushed it up, and she didn't think she could delay it again without making people suspicious."

"It's not her fault. Ben doesn't regret helping out. But, even without knowing Ben was their source, the media has been brutal, and people on social media have been..." He clenched his jaw, fists braced on the countertop as his face darkened with anger.

"I know," I said. "I've been watching it all unfold, checking up on his Twitter mentions to stay aware of public opinion."

"His publicist thinks it's time to hire people to manage his accounts for him."

"That sounds like a good idea."

Hani nodded, wiping a hand over his face. He looked utterly exhausted.

"Do you want to take a break for a while?" I asked. "I can hold down the fort, clean up, get some meals prepped and in the freezer for you to reheat later."

He nodded. "Thank you, Ella."

"You're welcome."

He patted me on the shoulder and moved toward the hallway. At the door, he paused and turned back. "I'm glad you're here. I'm glad Benny has someone like you in his life. That you've been here for him when we couldn't be. I hope you stick around through this."

I nodded at him, afraid to speak.

He turned and shuffled away. I listened to him climb the staircase. I waited as the floorboards creaked on the landing. Upstairs, a bedroom door closed, and I let go. The tears I'd held at bay sprang to my eyes and slid down my cheeks. I folded my arms on the countertop and buried my face in them to muffle my sobs.

Ben. Oh, God, Ben.

I cried so hard that I started to feel nauseous, something I hadn't done since I was a child. All my preparation for a worst-case scenario felt useless in the face of his diagnosis. Because I'd never really given up hope. Even in my worst moments, that tiny spark of light had remained, guiding me on. Now it was snuffed out, and I was left bereft in a sea of darkness.

Enough, I finally told myself.

I stood. Tears still streaked from my eyes, but I forced myself to work through them. First, I finished unloading the rest of the groceries. Then I saw to the dishes in the sink, loading the dishwasher and hitting run while the pots and pans dried on the towels I'd spread over the counter. I went to the broom closet and swept the entire first floor.

Scrubbed the bathroom down. Took out the trash. Got the pellet stove going in the basement. Lit a fire in the sitting room.

I worked for three hours straight without hearing a sound from anyone else in the house. It was like I was there by myself. Darkness started to fall, and I returned to the kitchen. I pulled up a recipe app and searched through the contents of the kitchen, finding all of the ingredients for a huge pot of chicken soup. While it cooled, I got started in on a hearty beef stew. The meal prep served as a good distraction. Chopping, dicing, straining, stirring, measuring – these things forced my focus. As the broth for the stew simmered, I poured out the chicken soup into smaller glass jars, then snapped the lids on and stacked them in the freezer.

Hani ambled back into the kitchen just as the timer for the stew went off. "Smells good. Can I help with anything?"

"Nope," I told him. "Did you want some?"

"Yes, please."

He tucked his large frame down onto one of the barstools, and I ladled him out a bowl.

"When was the last time Ben and Klara ate?" I asked.

"Breakfast," he answered in between spoonfuls. "I can take some to Klara when I'm done." He looked up at me then. "Do you want to take Ben his?"

Did I? Was I strong enough to hold myself together in front of him right now? Did I even need to hold myself together in front of him right now?

"I do," I made myself say.

Hani finished his stew, and I handed him a second bowl to take to his wife. I ladled out another for Ben, and set it aside for a minute to pour the remaining contents of the pot into freezer containers and pop them in next to the chicken soup. Then I gathered my courage and headed upstairs, pausing outside his door.

No sound came from within, so I knocked. "Ben? It's Ella."

"Come in," he answered.

I took a deep breath and opened the door. The room was pitch black and smelled kind of like a bear den: musky, a little sour.

"Hang on," he said, voice low and hoarse.

His nightstand light clicked on, illuminating his bedroom. Clothes littered the floor. His comforter was half off the bed. The sheets twisted around his legs. He was shirtless, his skin looking three shades lighter than the last time I had seen him. There were dark circles under his eyes, and his hair was a mane of tangled curls.

His bloodshot eyes met mine. "Ella."

My heart broke at the sound of so much loss and grief packed so tightly into my name. I shut the door behind me, set the soup on his dresser, and went to him.

He reached out and pulled me down onto the bed, hugging me tight to his chest.

"I'm sorry, Ben. I'm so fucking sorry," I told him, helpless to stop my tears.

He shook beneath me, pulling me closer. "Stay with me?"

"Of course I'll stay."

Chapter 22: Ben

When I asked Ella to stay, I meant for a few minutes. An hour, at most. How many days had she been here with me now, in this bedroom, trapped with my grief? Three? They were mostly a blur. I'd spent a lot of that time sleeping, I think. Or so out of it that I might as well have been unconscious.

I ate when she told me to eat. Got up and into the shower when she urged me to. I even managed to help her change the sheets once or twice. My sessions with Brian were the only other points of memory over the past few days. Or was I into weeks now? How long had it been since I'd left the clinic in Boston?

Beside me, Ella shifted. It was the middle of the night; of that I was sure. Darkness bathed the room in shadows, and the only light source was the neon glow from the clock on my nightstand. It read 1:45.

I planted my hands on the bed and pushed myself up, the sheets falling to my waist as I rested my back against the padded headboard. Ella, sensing movement, rolled toward me. The clock provided just enough illumination that I saw her hand reach out as if in search of me. Her fingers brushed against the fabric of my boxers, and she sighed in her sleep and snuggled closer, snaking an arm over my lap and draping a long leg over my own. She nuzzled her nose into the skin at my waist and sighed again, breathing deeply, her face a mask of contentedness.

I reached down and ran my fingers through her hair. How could I ever thank her for being here like this? For acting as my lifeline? Even though I'd been out of it, she'd helped. With her here, the loneliness abated. The crushing grief eased a little. Waking up to feel her beside me, to be able to roll over and curve myself around her, to have her cling to me as though she could hold me together through sheer willpower alone, had done more for me than I could have ever imagined.

Brian was right. I needed her. And not just to use as a crutch or a distraction. But was it fair to need her like this? To ask her to be with someone like me? A man who might lose himself to a debilitating disease? These thoughts left me feeling unsettled and...guilty. Like I'd still be using her, or lying to her somehow, or unworthy of her.

You are worthy, I reminded myself, the words sounding out in Brian's voice. How many times had he told me that? How many more would it take until I actually felt like I was?

I brushed a few loose strands of hair back from Ella's face, and she shifted again, hugging me closer.

"Mmm," she murmured. "That feels nice."

I clung to her words and continued to run my fingers through her hair, wanting to keep making her feel good, like I could somehow pay her back for everything she'd done for me the past few days – or was it weeks?

She turned her head toward me, eyes still closed, lips curling into a lazy smile. "I was having the best dream."

"Yeah?" I asked, voice raw from disuse.

"Mmhmm. We were in Hawaii. It was warm. Remember what warmth is like?"

I smiled down at her. "Vaguely."

"I miss it," she said, snuggling closer.

The sheet fell away from her. She wore a threadbare nightgown, and the thin strap had slipped down her shoulder. Her skin was like liquid moonlight in the darkness. Her breasts pressed against my upper thigh, warm and soft. Unbidden, a swell of lust coursed through me.

I was grieving. Ella was grieving. Seeking an outlet that reminded you that you were still alive was a natural response to grief. Sex was one of the most common of those outlets. Up until this point, I'd been too out of it for sex, and this sudden raw, aching need I felt for her surprised me. I wanted to bury myself inside her and stay there forever.

I wrapped my fingers in her hair, trying and failing to corral my desire. My dick was starting to lift my boxers, and with her arm thrown over me like this, there was no way she would miss it.

A little crease formed between her brows. She turned her head up and opened her eyes. Her gaze landed on my face and then fell, slowly, to my waist. She blinked, long and slow, and then leaned closer and pressed her lips to my hip. The movement caused her tightened nipples to rub over my thigh, and the feel of them unraveled what little resistance I had left.

I gave her hair a gentle tug. "Get up here."

She pushed herself up and swung a leg over my waist, straddling me in one fluid movement. She lowered herself slowly, so that the V of her thighs settled right over the hardening line of my dick. Her hands cupped my cheeks, angling my face up so that she could press her lips against mine. Thank fuck she'd forced me to shower and brush my teeth before we'd gone to bed.

I wrapped my fingers around her legs and gloried in the feel of muscles bunching beneath my grip, the dichotomy of their strength and the softness of the small breasts pressed against my chest.

"Thank you for being here," I told her when she pulled away. "You didn't have to stay so long."

"Yes I did."

There was so much emotion in those three words that I actually believed her.

I wrapped an arm around her waist to stabilize her, then sat up straighter, my back against the headboard. Her nightgown bunched around her thighs, and she reached down and pulled it up over her head, baring herself to me. I snaked my hands around her back and pulled her close so I could kiss her clavicle. She rested her weight against my hands, trusting me to hold her up as she arched her back, offering up her breasts, simultaneously rubbing her sex over the length of my cock.

I groaned and dropped my head to pull her nipple into my mouth. A soft gasp slipped from her lips as I rolled my tongue over and around her tightened bud. It stiffened further when I clamped it, gently, between my teeth. I released it only to repeat the process with her other one. She undulated her hips forward and backward in rhythm with my tongue.

With a small noise of frustration, she sat back a little, even as I continued to ply her nipples, and tugged the band of my boxers down just enough to free my dick. She wrapped her fingers around my length and stroked me until I strained within her grip. Her other hand dropped to the seam of her underwear, tugging them aside. She stopped stroking me and guided the head of my dick to her opening.

She was wet already, and it made me wonder what we'd been doing in that sunny Hawaiian dream of hers. I stopped wondering the moment she slid down my length. There was no stopping and starting now, like our first time. Her body felt like it had already become accustomed to my size, and she took every inch of me inside her in one gloriously slow descent.

"I love this feeling," she said, voice soft as she leaned back and planted her hands on either side of my legs.

"What feeling?" I asked. I wanted to hear her say it.

"Being so full of you I feel like I could burst." She arched back and thrust her hips forward, just once, as if to accentuate the words.

I reached down and gripped her ass. "Do that again."

She moved just as slowly as the first time, her body supple and languid as she lifted her hips and flexed her stomach. I fully approved of this slower pace. It allowed me to look my fill of her. To watch her thighs clench. Her breasts rise and fall with every breath. To glance lower still and stare at where we were joined, see her sliding down over my shaft even as I felt her inner muscles gripping me tightly, pulling me deeper.

It was almost too much right now. Feeling overload after I'd been numb for so long. Instead of letting myself be overwhelmed by it, I let myself be reminded by it. This sensation, this thrill of being vibrantly alive, deep inside a woman who cared enough about me that she had literally plastered herself to my side while I went through one of the hardest moments in my life. This woman who had seen me deep in a depressive state, and instead of running away, had brought her light closer, keeping the worst of the darkness at bay.

I didn't have the words to thank her right now, so I let my body do the talking. I took a hand from her hip and let it roam, pausing to cup her breast, ply her nipple, and then fall, fingers splayed, down over the warm, taut skin of her stomach before I pressed my thumb against her clit.

She moaned softly and sat forward, gripping my shoulders, still moving in that slow, torturous rhythm. I followed her sounds and her movements, giving her everything, reading the signs her body sent me. There, right there. *That* was how she liked it. This deep, penetrating angle paired with my thumb stroking her clit.

"Ben," she breathed, her hips picking up speed.

"You're so fucking beautiful," I told her.

I memorized the sight of her, back arched, head thrown back, shadows and highlights playing over her muscles and softness as she lost the rhythm and came, whispering my name.

I clenched her hips and spilled myself inside of her.

Afterward, we were both out of breath. She slumped forward against my chest and tucked her head beneath my chin. I wrapped my arms around her and pulled her closer.

I love you, I wanted to tell her.

But I didn't. Because at that moment, I wasn't sure if I could trust the words, or the feeling. Was it my grief talking? My thanks? This brief emotional bliss brought on by sex? Or had I really fallen in love with her?

***

I managed to leave my room around noon the next day. Ella had slipped from the bed much earlier to make breakfast, and I think I must have fallen back asleep after she coaxed me into eating.

The sound of laughter was what pulled me from my mattress, that and a series of little, yipping whoofs that I knew so well. The puppies were back.

"They are so stinking cuuute. Hani, look at them!" Mom said as I rounded the corner of the living room.

My parents and the woman I may or may not have loved sat on the floor between the couch and the fireplace, their backs to me as two living marshmallows tumbled over their legs. I leaned my shoulder against the frame of the door and watched, letting the scene fill my mind, committing the sight to memory, as I had with Ella last night, so that later, maybe in just a few minutes, when my future seemed so fucking bleak I felt crushed beneath the weight of it, I could remind myself that there were still good moments.

"Can we get puppies when we get home?" Mom asked, picking Doodle up and burying her face into his side. The puppy turned his head and tried to eat her hair.

Dad reached out and pulled the strands free. "If we actually commit to training them this time, sure."

Mom set Doodle down. "Ella can help. Benny said she knows all about training dogs. You'd give us some tips, right, sweetie?" Mom asked her.

"Absolutely," Ella answered.

Mom turned back to Dad. "Plus, pets have been proven to help combat depression, and God knows we need all the help we can get right now."

Her words stabbed at my heart like a knife. I'd been so busy dealing with my own grief that I'd completely neglected thoughts of what this must be doing to my parents. It made me want to apologize. To beg their forgiveness for putting them through this.

This isn't your fault, Ben, Brian had told me, over and over, as if he'd known a moment like this was coming.

I took a deep breath and tried to force myself to absorb his words. It was going to be hard. It was going to be so fucking hard not to constantly apologize to the people I loved when I was the reason they were in pain, even if that pain was out of my control.

Hopefully Mom's therapist had been able to help her. The guilt after Zach's death nearly crushed my parents. My diagnosis must have felt like added torture.

How the fuck were we going to get through this?

One day at a time, Brian had said. *Just take it one day at a time for the foreseeable future, Ben. Don't even think about tomorrow. Focus on the short term for now.*

Boots was the first one to see me. He chased a rogue squeaky toy, bounding in my direction, and caught sight of me standing just past it. His little head whipped up, and then he let out a yip-bark and came barreling straight toward me, jaws wide, ears forward, tongue lolling out in excitement.

I picked him up and snuggled him to my chest. He started licking my neck, and I was too happy to have this wriggling, hyper baby animal in my arms to stop him.

"Benny," Mom said.

I looked up. She and Dad had turned toward me. There was no easy way to put it; they looked like hell. Mom's eyes were bloodshot. Her skin was pale and paper-thin. Dad looked like he hadn't slept in a week.

I'm sorry. I'm so, so sorry, I wanted to tell them.

From the way Mom's mouth pinched, it looked like she was holding in words of her own. Or tears.

Ella broke the tension. "Hey there, handsome," she said, rising to greet me. She stood on her toes and planted a kiss on my cheek, like this was just another normal day, and then ruffled the fur between Boots' ears. "Jack didn't want to let these little rugrats go. They haven't eaten yet. Did you want to feed them?"

Over the past few days, I'd put Brian on speakerphone a couple of times, so she could hear our sessions. He'd given us both advice on how to work through our grief. She employed one of his tactics now: giving me something to take care of aside from myself.

I nodded and turned toward the kitchen. "Come on, Doodle."

Ella stayed behind, putting the ownness of caring for the dogs on me alone. I heard muted conversation coming from the room as I walked down the hall, their voices low like they didn't want them to carry. I was sure they were talking about me, but I wasn't bothered by it. No doubt there would be a lot of similar conversations in my future. Better get used to them now.

I focused instead on the task at hand. On these small, simple motions. Taking the puppy food from beneath the cupboard. Picking up their bowls from the floor. Doling out the appropriate servings for their age and size. Setting them back down next to each other. Watching the dogs as they messily inhaled their lunch. Cleaning up after Boots when he stepped on the edge of his bowl and sent kibble bouncing all over the kitchen floor.

Ella joined me a few minutes later. "You hungry?"

"No. But I should eat."

She opened the freezer. "What are you in the mood for? There's lasagna, chicken soup, beef stew, chana saag, and chicken parm in here. Or there's eggs and potatoes, or pancakes, or..." She turned away to search through a nearby cupboard for more options.

I walked over and pulled her into a hard hug.

"Oof, my ribs," she said.

I loosened my arms. "Thank you for cooking so much food."

"You're welcome," she said into my chest. "It served as a good distraction."

"Benny?" Mom said from behind us.

Ella and I broke apart to see her and Dad in the doorway.

"Yeah?" I said.

"Your father and I were going to step out for a bit. Maybe grab a bite down in town, if that's okay with you?"

"Of course," I told them. How many days had they been housebound now? They must have been desperate to escape, if only for a few hours.

"Mind if we take the Jeep?" Dad asked.

"Go right ahead. The keys should be by the front door."

"Make sure you take the back way," Ella said from beside me. "You still have the directions I wrote out for you? Cell reception can be tricky up here."

Mom nodded. "We do. Thank you, sweetie."

Sweetie. That was twice now she'd called her that. Mom only used pet names and endearments with people she considered to be part of her inner circle. Which meant she was already attached to Ella.

I glanced over at Dad. He smiled at Ella in a way that reflected Mom's feelings toward her. It would be terrible if a few days from now Ella realized this was all too goddamn much for her and bailed. For them, and for me.

As we said goodbye to my parents, I resolved myself to have a hard conversation with her. One that might end with her in full understanding of what she'd be getting herself into if she stayed, or with her walking out of the door and out of my life forever.

Chapter 23: Ella

"I think you should go home," Ben said after his parents left.

We stood on opposite sides of the kitchen island. I leaned my hips against it and tried to process his words, placing my hands on the massive slab of butcher block we nearly broke our backs installing. Beneath my fingers, the wood was as smooth as butter. I'd seasoned it myself a few days after the installation, rubbing food-grade mineral oil into its surface with painstaking care while Ben started on the herringbone tile kitchen backsplash. I had wanted this countertop to be perfect. I had wanted him to look on the job I had done with pride, see my usefulness, and decide to let me hang around a little while longer.

Now he was pushing me away.

"Did I do something wrong?" I asked.

"No," he told me. "I don't have the words to thank you for being here the past few days. I may never have them. But this," he said, motioning between us, "this is starting to feel unhealthy."

Calm. Stay calm.

"How so?"

He leaned against the counter, mirroring my posture. "All I do is take from you. I've been reliant on your humor and your energy to keep me distracted and act as a crutch when my mood went to shit. You've had to lie, either outright or by omission, to nearly everyone in your life since we met. I've kept you here, as free manual labor, working on my home reno when you could have been hanging out with your family or friends, living your life."

"Those were all my choices to make," I said.

He barreled on as if I hadn't spoken. "And now you've dropped your entire life to come help me. You're losing money, maybe even clients. You can't deny that. You can't ignore the way our relationship is negatively impacting you, at least financially."

I dug my fingernails into the countertop, willing myself to keep my tone level. "I took care of my clients before I came here, and I have my phone in case anything important pops up. It was my decision to make you my priority. Did you ever stop to think about why I chose to help you with the reno? That maybe you were distracting me too?"

He frowned.

I took a deep breath before responding. Sofia told me he might do something like this – try to end things between us because he either couldn't handle anything romantic right now, or because he was trying to "save me" from himself. If this was motivated by the former, there was nothing I could do but respect his wishes, but if it was the latter, I might be able to make him see reason.

Please, please let it be the latter.

"I spent so much time here because I really like you," I said. "You're fun. You're funny. You are really nice to look at. Your parents inflate the hell out of my ego with their compliments. You inflate the hell out of my ego with your terrible cribbage play. I like working with my hands. It is literally what I do for a living, Ben. Give me a home improvement project, and I will gladly offer up my free labor because I get so much out of seeing a dream or an idea become a reality that being part of bringing it to life is payment enough for me. But aside from that –"

I had to pause for a moment to get my tone back under control. Anger had started to corrupt it. "I'm sorry. I'm not mad at you. I'm mad at myself," I told him. "You think you haven't been treating me fairly? Well, I haven't been treating you right either. I've been hiding things. Tamping down on any negative emotion around you because I wanted to be this shiny, happy part of your life to balance out all the bullshit you have to deal with simply by being famous and outspoken about things that matter.

"Winters are hard for me, Ben. I'm actually not losing that much money by being here. Business slows to a crawl at the end of January, picks up a little around Valentine's Day, and then drops off again until spring. I have to save all year just to make it through."

He straightened, eyes wide in surprise. "I'm sorry Ella. I didn't know. But doesn't that prove my point about how one-sided this relationship has been? How much I've been taking advantage of you?"

I shook my head. "Not really. All it proves is that I'm as complicit in this as you are."

"What?" he asked, deadpan.

"I didn't tell you any of this because I was..." I ran a hand through my hair, trying to think of how to phrase this. "I don't know, babying you isn't the right term here, but I was definitely trying to shield you from anything negative."

His expression hardened. "I'm a grown-ass man, Ella."

"I know you are. I'm sorry for what I did. Trust me." My laugh was a bitter thing. "And it wasn't just that motivating my actions. Part of why I didn't say anything was because, really, what's a few months of tight living compared to all the hate you receive on Twitter? What are my problems compared to yours?"

Ben crossed his heavy arms over his chest. "Just because our problems are different, it doesn't mean yours don't matter."

"I know that now," I said. "My sister-in-law helped me to see that. What *you* need to see is that this imbalance between us isn't entirely your fault."

Ben tried to respond, but I barreled over him, having held so much in for so long that I couldn't seem to shut the floodgates now that they'd burst open. "Look, you want the whole truth, this is it. We spend so much time snowed in up here that I rarely see my friends during the winter. As for my family, my mother's depression spikes after the holidays. She ignores everyone's advice and self-medicates with pot instead of taking the pills Dad prescribes her. It's really hard for me to be around her when she's like this. That might be shitty for me to say, but it's the truth.

"I stress out for the entire month of January when Jacob is in Somalia. It's so dangerous over there, and he's already had several close calls. When he gets home, he and my dad are flat-out at the practice with flu season. Sofia is flat-out at hers too. Mental illness is really common up here, and so is addiction, both of which seem to get worse this time of year. Megan and Stacey are in Boston, Charlie is back at college, and Anabel is busy with school and sports and friends. Most winters that leaves me with my dogs, Jack, Jane, Dave, and Willow. You know how outgoing I am, how social. Having you here has been just as much of a distraction from my own shit as I've been for you."

Ben scrubbed his hands over his face. "Is that supposed to help? You telling me all of this now? Because it only makes me feel worse for not knowing any of it."

"And that's my fault," I said. "I'm sorry that I didn't tell you. I should have known you could handle it."

He sighed. "I'm sorry too. For not asking."

"It's okay. How could you have known?"

We fell quiet. I stared across the island at him, taking in his expression, noting the way he still seemed to be fighting some sort of battle with himself.

"But you still want me to go home," I said.

He nodded.

My heart started to break. "Why?"

"Because I'm afraid that if you stay, I'll use you as a crutch. That when I'm sad, instead of examining why and trying to find a way out of it for myself, I'll cling to you, as I have been. When I feel like I'm fucking dying, I'll turn to sex with you to remind myself I'm still alive. If I continuously use you as a coping mechanism, I'll never give myself time to grieve or process."

"That makes sense," I forced myself to say.

"And I want you to go because I think you need time to process this. I think you've been so caught up in helping me that you might not have given yourself any time to really think this through."

I turned on my heel and marched out of the kitchen.

"Where are you going?" he called after me.

"To get my e-reader!"

I grabbed it from his room and pulled up my library of e-books on the way back down. "Here," I said, shoving it across the counter toward him.

"What is this?"

"This is four books on the study of the human brain, three on head injuries, two on effective strategies for combatting depression and anxiety, two filled with memory exercises, three self-help books for dealing with grief, one on dealing with loss, three more on coping with chronic illness, and I don't know how many others that I just can't remember right now," I told him. "While you've been asleep, I've been reading. I've been doing research. I've been strategizing ways to help you. Trust me, I've thought this through."

He pushed my e-reader away. "Planning is all well and good, but it might do nothing to prepare you for the reality."

"I know that."

"Do you?" he asked, voice rising. "They said my anger flashpoints are lower than they should be. It's taking everything in me not to yell right now. What if it gets worse? What if I snap? What if I end up becoming violent?"

"I'll start taking self-defense classes and keep taking them until I can kick your ass," I said. It was a struggle not to match his elevated tone.

"I outweigh you by a hundred pounds, Ella!"

He was trying to scare me. Push me away. It wouldn't work. I planted my fists on the countertop and leaned forward, feeling desperate now. "Then I'll fight dirty."

His expression was full of disbelief. "You're too nice to fight dirty."

"No, I'm not," I told him. "You don't know me well enough yet to say that. You haven't seen me when I vent my anger. All I've ever been around you is happy, bubbly, Ella. Just because that's a huge part of my personality, it doesn't mean it's the entirety. I get fucking sad, sometimes. I get so mad I end up crying, because if I don't cry, I'll scream. Certain times of the month, I can even be an overly sarcastic, borderline bitch. Because I get hormonal. And who's to say our relationship will last long enough for me to find out what symptoms you end up manifesting?" I asked. "I'm telling you I want to be here for you. Now. That I want to be with you. Now. That I want to help you through this. That doesn't mean I want to get married and have your babies. I'm twenty-three. I don't even know if I want children. Literally anything could happen between us. We might be great for a solid two years and then not be able to get over our communication problems and break up. Or five years and fall out of love. There might be a nuclear apocalypse. Mother nature might finally say, 'ENOUGH!' and decide to murder all of us."

He gripped the edge of the counter and leaned back, head down, breathing deeply. "Don't you understand, Ella?" He looked up at me from behind a curtain of hair. "I can't even think about any of that. I can't imagine what could happen between us. In all your imaginary scenarios, you're forgetting one thing. I might not even be *me*." He straightened and pounded a fist against his chest. "This me. The me I am right now. I might be someone I don't..." tears welled in his eyes, "...someone I don't recognize."

Oh, fuck.

I stood there and stared at him, so sad that I couldn't even cry. So stunned that I had nothing to say in response. Because he was right. He was absolutely right. I'd been overly optimistic. In my planning, Ben's symptoms were manageable. They manifested slowly enough that we had time to recognize them and react.

What if they weren't? What if they didn't? What if he was fine one day, and then the next he had trouble remembering my name? What if I heard a noise, walked around a corner, and discovered him on the floor, in the throes of a seizure? What if he got mean? *Really* mean? Or he tried to seriously hurt me, or his parents...or himself?

That's what he was trying to get me to see. That's why he wanted me to go home. Because I did need to think about this. I'd been ignoring some of Sophia's most important advice. I hadn't gone down every worst-case scenario.

What if things did work out between us? What if they were great for five solid years? What if we got married and had babies and everything seemed manageable and then **boom** his CTE suddenly manifested in some devastating way? Being with him might be so hard on me that

I lost myself too. Was I willing to risk that? Was I willing to endure years of heartache and pain watching someone I loved succumb to a debilitating chronic illness that I could do nothing to control or make better?

Anticipatory grief hit me like a battering ram. It hit me so hard that I realized I didn't just like him; I was falling in love with him. But love wasn't the end all be all. It wasn't some miracle cure. This wasn't a movie or a romance novel where we could say the words "I love you" and then ride off into the sunset together to live happily ever after. My love couldn't "fix" Ben. I couldn't "fix" Ben. Hell, I might not even be able to help him if his symptoms were worst-case scenario.

"You're right," I told him.

He wiped impatiently at his cheeks and didn't meet my eyes. "I know."

"I'm going to stay until your parents get back, at least."

"Okay," he said, nodding.

I hated this. I fucking hated this. I wanted to stay. I didn't want to leave him. I didn't want to lose him. If he was only trying to push me away for my own wellbeing, I would fight him more on this, but it was clear that he needed this break as much as I did. Ben had to come first right now. His mental health needed to be the most important thing.

But God, this hurt. My stomach was in knots. It felt like someone had reached into my chest and was trying to pull my heart out through my ribcage.

I struggled to push the worst of the pain down as I rounded the corner of the island and went to him, wrapping my arms around his waist. His own came up and gripped my shoulders, hugging me so hard it was almost painful.

An hour later, I pulled out of his driveway.

I made it halfway up the hill before I had to stop on the side of the road, unable to hold myself together any longer. The steering wheel was cold against my forehead as I cried.

Was this it? Was this how it ended?

Chapter 24: Ben

"You did the right thing, Ben," Dad said after he and Mom returned from their brief foray into town.

"She'll be back," Mom added. The confidence in her voice was absolute.

I made a noncommittal noise. Did I do the right thing? Would she be back? Or did I just lose Ella forever?

God, the look on her face when she walked out the door.

Mom pulled a white paper bag from her purse and handed it to me. "Here you go."

"Thanks for picking these up," I said.

They were my new meds. Brian and I agreed it was best to raise my dosages for the short term and then see how things stood after a month. At this point, I welcomed the increase. Staying down here in the kitchen with my parents instead of climbing back into bed was taking all of my willpower. I needed outside help to take some of the edge off of all of these emotions.

A soft whining echoed from the front of the house, providing a welcome distraction.

Dad turned toward it.

"I got it," I told him.

Ella had done the right thing bringing the puppies back. They would give me something to focus on. When Mom and Dad eventually went home, I'd be forced to get up, to let them out, to feed them, and to train them if I was going to live up to being the responsible dog owner I promised Ella I would be.

Doodle waited for me by the front door. I shoved my feet into my boots and pulled it open. It was snowing again, another dense, inexorable blanket of white flakes falling from low-lying clouds. The snowbanks on either side of my driveway were already four-feet-high. At this rate, it'd be July before they melted.

Doodle didn't go very far, dropping his little butt down just to the side of the porch stairs so he could pee. The second he finished, he bounded back up them and sped past me into the warmth of the house before I could catch him. Little puddles of melting snow marked his path. I sighed, grabbed a towel, and cleaned up after him.

"Gonna be a hell of a storm," Dad said when I walked back into the kitchen. He frowned down at his phone, forehead creased.

"What's the predicted snowfall?" I asked.

"Twenty-eight inches."

Good. This was good. There was prep work to do for the storm. I could spend today focusing on that instead of my diagnosis or the stricken look of heartbreak on Ella's face when she'd left.

"I'm gonna eat real quick," I told my parents. "And then, Dad, did you want to help me stack some more bags of pellets near the stove in the basement? After that, Mom, we could use your help to salt the porch steps and the walkway so they don't freeze, then haul in some more wood for the fireplaces and check on the generator. We lose power up here a lot."

Mom nodded in response.

"Sure thing," Dad answered. He looked excited. This would be their first snowstorm since my rookie year in the USFL. They'd come out to watch me lose my first playoff game and had to reschedule their flight home after we'd been pummeled by heavy snow and winds the next day.

I went to the freezer and pulled it open. There was enough tupperware stacked inside of it to feed a football team.

"Try the lasagna," Mom said from behind me. "Top shelf."

I pulled it free and set it on the island. I'd lost weight. My muscle tone was deteriorating as my body cannibalized itself. I needed these calories, but since coming home from Boston, food held little appeal and tasted like ash on my tongue.

I heated the container up and tucked into the lasagna. Maybe it was the fact that Ella had made this and it was all that was left of her in my house, or maybe I was finally starting to come out of the depressive fugue I'd been in, but for the first time since my diagnosis, food tasted...well, not good, but like food again. There was the sharpness of the cheese, the tang of salt, the sweetness of the tomatoes, and the subtle bite of spices. I cleared my plate and then reheated a second serving. If I was going to be on my feet all day, I needed the fuel.

I turned to Dad when I was done. "You ready?"

"Let's do this," he said with a grin.

Chapter 25: Ella

Two weeks had passed since Ben and I...broke up? Was that the right term? Since we amicably split? Consciously uncoupled? Willingly diverged? Whatever the phrase was, I was not handling it well.

Business had slowed to a crawl. We'd been hit by one storm after another, deep winter digging its claws into us. It was so bad we made national news. A meme was circulating that showed a picture of a state plow on the highway. The snowbank next to it towered over the vehicle, an impenetrable wall of winter that looked like it could hold back an army of white walkers. Beneath it, some enterprising person had written, *"Meanwhile, in Aroostook County..."*

The storms left me cut off from my friends and family. The lack of daily human interaction, which I'd gotten used to since Ben had come into my life, only served to highlight how much I needed social engagement. And with nothing to distract me from my misery, I was having trouble just forcing myself out of bed.

Complicating matters was the fact that anytime the dogs did something cute, I wanted to send Ben pictures. When something came on TV that reminded me of a conversation we had, I wanted to call him. When my loneliness and heartache and worry were at their worst, I wanted to drive to his house and beg him to let me in. The only thing that stopped me was his own need for time apart.

The one bright spot was Jacob's coming home party. I cried when he walked through the door, at first out of relief to have him back, but then I had to excuse myself to him and Sophia's upstairs bathroom, so no one worried when I broke down sobbing.

Jane came to find me several minutes later, knocking softly on the door until I finally let her in. She sat with me on the cold tile floor, our backs against the tub as we talked.

"He has CTE, doesn't he?" she asked.

I didn't hesitate to answer. I knew she would take the information to her grave. "The doctors think so. There's this new test that lights up the tau proteins, and they found them in his brain."

I didn't have to explain tau proteins or PET scans to her, because she'd done so much research for her NYT article that the medical jargon surrounding brain injuries had become as familiar to her as it was to me.

"I'm so sorry, Ella," she said.

"Me too."

"Is that all you're upset about?"

I shook my head. "We're taking a break. He needs time to grieve and to start the recovery process. And I need time to think about whether or not I'm strong enough to be with someone with a chronic brain disease."

Jane passed me her glass of wine. "You need this more than I do."

"Thank you." I took a big swig of it.

"You love him, don't you?"

"I think so," I answered, my voice small.

"You wouldn't be this upset if you didn't."

"But is that enough?" I asked her. "Am I strong enough to watch someone I love suffer for years without hope of it ever getting better?"

"Yes," Jane said without preamble.

I stared at her.

She shrugged. "You're one of the strongest people I know. You were there for Jack and Renee in a way the rest of us weren't. Not even Dad. You stayed up there on that hill with him while he fell apart after her death, and you helped to pull him out of his grief."

I leaned my head against the tub and closed my eyes, thinking back. "You make what I did sound so easy, Jane. You're right. The rest of you weren't there. You don't know what it was like. It was fucking terrible. Renee was so sick. And in the end, there was nothing we could do to keep her there with us. After she passed, there were days I thought Jack would die from heartbreak. The only saving grace was that she went so quickly at the end. How much worse would it have been if it had dragged out for years?"

I turned to look at her. "That's what I can't stop thinking about. You seem so sure of my strength, but the thought of watching Ben remain physically healthy while parts of his brain die off terrifies me in a way that I can't think past."

She frowned. "But you can't be sure that'll happen. He might only have minor symptoms."

"He's twenty-eight, Jane. And the doctors already found behavioral and psychological problems they think are directly related to his current level of tau tangles."

"That's no reason to give up hope. Someone might discover a way to treat it. Wasn't there something...hang on." She shifted sideways and pulled her phone from her pocket. Her fingers tapped on the screen for a few minutes. "Here. Found it," she said, shoving it toward me. "There's a doctor at Georgetown that thinks he can slow CTE way down."

My eyes flew over the article. The doctor had discovered that a leukemia medication, already approved by the FDA, could work in conjunction with others to reduce the toxic buildup of tau proteins in the brain. It wouldn't cure the existing damage the tau had caused, as brain regeneration was still so far outside of our medical capabilities, but it would stop the disease from causing more deterioration. Ben might never have to worry about further memory loss or violent mood swings.

"I have to send this to him," I said, texting myself the link. "He might not have seen it yet."

"That's what I was wondering," Jane said.

I turned sideways and pulled her into a hug. "Thank you so much for this."

"You're welcome," she said, patting my back.

I let her go and dug my phone out of my handbag.

Ben, I texted, *I'm sorry for maybe overstepping here. I know you still need your space, and I fully respect that, but I'm not sure if you've seen this study or not. It's brand new. There's a doctor at Georgetown that thinks he's found a way to clear tau buildup from the brain.*

His response came much later that night, after I got home from my brother's party and had given up all hope of hearing back from him.

You're not overstepping. Please don't apologize. I hadn't seen the study. Thank you. We're looking into it now.

Three days passed, and every time I picked up my phone, I wanted to text him back. I was dying to know what he and his parents had found out, or if their foundation could fund further clinical trials, since, for some mind-boggling reason, the doctor who had made the discovery was having trouble raising money for testing.

You'd think with how much CTE had dominated headlines recently, organizations and institutions would jump at the chance to have their names tied to a study that actually promised hope. If you couldn't count on people wanting to help other people because it was the right thing to do, you could almost always count on people wanting to help other people because it made them look good in the process.

It made me wonder if the USFL was putting pressure on companies and entities to *not* fund the research. Or if those same enterprises didn't want to fund it because they were worried about attracting negative attention from such a juggernaut like the USFL. The more I learned about the league, the more I'd come to think about them in the same way I did big tobacco and pharmaceutical companies. The bullying, the lying, the coercion, funding "alternative fact" studies, the bribery. It was all there.

I'd never watch another football game again. Between my disgust at the league and how hard it would be to witness every single tackle, wondering if that was the one that resulted in a player having TBI or CTE, I was done with the sport.

***

Friday night, my phone rang. I had the TV on, but I wasn't really watching it. Just like I hadn't really been doing any of the activities I'd attempted recently, whether it was painting or reading or shoveling. My mind had been elsewhere, preoccupied with thoughts of Ben and the Georgetown study.

What if he was able to take part in the next phase of trials? What if they successfully halted his progression of CTE? And more importantly, what if they didn't? I'd been running circles in my mind, always coming back to worst-case scenario, stuck in a loop that I couldn't pull myself out of.

Thankful for this momentary distraction, I picked up my phone and saw a text from Megan.

We're moving in a few weeks. To an apartment that allows pets. Dad said business is slow and you haven't been doing too good. Want to come down and help us? We'll pay you in beer and pizza.

Yes. Thank you so much, I texted back. *Are we going puppy shopping while I'm there?!?!?!?!*

Maaaaaaaybe, Megan answered.

My phone chimed with a text from someone else, and I laughed aloud reading it, for the first time in weeks. It was from Stacey.

By maybe, she means OHHELLFUCKYES.

Chapter 26: Ben

"Hey, Jack," I said, shutting the Jeep door behind me. "Thanks again for watching the puppies."

He jogged down the porch steps to greet me. "No problem. I'm sure they'll be happy to spend some time with their older cousins."

I heard a bark and turned to see Fred and Sam's faces appear and disappear in one of the front windows as they jumped up and down trying to look outside.

"Is Ella here?" I asked, unable to keep the hope from my voice. Her truck wasn't in the driveway, but he could have picked her up, or she could have gotten dropped off for some reason. Over a month and a half had gone by since she'd walked out my door, and the thought of her sitting in Jack's living room right now made me want to sprint past the man and rush inside.

Jack shook his head. "She's down in Boston for a few days, staying with Megan and Stacey."

My brief flash of hope was drowned by a tidal wave of disappointment. "Oh. How's she doing?"

"The truth?" Jack asked.

I nodded, stomach knotting.

Jack sighed. "I haven't seen her this torn up since the year both her grandfather and Renee passed."

I took a deep breath and held it, counting to ten. I did this a lot lately. Both Brian and Christina – my new behavioral therapist – had recommended I start employing this exercise more often. We'd dropped my dosage down last week, and feelings were becoming sharper again, and at times, more painful. These ten seconds gave me a chance to pause and adjust to whichever emotion I struggled with. Hearing that Ella was so upset felt sharp enough to cut. Ten seconds weren't nearly enough.

"So, where are you off to?" Jack asked.

I latched onto the subject change like a lifeline. "D.C. There's a doctor down there that might have found a way to treat CTE. Or at least pause the degenerative process of it. Our foundation and a few other organizations are going to fund the next phase of trials, and I'm offering myself up as a guinea pig."

He frowned. "It safe?"

"Pretty safe," I said. "The medications don't interact negatively with the ones I'm already on, and they have minimal side effects, considering the fact that they're leukemia drugs."

"Just be careful," Jack said. "Renee ended up on the extreme reaction side of one of her cancer medications, and we almost lost her before she even had a chance to fight."

"I will," I told him.

He clapped a hand on my shoulder. "I really hope it all works out for you, Ben. Good luck."

"Thank you."

"You'll be back, Friday?" he asked, releasing me.

I nodded.

"So will Ella," he said. A small smile played over his lips.

"Thanks for letting me know," I told him, even though I wasn't quite sure if I was grateful for this knowledge or not. It made me want to do something about it, and though today definitely highlighted how much I wanted to see her, I had no idea if she was ready to see me. And if she was, would it only be so that she could tell me it was over?

Is it over?

That thought had been fucking killing me the past two weeks.

I turned away from Jack and opened the rear door of the Jeep. Boots and Doodle were big enough now that they could jump down from it on their own. They were growing so quickly, both in size and in personality. Boots was Trouble with a capital T. He constantly got into things he shouldn't. I was beginning to suspect that Doodle had been egging him on somehow, because whenever I caught Boots in the act, his brother was always nearby, sitting innocently aside with a look on his little face like, "*I didn't do anything, Dad. Boots did it.*"

"Make sure your trash can is bungeed to something," I warned Jack.

He laughed. "Boots still knocking yours over?"

"Every chance he gets. He doesn't even eat anything out of it. I think he just likes to see garbage spilled all over the kitchen floor."

"He might be doing it to get a rise out of you. Renee and I had this cat once that could open our laundry room door because it was one of those sliding ones. He'd get his little paw right under the joint where the hinge was and pull it open. Didn't ever go in there, because the machines scared him, just popped it open and walked away. He could be dead asleep, and if he heard Renee close it afterward, he'd jump up, and as soon as she was out of sight, the little shit would open it right back up again."

"A battle of wills with a cat," I said, surprised into laughing.

"One that we lost every time," Jack answered, grinning good-naturedly back at me. "It's good to see you laugh again. How you handling things?"

"Better now. Taking action is helping. I've been seeing a behavioral therapist, scheduling more tests, like this one in D.C., helping my parents with the foundation, speaking with my doctors about other treatments. It seems...more manageable now, if that makes sense."

"It does," he said, nodding.

Of course he understood, what with his history with Renee. I should have talked to him about all of this sooner.

Together, he and I reintroduced the dogs. It was like they'd never been apart. Fred and Sam immediately rushed the puppies and gave them a thorough sniff down, all four of them soon yipping and barking in greeting. Jack was going to have a rowdy house the next few days, but from the grin on his face, he looked forward to it.

Once they'd said hello, the older dogs turned their attention to me. I dropped to a knee and let them leap all over me. Fred jammed his head into my hands when I wasn't fast enough to pet him.

"I missed you two," I told them. "You better have been taking care of your mom." The last I added under my breath, so Jack wouldn't hear.

I stood a few minutes later, feeling overwhelmed. Jack and I said goodbye, and I thanked him again for watching the puppies before climbing into the Jeep and heading back down to my place.

"How's Jack?" Mom asked when I walked in.

"Good. Fred and Sam were there."

Her face brightened. "Ella too?"

I shook my head, and her expression fell. "She's in Boston, visiting her sister. He said she'll be back Friday."

Mom gave me a pointed look. "Same day as you."

"Same day as me," I said, nodding.

My parents were flying down to D.C. with me, but we planned to part ways afterward. They needed to get home. Back to their lives. We'd been arguing about that a lot over the past few days. They wanted me to put this place up for sale and move back with them. I'd been dragging my feet about making the decision. I wasn't sure I was ready for that. A return home felt like a return to the spotlight. Plus, a lot of the specialists that had agreed to treat me were out here on the east coast. It was much faster to fly to New York from Maine than it was from Hawaii.

And I had unfinished business here. I couldn't bring myself to leave until things were settled with Ella. One way or another.

"Are you going to talk to her?" Mom asked.

I sighed. "I want to. But I don't know if she's ready."

Mom frowned. "Ella is an empath, Ben. She'll give you space even if she doesn't want to, because she won't want to pressure you into something you're not ready for. If the opportunity presents itself, you need to be prepared to take the first step toward bridging this gap between you two."

"I will." I sighed and scrubbed a hand over my face. "We have so much shit to wade through though."

Mom nodded. We'd talked about this a lot as a family. She and Dad had sat in on several of my therapy sessions. "I think Brian was right when he said that the first thing you two need to do is promise to be open going forward," she said. "You need to talk to her about Zach and your diagnosis. She needs to talk to you about her own struggles."

"I still don't know why she didn't open up to me about them. Especially since we'd talked so much about other hard topics. She was fine to tell me about her adoption story, but not her own lows during winter?"

Mom just looked at me. "Really? You don't get it? You didn't think that maybe it was for the same reason you never said anything about Zach? Or, like she said, because you weren't the only one putting unseen pressure on her to be a point of brightness and positivity in your life?"

I held up my hands. "Okay. I hear you."

"You can't change the past, Benny," she said. "You can only try to do better going forward."

Chapter 27: Ella

Megan dropped her fork onto her plate with a loud clatter. Several people from nearby tables turned at the sound.

"You're being a fucking coward," she said.

The other patrons quickly looked away. Beyond them, darkness had descended upon Boston. The people that walked by the restaurant windows were half in shadow, half bathed in pink and blue and green as they passed beneath the electric strobe of neon lights. It looked nice out there. Welcoming. Free from older sisters hell-bent on lecturing me.

I forced my gaze away from the beckoning glow of the Exit sign and back to my sister. "Can we not do this here?"

"Oh, we're doing this," she said.

Stacey frowned. "Be nice, Meg. Anyone in Ella's shoes would be struggling."

Megan shook her head. "She's not struggling. She's hiding down here with us so she doesn't have to make a decision."

I leaned back in my chair. "Funny. I could have sworn that I've been down here breaking my back moving your furniture halfway across the goddamn city."

"We finished moving two days ago. What are you still doing here?" she asked.

That hurt. So much for our celebratory dinner. Up until now, this had been a nice trip. A needed trip. Between lugging all their earthly possessions from East Boston to Chelsea, helping them deep clean their old apartment so they didn't lose their deposit, picking out paint samples, reveling in the warm weather (how sad was it that 50 felt warm?), and eating out at diverse, eclectic restaurants for just about every meal, I'd been able to get out of my own head.

"Love you too, Megan," I grumbled.

"Don't do that," she said. "Don't deflect or try to turn this around on me. We're worried, Ella. You've been mopey and sad and quiet this entire trip. You haven't cracked a single fucking joke. I don't think I've even seen you smile. That's not you. You've crippled yourself with indecision. Since when have you ever hidden from your problems?"

I started to get angry. "This isn't one of my normal problems. The man I love just received a life-altering diagnosis." I hadn't really outright lied to them, more like skirted around details and said that Stan had recently found out he had a chronic illness that could potentially make a future with him incredibly difficult and painful and possibly even dangerous.

"And your response is to abandon him?" Megan asked.

"He. Kicked. Me. Out," I said through clenched teeth. "Because he needs this time more than I do."

"Fine. But it's been over a month. That's plenty of time for you to figure out if he's worth fighting for."

I threw my hands up. "Of course he's worth fighting for. Him, as I know him right now. But this disease might change him."

"And who's to say you won't love the new him just as much? Despite his flaws? Alternatively, he could remain exactly as he is right now. You said so yourself; there's no way to know."

I shook my head. "You can't think of a chronic illness like that. You can't put your blinders on and hope for the best. Doing that wouldn't have saved Grandpa or Renee, and it sure as shit won't save Stan."

"If my years of anxiety have taught me anything, it's that you sure as shit can't go through life continuously thinking up all the ways that everything could blow up in your face. Listening to the way you're talking right now, I'm amazed you managed to finish that salad without being terrified that it was filled with arsenic-laced rat shit that might end up killing you."

The woman at the nearest table set down her napkin, meal half done, and called for the check.

I leaned forward. "You're disturbing the other patrons, Megan."

She looked over at the woman. "I eat here all the time, and I've never gotten sick. If there's arsenic in the rat shit, it hasn't reached levels toxic to humans."

The woman paled.

"Oh my God, Megan," Stacey said, sinking down in her chair.

My sister turned back to me. "I hate seeing you like this. I meant what I said a minute ago. You can't let fear dictate your decision."

"I can't just ignore it, either."

"I would never tell you to ignore it. But you also can't ignore the possibility that it might never get that bad. You need to accept these outcomes and then decide if he's worth both of them."

I shifted in my seat. "That's what I've been trying to do."

"For over a month?" She sat back, arms crossed over her chest. "Have you been miserable the whole time?"

I nodded.

"Has it gotten better or worse?"

"Worse."

"Good."

I stared at her. "How is that good?"

"Because it tells you that you'd be miserable without him. Imagine it, Ella. You've gone worst-case scenario on his condition, but what about with your own wellbeing? You're not happy right now. You think you'd just bounce back after deciding to let him go?"

I shook my head.

"Would you ever stop thinking about him? Worrying about him? Wondering what might have been if only you'd had the ovaries to stay with him?"

"Probably not," I said.

"There you go then. If you stay with him, there may be a lot of tough times ahead. If you leave him, you know for a fact that you'll be miserable and filled with regret."

Stacey handed Megan her steak knife.

Megan took it, frowning. "What's this for?"

"I thought you might want to stab her for the finale," Stacey said.

Megan set the knife down and leaned forward to clasp my hand. "I'm sorry, Ella. I know this sucks. But you need to make a decision. For you, and for him. You think he hasn't thought of you this whole time too? Wondering if you've left him forever? You think he needs that on his plate with everything else he's dealing with?"

I sniffed, fighting off tears. "No."

Stacey scooted her chair around the table and hugged me. "It's okay," she said.

I put my head in my hands. "It's not," I told her. "I miss him. So goddamn much."

And not just in an, *I missed having company kind of way*. I missed the way his eyes crinkled up when he smiled. I missed the way he tilted his head sideways and said "Yeah?" when I complimented him. I missed the way we teased each other. I missed hearing his perspective on current events. I missed the way he flirted with me. I missed that non-stop feeling of butterflies when I was around him. I missed the puppies. God, they must be so big now. Three times the size of the fuzzy little mutt Megan and Stacey picked up at the shelter yesterday.

"Sounds like you've got it bad," Stacey said.

I nodded. "I've never felt like this about anyone. No offense," I told Megan.

"None taken," she said.

I wrapped my arms around my stomach. Between the stress and the anxiety, it was starting to hurt. "This is worse than when Renee and Grandpa died."

Megan grinned. "Listen to what you just said, Ella. Being away from him is causing you more pain than losing a family member. You didn't walk away from Renee when she was dying of cancer. Can you really live with yourself if you walk away from someone who might be the love of your life?"

I let out a heavy breath as the realization hit me. No. I couldn't.

She was right. If I loved him, I would be a fucking coward not to fight for him.

***

I was zipping up my bag the next morning when Stella, the fuzzy little mutt that Megan and Stacey had adopted, raced into the room, tripping over the bra she carried in her mouth. I was too slow to catch her, and she dove past my outstretched hands and disappeared under the bed.

"Get back here, you little a-hole," Megan said, barreling into the room. Stacey was hot on her heels. Despite my sister's raised voice, I could tell from her expression that she wasn't even remotely angry that, for some bizarre reason, Stella kept stealing articles of her clothing and hiding them all over the apartment.

"She's adjusted pretty quickly," I said to Stacey.

"Which one?" Stacey asked, side-eyeing Megan as my sister scrambled beneath the bed after the puppy.

I grinned and swung my duffle bag over a shoulder. "Thanks so much again for having me. Sorry I wasn't better company."

She gave me a quick hug. "It's okay. You're welcome any time. You know that." She pulled away and coughed in a way that sounded like a prompt.

"Uh..." Megan said, voice muffled. "I'm sorry again for calling you a coward."

"It's okay," I told her. "I needed to hear it."

"You weren't being a coward," Stacey said for what must have been the fifth time.

I shrugged. "Maybe not, but I was definitely losing my battle with fear."

Megan reappeared from under the bed, bra in hand, expression victorious. "Got it." She turned to look up at me. "You going to get a therapist recommendation from Sophia?"

"As soon as I get home." I still had things to work through, and it wasn't fair of me to continuously burden my sister-in-law with them.

Megan and Stacey walked me down to my truck a few minutes later. It was mid-morning, and the wind that whipped off the Charles River was frigid, reminding me of the deep cold I was about to return to.

"Have a safe ride home. Text when you get there so I don't worry," Stacey said.

I chucked my bag into the passenger seat and turned to her. "I will. And thank you both again so much."

Megan surprised me by pulling me into a hard hug that lasted a few beats longer than normal. "I really am sorry," she said. "You're not a coward. That was a shitty thing to say. I just love you so much, and believe in you so much, that I felt like I needed to do something drastic to snap you out of it. I don't think I've ever seen you as down as when you got here, and honestly, it freaked me out. I didn't handle it well."

I squeezed her before letting go. "I get it. And I accept your apology. Love you too."

"I hope things work out with you and Stan," she said.

"Me too," I told her.

I said goodbye to them and then carefully pulled out into traffic. Parallel parking the truck had been a bitch, and I was thankful no one had parked in the space in front of me.

The drive out of Boston took all of my focus. I swear the Massachusetts Department of Transportation was run by some sort of sadist who took pleasure in the misery of commuters. Half of the streets I traveled down were familiar, because, over the years, I'd visited Megan enough to learn them. I knew which ones were *supposed* to be two-way streets, but twice I came to intersections expecting that and was instead faced with "one way only" signs, the last of which led me straight to a brand-new toll.

Imagine that.

"You win today, MassDot," I said, merging onto the highway and heading toward the Tobin Bridge, where I'd get to pay yet another toll.

Traffic stayed heavy out of Mass and well into New Hampshire. By the time I hit the Maine bridge on I-95, it started to clear up a little. After exit 75, I was the only vehicle on the road.

I spent the rest of the long drive stuck in my own head. At dinner, Megan had kept harping on the fact that over a month had passed since Ben and I had last seen each other. Was that enough time for him to decide if it was healthy to let me back in? How did I even broach the subject without him feeling like I was pushing him?

I ended up doing that thing that I'm sure everyone does when they're nervous: I rehearsed the conversation in my head, coming at it from all angles, practicing what to say if he seemed uncomfortable or uneasy or even standoffish. This exercise took up the entire last leg of the drive, because apparently Ben still brought out the neurotic side of me.

The sun sank behind the mountains as I crested the hill leading to Jack's, its dying rays staining the sky an ugly, mottled puce that spoke of another storm rolling in.

Jack waited for me on the front porch.

I got out and hugged him.

"Hey there, kiddo. Glad to have you back."

"Glad to be back. Thanks again for watching the dogs."

"You're welcome. They're pretty worn out."

I let him go. "Did you take them snowshoeing?"

He turned and led me up the porch. "Nope. I had Boots and Doodle too, and those little gremlins have even more energy than yours do."

I paused halfway up the stairs, shell shocked. "Is Ben here?"

Oh, God. Was I ready to see him right now if he was?

Jack chuckled, and for once it felt like our roles were reversed and I was the one to miss the joke. "Nope. He picked 'em up about an hour ago."

"Oh."

I took the stairs up. I wanted to ask so, so badly why he'd watched them, but that suddenly felt intrusive. Which was weird after Ben and I had been all but attached at the hip.

"He asked about you," Jack said, pushing the front door open.

I tried and failed to crush my rising hope. "Yeah?"

"Yeah," he answered. "Seemed like he missed you."

It felt like my hope lifted me clear off the ground. I floated into the living room. The dogs lay by the fire, sprawled out in exhaustion. They saw me, and with what looked like a heroic effort, they heaved themselves up and came over, tails wagging.

I crouched down and hugged them both. "Hi, you two. I missed you."

The dogs whined and cried like we'd been apart a year instead of a week. Fred nearly knocked me over. Sam tried to crawl into my lap, whimper-howling in a way that made me want to promise that I would never leave them again.

Dogs. They'll break your frigging heart.

Eventually I calmed them down enough to take them out and buckle them into the truck. I paused at the driver's side door. "Thanks again for this, Jack."

"Anytime. Hey, maybe give Ben a call before you head home." He held his hands up. "Just a suggestion from a meddling old man."

"I'll think about it," I told him.

I got into the truck and put it in reverse. What would I even say to Ben right now? Which of the seven hundred and eighty-six scenarios that I'd thought of on the drive up was the right one?

I made it to the end of the driveway, lost the battle with myself, and shifted into park and pulled out my phone. Instead of calling, I texted, because I had no idea if I could handle speaking to him without breaking down. I had a few voicemails from him saved on my phone that I'd listened to on repeat over the past few weeks, and they always made me cry.

Hi, I texted. Simple. So simple it didn't have to mean a goddamn thing.

Hi, he immediately responded. *You back yet? Jack said you were on your way.*

My pulse spiked, adrenaline flaring like I was getting ready to run a race. *Yeah. Just picked up the dogs.*

Want to swing by? he asked.

Yes, I answered.

The butterflies in my stomach shapeshifted into a herd of stampeding wildebeests that seemed hell-bent on trying to break free. I felt like I could laugh or cry or vomit. Maybe all three at once.

That had gone so much better than anything I'd rehearsed. In all my scenarios, I was the one to broach the subject of meeting, carefully, and without strings attached. That Ben immediately invited me over gave me so much hope to cling to that if this went sideways, I'd be beyond devastated. I'd be wrecked to the point that I didn't know if I could ever come back fro –

"No," I told myself, shaking my head against those thoughts.

I couldn't allow myself to think of worst-case scenario right now. I was about to see him face-to-face for the first time in over a month. I needed to focus on that, take it one step at a time.

I pulled into Ben's driveway a few minutes later. He stood on the porch waiting for me, a big, looming shadow because the sun had just slipped over the horizon. He stepped into the floodlights, and the sight was enough to still my heart. He wore jeans and a blue button-down. His hair fell in loose waves to his shoulders, stirred by the breeze. He tucked it behind his ears as he took the stairs down.

I got out of the vehicle and unbuckled the dogs before he reached us. They padded straight over to him.

"It's only been an hour, you two," he said, leaning down to pet them. The sound of his deep voice rumbled through the twilight. Hearing it felt like coming home. He straightened, and our gazes caught, a half-smile still frozen on his face. "Ella," he said.

"Ben."

And then I was moving forward. I didn't even question this overwhelming need to hug him. There was some invisible force, drawing us together. The look of open longing on his face made it clear I wouldn't be rebuffed.

What I didn't anticipate was him hauling me completely off the ground. I wrapped my arms around his neck and held on for dear life to keep from slipping.

"I fucking missed you," he murmured into the side of my neck.

Oh, God. Don't cry.

"Are you...Ben, are you sniffing me right now?" I asked, teasing him, because if I didn't, I'd break down instead.

"Yes," he said, unabashed. He shoved his nose into my skin and took deep, panting breaths like he was some sort of deranged werewolf scenting his mate.

"Your beard!" I said, struggling to pull away.

His response was to let loose a muffled, "*Muah ha ha ha ha!*" and sniff his way lower, until it tickled so bad I started to squirm.

He finally let me down when a scream-wheeze-laugh burst from my mouth, but the second he released me, a sob followed.

Great. So much for keeping my composure.

"Shit, are you okay?" He leaned down to look at me. His hair fell loose over his shoulders with the motion. I wanted to wrap my fingers in it and never let him go. Even in the darkness, his eyes were an almost inhuman color.

"I just really missed you too," I told him. And then it just. All. Poured. Out. "This has been the worst month of my life. Are you okay to have me back in yours? We don't have to be anything romantic yet, if you can't handle that. I can just be here to puppy sit and work on the reno and be your friend and maybe verbally abuse all your Twitter haters."

He took me by the shoulders. "Ella."

"And I know that sounds desperate, and maybe kind of pathetic, but I don't really care. I just know that if you're ready to have me back in any capacity, I would happily take that and I won't even try to touch your butt or anything."

"Ella," he said with a little more force.

"And before you question whether or not I'm really ready for this, you should know that I've been stuck at worst-case scenario for weeks, so I've had plenty of time to think about whether or not I can handle that and I can because...because I love you, Ben."

Oh, shit. Oh, shit, oh, shit, oh, shit. I just said that. Out loud. To a man who might not be in a place to hear it, or a place to accept it, or who might not return the emotion.

What the hell had I done?

He opened his mouth to respond, but I barreled over him. "You don't have to say anything back to me. How you feel doesn't matter." I wanted to open a hole in the earth and bury myself alive in it. "Oh, Jesus, I mean, obviously how you feel *matters*, but I just meant that -"

And then his lips were on mine, and hope began to rise like a phoenix within me, swelling with so much heat and ebullience that it might do real damage to me if it was allowed to grow any bigger.

I laugh-hiccup-sobbed against Ben's lips.

He pulled back just enough to whisper, "I love you too."

Epilogue: Ben

I woke to the sound of distant, pounding ocean surf and soft chanting. A warm breeze floated through the open windows, bringing with it the tang of salt. The bedsheets were wrapped around my legs, a reminder of me and Ella's midday sex session.

I must have fallen asleep afterward. Our impromptu fall vacation was taking way more out of me than I thought it would.

This was Ella's first trip to Hawaii, and the woman wanted to do *everything*. Yesterday, we woke up at the ass crack of dawn for surf lessons. She was terrible. I had so much video blackmail to get back at her for that cross-country ski incident last winter that I gleefully looked forward to the opportune moment to unleash it. Maybe I could enlist Jane to help. She had the kind of devious mentality that would be perfect for this. Must be where Willow got it from.

Once Ella's fail-surfing was over, we'd spent the late morning on a chartered whale-watching vessel. After landing, we ate lunch, then headed further inland to hike the volcano and watch the sunset from its western summit. Thankfully, someone picked us up in a vehicle afterward, and we were chauffeured back down to the base. We ended the night with dinner at my parents'.

And this was just one day of activities. We'd been here for a full week, and I was so sore that it hurt to turn my head toward the sound of her chanting.

"*Sipping Mai Tais on a beach, sipping Mai Tais on a beach, sipping Mai Tais on a beach,*" Ella sing-whispered over by the drink cart. She wore a green string bikini, butt twitching back and forth to the tune of the song she'd made up.

I had no idea where she got this boundless energy. I knew she was sore too. Her feet had blisters on them. She woke me up at one this morning swearing and hopping up and down next to the bed, trying to alleviate the Charley horse in her leg. And yet here she was, several hours later, practically vibrating with energy. If anyone ever found a way to bottle it, they'd be a millionaire.

She lifted a silver drink shaker and rattled it over her head along with the rhythm, doing a full-on dance now. One that looked disturbingly similar to Skunkarooney Time, complete with hip-thrusts and elbow flares. The sight probably shouldn't have turned me on, especially since I was so tired I didn't know if I could even get it up, but…

"I like the way your ass jiggles when you do that," I told her, voice still rough from sleep.

She froze, looked at me over her shoulder, and then sent me a devastating grin before shaking her hips even faster than before. A second later, she set the drink mixer aside and belly-flopped onto the mattress.

"Let's move here," she said.

"You're only saying that because it was forty when we left Maine."

"Nope, I'm saying that because this place is amazing." She reached out and smushed my cheeks together, expression slightly manic. "You grew up just being able to go outside all year round?"

"Yes," I said, batting her hands aside. "We can't move here. We have the dogs and your family and all my appointments."

She rolled onto her back and mulled it over for a second, chewing her bottom lip in a way that would forever make me want to pull it out of her mouth with my teeth. "We could shave the dogs. I could start a huge fight with everyone in my family and become estranged from them. And we could schedule all your appointments for the summer and then winter here. What about that?" she asked, craning her head sideways to look at me.

"I don't think so," I told her. "Boots and Doodle would look ridiculous shaved. And I like your family too much to be estranged from them."

That was the goddamn truth. Late last spring, after we'd reconciled, I met all of them in one go. Ella's parents had thrown a dinner party that even Megan and Stacey came up for. A few of her family members had *holy shit* moments, much like Ella had when we'd first met, but they quickly brushed aside my fame and absorbed me into the family in a way that made me feel like I'd been there all along. Our moms now talked so much that they jokingly called each other "besties".

"Okay, how about this," Ella said, sounding desperate now. "I move here with all the dogs, you stay alone in the frigid north, and we try the long-distance thing?"

I pushed my tired, aching body up and rolled on top of her. "Abso-fucking-lutely not," I said from inches away.

She frowned at me. "Fine. *Fine!* But can we come out here more often? I really mean it when I say that I love this place."

"My parents would definitely approve of that," I told her, smoothing her hair back from her face. "And maybe we could bring your parents with us too."

"That would be really good for Mom if we came during the winter."

"Then that's settled. Plus, now that the foundation is growing, we might need to come out here at least quarterly to help out."

She smiled up at me, the look more feral than warm. "Gotta put all that lawsuit money to good use."

"You're doing that thing again. With your face," I told her.

"Right," she said, blanking it. "Letting my, *"Ah-ha-ha, fuck you, Mr. Ex-Commissioner,"* feelings run away with me again."

"That's it."

She was so good throughout the trial. Her backbone and her steadfastness and her constant reassurances and her unending belief in me had raised me up when it felt like the whole world was trying to keep me down.

I dropped a kiss of thanks on her brow and then moved to place one more on her button nose. "It's like your entire skin has become one giant freckle."

She narrowed her eyes at me. "Har."

"Don't give me that look. I mean it in a good way. Your freckles make me want to trace them down and see just how much of your skin they cover."

She shifted her legs so that our hips fit together. "Please do."

"Don't start that. I'm so tired," I said, leaning down to kiss her, quickly, because I didn't trust myself to linger. We could have sex again right now, sure, but then I'd probably fall asleep again, and we'd miss my cousin's birthday party that I promised my aunt we would be at. She was *not* the aunt you disappointed. Not without never hearing the end of it.

"Oh good," Ella said, grinning. "Then it's not just me."

"It's not just you," I told her. "You're beautiful," I added, because I couldn't say it enough.

Her sideways grin turned into a blinding smile as she snaked her arms around my neck. "So are you."

The past year and a half with her had been a rollercoaster. Most of the time, we'd been up, laughing and teasing and loving each other just like this. We'd had our lows, too. I tried to push her away a couple of times when things got bad. The clinical trial I took part in was rough. One of the side effects of the meds was nausea, which I completely ignored because that was a listed side effect for just about every medication I'd ever been prescribed, and I'd never experienced it.

Oh, what a sweet summer child I had been. I spent the entire time I was on that one feeling like I was one deep breath away from projectile vomiting. It was miserable. I lost a lot of weight. I was forced to cut back on my workouts, which dropped my endorphin levels. I ended up getting short with her.

There were other factors driving my mood down at the time. In the middle of the trial, I had my second, more detailed PET scans done, and the results showed that I'd have to be on antidepressants for the rest of my life.

My response had been to try and "save her" from myself. Ella ignored me. She was stubborn in a way that would be annoying if it wasn't so impressive. God, was I thankful for it now, regardless of how infuriating it was at the time.

Really, I should have known better than to push her away. She meant it back when she told me she was all in. Every day, even while we'd been out here, she was the one to block out time for us to sit down and play some sort of brain game that was advertised as "fun!" but without her would be boring as fuck.

She insisted on giving me scalp massages before bed every night because one of the scans made the doctors think I could be prone to headaches. She attended half of my therapy sessions. She'd even booked regular time with a therapist of her own to unpack everything with her and help her work through some of her own mental health issues.

And she never, ever complained when I backtracked or had a depressive bout. Or when I was forced to up my meds, putting a temporary halt to our sex lives and becoming a shadow of my usual self.

She was just...there for me. Always. In a way that made me think she always would be. In a way that made me so fucking happy and thankful that some days I just kind of sat and stared at her, wondering how I got so lucky.

Would it always be like this between us? I had no idea. The clinical trial actually worked. Most of the tau was gone from my brain. The treatment was now in the approval process by the FDA. But my brain wasn't "fixed". It never would be. There might be hidden damage we hadn't yet discovered. I could still experience further symptoms. The headaches I was warned about, possibly even seizures, mood swings, memory loss. There was no way to know.

But one thing I did know was that unless we did something else to fuck it up between us, Ella would be there with me through it all.

"I love you," I told her.

"I love you too," she said, pressing her lips to mine.

It was several moments before we broke apart, but when we did, her gaze skirted sideways, toward the open windows and the ocean breeze blowing in through them.

She looked back at me, and under her breath, began to chant, *"Sipping Mai Tais on a beach, sipping Mai Tais on a beach."*

Acknowledgements

I started working on this book shortly after my paternal grandmother lost her decades-long battle with Alzheimer's, a disease with a lot of similarities to CTE. Much of the inspiration for *Snowed In* came from her struggle and the idea of love enduring even in the face of such adversity.

While this book is rooted in my real-life experiences, Ben and Ella's story wouldn't be what it is without the advanced readers of *Snowed In*, Katie, Eric, Mónica, Gretel, and Sarah. Your honesty and critical feedback helped to make this a better book.

Tremendous thanks go to Victory Editing. Anne set me on the path to success early with writing courses and self-publishing how-tos, while Keri's insight and expertise smoothed out this book's rough edges and honed it into something stronger and leaner. Any final mistakes are obviously my own.

About the author

Navessa Allen lives on the shores of the Chesapeake Bay with her husband and their spoiled cats. *Snowed In* was her third novel. For fun behind-the-scenes, character art, and sneak-peeks at her next project, please visit her Patreon page: https://www.patreon.com/navessaallen